KAPHEUS
FIRE

MARGUERITE TONERY

Published by Tribes Press 2018.

This paperback edition first published in September, 2018.

ISBN 978-1-912441-02-0

www.tribespress.com

To my friends
who have been by my side
through the dark days as well as the good.

To Nina,

Believe in your dreams...

Marguerite Jonery

Chapter 1

Mother Badger's Dream

He breathed heavily as he slowly trudged uphill supported by the large hawthorn stick in his right hand. He tucked the collar of his long brown waxed coat tightly against his cold neck and turned the wide brim of his brown hat downward to shelter his face from the cold sharp breeze that swept across the land. Although the new year had dawned with the promise of a new spring, it brought with it a chilling wind that cut through the land of Kapheus that morning. The man coughed a couple of times and this simple distraction caused him to slip on a stony outcrop. He dug his hawthorn stick into the earth and gripped tightly to save himself from falling.

"Ugh", he grumbled before regaining his footing. He kicked the muck off his brown leather boots and walked on.

High up on the barren hills where only goats and wild animals survive stood a cottage that was unlike any other in Kapheus. It was a modest home, yet it was distinguishable by the unusually large round granite stones used to build it. The land was grey and the mountains were grey, but the stone of this cottage was beige in colour with glistening flecks of silver mica embedded in it. It was a warm and inviting home with large red-sill rectangular windows that overlooked the valley to the front, accompanied by smaller windows at its gable end that provided little view of anything in particular. A billow of smoke always rose in an unusual fashion from the chimney of its thatched roof and whomever looked at that smoke was often lulled into a state of peace and tranquillity. There was a large rock at the front of the cottage on which the words *La Petite Maison Le Fèvre* were engraved in gold lettering and this was something that no other cottage in Kapheus had.

The man had almost reached his home when he stopped and bent down. He pulled his woollen gloves off and with one hand that seemed as large as a shovel to the little leveret, he pulled back a stone and lifted her up.

"There now, shush," he said, "your struggle is over." The leveret stopped shaking. She looked upwards. "You know, our lives are forever linked now that we've met," he said.

He pulled a twig from his pocket and broke it in two, placing one piece on each side of the leveret's leg. The man then tore a strip from his handkerchief and used it to tighten the splint and as soon as he was finished, he laid her down on the hillside next to a tuft of bog grass.

"It'll be a bit awkward in the beginning," he said, releasing her from his grip.

He chuckled as he recalled the time he mended the leveret's mother's leg on that very spot when it was caught under that same stone. He picked up the stone and shoved it into his large coat pocket.

"Take your time," he said, pulling on his gloves, "by the time you've chewed your way through *that* bandage, your leg will be just about right."

The young leveret, however, couldn't understand why this man had saved her only to cause her such struggle. With great difficulty she gathered her leg under her body and began a number of awkward attempts to hop home. The sky turned dark and the wind changed direction all of a sudden. When the man looked over his shoulder he saw a large and menacing black cloud rolling over the distant mountain range and moving towards him at a fast pace. Lightning flashed inside the cloud and he grew afraid.

"Hurry! Hurry! *Get to your mother,*" he whispered to the leveret. He sounded a sharp three-stepped whistle, and the hare appeared. "Hurry!" he insisted. The hare grasped her leveret by the neck and fled.

The man pulled himself to his feet and ran to the door of the cottage, quickly opened it and then slammed the door shut. He dropped the large wooden latch across the inside of the door.

"Dampen the fire!" he called to his wife while he rushed to close the window shutters.

"*What's wrong,* Micah? Is someone *after you?*" Rós asked.

"The darkness is coming," Micah said, quenching the candles. "I saw it over the far hills. It's *Donn. I'm sure* of it."

"Wait! *What time* is it?" Rós asked, frantically grabbing hold of the one remaining lighting candle. "*Is it time? What time* is it? *Whose fate* is at stake? *Whose light* is the darkness trying to *quench?*" she asked, desperately searching the clock faces.

Although this cottage seemed small from the outside, it was in fact larger than one would believe within. Every available space from table tops to mantel piece to counter tops to walls were filled with wooden clocks, each exquisitely carved from the finest pieces of wood and in the shape of miniature houses. Rós hurriedly searched each clock face for an answer to her question of whose fate was at stake. She looked through the tiny windows of each little clock house, but Rós could only see children playing with toys, an old woman mending socks, a man sleeping and a woman cradling a baby in her arms. There was nothing unusual. She looked carefully to see who may be sick or frail, and if this person was the light the darkness sought to quench.

"*Whose life is it?*" Rós asked. Her anxiety rose with each failed search.

"It's coming!" Micah called, "it's *crossing the valley now.*"

"Quench the fire, Micah!" Rós ordered.

Rós rolled her chair onto a ramp and locked it in place. There were two railings on this contraption on either side of her metal wheelchair with a very large handle on one side. Rós placed a glass cover over her candle stand and stood it on her lap. She held onto one of the railings and pushed down the large wooden lever. An intricate mechanism of wheels, weights, springs and spindles engaged to transport Rós to the next level of the cottage. She rolled off the ramp and along the path made especially for her.

"Rós!" Micah called, but she ignored him.

The pendulums swung over and back in the smoothness of time as Rós searched inside those little houses. Each one had a story to tell of love and loss, of triumph and defeat, but none had the story of impending death. Then a thought came over Rós, and it was the most serious of thoughts. Her face turned ashen.

"*Listen*... can *you hear* the pendulum swing *in Éire?*" Rós asked Micah.

"In the house of *Elisa and Jamie?*" Micah asked.

"*Yes*... can *you hear* it?"

"*Shh*... they're here," Micah said. Rós quenched her candle and they both fell silent.

The wind howled loudly outside. They heard it catch hold of a bucket and toss it into the air before it landed hard onto the ground and rolled away. Then silence. It was a deafening silence that seemed to last forever. Micah and Rós looked at each other. Their hearts began to beat faster and cold shivers ran through their bodies. Micah was fixated on the latch of the front door. He thought about running to it and holding it down. He looked at Rós and she shook her head. Micah stilled his body again and waited. Then they heard voices outside their door but couldn't hear what was being said. The voices soon grew silent, and when they did, a dark shadow approached the front door of their cottage. Rós could barely contain her fear. She took a deep breath. Micah looked at her willing her to be still. The dark shadow slowly moved along the outside of the cottage, and then stopped at the large rectangular front window. The shadow moved on. Nobody stirred inside.

The wind howled loudly outside La Petite Maison Le Fèvre and the walls began to shake. The clocks shook, knocking their inhabitants over and Micah and Rós didn't move. Rós scanned the whole room wondering how she would save any clock that would fall. She watched them all shake while planning her move, and when a clock dislodged from its holding bracket and fell through the air, Rós swiftly reached out and caught it before it came crashing to the ground. She held it on her lap and watched the other clocks shake. The wind blew stronger outside and Micah tracked the shadow's movement from window to window. There was only one small gable end window left for Donn to peer through and having noticed a crack in the shutter, Micah rushed towards it. Lightning struck at the moment Micah reached out his hand to cover the open crack in the window shutter. He grimaced in pain as the lightning burned through his glove and to the palm of his hand, yet he didn't make a sound. Donn could not see inside the cottage and gave up. The wind howled loudly one last time and then eased. Micah had done enough; he dropped to the floor. The dark cloud drifted over the hills and Donn was gone.

"It's time to build another timepiece, my love. It'll be the one for all the ages" he said with a cheeky grin. He pulled his glove off to look at the open wound on his hand.

Rós didn't respond but rather looked at her husband with a vacant stare. Her thoughts were with Éire and the Children of Light. Rós placed the clock onto its wall bracket and was only briefly distracted when she looked across to the far hillside when Micah opened the large front window shutter.

On that far hillside, Fiona stepped inside Éataín's cottage and quickly closed the door behind her. She pulled off her coat and hurriedly made her way to the fireplace to warm her hands.

"*Did you see that*, Éataín?"

"What?" she asked, stoking the fire.

"That flash of lightning over the far hills. It seems to have passed over," said Fiona, looking towards the window.

"*Humph,*" Éataín responded.

"Spring will be here soon, Éataín," Fiona said. "You're always the first to start the dawn chorus and one of the last to stop singing at night," she said, leaving to get her apron in the kitchen. She returned to the living room. "I haven't heard you sing since little Fódla passed away." Fiona tied her apron around her waist. "*I was sure* that flash of lightning would have you out singing."

"I think I'll sit by the fire today," Éataín said.

"*Would you not like* to visit La Petite Maison Le Fèvre? It might do you good to see Rós."

"You sit by the fire *every day now,*" said Fiachra, "maybe Fiona is right."

"So, what if I do?" Éataín remarked with a sigh. She placed the poker back onto its holder next to the fireplace.

"*Would you not like to fly?*" Fiona asked.

"Aw, leave her be, Fiona," Fiachra said, disappointedly. "You're wasting your time. After all, a bird cannot sing with a broken heart. She'll find her way when she's ready." Fiona looked at her husband with absolute discontent. "*When she's ready,* Fiona," Fiachra insisted. Éataín did not respond, but instead drifted in her thoughts to the little pink dragon who had filled her heart with so much joy and who was now gone to meet her ancestors. Her mind was consumed each day with thoughts of Fódla and her heart needed more time before she could laugh and be joyful again.

"I wonder what the children of Éire are doing right now," Fiona said, opening the front door. She desperately hoped that thoughts of Elisa and Jamie might stir Éataín from her sorrow but when she looked around it seemed that Éataín was lost to another place in her mind.

"I'm sure the children are getting on with their lives," she said.

The wind carried her words from the hills to the valley below, and before long, a sharp breeze blew from the Kaphien meadow to the boundary between two worlds and into Elisa's room as she lay in her bed that morning. The breeze howled under her bedroom door and down the stairs to the living room below. Aideen took notice of that breeze and hurried from the kitchen to the bottom of the stairs. She placed her hand on the bannister post and looked up, but then she saw Jamie opening Elisa's room door. Her head dipped, and she walked back to the kitchen.

Jamie entered Elisa's room and stood at the end of her bed. Elisa's bed clothes were pulled up over her head with only a fraction of her face visible beneath the covers.

"Elisa, are you not getting up?" Jamie asked.

"I will in a while."

"But *you're awake*."

"I'm asleep."

"We've a new calf. *Rosie had him* last night. *I was there*."

Elisa turned around in her bed and faced the wall with her back to Jamie.

"Alright. Well, if you want to come down later, let me know," he said, and closed the door. Jamie stalled in the hallway and then opened Elisa's door again.

"Elisa, I love you," he said, and then closed the door.

Elisa turned over again and lay flat on her back staring at the ceiling. She began to cry. It wasn't long before Joachim climbed onto her bed and lay down next to her until the tears subsided. Elisa looked at his large black paw and caressed it.

"You know, things are different now and they will be forever more, but you need to put one foot in front of the other and do just the basic things every day, Elisa," said Joachim.

"Like what?"

"Like get out of bed at the usual time and get washed and dressed," he said. The black wolf sat up on her bed.

"And what then?" Elisa asked.

"Then have your breakfast," he said, softly. "It's not about doing big things. It's about doing normal things when you're feeling sad." Joachim jumped onto the bedroom floor. "Will you give it a try?" he asked.

"Okay," said Elisa, and she pulled the covers from over her. Joachim scratched the door of the wardrobe with his paw and then yanked it wide open with his snout. He pulled Elisa's navy trousers from the hanger and then snatched her warm red jumper from the shelf.

"Thank you, Joachim," Elisa said, receiving her clothes from the black wolf. She opened the drawer of her dresser and took out the remaining clothes she needed. "I'll go wash," she said and left the room.

As soon as the room door closed, Joachim pulled the clothes from the bottom of the wardrobe and threw them onto the floor. He nuzzled at Fódla's satchel, rocking it over and back and then finally shoved it against the backboard of the wardrobe. He reached for the clothes on the floor and grabbed them with his teeth and paused. He waited until Aideen's footsteps moved on from the top of the stairs. When Aideen had reached the halfway point in the hallway, he resumed his work, piling the clothes from the floor on top of the satchel containing the dragon egg. Once completed, he climbed into the wardrobe and lay down with the dragon egg to keep it warm. He was just snug when Elisa returned to her room with her pyjamas in hand. By now, she had become used to Joachim hiding in her wardrobe and thought nothing of it.

"Bye Joachim. Sleep well," she said.

Elisa closed the wardrobe door over until only a small opening was left for Joachim to see through, and then she left. Joachim was now content that his work was done for the morning, and so, he closed his eyes and drifted to sleep. His chin relaxed on the pile of clothes as he fell into the dreamtime.

Suddenly, there was a loud bang on the wardrobe door and it shut tightly. Joachim was furious, and he did what any wolf would do at that moment and broke the lock with brute force.

"*Who's there?*" he growled, throwing the door open. "*Who dares* enter Éire *without my consent?*"

"What has *you so grumpy?* You're like someone who got out of the wrong side of the bed," said Mother Badger, hiding beneath the wardrobe.

Joachim landed onto the bedroom floor and crouched down to see who was beneath the wardrobe. It was then that he was knocked over by a family of badgers tumbling through the boundary between the two worlds. Joachim quickly brought himself to his feet. He had had enough. The black wolf howled to his pack.

"*What are you doing?* We are here to help you! *Don't call* the pack! You *know* how I feel about wolves, Joachim," said Mother Badger, distressed. "I had *such a dream* last night that I knew I *must* come to *your aid,*" she said, crawling out from under the wardrobe. "*You know* how it is with us badgers, *one for all and all for one,*" she said, looking into the wardrobe. "*Not* that it is *any of my business,* but you could keep your wardrobe a *little tidier. When* did *you last clean* the bottom of this wardrobe?" she asked.

"*Mother Badger*, you didn't come all this way to discuss *my level of cleanliness!*" Joachim snapped. "*What is this about?*"

"*Well, let me tell you…* oh, by the way, could you call Éataín? We'll need her for this one."

"*What… what one? What are you doing here?*"

"*Oh,* just please call her."

Joachim howled for Éataín. That howl was heard by his pack, who were filing down the hillside towards the meadow. They carried that howl and projected it back up the hillside towards Éataín's cottage. Inside the cottage, Fiona stopped kneading the bread on the kitchen worktop and listened. Éataín too heard the call and turned her head to the sound for a moment before returning to look into the fire.

"Éataín, *they're calling you*. It's the wolves!" urged Fiona, walking into the living room. "Éataín, you must go. It *has to be* Joachim. There must be something wrong in Éire," said Fiachra.

Éataín stood up, walked to the door of the house and within a second, she had taken flight.

"We'll have to thank that wolf one day for getting her to fly," said Fiachra, scratching his head.

"I hope it's nothing too bad in Éire," Fiona said.

Onwards that robin flew from the hillside through the valley and to the boundary with the determination and zest that defined her. No matter what happened in her life, she was not going to allow any more sorrow come to Elisa and Jamie. She was determined that whatever was happening in Éire that she would find a way to sort it out.

"Did you hear something?" Cathal asked Jamie. He opened the door on Buddy's stable.

"No," said Jamie, lifting the manure with his pitch fork.

"I thought I heard a wolf howl."

Jamie looked at his Dad and then handed him his fork and ran from the shed, across the yard and burst through the front door of the house.

"Take off *your boots!*" his mother shouted from the kitchen.

Elisa watched her brother stumble as he pulled off his boots and ran upstairs with all his might. She dropped her spoonful of porridge back into the bowl and chased up the stairs after him.

"*What's going on?*" Jamie asked, trying to push his way into Elisa's room. "Elisa, is your door *jammed?*" he asked, using all his strength to open it.

"*It's Elisa,*" whispered the badgers inside.

"*Oh,* and I haven't *even brushed my coat* this morning, I was in *such a rush* to leave the sett. *Oh, dear, oh, dear,*" said Mother Badger, attempting to comb her hair with her claws.

"Let me in!" Jamie shouted. "I can *hear* you!"

The badgers held steady against the door to stop Jamie entering.

"*Let* Elisa in," said Mother Badger. "Oh, *dearly me.*"

The badgers stepped back from the door, and at the exact moment one badger opened the door for Jamie, Jamie ran at the door to break it open and came flying into the bedroom. Jamie stumbled, tripped, landed and then slid across the floor of Elisa's room.

Elisa laughed so hard at her brother that it made Jamie smile. They hadn't laughed together in quite a while and he liked how it felt. However, that didn't last too long as the badgers climbed on top of him to hold him down.

"*What's this about?*" Jamie argued, but it made no difference.

A badger placed one paw over his mouth and the outstretched claws of another over him in a threatening manner.

"Oh, *my dear Elisa,*" said Mother Badger, bowing before Elisa. "It is *a wonderful honour* to meet you again, *and now* as the *goddess of Éire.* I hope you don't mind me visiting you in your home in Éire."

"Mm, mmm, mmmm…" Jamie mumbled.

"I'd be a lot happier to see you all if you let Jamie free," Elisa said.

"*Boys!*" scolded Mother Badger, and the badgers climbed off Jamie, but not before one of them threatened his claws on Jamie one more time for good measure.

"Thanks, Elisa," said Jamie, getting to his knees.

"Dia duit, Elisa," said Feehul, stepping through the drawing on Elisa's wall.

"Hi Feehul!" said Jamie.

"Oh, hi Jamie. I didn't see you there."

The wolves slowed down close to the boundary. They smelled the ground for a few seconds and then howled. Only one, the large grey wolf, stepped through. She had long been Joachim's mate and stood by his side in Elisa's room.

"There is *really no room for all of you* here," said Mother Badger, trembling. She took a step back from the two wolves.

"Jamie! Elisa!" Aideen called from downstairs.

"*Yeah, Mam?*" Jamie asked, opening the door.

"Your Dad and I are going to town for a short while. We won't be long. Will you two be alright there?" Aideen asked.

"Um… yeah, Mam."

"Alright then. We should be back by two. Don't let anyone into the house even if you know them," Aideen said, pulling on her coat.

"Yeah Mam."

"Did *you hear me?* Don't open the door to anyone!"

"Yeah, alright… Mam?"

"Yes," Aideen said, wrapping her scarf around her neck.

"Could you bring back some hot chocolate cocoa?"

"Alright then if you promise not to burn the house down," Aideen said, and she closed the door behind her.

"*Hot chocolate? How can you think* of your belly at a time like this?" Elisa asked.

"No. I thought I'd give Mother Badger some of our hot chocolate to bring home and I was going to make some for everyone," Jamie said.

"Well then, if *that's the case*, I'll have some too," said Éataín, stepping into Elisa's bedroom.

"Éataín!" Jamie called with delight.

"It's wonderful to see you too, Jamie," she said, embracing him.

"And you, Elisa," Éataín said with a smile. "Come on! Let's make that hot chocolate."

"Rosie had a calf this morning, so we don't have as much milk. She needs it for her calf."

"That's no problem," said Éataín, "we'll work it out."

It wasn't long before they were all sitting together at the large living room table with mugs or bowls of hot chocolate, depending on their preference. Mother Badger cast an odd discerning look at those family members who slurped their hot chocolate or licked their faces rather than using a napkin, but all in all, things didn't go too badly for Jamie. They all made a toast to the cook and this pleased him greatly. Elisa felt distant from the group and struggled to be jovial, but it didn't matter, because Éataín and Joachim stayed close to her to keep her company and their warmth comforted her.

"Push over, Elisa," Jamie said, shuffling onto her chair. "They like my hot chocolate," he said and smiled with lips of chocolate froth.

"It *is* the best, Jamie," Elisa said.

Everyone turned when they heard footsteps on the stairs and watched as the stranger walked down each step with a fox following closely behind until they could recognise him. It didn't take long for them to realise it was Feehul and to warmly welcome him to the table.

"Thank you for coming, Madra Rua," Mother Badger said.

"*Madra Rua?* Is *that* her name?" Jamie asked. "But *she never speaks* and she *has never* been in *our house* before."

"Please don't refer to Madra Rua as *she*. It is not very kind," said a badger.

"I'm sorry. Tá brón orm. I didn't mean to."

Madra Rua negotiated the steps of the stairs with relative ease and gently placed her feet on the living room floor. She scanned all the faces in the room and when she was ready she sat close to the base of the stairs to observe Elisa.

"She's looking at you," Jamie said to Elisa.

Elisa nodded to Madra Rua and then lifted her cup to her mouth.

"Elisa, she's watching us. I think you should probably say something," Jamie said, softly.

"*Jamie her name* is Madra Rua. It's very impolite to say *she, and really,* could you *please* call Madra Rua by her name," said Mother Badger.

"Just enough left for the two of us," said Feehul, placing a bowl of water on the floor next to Madra Rua. "So, does anyone know why we are here?" Feehul asked.

"*You don't know?*" Jamie asked in surprise.

"No. I followed the fox."

"We followed Mother Badger," said Timothy Badger.

"And *I* followed the wolves who heard Joachim call," said Éataín.

"And all *I* wanted to do was rest," said Joachim. "*Mother Badger* you have a bit of explaining to do."

"*Well*, let me tell you about my dream," Mother Badger began.

"It better be good or *this* badger is in serious trouble," Jamie muttered before getting his foot stood on by his sister.

Mother Badger took another sip from her hot chocolate served to her in Aideen's finest delft cup. Then she gently placed the cup onto the fine bone china saucer and began. She recalled her dream in the most magnificent way. She spoke of smoke billowing from a cottage high in the hills and flames of fire as high as giant trees, and the elf that sung to the water that rose to the sky to quench the dragon's flames.

"The elf was *so* beautiful, the most beautiful I've ever seen with long wavy blonde hair and searing blue eyes," she said, and then suddenly stopped speaking as if she had seen a ghost.

Everyone looked to where the badger was staring and there was Sinann walking downstairs followed by her brother Lug.

"*Go on...* tell us more," urged a badger.

"Well... um... I... I don't think I should," stuttered Mother Badger.

"Lean ar aghaidh. Please continue," said Sinann.

Mother Badger took a deep breath and then had another sip from her cup of smooth hot chocolate before neatly placing it onto the saucer.

"I saw them fly across the sky spitting flames of fire as tall as trees and then the wind changed direction, and everything was still for what seemed an eternity and... *clocks!* There were *clocks* everywhere!" she said.

"*Clocks?*" Joachim asked. "What *kind* of clocks? Describe them to me."

"Well, I don't think this is a conversation for children, Joachim, and I don't think..." Éataín interjected.

"It's alright, I *can explain this* to Joachim. I *assure you*, it was *only* a dream," said Mother Badger.

"Ní hé lá na báistí lá na bpáistí. There is a time and a place for everything, and this is *neither the time nor the place*," Éataín stressed, standing up to leave. She had only begun to lift her body from the chair when she looked up to see warriors walking downstairs. "Is there *anyone* left in Kapheus?" Éataín asked and sighed.

"*What* are the Tuatha Dé Danann *doing here*, Elisa?" Jamie whispered.

"We followed the fox. We thought there must be something serious about to happen if the fox left her den and crossed the valley to jump through the boundary between the two worlds. *So, what is it?*" Dagda asked.

"Mother Badger had a dream," Jamie said.

"It must've been *some* dream," said Dagda.

"Yeah, I said the same thing."

"Was it a dream or a premonition?" Dagda asked Mother Badger.

"Well, you know I have premonitions all the time and that is *well known* on *all the plains* of Kapheus. And you know how my premonitions have helped the children before," she said, becoming more nervous with every word she spoke. "Well, I must have had too much nettle tea before bed or maybe it was the blackberry jam I ate earlier," she said, all flustered. Her paw shook so much that she spilled hot chocolate on the table cloth. "Oh my, oh my, oh my," she said.

"It's alright," said Jamie, running for a cloth.

"Was it a premonition?" Dagda asked again.

"Yes."

"Dagda, the children are here," said Éataín.

Dagda appeared a little frustrated by what Éataín had said, but he knew she was right. Elisa and Jamie and the young badgers didn't need to hear about a premonition that would cause them fear or to have bad dreams.

"Just tell me this. Is it what the ancestors have spoken of? Is it the foretelling of... is... is the time of fire... well... is..."

"Yes."

The room grew silent and enough had been said in those few disjointed sentences to disperse the group. The fox had heard all she needed to hear. Madra Rua stood up, turned and climbed the stairs. Dagda didn't say a word, but in the silence, he and his warriors retreated from the living room to Kapheus. Feehul then left with his sister and brother with the thoughts of prophecy weighing heavily on their minds.

"I need to go," said Éataín. She seemed equally distressed. "I'll call to see you another day," she said to Elisa. "Please thank Jamie for the hot chocolate. It was delicious."

"*Éataín*..." called Mother Badger.

"I don't want to know," she said, placing her hand on the bannister post. "This old mind has heard too much," she said.

Éataín climbed the stairs with the weight of a body that had lived one hundred years. Each foot she placed on a step seemed equal to the struggle involved in climbing a mountain. She was a changed woman now. The events of Kapheus had taken more from her than anyone had ever realised, but in this one act, Joachim saw the brokenness of her sorrow.

"What did I do *wrong?*" Mother Badger asked Joachim.

"You did nothing wrong. You just saw what they didn't want you to see. Nothing more," said Joachim.

He stood up, and like the others, he made his way to Elisa's bedroom. He climbed into the wardrobe, lay down next to the dragon egg and closed his eyes. The grey wolf followed him, and once Joachim's eyes were shut, she left for Kapheus.

Chapter 2

Troubled Times

"Feehul, rest now," said Grandmother Oak. "You haven't had time to grieve with all this work you've been doing."

"I *need* to work, Grandmother Oak. *I need to work,*" he insisted, tending to the soil around her roots.

"I think I'll be alright now," she said. "You've done so much work to heal the wounds of that terrible fire. The trees and all of the earth beneath them are very grateful to you… *I even* saw snow drops the other day. Did *you* see them?"

The spirit of the great oak tree stepped from the security of her bark and stood next to Feehul. It's one of the rarest things to see in a woodland, but sometimes, if a child or even an elf are lucky, she will reveal herself. Feehul was bent down with a trowel in his hand, digging at the soil around Grandmother Oak's bark.

"Yes, I did," said Feehul without noticing the spirit of Grandmother Oak.

"Why do you work so hard, Feehul?" she asked, placing her hand on his shoulder.

"I don't want to remember," he muttered.

"There are many things I wish had never happened too."

Suddenly, Feehul realised that Grandmother Oak's spirit had touched him. He turned around quickly and in his shock he fell over.

"Tá brón orm. My apologies, Grandmother Oak," he said, scrambling to his feet while at the same time trying to bow to her. Grandmother Oak reached out her hand and touched Feehul's face. He looked up, but then hurriedly attempted to bow again.

"Feehul, we are friends. You don't need to bow to me," she said. "I know your sorrow. I see it every day in your work and I hear it in your voice."

In that short silence between them, Feehul had allowed her words to penetrate his heart.

"I miss her, Grandmother Oak," he said, and his eyes filled with tears.

"Yes."

The silence returned, and Grandmother Oak did not wish to fill it with nonsensical words. She waited for Feehul to speak, but there were no words. She saw his body tense as he held back his sorrow. "There is something else," she said. Feehul's breath grew shallow. "Tell me what it is, Feehul."

"It's my fault. I didn't do enough to protect her," Feehul said. "I could have saved her. I…"

"She was the bravest little dragon I've ever seen. Fódla was so full of life and energy and love," said Grandmother Oak, and they both smiled remembering the little pink dragon. "Take a break from all this work. Your job is done here and we are *so* grateful to you… Find a place now where you can rest and feel your sorrow," she said. Feehul nodded.

"Cry, my dear Feehul," Grandmother encouraged.

Feehul nodded again.

"Mother Badger had a dream," he said.

"Don't you worry about her dream, Feehul. You take some time to rest and grieve. Go on, now," she said and with that Feehul took leave of Grandmother Oak and walked into the woodland.

Grandmother Oak watched Feehul for a short while before the spirit of the oak tree stepped back inside her bark.

"Dagda, you could do something useful with yourself and call to Mother Badger. I want to hear of her dream," Grandmother Oak said.

Dagda stepped out from behind an ash tree and when he did, the rest of his warriors appeared from behind the surrounding tree barks.

"I don't think she'll leave that dragon egg," Dagda remarked.

The trees shook with such ferocity at that moment that the birds fled from the woodland screeching. Then the earth shook beneath the Tuatha Dé Danann's feet as the roots rose up. The mighty trees pounded the ground. The badgers ran from their setts beneath the earth and the rabbits frantically escaped from their burrows. The tree branches wielded through the sky and down on the warriors like huge axes hacking at the earth beneath them until they struck their targets. There was rage in the woods of Kapheus and the Tuatha Dé Danann fell to the ground in terror.

"*Do not* mention that again! Words are carried in the wind!" Grandmother Oak shouted. "Call Mother Badger! *Tell her* that *I am waiting* and it's already *past the hour of her invitation.* Go!" The trees grew still. Dagda took one last look at Grandmother and ran with his warriors from the woodland to the boundary between the two worlds.

Far away in La Petite Maison Le Fèvre, Micah patiently waited as Rós sat at her workstation close to the window and carved. He walked over and back along the gleaming oak floor, pausing every once in a while to think. However, those thoughts did not actually materialise into anything of any great significance. He watched his wife carve by the light of the sun as it streamed through the window pane and shone brightly upon her and felt powerless to help her. He noticed her strong hands, and as she carved, he saw that she was lost to time. It was as if nothing else existed other than that piece of wood and the fine chisel she used. The tapping sound of the small round mallet was sharp and high pitched against the chisel and wood, and with each tap Micah became ever more flustered. He couldn't wait any longer and he left the living room. Micah stood at the back door of the cottage. It was a thick wooden door, adorned with the symbols of life from birth to death. There was the symbol of a pregnant woman, a child held in a mother's arms, children playing ball together in a yard, teenagers congregating, a couple in love, and with each phase of a person's life, there was a story carved into the wooden door until death. Yet, death did not seem to be the end as the cycle moved on to a small carving of birth. Micah stood in front of the door and took a careful look at the craving of the child held in the arms of the mother, and then pushed a secret button at the baby's stomach that only the knowing eye could see, and the carving moved to the sound of a 'click'. He then placed his finger on the ball the children played with and moved it high into the air to the top of the large granite wall in the engraving and 'click'. He continued to the couple who were in love and as he had done before, he carefully scrutinised them sitting by the river with their feet in the water. He touched the woman's foot and 'click', her leg lifted from the water.

Micah needed a moment to think. He scratched his head and then he remembered. Micah ran his fingers down along the Celtic symbols that weaved along the outside of the large wooden engraving in the knotted fashion of ivy on a tree. He followed the weave downwards until he pricked his finger on a thorn. Micah immediately withdrew his finger and then turned around for fear that anyone was watching, but there was no one there other than the sound of his wife carving. He flicked the thorn to the right and 'click'. Rós looked up from her carving.

"Bring your oil can," she called before returning to her work.

"*That woman* hears everything," Micah whispered.

"I heard that," Rós replied, jovially.

Micah focused on the writing above the circle of life. The words were engraved in the ancient writing of ogham. To the untrained eye the letters appeared as scratches on an otherwise exquisitely carved wooden door, but these parallel strokes were the final key to this combination lock. Although Micah had done this so many times before, he still needed time to think of the combination. If he didn't find this final key all other keys would lock and he would have to start all over again. But it wasn't as simple as that. There were five hundred and fifty- five different combinations to this door and each symbol to unlock was different depending on that given combination.

"It's the cloud you just saw," Rós called out.

"*How do you know? You're not even standing here?*"

"I know by the sound of those clicks," she said and laughed.

"*Are you sure?*"

"Yes, I am."

Micah reached down to death. He passed his fingers along the length of her hair and then hesitated for a second before he pressed on the Banshee's comb. 'Click'. He breathed a sigh of relief.

"Thanks!"

Micah pushed open the door to a tunnel filled with clocks that reached into the heart of the mountain. He grabbed hold of his oil lamp and stepped inside. Micah bent down and lit the paraffin in the small channel on either side of his feet, and when he did, a

paraffin flame shot down through the channels and along the
tunnel for as far as the naked eye could see.

Micah lifted his oil can and then took a rag cloth from the bundle
he had neatly folded in the alcove next to the door. It was a regular
daily routine for Micah to stand in this tunnel to maintain the
timepieces and it was work that always helped him to unwind. He
walked down through the tunnel until he came to the point where
he had finished the day before. He placed his oil can on the floor
and checked his pocket again to see if he had remembered his small
toolkit that he kept rolled in cotton cloth. All around him
Grandfather clocks stood like tall statues on the granite floor of
the mountain tunnel. Each large round pendulum swung inside
each glass cabinet beneath three heavy weights to the 'tick tock'
sound. Yet, for all the glory of the pendulum swing, it was the
specific wood sourced from woodlands far and wide that gave each
clock character. The beauty held in the grain of the wood, the tall,
spiralling pillars carved from select branches, the tapestry of the
engraving from wooden foot to wooden crown was what gave a
sense of the unrivalled power of beauty. A beauty that would
transcend all the thoughts that filled the mind and disperse them
for a few seconds of awe.

"What a life you've lived," Micah commented, opening the glass
cabinet.

It was as if the clock knew what he had said. The hour handle
struck twelve on the golden clock face and it began to chime.
Micah smiled. He examined the clock face mechanism, and when
he was ready, he shut the door on the glass cabinet.

"You'll be around for another while yet," he said and moved onto
the next clock.

Smaller clocks similar to those inside the cottage were hung on the
walls of the tunnel. As with those inside the cottage, these were
carved in the shape of a house, and each one told the story of all
who lived in that home. The sound of ticking clocks was loud and
magnified in the tunnel, but, in some way, the sound harmonised
to the rhythm of the soul, and so, it felt peaceful.

Peaceful, however, wasn't how Mother Badger felt standing in front of Grandmother Oak and surrounded by the Tuatha Dé Danann that morning. The hairs stood on her coat and she was petrified. Her family of badgers who were equally as scared huddled close to her.

"*What's this* I heard about a dream?" Grandmother Oak asked.

"You know my dreams, Grandmother Oak, they amount to nothing," Mother Badger nervously responded.

"Well, you travelled *a long and dangerous distance* for a dream that *meant nothing* to you. I know you would *never* leave these woodlands with *all the dangers* that exist in the valley if you thought this dream was not prophetic," Grandmother Oak said.

"It was nothing really… nothing at all Grandmother Oak," Mother Badger insisted with a quiver in her voice.

Mother Badger then tried to clear her throat, but she was unable. She gathered her family closer to her. Seeing Mother Badger so distressed filled Grandmother Oak with compassion for the badger who now had twice risked her own life to save the Children of Light.

"You risked your *own life*, Mother Badger, to save Elisa and Jamie and all the creatures of Kapheus. You are a wonderful and brave badger, and I commend you on that," she said, softly. "You'll need to tell me of your dream."

The trees shook, and the dead leaves of autumn rose from the ground.

"Hurry! *Run to the sett*," Mother Badger cried.

A column of air rotated around Grandmother Oak and Mother Badger, carrying the leaves into its tornado-like funnel. The badger family grew very afraid and called out to Mother Badger, but she couldn't reach them. Without warning, a young badger tried to jump into the funnel, but Dagda reached out and caught him in time.

"Grandmother Oak won't hurt your mother. Wait here," he said, and the badgers ran to Dagda and surrounded him.

The tornado of leaves reached high above the badgers and the Tuatha Dé Danann, so high that it was visible from the meadow.

"There's nothing to fear," Grandmother Oak said. "This is so that your dream doesn't fall on the wrong ears."

The brave badger told the great oak tree everything she saw in her dream, and Grandmother Oak asked question after question until she was certain that she had heard all she needed to know. Beyond the encircling leaves, the badgers and the Tuatha De Danann waited for what seemed an eternity to the young badger family.

"Speak to no one of your dream," Grandmother Oak said as the leaves fell, and answer your door to no one.

"Yes, Grandmother Oak," said Mother Badger. "Come along children. I'm sure you're hungry. I'll make some scones for us all," said Mother Badger, and with that the badgers happily scurried along the ground and down into their sett.

Dagda waited around to hear about the dream, but Grandmother Oak took no notice of him. He lingered around her bark for another minute and hoped.

"What was the dream about?" Dagda asked in the end. "Is it the time of fire?"

"Do you wish to have *my wrath*?" Grandmother Oak asked, angrily.

"No... fair enough."

"You could make yourself useful, Dagda, and take a message to Joachim."

"What is *it?*" Dagda curiously asked.

"When you reach Elisa and Jamie you can tell Joachim that I have spoken to Mother Badger and that I trust in his judgement," she said.

"*Is that it?*" Dagda asked.

"*Do I need to explain myself further?*" Grandmother Oak asked.

"We'll be on our way," said Dagda. "Come on, we're on our way to Éire," he said and the Tuatha Dé Danann left with him for the boundary between the two worlds.

On the other side of that boundary in Éire, Jamie sat at the desk beneath his bedroom window. His bed was unkempt as always with blankets almost at the tipping point between dangling from his bed and landing in a heap on the floor. His pillow was awkwardly thrown against the bedroom wall and his clothes were

left in their usual hanging place on the bedroom floor. In the
months that passed since Fódla died, Jamie spent more time in his
room. His mother and father had called him on so many occasions
to do chores, something they rarely had to do before, and as soon
as they were completed he returned to that desk. The house was a
very different place now. The playfulness and camaraderie between
siblings had been difficult to find and although both Jamie and
Elisa tried their best, they were both struggling alone with their
grief.

"What are you doing Jamie?" Elisa asked, stepping inside his room.

"Nothing," he said, closing his sketch book. Jamie scratched his
head with his pencil. "What do you want?"

"I just wanted someone to talk to."

"What about?"

"Nothing really," said Elisa.

Elisa opened the front cover of the sketch book. She picked it up
and walked from Jamie's desk to sit on his bed.

"I thought you didn't miss her," Elisa said. "You never speak about
her."

Elisa slowly turned the pages filled with drawings of the little pink
dragon they both loved. Jamie wasn't able to ask Elisa for his book
back, the words were blocked by the enormous lump he felt in his
throat. Elisa touched the sketches on each page wishing to caress
Fódla one more time and to feel her warmth. For those few
minutes Elisa turned the pages, Fódla was alive again. She was as
real as the moments Jamie had captured of her following him in
the long grass or flying to him with Banbha or climbing on his back
or… Elisa's eyes filled with tears as she saw little Fódla lifeless on
the flagstone.

"Don't cry Elisa. I didn't mean to make you cry. I miss her too,"
said Jamie. "Everyday."

"*What's* going on in here?" Aideen asked, standing at the doorway.
"*What* are *you crying* for? Grow up!" she scolded.

"I'm *not* crying," said Elisa, defiantly. "I don't cry!"

"I *hope not,*" snapped Aideen. "You're getting *a bit too big* for that
carry on. Go on out and sweep the yard! Do *something productive* with
your time."

"Jamie will you take your bike, my love, and go to the post office for me? I left the letters and the money for the stamps on the living room table," Aideen said.

"Alright, Mam," said Jamie. He took his sketch book from Elisa, shoved it under his mattress and followed his sister from the room. Aideen stood at the bedroom door until she heard the front door close. The clothes lying on the floor didn't seem to bother her on this occasion. She stood gazing into space for what seemed an eternity until for whatever reason, she suddenly came out of her daydream and walked with determination towards Jamie's bed. Aideen pulled the sketch book from under the mattress and sat down on the bed. She looked at the worn out cover with unrecognisable scribbles. She passed her hand over its coarseness and hesitated before opening it.

Micah's hand passed over the intricate engravings one last time before he closed the door solidly on the tunnel. He left his oil can to one side, washed his hands at the sink and then slowly made his way to the living room. By the time he had reached Rós, she had put down her mallet and chisel and was staring out the window. He said nothing for a while. Rós often needed a moment to think while she was immersed in her carvings. Micah added two pieces of wood to the fire, the sound of which pulled Rós from her daydream.

"You might as well throw this in the fire too," she said, holding her piece of carving. Micah appeared confused.

"It's no good," she said. "The grain in this wood is all wrong. I *cannot* make it work. *It's not the right wood.*"

"This is the finest wood we have. I sourced it *myself* for you… *in the woods of Kapheus,*" Micah remonstrated.

"It *won't work.*"

"It *must work.*"

"I am *telling you now*, Micah, this will *not* work."

They looked at each other. There was only one tree that could be used to build this clock.

"We need Grandmother Oak's branch," Rós said.

"*That's not possible*. She's *not just* going to allow me to cut her branch. *No tree* allows you to cut them down unless they are in pain or their branch is ill. She is being nurtured each day by Feehul. *Feehul* is the *greatest medicine elf* who ever lived! Grandmother Oak is in *incredible health* these days."

Rós looked away from her husband. There was no other tree from which she could carve this clock. Rós couldn't get to her in her wheelchair, but she thought that if she could only sit face-to-face with Grandmother Oak in the woods of Kapheus that woman-to-woman for the good of all who lived, Grandmother Oak would do this.

"Don't do this, Rós! *Don't start thinking…* it's a dangerous thing *when you* begin to concoct a plan," Micah said. Rós ignored her husband and thought.

"I *won't* do it! Whatever you're concocting in that *head of yours*, you can *count me out*,"

he said. "I'm making *the dinner*. I'm *not standing here* to listen to some *hair-brained plan*," Micah said, and shaking his head he left to find something from the pantry for both of them to eat.

Rós closed her eyes. She imagined herself leaving her house and she heard the latch 'click' in her mind's ear. She walked down from the hills and into the valley. She looked up and saw Iolar, the golden eagle, gliding across the sky. She passed through the campfires with the elves cooking and children playing; she walked to the woods of Kapheus.

Micah took a peak around the corner to see his wife with her eyes closed in dream.

"She's *at it again*," he muttered and then returned to stirring the pot.

Rós passed by the fountain of hope and saw the leprechauns standing there like bold school boys. She walked onwards and passed through the translucent veil of the Meadow of Discovery and met the frog on the other side. She nodded and smiled, and with one 'ribbit' the frog hopped away. Rós saw the wood of Kapheus, a wood that she had longed to visit for so many years. She took one more deep breath. She looked down at her strong legs, her leather boots, and her dark grey trousers and smiled. Rós called to Feehul and he came from the woodland. She saw him standing at its edge and it filled her heart with delight. Rós ran to him and they embraced and Feehul then escorted her to Grandmother Oak. They spoke of all things Kaphien and some of the Children of Light.

'They'll need a little more time. Don't rush grief,' she said in her dream, and then looked at Feehul more intently. '*Don't you rush* your grief, Feehul. This is Éire and we don't expect that of you. No one does.'.

Feehul nodded.

'It's great to see you, Rós. It's been so long without you here.'

'Grandmother Oak?'

'She's well. The fire did a lot of damage and I thought we were going to lose her, but she's doing well now,' said Feehul in the dreamtime.

'She's lucky to have you.'

'It's good to see you, Rós,' Grandmother Oak whispered. Rós smiled.

'It's wonderful to see you,' Rós said in her dream.

As Rós looked around her she saw the elves appear from the hidden parts of the woodland and the dragons from their nests in the treetops high above. Rós was a rare sight to behold and curiosity overtook them. They gathered around her as if welcoming a family member home. In the distance, Dagda stood cloaked by the dark shadow of a tree and watched his sister. A peace fell over him as he watched her there. Her legs were strong and she stood tall. She was the Rós he remembered.

"Women! *They're impossible* to understand," said Micah while setting the table.

He placed each fork and knife on the table and looked to his sleeping wife again. His heart filled with love and his mind knew that he could never reach her where she was.

"There's no point. She is far more powerful than I could ever be," he said. He decided to sit down and wait for Rós to awaken from the dreamland.

As Rós spoke to the creatures of Kapheus, the badgers came from their setts, the rabbits from their burrows and the birds flew down to listen, for what was being spoken affected them all. A large elk slowly approached Dagda from behind. He was a creature of spirit, and when he reached Dagda he bellowed loudly. Dagda froze. Suddenly, Rós saw Dagda, her brother, in the distance and woke from her dreaming state.

"It's alright, it was only a dream," said Micah from the table. Rós reached down to grab her handkerchief to wipe her tears away. "It was *only* a dream Rós."

Micah stood up and brought the casserole to the table, placing it in the centre. He looked at Rós again before fetching glasses of water.

"Do you want to tell me about your dream?" Micah asked.

"No," Rós said, making her way to the table. "Thank you for cooking, Micah."

They both sat together in silence and ate. Micah didn't want to upset Rós further by asking her again about her dream or the clock or the grain of wood. Rós on the other hand did not want to tell Micah of what she had seen or where she had been in the dreamtime. It was too wonderful and too painful, and she felt he would not understand. Suddenly, there was a loud knock on the door.

"*Who's* that?" Micah asked, curiously.

"Could you give this to Rós, please? Grandmother Oak wants her to have it," Lug said when Micah opened the door. He was then snatched by Iolar and taken back to the woods of Kapheus.

"*Rós*," Micah called, "Grandmother Oak wants you to have this." He looked bemused. Micah held in his hand a substantial branch from Grandmother Oak and he stood like a statue staring at it.

"Your dinner is getting cold."

"*My dinner?*... Women! I'll *never* understand you."

Grandmother Oak's healthy and robust branch was gone and now she stood in much pain in the woodland. It was a pain of which Feehul was very much aware. He had tended to so many trees who were crying in pain from the burns they endured in the fire, but when he was told of this self-inflicted wound, it made no sense to him. Feehul climbed the branches of Grandmother Oak with his satchel draped across one shoulder. He sat down and took out his mortar and pestle. Grandmother Oak watched as Feehul pulled out a handful of dried parts of woodland plants from the front pocket of his satchel, placed them into his mortar bowl and ground them down with his pestle. She saw him pull a small clear glass jar from the inner pocket of his satchel and unplug the cork top.

"I had no choice. It was for the greater good," Grandmother Oak said.

Feehul tapped the jar twice with his finger and this was the perfect measure of ground seaweed and then placed the jar back into his satchel. He mixed the contents of the bowl again and then reached down into his bag for the small leather water pouch. Once the perfect amount of water was added, Feehul began to stir the contents until it formed a thick paste.

"Thank you for coming, Feehul. The pain is great," Grandmother Oak winced.

Without saying a word, Feehul turned to the wounded oak tree and bathed her cut in a thick layer of his brown paste. As soon as the paste dried he made another mixture of a different sort. "You're a good elf," Grandmother Oak said.

Feehul spent the whole afternoon bathing her wound and continuing to mix varying contents to form the perfect potion for each stage of the old tree's healing. It was dusk when he closed over the large leather flap of his satchel and climbed down from her branches.

"Go raibh maith agat, a Feehul," Grandmother Oak said. "Thank you, my dear elf."

There was no response. Feehul walked into the wood.

Chapter 3

The Sweet Shop

That morning Elisa's mother decided to tidy her daughter's room. Elisa's bedroom was always neat and tidy, so Joachim knew that something was not right when he saw Aideen through the narrow opening on the wardrobe. He watched Aideen place the clean sheets on the chair and then saw her pulling off Elisa's bedclothes. The blankets landed with a thump on the floor just as Joachim stretched his snout a little further to watch. Aideen placed a clean under sheet on the bed and tucked it in on all sides. She then turned around and lifted the pillow off the floor to remove the pillow case. Aideen was looking for something. She put her hand into the pillowcase, searched around inside it and then tossed it to the floor. Aideen paused for a moment and then thought of searching the bedclothes. She pulled the sheets from the floor and shook them vigorously. Nothing. Aideen hurtled them against the bedroom door in frustration. She reached down and pulled up the blankets and shook them. She separated them from each other and shook them again. Aideen looked down, but nothing had landed on the floor.

Joachim withdrew inside the wardrobe. He nuzzled the clothing, covering Fódla's satchel until he found the satchel strap and caught hold of it with his teeth. Joachim crouched down and prepared himself to run if Aideen opened the wardrobe. He watched as Aideen put her whole arm under the mattress and moved it down along its length. She felt nothing. Then she decided to lift the mattress and look under it. Nothing.

"Hi Mam!" said Elisa, walking into the room.

"Oh, hi!" Aideen said, dropping the mattress back down onto the base.

"What are you looking for?"

"Nothing! I was turning your mattress, that's all. It's good to turn your mattress every once in a while," she said. "Why are you back so soon?"

"Dad said the yard didn't need to be swept. He said he'd prefer if I went to town to meet Jamie. He gave me money for sweets, so

I'm getting my jacket," Elisa said, placing her hand on the wardrobe door to open it. "Oh, do you want me to stay and make my bed?" Elisa asked.

"No, you go on. I'm nearly finished," said Aideen.

Elisa opened the door and reached into the wardrobe for her red jacket forcing Joachim to retreat to the shadows. Elisa smiled at him and then carefully closed over the wardrobe door, leaving just a slit for air. She left the room and made her way downstairs. However, halfway down the stairs, Elisa remembered that she had forgotten something and returned to her room.

"Mam, what are you looking for?"

Aideen was halfway under the bed.

"Dirty socks!"

"There *aren't* any. I put my clothes in the washing machine this morning," Elisa said.

"Are you alright, Mam?"

"Elisa, I thought you were gone," Cathal said, standing at the doorway. "Aideen, *what are you doing?*"

"She's looking for socks."

"Did you find them?" he asked.

"I wish *everyone would stop asking me questions* and *mind their own business!*" Aideen snapped, crawling out from under the bed.

"I'd say you'd have better luck finding a sock under Jamie's bed," said Cathal. He laughed.

"Oh, here! Are *you not supposed* to be somewhere, Elisa?"

"Yeah, I forgot my watch," Elisa said, making her way to her bedside locker.

"And *you?*"

"And me!" Cathal exclaimed and laughed. "Why do you want to give out to *me?*"

"*I've had it* with everyone around here!" Aideen shouted and left Elisa's room to go downstairs.

"I only remember two other occasions when you were like this Aideen," said Cathal, and he laughed heartily. He suddenly stopped laughing and a serious look came over his face.

"What's wrong, Dad? You look like you've seen a ghost," Elisa said. She ran downstairs and into the yard to get her bicycle.

Jamie had already reached town and by now stood waiting in line at the post office. It was the main post office in the town, and as such, it was always busy. He stretched his neck to count the number of people in front of him. He counted eight and then stood up straight again. He looked at the green paint on the walls and the grey cobwebs in the corner. The place smelt old and dirty, and even the man in front of him smelt of old gone-off, smelly, leather boots. He looked away. The countertops were old and made of dark polished wood with large brass grilles above them leaving just enough room for a person to pass their letter beneath. The brass post boxes were lined against the wall closest to the large windows that almost touched the ceiling. He heard letters dropped into the boxes from outside and saw people at the window. Jamie looked down at his feet to see the industrial grade carpet, which had turned from light to dark grey with blotches of brown here and there where people had dropped their rain-soaked bags or stood their dripping umbrellas. Everything seemed to Jamie to have been there since time began. The longer he had to wait the more frustrated he became with each thing he saw, and it seemed to him that everything was created in perpendicular lines. Nothing was meant to bend, not even the tellers. They looked as straight as everything else in the post office, and they never seemed to smile.

"Cúntar a sé," he heard from the teller announcer as the number six lit above counter six.

'Seven more people to go,' Jamie thought.

"Gabh mo leiscéal, gabh mo leiscéal a mhac," said an old woman standing behind Jamie.

She tugged at his sleeve, and Jamie turned around. She was a little old woman with a bend on her back and a very wrinkled and old face.

"Gabh mo leiscéal," she said again.

The woman pushed a few stray strands of hair back under her cream-coloured satin scarf that was covering her head. She pulled uncomfortably at the scarf's pink trim that tied in a knot under chin.

"Yes," said Jamie.

"Mo litir. Tóg í," she said.

Jamie looked down to see her holding the letter tightly in her hand. She pressed him to take it.

"*Why* do you want me to take your letter? Are you not feeling well? Do you want to sit down?" asked Jamie.

It was then that the woman dropped the letter from her hand and Jamie reached down to get it. Beneath her long cream coat she wore a black skirt over her black tights and short black leather boots and Jamie thought that she must have been a nun.

"I'll get somewhere for you to sit," he said, standing up. He scanned the room for a chair, but there was none.

"Um…" he uttered. He looked back to see how many more people were ahead of him in the queue. Six people. He turned around to the woman, but she was gone.

'*Where* did she go?' Jamie thought. '*How* could she have moved that fast?'

"Cúntar a dó," he heard on the loudspeaker then "cúntar a trí." Jamie shuffled along behind the others.

'*Where did she go?*' he thought, searching for the old woman.

"Cúntar a seacht."

Jamie didn't know what he was supposed to do. He only had enough money for stamps for the letters his mother had given him.

"I'll take you here," a voice called. The teller had turned the face of his sign around so that it read '*ar oscailt*'. "I'm open now. I can take you here," he said.

"Um… alright," said Jamie.

He handed the man the letters, four from his mother and one from the woman who stood in the queue. Jamie watched as the man looked at the envelopes. He set one aside and then placed stamps on the other four.

"That will be €4," he said. Jamie handed him the money.

"There you go," the man said. "You can put the letters into the letter box at the window, and here, take this one with you," he said. Jamie looked down at the letter the teller handed him. He hesitated for a moment.

"Next!" the teller shouted. "Cúntar a h-ocht," sounded out on the load speaker. Jamie stood out of the way.

He walked to the post box and deposited the four letters his
mother gave him. He looked down at the final letter and to his
surprise he saw written:
Elisa and Jamie Dé Danann,
Tobar na nGuíonna,
Coill Garbh,
Conamara,
Éire.
Jamie looked around, but nobody seemed out of place in the post
office.
"Hi Jamie," said Elisa, walking through the post office door.
"I'm *so glad* you're here," Jamie said.
"Why?"
"*Come on.* I'll tell you outside."
Elisa and Jamie picked up their bicycles leaning against the wall of
the post office and Jamie began to lead Elisa home.
"Wait, Jamie! Dad gave me money for sweets. Can we go to the
sweet shop first?" Elisa asked.
"Oh, yeah. Sorry," said Jamie, and he climbed down off his bicycle
to follow Elisa to the shop.
"Elisa, the *weirdest thing* happened when I was in the post office,"
said Jamie. He reached into his pocket to pull out the letter and
just as he was about to take it from his pocket, a tall man
approached him and pushed his hand back down into his jacket
pocket. The tall dark-haired stranger shook his head and walked
on.
"What happened?" Elisa asked, turning around after placing her
bicycle against the shop window.
"I'll tell you later," said Jamie, "when we're at home."
The bell rang over the shop door as Elisa and Jamie entered.
"Good morning, Eve," Elisa said.
"Good morning, dear Elisa. How are you, Jamie?"
"Alright," Jamie replied.
"What can I get you two today?"
"How much money do you have?" Jamie whispered.
Elisa pulled the coins from her pocket.
"Three euro," she said.

"You two take your time," said Eve.

The shop was only small but was filled from floor to ceiling with all sorts of sweets. Inside the wooden framed counter with the glass panelling were shelves of handmade chocolates from dark chocolate truffles, milk chocolate pralines and orange chocolate caramels to white chocolates. Elisa scanned the chocolates inside their glass cabinet.

"Yours is the chocolate caramel with the hazelnut hidden inside," said Eve.

"Elisa, we *haven't enough* money for them," snapped Jamie. Elisa disappointedly walked away.

"You like the apple drops, Elisa. Why not have a few of them? I'll make sure your Dad buys a few chocolate caramels for you for Easter," she said with an expression of promise on her face. "Would you like apple drops?"

"Umm…"

"You take your time, Elisa."

Elisa looked at the large glass jars of sweets behind the counter. They were sitting on tall shelves that stretched from the floor to the ceiling. There was a whole row of hard boiled sweets, which Elisa loved. Her mouth watered at the sight of the black and white bulls eyes, the butter nuggets, cola cubes, clove rocks, lemon sherbets, her favourite apple drops, and fruit mixtures.

"I'll have some apple drops," she said.

Eve lifted the large jar from the shelf to the counter. She screwed off the top and scooped out a portion of apple drops with her gleaming brass scoop. She placed them into her shiny brass bowl that sat neatly on the weighing scale and then reclosed the lid of the jar.

"Would you like anything else?" she asked.

"*How much is that first?*" Jamie snapped.

"You're very concerned about money today, Jamie," Eve said.

"Don't worry. Elisa has enough money to pay for her sweets. Have you decided on what you'd like?" she asked.

"I'm still looking," said Jamie, reading the contents of the sweet packets on the shelves in the alcove.

"What else, Elisa?" Eve whispered.

"Elisa! *Don't buy* too much. You *don't* have enough money," Jamie argued.

"What else would you like?" Eve asked, secretly.

Elisa loved liquorice all-sorts and the giant sour strawberry jellies Eve had. She pondered on which to buy.

"You can have both," said Eve.

"No", said Elisa, looking down at the money in her hand.

"I say you can. Will you trust me? I say you can have both."

"Elisa, I *don't* think you can buy anything else. *You don't* have enough money," quipped Jamie.

"Will you trust me when I say you can have both. Trust me, Elisa," said Eve.

"Why?" Elisa asked.

"Because abundance is one of the riches of the world, but you do need to allow yourself to have it. Otherwise it won't appear," Eve said.

Elisa was shocked to hear this. She remembered Taragon, the earth dragon, at that moment who told her about play and how it was one of the riches of the world. He told her to find the others and Eve knew one of them.

"I knew him too, Elisa," she said. "Will you trust me?"

Elisa nodded her head. With that Eve took down her large jar of liquorice all-sorts and scooped some into her shiny brass bowl. She returned the jar to the shelf and then opened her jar of giant sour strawberry jellies and poured a few onto the weighing scales.

"That will be €1.50 in total," Eve said.

Elisa looked at the scale and then looked down at the money in her hand. She had exactly the right amount of money to pay for all the sweets she desired. She looked over at Jamie, but he hadn't noticed what had happened.

"There you go, Elisa," said Eve. "Jamie, have you decided on what you'd like?"

"Yeah, I'm getting these," he said, showing her the packet of sweets in his hand.

"That will be three euro,"

Elisa handed Eve the exact amount.

"Thank you, Eve," said Elisa.

"You're welcome, dear Elisa."

Jamie pulled the letter out of his pocket, so that he could stuff his packet of sweets into it. All of a sudden, Eve became agitated. She rushed to the door of her shop and turned the sign to read *dúnta*. She turned the lock on the door, pulled down the small door blind and then quickly pulled down the large blind on the shop window. Apart from the bare amount of light that could penetrate the shop blinds, the shop was in darkness.

"*What's wrong*, Eve?" Elisa asked.

"Come with me," she said, ushering the children into her home at the back of the shop. She nervously looked back at the shop window.

"Mam will be wondering where we are. We'd better go home," Jamie said.

"You don't need to worry about that. I'm not the one who wants to harm you," she said. "Sit down there you two."

Jamie and Elisa sat on the soft couch and were totally confused. It always felt strange sitting in Eve's living room. The wallpaper was very unusual. It had the images of a phoenix bird flying and then dying and then rising to life from the ashes all over the walls. She even had a bird cage sitting on a large stand next to the fireplace, but in all the times they had visited Eve's house, they had never seen a bird in it. Elisa knew that her father and Eve went to school together and that they were best friends growing up. Their father always said that she was an old flame, whatever that meant, and both Elisa and Jamie always felt she had their best interests at heart, even if she had a strange way of showing it today.

Eve picked up her phone to call Cathal to collect the children.

"Ó! Dia duit, a Aideen. Cén chaoi a bhfuil tú? How are you?"

"It's Mam," Jamie said. "She's *gonna kill us*."

"...as soon as Cathal can get here. They're safe with me for now... alright... don't worry..."

"She's *definitely* going to kill us," said Jamie. "*You're* probably *really going to get it now. I wanted* to go home. I didn't know *you wanted to get sweets.*"

"Don't be *so mean*, Jamie. *You wanted* sweets too," Elisa said, squeezing her paper bag tightly.

"Alright then. Your Dad is going to collect you," said Eve.

"But we can cycle home. Our bikes are outside," said Jamie.

"Oh, your bikes! I forgot. I hope no one notices… we'll have to take the chance," she said.

Eve gathered old newspapers, crumpled them into loose balls and placed them onto the fire grate. She lifted the lid on her brass plated coal chest and took out the kindling.

"Jamie, you have a letter in your pocket that you need to open," said Eve, placing the kindling onto the newspaper.

"Stop! *Don't do a thing!*" she yelled, hurrying to close the curtains. She sighed deeply and placed her hand on her heart. "*Now* you can open it," she said. Eve reached behind the clock on the mantelpiece to fetch her matches and bent down to light the fire.

Jamie looked at Elisa in puzzlement, but Elisa had no answer for him. She didn't even know he had a letter other than those he had to deliver to the post office.

"Well! Open it!" Eve insisted.

Elisa waited as Jamie tore the envelope open.

"It's addressed to the two of us, Elisa," said Jamie, "do you want to read it?" Jamie handed the letter to Elisa.

"My Dearest Elisa and Jamie,

It seems a lifetime has passed since I last sat with you both on the floor of your bedroom Elisa. I left you with one piece of advice then and that was 'how you believe the world to be is how the world will be'. This is never more true as it is today and will be in the days ahead. My heart is filled with sorrow that, though so young, you have experienced such grief at the loss of your dear friend Fódla.

The time of fire is almost here. It will be a time of wonderful opportunity or uncontrollable greed. The stream of abundance will flow to you and you must remember that in isolation you will fail, but together in union with your fellow Kaphiens you will succeed beyond your expectations. My advice to you is this. Stay together, work together and support each other.

Le gach dea-mhéin,
Davin."

"*Give it to me quick,*" said Eve. Elisa handed it to her and Eve threw the letter into the fire. "*Who* gave it to you?" she asked Jamie.

"An old woman in the post office. She disappeared. I couldn't find her when I turned around," he said.

"Oh, it doesn't matter. She may have been a shape-shifter," Eve said.

"How *do you know* so much?" Elisa asked. "*Are you* from Kapheus?"

"Kapheus! Not at all," Eve said. It grew dark outside the window all of a sudden. "It's here," Eve whispered.

Elisa and Jamie didn't move a muscle, but instead watched Eve for their cue. The house felt cold as the darkness saturated every layer of the thick concrete walls. Then suddenly, the fire went out. They both looked at Eve. The wind howled outside the window and then a loud shrill flew down the chimney. Eve grabbed hold of the wooden fire screen and pressed it hard against the fireplace. The wind shrieked loudly and forced itself against her wooden screen. It screeched as a slight breeze squeezed through. Jamie and Elisa saw the darkness form what looked like the fingers of a hand. It gripped hold of the wooden screen and attempted to wrench it away from Eve's grip. Elisa and Jamie jumped up from the couch and forced the wooden screen flat against the open fireplace with all their strength. The shriek was now so loud and the force against them so strong that they could barely hold out. Jamie forced his shoulder and then his back against the fire screen, dug his feet into the floor and pushed against it. The dark fingers were sucked back up the chimney flue to the top of the roof with a loud shrill.

"We're not out of the woods yet," Eve whispered, looking upwards.

Three loud thumps landed on the front door of the shop. Eve didn't move. Jamie gulped. They all looked at the front door in dread.

"Eve! Are you in there?" Cathal called, knocking on the door.

"It's your father, buíochas le Dia," Eve said.

"Eve, is *everything alright?*" Cathal asked.

"Well, it's a lot better now that you're here."

She pulled Cathal inside and shut the door quickly behind him. As fast as she tried to shut the door a black leather shoe wedged the door open. Cathal immediately looked around. Then a man's arm reached around to grab Eve.

"Get out!" Cathal shouted, and the arm withdrew. "Get out of here!" he shouted again, and the dark figure withdrew his foot. Cathal forced the door shut.

"Eve, *is this* what I think it is?" Cathal asked.

"I don't know. Maybe we're imagining it."

"I didn't imagine *that*. Elisa! Jamie! Are you alright back there?"

"Yeah, Dad," said Elisa.

"Speak for yourself," Jamie muttered.

"You're staying with us tonight, Eve. I'll come back tomorrow to check everything with you," he said, making his way to the sitting room. "I've your bird cage. *Come on*, Elisa and Jamie." Cathal grabbed the throw from the armchair and threw it over the cage. "Are all the doors and windows locked?" he asked, scanning the back of the house.

"Yes," said Eve.

"Jamie, Elisa, stick together and *don't get separated* in the crowd. The car is up the street," Cathal said. "Stay close."

Jamie and Elisa picked up their bicycles from the front of the shop and waited with their father for Eve to lock the door. It wasn't even midday and it seemed so weird that the shop was now closed for the day. Cathal was hyper-alert, constantly looking around them as Eve turned the key on the first, then the second and finally the third door lock.

"*Come on,*" he said.

Cathal scanned the faces of the people walking up and down the busy street as they walked. He searched each one for signs of anything unusual, but in spite of his search, he merely saw individuals and families going about their day. He scrutinised the man playing the fiddle outside the clothes shop. He looked to see if there was anything unusual about the trousers or the hat or even the shoes he wore. He observed the small crowd that had gathered around him and looked for the black leather shoe that had wedged itself in the door of Eve's shop.

"Are you all there?" he asked, looking behind him. Everyone nodded.

Cathal's eyes then tracked the movements of a couple who stood at the window of the jewellery shop to choose their engagement ring and then he diverted his gaze to the far side of the street to a small boy pointing out the pair of runners he wanted his mother to buy him for his Birthday.

"It's over here," he said, hurrying them along.

Elisa and Jamie waited as Cathal helped Eve into the car with her bird cage. He closed the car door and quickly looked around.

"You two jump in. I'll put the bikes on the roof rack," he said, and then lifted Elisa's bicycle. He hurried to secure both bicycles onto the roof all the while watching for any signs of danger. "Lock your doors," he said, and they all pressed down the buttons on the car door next to them to secure themselves inside. "Nice morning!" he said to the man passing by on the footpath, and then quickly hopped into the driver's seat. He locked his door. "We'll be home soon," he said, and drove off.

When they reached the crossroads at the edge of town, Jamie saw his father look at Eve with an expression of concern. He then noticed his father place his hand on Eve's hand before driving straight through.

"It'll be alright now. Is she alright in there?" he asked.

Jamie was more confused than ever. Beyond the crossroads, Jamie noticed an old man dressed in a long black trench coat with his arm outstretched looking for a lift. Jamie watched the man become enraged when they drove past him. He saw him raise his hand and throw a stone at the car. Jamie ducked. The stone struck the back windscreen with a loud bang leaving a hole. Jamie quickly looked up again and saw the man turn into a black dog and run across the road and into the fields.

"*Keep down* you two!" Cathal shouted.

Elisa and Jamie shrunk down in their seats. Jamie really needed Elisa's courage at that moment, and so he reached out his hand to hold Elisa's. Once he held tightly to Elisa's hand he felt stronger. Jamie watched his father again as he spoke in a low tone to Eve. He couldn't hear what they were saying, but by the low and deep tone of their voices, the stiffness in their bodies and the slow and drawn out facial expressions, he could tell that this was something they had seen before or maybe even been through as children. They were best friends then after all, and his father always said that Eve was an old flame, so that must mean that they shared a lot. He looked out the window and could only see white clouds in the blue midday sky. He held on tighter to Elisa's hand. It wasn't long before he could see the tree tops and when he did, he slowly lifted himself onto his seat properly. Jamie could see the front door of his house and his heart delighted. He was home. He released his grip on Elisa's hand, opened the door of the car and ran to his mother.

"*Mam*, are you there?" he called, bursting through the front door.

"I'm in the kitchen, Jamie," she called.

"Mam, *you wouldn't believe* what happened. We went to see Eve. She's outside, and everything went dark, and…"

The knife dropped from Aideen's hand and landed on the kitchen floor. She didn't hear or see her son from that point onwards. She left the kitchen in a complete daze and ran to Elisa. She threw open the door of the car and Elisa, already slumped on the seat, fell from the car and into her mother's arms.

"Elisa!" Aideen cried out.

Cathal had only placed Eve's bird cage on the living room chair when he heard Aideen's cry. He immediately ran to Aideen and Elisa, and lifting his daughter into his arms, he carried Elisa back to the house. Aideen fell to her knees and let out a loud cry. The darkness heard her cry and filled the sky in a black cloud. A large black dog with frothing mouth and deadly black eyes chased up the road towards Aideen, and as fast as that darkness ran, Cathal ran faster. He lifted Aideen from the ground and they both ran into the house.

"Jamie! Close the door!" he shouted. Jamie ran to the front door and the instant his parents crossed the threshold, he slammed the door shut behind them and locked it.

The dog transmuted into the human-like figure of darkness when he reached the yard in front of their home. He pulled the hood down from over his head to reveal an ashen face with a fiery red scar along its left side. Donn threw open the car door and looked inside. He saw the hole in the window and searched all around the seat and floor of the car for the stone he threw. He couldn't find it. Donn stood out of the car and slammed the door behind him. He squinted his black eyes and then approached the door of the house.

"The shutters!" Cathal shouted. Jamie ran to close the window shutters. "*Stay down,*" Cathal called to Eve. Aideen tried to get to her feet to reach Elisa, but Cathal pulled her back down. "Stay down," he whispered.

Three heavy and dull knocks sounded at the front door. No one moved inside. Lightning struck outside the house and in that moment a loud cry came from the bird cage. Jamie looked questioningly at the cage. He had never seen a bird in it. A heavy rain shower began to beat down on the house. Louder the rain sounded outside and then the wind rose up and shook the tiles on the roof. Then everything grew still. Another three knocks sounded at the door.

"It's Danú. Let her in," said Aideen.

"Are you *crazy*?" Cathal asked.

"*Jamie,* let her in," Aideen ordered, and Jamie opened the door.

"Dia daoibh!" Danú said.

"Dia is Muire duit, a Dhanú," Jamie said.

"Good lad, Jamie. You lock the door again now… and keep those shutters closed for another while," Danú said in a pleasant tone. She nodded her hello to Eve.

"I think Elisa fell asleep in the car or something, but Mam is freaking out," Jamie told Danú.

By that time Aideen was examining the unconscious Elisa on the couch to see where she was wounded.

"*What happened?*" Aideen asked.

"Cathal, could you carry Elisa to her bed?" Danú asked. "The doctor is on the way."

"*How did you know* to call the doctor?" asked Cathal, carrying Elisa upstairs to her room.

"Jamie you help Eve with her bird cage. Good lad," Danú said, and with that they were all making their way upstairs to Elisa's room.

Cathal laid the limp Elisa onto her bed and began to remove her shoes. Joachim watched from the wardrobe.

"You can leave those," Danú said, "we'll take it from here."

"What will I get her?" Cathal asked, walking towards the wardrobe.

"Um... a hot water bottle," said Danú.

"I'll get her another blanket from the wardrobe too," he said, placing his hand on the edge of the door.

"A hot water bottle would be great, love," Aideen said, softly. Her face was as pale as the sheet on Elisa's bed and her body was cold.

"I'll get one for you too, Aideen. I won't be long," he said, and walked to the door of the room. "Jamie, come on," he said.

"No, leave Jamie here. He needs to be with his sister," Danú said, and Jamie walked over to Elisa's bed and sat down next to her.

"What happened to her?" Jamie asked.

"It seems she's had a bump on the head," said Danú, feeling the back of Elisa's head. "She's in the dreamtime now," she said, "and you need to be here to call her out of it."

Danú reached down and found the stone at the back of Elisa's collar. She held the coarse black stone in her hand for a few seconds and had a terrible feeling in her heart. She looked at Eve with grave concern.

"You know what to do," she said, handing the stone to Eve. "The time of fire is here."

Aideen sank on the bed on hearing those words and began to wail uncontrollably. Jamie looked at his mother and didn't know what to do. He had never seen her cry like this. He looked at Eve for some answer to his mother's tears, but it was clear that her mind was distracted by that black stone.

"I'll go then," Eve said in a soft voice. "I... I..."

"Go n-éirí leat. Good luck," Danú whispered.

It was then that Éataín stepped through the boundary and into Elisa's room.

"I'm here now, Aideen," said Éataín.

She hugged Aideen tightly while she cried from the depths of her soul. The struggle had been too much for Aideen and there had been years of pain that she had not wished to visit and a loss so great that she had not wished to cry. Jamie watched his mother cry and shake and knew he could do nothing to make her feel better. Éataín nodded to Eve, and Eve stepped through the boundary between the two worlds.

Eve stood in Kapheus for a short while to survey her surroundings before removing the throw from over her large, gleaming, brass birdcage and opening the latch on the door. Within a few short seconds Eve had transformed into a large phoenix. Her body and wings were fiery red in colour, and at the wing tips, the red faded to orange and then to yellow. Her very long tail that was the length of her body again swished as she turned her fiery-red head to look around again through piercing blue eyes. She stood tall on her very long fiery-red legs before stretching her wings. Her wing span was enormous stretching at least ten feet. The phoenix ran quickly in steps that were in synchronicity to her wingbeats and then took flight. She tucked her legs under herself to create a streamlined body shape and she was airborne. The phoenix continued her flap-flap-glide sequence through the sky and fanned her magnificent tail to battle the ocean crosswind passing through the valley.

"Jamie, will you pick up Eve's birdcage. She left it in Kapheus," Danú whispered.

Jamie was shocked to hear those words, and after all, his mother was sitting at the end of the bed. She didn't know about Kapheus.

"Go on! Be quick about it," Danú whispered.

Jamie stood up and tried his best to step around his crying mother without being seen. He took one look back at his mother and stepped into Kapheus. Once inside Kapheus, he reached down to pick up the birdcage directly in front of him and then return, but he saw something in the corner of his eye and heard a bird cry out in the sky. Jamie looked up and saw the most magnificent creature in flight. Jamie was in awe as he watched the phoenix glide across the valley. He wanted to stand there forever watching her majestic flight, but knowing that Danú was waiting on the other side, he quickly picked up the throw on the ground, grabbed hold of the cage and quietly re-entered Éire. Jamie gently placed the birdcage on the floor at the end of Elisa's bed while trying not to be seen and then quietly placed the throw over it. He tiptoed around his mother and sat back down on the bed beside Elisa. His mother hadn't noticed a thing.

The phoenix flew high above the valley. The first to see her were the elves on horseback returning from the far fields.

"Tine!" a horseback rider shouted, pointing to the sky. All the others looked upwards to see the phoenix gliding high above them. The word spread like wild fire that the phoenix had returned to Kapheus. She flew high into the hills and hovered close to Éataín's cottage.

"The phoenix!" Fiona exclaimed.

Fiachra looked out the window to see the phoenix turn and like a dynamo plummet to the lower valley at high speed. She stretched out her wings above the long grass for all to see that she had returned to Kapheus, and then lifted herself high above the earth once again. The phoenix pushed ahead in her flap-flap-glide sequence with increasing flight speed until she reached the veil of the Meadow of Discovery. She tucked her wings close and pierced the veil as if it didn't even exist. Onward she flew, flap-flap-glide, flap-flap-glide, until the woods of Kapheus were only a wing's length from her, and then she disappeared inside. The elves looked up from their work to the phoenix standing in front of him. The phoenix bowed to the elves and they to her, and then the phoenix took flight again. She lifted her body upwards and then swirled high into the woodland beneath the canopy of tree tops. The bird of fire came to rest again on the branch of Grandmother Oak. The phoenix looked at the tree and noticed the work Feehul had done to heal her wound. With one breath from her fiery beak, she cast her flames onto Grandmother Oak's wound and as a sapling grows from the fragility and delicacy of youth to the strength and wisdom of old age, Grandmother Oak's branch regrew with no trace of its wounding.

The phoenix then stood tall, released her grip on the branch and floated downward. Flap-flap-glide, flap-flap-glide and she had left the woods of Kapheus. Dagda raced to reach her. He desperately wanted to speak to her, but by the time he had reached the edge of the woodland, she was gliding across the plains. He watched her fly in the direction of La Petite Maison Le Fèvre and he willed her to heal Rós.

In Kapheus, Jamie like Dagda willed his sister to heal. He watched her sleeping in her bed and could do nothing for her. He looked around him and everyone seemed to be preoccupied with their own sorrow. Even Danú kept rubbing Elisa's hand and whispering words to her in the ancient language that Jamie had never heard anyone speak before. Not only that, Jamie couldn't understand how Éataín could hear his mother crying and walked through the boundary to be with her. This was so weird, and the weirdest part was that his mother didn't seem to mind being hugged by a stranger that appeared out of nowhere. Jamie needed space and he stood up and left Elisa's room. He walked downstairs to his father and sat at the living room table.

"How's Elisa?" Cathal asked.

"I don't know, Dad. I think she's going to be alright. Everybody is thinking of other things up there," he said, resting his head down onto his folded arms on the table.

Jamie looked at the glowing red and orange embers in the fire. They lured him in as he watched the embers' edges turn to grey and die. Jamie remembered the phoenix. She was bursting with life and fire, and yet he had never seen her in the birdcage. 'My destiny mustn't be linked with hers,' he thought. Jamie remembered the time Jeremiah taught them all he knew about the earth in the woods of Kapheus and how you will only see a creature if your destiny is linked to theirs. He thought that this was a very strange thing. They didn't seem to have any connection to each other in Éire, but in Kapheus she was alive and magnificent beyond words. He saw every feather on her body and her majesty in the sky.

Jamie wondered where Eve had gone. He hadn't seen her in the meadow. He sighed and thought of Elisa and wondered what would happen to her. He couldn't understand why anyone would want to hurt her. She didn't do anything.

"What is it?" Cathal asked.

"Huh?" Jamie asked.

"What's happening?"

"There's a lot going on up there, Dad," Jamie said.
"Like what?"
"Mam's crying."
"I know she is, Jamie. I hope the doctor comes soon," Cathal said.
"I don't think she is crying about Elisa."
"What is she crying about, Jamie?"
"I don't know."
Cathal secured the lid on the second hot water bottle and handed
them both to Jamie.
"*Here*, take them to your Mam," he said. "I'll keep a look out for
the doctor."

The phoenix flew majestically above the valley until she reached a
high ledge on the hills. She gracefully came to rest there and looked
across the land of Kapheus once more. She looked far out to the
western seas and the island beyond the coastline of Kapheus. She
watched the river run off the edge of the cliff and come thundering
to the earth and the large rainbow guiding the water's fall. She
watched the birds flying across the land and then she saw it looking
straight at her from the opposite hills. Iolar took flight and flew
towards the phoenix at speed, she then hovered in the air above
her before landing on the ledge next to her. Once on the ledge,
Iolar, who rarely uttered a sound, released a high pitch, rhythmic
and whistled cry forcing the phoenix to leave the ledge to continue
her journey, and she did. She flew to her final destination and that
was the door of La Petite Maison Le Fèvre.
"Do you hear it?" Micah asked Rós. He walked towards the front
door of the cottage.
Micah opened his front door to see a large and majestic phoenix
standing directly in front of him. He took fright.
"How did *you get here?*" he asked, but the phoenix did not oblige
him with an answer.
She looked straight at him, her fiery red head turning from side to
side and her beady blue eyes examined every inch of him from the
hair on his head to the laces on his shoes. Micah looked down at
his shoes. The lace was coming loose and he felt like a boy who
had just been scolded by his mother to tie his lace. He didn't dare

reach down to tighten his lace in case the phoenix might do something unexpected. By the time he looked up from his shoes, the phoenix was staring directly into his eyes. She had an expectant look that made Micah grow very uneasy. He desperately wanted to turn around and retreat into the security of his home but was afraid to withdraw eye contact in case the phoenix might take a plunge towards him. He took one step back.

"Umm… Rós… love… Rós?"

"What is it, Micah?" she asked, not wishing to leave her work.

"Rós, I think you should come out here. There's a phoenix…" he said, holding the door wide open.

Rós immediately dropped her chisel and mallet and turned her wheelchair around. She propelled herself to the door at a quick pace. The phoenix reached her long neck through the doorway as Rós approached.

"I think it wants you," Micah said.

"Leave us," Rós said, softly.

"Happily," he said and stepped inside. Rós closed the door behind her.

"Eve! *Why have you come?*" she asked.

The phoenix dropped the black stone from her beak onto Rós' lap. Rós' face turned ashen as she held it in her hand. She rolled it over and back along the palm of her hand.

"I… I… It's," she said, handing it back to the phoenix. "It's too late for me. I'll *never* walk again," she said, looking up at the phoenix. The phoenix tilted her head from side to side. "I… It…" Rós said, struggling to find her words. "Too much time has passed since I was struck by this stone," she said, but the phoenix merely looked blankly at her. "I can *do nothing* now," Rós said.

"It's Elisa, Rós. Elisa's been struck by it," Éataín said, approaching them.

Chapter 4

Phoenix Rising

"*Elisa got a bang on the head,*" Jamie scolded, holding the door of the wardrobe open. "*She's sleeping.* We just have to stay with her tonight to watch her to make sure she doesn't get any worse... *You were supposed* to mind her. Grandmother Oak *told you to.*"

Joachim remained huddled next to the dragon egg in the wardrobe of Elisa's room, and said nothing.

"You're *a useless wolf!*" Jamie shouted, and slammed the door of the wardrobe, but it crept open again. Jamie slammed it again and then again.

"Stupid lock is bust!"

Jamie looked at Elisa sleeping and took a deep and angry breath. The anger now raged inside him and he wanted revenge. He thought about...

"*What's this* I'm hearing?" asked Ruan, stepping through the boundary with his brother Lir.

"*That wolf was supposed to mind* Elisa, and *she got hit in the head,*" Jamie retorted.

Ruan stood with his hands on his hips and his chest out. He did his utmost to make himself look tall and strong at that moment, but Jamie had already grown taller than him and it was quite a difficult task for him to appear larger than Jamie.

"*And why* does that give you *the right to treat him* so?" Ruan asked.

"He's *useless!*" Jamie snapped.

Ruan glanced into the wardrobe and saw Joachim. He had never seen him huddled in the corner of anything, and probably had not huddled anywhere since he was a young pup.

"*It seems to me that you,* my lad, think that you have *more power than this black wolf* and that *you are doing your best* to make him *feel less* than you... Where is it written *that you* have permission *to do that?*" Ruan asked.

"I can do what *I want!*" Jamie yelled.

"You can do many things," said Ruan, "and shooting him dead is not one of them. I can read your thoughts, Jamie. Remember that."

"*I don't care,*" said Jamie, walking towards the door.

"That wolf could kill you right now in this room, and if he chose it, he could drag you to Kapheus and feast on you with his pack. *That wolf* is far more powerful *than you,* but he understands his power and *chooses to live compassionately towards you* at this moment," Ruan said in anger. "Remember that!"

"I'm leaving," quipped Jamie, and he stormed out of the room.

Ruan scratched his head and looked around. When he saw Elisa lying on her bed, he crept slowly towards her and saw that her breathing was shallow, her face was pale and her body lifeless.

"My dear, Elisa. Stay with us," said Ruan, holding her hand.

Ruan was then distracted on hearing Joachim moving in the wardrobe.

"I'm sorry, Joachim. He made my blood boil," said Ruan. "I shouldn't have been so angry with him."

"I could not save her, Ruan. It was written long since before Elisa ever set foot on Kapheus that this would happen to her. Destiny had predicted this moment and nothing I would have done could have prevented it," Joachim said, stepping out of the wardrobe.

The black wolf walked to Elisa's bed and nuzzled at her bedcovers as she lay sleeping.

"She is slipping into the depths of her being," he said. "Were you called to take her with you?" he asked.

"No. We were sent to be your watchers and messengers," Lir said, proudly.

Joachim climbed onto Elisa's bed.

"What have the stars told us? It's been a while since my paws set foot on Kapheus. Be my messenger now and look to the night sky. Tell me what is written in the stars. Ask Taragon if need be," he said, and then Joachim pulled the bedcovers up around Elisa's neck to keep her warm. He lay down next to her and placed his head close to her heart.

"You heard what he said, Lir," said Ruan. He held Elisa's hand for a few seconds longer and then left with Lir to view the Kaphien night sky. "If only Jamie wouldn't make my blood boil so much. I could do with a walk right now anyway. That boy!"

Jamie sat at the living room table and lay his head down on his folded arms. He stared into the fire and watched the burning embers spark and then fade and die. The longer Jamie sat there the more enraged he became. He thought that Ruan had no right to give out to him in his own home. It was none of Ruan's business how he treated the wolf, and anyway that wolf was useless. He was supposed to mind Elisa and she's in bed now. Jamie thought of all the times that injustices were done to him in Kapheus and all the times Elisa and the elves and everyone laughed and made fun of him. He was fed up of them all and he could say and do as he liked. He thought that when Elisa woke up that he would sort a few things out with her about Kapheus.

"I'm beginning to wonder if *it was you* who was hit with the stone," said Danú.

"*What's that supposed to mean?*" Jamie snapped.

"There is a rage inside you, Jamie, that I've never seen so strong," Danú said.

Cathal looked over from his chair by the fire to see Jamie's face full of rage. He put his newspaper down at the side of the chair and observed him.

"It's *none of your business,*" Jamie muttered under his breath.

Jamie stood up and went to the kitchen to make himself a sandwich. One after the other, he slammed the doors of the kitchen presses until he finally found the bread loaf on the countertop where his mother always left it. He cut himself two slices of bread, he lifted the lid off the butter tub and picked up a knife from the cutlery drawer, slamming the drawer shut. Jamie then walked to the refrigerator to find a piece of ham and a portion of cheese and slammed that door. He sliced the ham and cut two pieces of cheese to add to it, and eventually, his sandwich was made. He poured himself a glass of water from the tap and left the kitchen. Jamie dropped his plate heavily on the table along with his glass of water all the while his father watched him in silence.

Jamie looked across the room and saw his father looking straight back at him.

"Finish your sandwich," Cathal said.

Jamie bit into his sandwich, chewed and swallowed. His father watched him. Jamie then took another bite and then another until he finished the sandwich. In all this time, Jamie was conscious that his father watched him. Cathal remained as still as a statue. Jamie reached down and lifted his glass. He took the final sip of water and put the glass back down on the table. His father's eyes were still watching him. He lifted his glass and plate to leave them back into the kitchen.

"Sit back down," Cathal said.

Jamie nervously sat down on his chair. Cathal said nothing for what seemed an eternity. Jamie's heart began to beat faster. In fact, it was not only Jamie that felt uncomfortable, but Danú too felt very uneasy with the tension between father and son. Jamie wasn't sure whether his father was trying to think of something to say or whether he was trying not to say something.

"*Your mother* is sleeping… and *your sister* is resting, and with *all my heart*, I hope Elisa will recover tonight. What is *your reason* for *your rude behaviour?*" Cathal asked.

"*I wasn't being rude*. I just…"

"You were rude to your mother by slamming all the doors in her kitchen. You were rude to your sister by making so much noise, and you were *clearly rude* to Danú. I saw it all with my own eyes and heard it with my own ears," Cathal said.

Danú didn't speak. She actually didn't want to move for fear that she would come between them.

"I was…"

"You are angry," Cathal said, "and you have taken your anger out on everyone and everything that has crossed your path this evening." Cathal picked up his newspaper. "What does that make you?" he asked.

Jamie lifted his glass and plate from the table to return them to the kitchen again.

"*Sit back down,*" his father said in a firm voice. "What does that make you?" Cathal asked again.

"I don't know," said Jamie.

"It makes you rude," Cathal said. "*Who gave you* permission to treat another person or their property poorly, because *you* are angry?"

"No one."

"No one," said Cathal. "If you're angry go outside and sweep the yard or clean out the stables, but don't take your anger out on any person, creature or property," he said in a very clear voice. Cathal looked intently at Jamie. "*Do I make myself clear?*" he asked.

"Yes," said Jamie, and he stood up.

"Danú is due an apology," Cathal said.

"Sorry," Jamie muttered under his breath.

"*With a bit of meaning, Jamie.*"

"Sorry, Danú. Tá brón orm," Jamie said.

Elisa's fate was hanging in the balance, and despite Jamie's optimism, the Kaphiens knew the level of danger she was in. News had spread that Elisa was hit on the head by Donn's stone and all Kaphiens knew that no creature who was hit on the head with this stone survived. They simply drifted into a non-waking sleep until their death. The light of the elves' lanterns streamed across the valley as they walked from the woodland and the meadow to climb along the narrow mountain pathway to La Petite Maison Le Fèvre. This was a monumental moment in Kaphien history and all Kaphiens wanted to either be there to witness the effort or to support Rós in any way they could. Some elves huddled together in their homes coming up with plans on how best to help Elisa, others searched for herbs and plants to create a potion that could in some way pull her from her deep sleep. Feehul became more disoriented with every hour that passed and was by now hidden from the Kaphiens in Sinann's home by An Abhainn Solais.

"I can't find it," Feehul said. "*I can't find what I'm looking for.*"

"What are you looking for?" Sinann asked.

"I don't know."

"Feehul, come sit with me. The elves are searching for a potion to heal Elisa," Sinann said.

"I must do that. I'm the medicine elf," Feehul said. He looked into his bag again for something. "*I need to leave. I need to go to Elisa,*" Feehul said, agitated.

"Rós will find a way. Come sit with me," Sinann said. "You can leave as soon as the sun rises."

Sinann sat Feehul by the fire and gave him tea and biscuits. She looked out of her home to see the train of lanterns making their way across the valley and upwards to La Petite Maison Lè Fevre. Inside that cottage, Rós sat at her workstation using the tip of her chisel to eliminate the undesired rough edges of the black stone. She worked diligently all the while Éataín stood next to her in anticipation. Rós was so focussed that she hadn't lifted her eyes from her work for well over four hours now. It was clear that finding the core of this stone meant more to her than to anyone else in Kapheus. This was the stone that had struck her spine and condensed her to life in a wheelchair and to live in a home far away from those she loved in the woods of Kapheus. Her thoughts drifted to the moment when she was struck, when she and the Tuatha Dé Danann fought against the darkness in the woods of Kapheus. 'It was all in vein,' she thought. 'The Dark One occupies Cormac's Cave and my family are in hiding in the woods that are our home,' she thought.

"Don't think like that," Éataín said. "Don't let despair and hopelessness take hold."

Rós saw the elves lantern lights outside her window and sighed deeply.

"Micah! You'll need to leave," Rós said, agitated. Micah put on his coat without saying a word and left their home.

Rós returned her focus, flattening and smoothing the stone's surface from top to base. As the night closed in, Éataín lit the paraffin oil lamps dotted all around the living room to give Rós more light. The elves supplemented this with the lantern lights they held up to the window while they peered through. Rós' hands were the colour of charcoal by now, and although tiredness was gripping her, she continued to work the chisel with the thoughts of every creature weighing on her.

Micah sat outside on a nearby rock and waited. He pulled the collar of his coat up higher on his neck to keep warm and on seeing this, the phoenix who had been lying down watching his every movement a short distance away opened her beak and lit a fire next to him.

"I don't know why you did that but thanks," he said. A cheeky grin appeared on his face. "I'm still not totally sure that you like me," he said, looking back at the phoenix. Expressionless, the phoenix stared back at him.

"Do you mind if we join in?" asked an elf.

"Of course," Micah said, inviting them to warm themselves by the fire.

"Do you think she can do it, Micah?" asked an elf.

"I don't know. I don't know enough about Kapheus to even know if she is succeeding or failing in there," said Micah, looking back to the large rectangular window and his wife inside.

"Feehul isn't doing too well," said the elf. "Their lives are both linked you know." The elf looked through the large rectangular window worryingly.

"I need a higher vibration," Rós said, rubbing her forehead. "*I need a higher vibration…* The darkness is *so strong* in this stone," she said. "I want to extract the metal from it and chiselling isn't working. I need a heat that will break it open. I need to get to the *heart* of this stone. This chisel is not enough," she said, placing her hands on her head. Rós pushed her chair back from the work table and made her way to the front door.

"I need to think Éataín. *I just need* a second to think," she said.

Rós opened the front door and went outside. Micah looked around and saw the expression on Rós' face as she looked up at the night stars. He knew by now that expression meant not to say a word, and rather than speak to Rós, he decided to look at the night sky too. The sky was so clear that it felt the universe was filled to capacity with planets and stars.

A young elf climbed onto Rós' lap and rested against her.

"You're up very late," she whispered, caressing her.

"*Look Rós*, it's the bright star Capella and the Big Dipper's bowl," said another elfin child, smiling back at Rós.

Rós smiled and then noticed Camelopardalis moving in the slow loping step of the camel in the starry sky.

"*I'm Orion the Hunter*," a young elfin child said, playfully holding his make-believe jewelled sword firmly in his hand. "These are my

hunting dogs Canis Major and Canis Minor," he said, pointing to
the imaginary dogs at his side.

Rós laughed.

"Is that the Milky Way passing through Canis Major?" she asked
the elf. He looked down at his imaginary dog a little confused. Rós
pointed to the sky and then he saw the milky way with its open
clusters passing through his faithful companion.

"See! Canis Minor is on my shoulder," he said, proudly recognising
his dog in the stars.

Rós remembered the wolfhound she had as a child. He became so
big that his paws reached to her shoulders when he jumped to
welcome her home. She watched the young elf playfully pet his
imaginary dog and remembered how her wolfhound loved to have
his belly rubbed.

"Have you ever seen the phoenix in the night sky, Eve?" Rós
asked, looking around. "I've never seen it, but I know it's there."

The phoenix looked at Rós blankly. She then noticed the stone in
her hand and looked at her more inquisitively.

"We're running out of time, Rós. It'll soon be morning," said
Éataín.

"*I know*, but I'm trying to think, and… it's just that the darkness in
this stone is so powerful. I can't reach its heart," she said, holding
it up. "I need to raise the vibration of it, and there *is no way I can
think to do it.*"

The phoenix slowly and quietly rose to her feet and then reached
out and in an instant she had snatched the stone from Rós. She
held it in her beak as everyone nervously looked on, and then she
tilted her head backwards, arched her neck and swallowed it.

"*What are you doing*, Eve?" Rós yelled.

The phoenix stared at Rós. Her eyes changed colour from crystal
blue to fiery red.

"Micah! Run! Rithigí!" Rós shouted.

The phoenix raised her wings to the sky and her feathers turned to
flames. A ball of fire rose up from the pit of her stomach and grew
larger until it enveloped the phoenix. She combusted. Ashes fell
from the air and landed in a heap in front of them. The little elf
held tightly to Rós, hiding her eyes in her bosom.

"I'll take her," said the elf's mother, and lifted her toddler from Rós' lap and held her in her arms.

"I've never seen a phoenix die," Micah said, curiously looking at the ashes on the ground.

"And you probably won't see it happen again," said Rós in jest.

They all watched as the fledgling phoenix rose from the ashes. Like a bird pecking at its shell with its small but sharp egg tooth and pushing itself free with its wings, the phoenix's beak first emerged from the ashes. Then her little head appeared. She struggled and fell over as she grasped the earth with her wings to pull her to freedom, but still kept going. With her wings now free, she pulled the rest of her body from the ashes and before long the fledgling phoenix stood in front of them with that all familiar vacant look in her crystal clear blue eyes.

Micah lifted her into his hands and he delighted in holding such a precious creature of Kapheus. He was a stranger to this land after all, and almost everything was strange and exciting to him. Before he came to Kapheus, he had never known an eagle to speak nor had he met any tree like Grandmother Oak. The elves were creatures to which he was very accustomed, but leprechauns and their ways were altogether peculiar to him. Now, he held in his hand one of the most magnificent birds he had ever known to exist. However, on this occasion, her feathers were wet and scraggly looking and a dirty ashen colour rather than the deep red of the mature phoenix.

"She's kinda cute in an ugly kind of way," said Micah. The phoenix opened her mouth wide and screeched. "*Oh*, here Éataín! I think she's looking for you," said Micah.

"Another fledgling to feed," said Éataín, taking her from Micah's palm.

"Stop!" Rós shouted, reaching out to Micah. He froze to the spot. "You were about to step on the ashes," she said. "Micah, will you look for the black heart?" Rós asked, searching the ashes. Rós then turned around and returned to the cottage with great enthusiasm. "The heart of the stone is in there. It's a metal ore. *Don't touch it* with your hands. Put your gloves on first," she said.

"And I'll need to feed this fledgling," said Éataín. The elfin children jumped up and down trying to get a glimpse of the little bird of fire.

"I know your parents wanted you to be awake for this moment in Kaphien history, *but really*," said Éataín, "are you *not* in the *least bit tired?*" she asked.

"Níl mé," said a little elf, "I'm not tired."

He opened his hands to show Éataín his pile of large black beetles he had collected for the phoenix. The beetles crawled up his arms and he laughed as they tickled him. Then the other young elves picked the beetles off his arms and reached up to feed them to the phoenix.

"Hold on, Elisa. We've found the way," Éataín whispered, and stroked the phoenix.

Elisa was barely holding on. With every minute that passed she fell deeper into the darkness of her mind. Something stirred Joachim. He woke and lifted his head from Elisa's chest.

"It's almost dawn," Joachim said. "Can you hear me, Elisa? You need to hold on," he said. There wasn't even a murmur from Elisa. "Hold on! I'm coming to find you," the black wolf said.

Joachim merged his heartbeat to Elisa's and dived into the dreamland to find her. In Elisa's dreamland, Joachim found himself standing in a dark wood. The trees were tall and plentiful, but the ground was almost dead and devoid of any life under his paws. He howled for Elisa, but she didn't hear him. He howled again and then one more time. Elisa woke from the base of a tree. Her head ached, and her vision was blurred. In that movement, Joachim heard her. He turned his head to track her scent.

'Where are you going, Joachim?' a dark figure asked, coming from behind a tree.

Soon Joachim was surrounded by twenty dark human-like figures. They wore long black cloaks that reached to their ankles with hoods that stretched over their heads making it impossible to see their faces.

'Where are you going, Joachim, the black wolf of Kapheus?' Donn asked. He moved closer. Joachim snarled. 'You *will not* save her,' Donn cried.

He reached out his hand and the nails of his fingers grew as sharp and as long as blades. He struck out and tore through Jaochim's body. The wolf dropped to the ground wincing in pain.

'You are not strong enough to break the spell in Éire,' Donn said. 'There is only one who has that power, and she has long been lost to Kapheus.'

'*Power...* power is not always found in strength,' said Joachim, breathing heavily. 'Power's in unity,' he said. '*You have not known me.* You're too young to have known my life. You made a mistake striking me,' Joachim said, pulling himself up with his front legs. His left hind leg was bleeding heavily now. Joachim howled loudly, and his pack appeared in the wood. He howled and then he was gone. Joachim had disappeared from sight.

Onwards he ran catching the scent of Elisa while his pack dealt with the darkness behind him.

"Elisa! Elisa!" Jamie called, but she didn't wake up for him. "Elisa!" he called again, but she didn't stir. "What is *that wolf doing* on Elisa's bed?" Jamie snapped. He lunged forward to pull Joachim off his bed, and as he pulled, Joachim came tumbling to the ground in the dark wood of the dreamland. Just then Danú walked into the room. "Jamie! Don't touch Joachim!" she shouted and ran to stop him. "Leave *that wolf* alone. He is trying to save your sister," she said, pulling Jamie away from him. "*Sit down* over there and *don't move!*" Jamie pulled himself away from Danú's grip and sat on the floor with his back against the bedroom wall. Danú sat down next to Elisa and held her hand.

Elisa tried to stand but stumbled and fell over. She tried again but felt so dizzy that she simply couldn't do it. The ground moved as if she stood on the deck of a ship in a storm. Joachim howled again, and she wanted to get to him. She stood up and stumbled as she reached out her hand to balance against the tree bark. She looked around, but all the trees appeared as moving objects in her dizzy state. Elisa heard Joachim howl again and she walked towards the sound of his howl but fell onto a fawn curled up on the ground. Elisa lay on top of the fawn unable to find her bearings, and while there, the fawn filled her with his light. Joachim saw that light in the north and ran to them. Elisa faded in and out of a sleeping state as she watched Joachim run towards her. She saw his figure getting bigger with each step closer and then Elisa felt Joachim nuzzle at her body. Finally feeling safe, Elisa gave up the fight and drifted from him deeper into the dreamland.

"Do you have it, Rós?" Micah asked.

"Nearly," she said, pouring the metal from the hot pan into the mould. The metal weaved its way slowly through the three rings of the Spiral of Life as they watched.

"Dawn *is almost here,"* Éataín said, panicking.

Rós patiently poured and watched the three rings fill.

"Here it is!" she said. "Did you call Iolar?" Rós asked Éataín.

"Yes, she's waiting outside."

"Here!" Rós said. She closed the mould and secured it on all sides with two separate straps and metal clamps. *"Here,* Éataín," Rós said, handing it to her.

Éataín hurried to give it to the waiting Iolar, and as soon as Iolar grasped it in her claw, she flew away to the far hills.

"Do you think, she'll make it?" Rós asked, watching the golden eagle in flight.

Iolar didn't falter for one moment on her path to free Elisa from the clutches of darkness. Onward she flew until she reached the eye of the mountain and flew straight through the cliff face and into the lungs of Dún Aonghusa.

"The mould will disintegrate in time and the straps will fall off. Someone will find it one day," said Micah, standing next to Rós.

Rós didn't want to hear that. She knew all those things, but for now, Elisa needed to be saved. Rós thought of Elisa lying in her bed and wanted so much that things would be different for her.

Elisa lay in her bed with Danú by her side holding her hand but not even Danú could reach her. Danú knew there was no crystal in all those crystals that she sold at the market that could save Elisa. The one elf that could probably buy Elisa more time was himself taken by the darkness that penetrated Elisa's brain, and by now, Feehul barely knew his sister's name.

"Come on, my sweet Elisa. Fall into the light of your soul. It'll save you," Danú said. She whispered to the goddess of Éire in the ancient language in an attempt to help Elisa summon the strength of her ancestors to her.

'Dúisigh a stór," Danú whispered. "Wake up, my love. Wake up."

"You never wear black boots, Danú," Jamie said, questioningly. He remembered the old woman in the post office who had worn black leather boots, black tights and a black skirt under her coat just like those Danú was now wearing. Danú looked at Jamie with a mix of annoyance and uncertainty. She was not his guardian and so she could not scold him for his poor behaviour as this would run the risk of falling out with Aideen and Cathal. Yet, in this silence, the balance of power had swayed in Jamie's direction.

"I think we have bigger fish to fry than the colour of Danú's boots, Jamie, and I don't want you creating a problem for anyone," Aideen said, standing in the doorway. "Go on to your room and get some sleep," Aideen said.

"*I'm staying here with Elisa,*" Jamie remonstrated.

"*You're going to your room to sleep*, and maybe you will wake up in a better state of mind." Jamie passed his mother by and walked into his own room, closing the door behind him.

"I'm sorry about that, Danú. I'll take over from you now. It's almost dawn," Aideen said.

Danú rubbed her tired eyes.

"Ceart go leor. I'll go downstairs for a cup of tea," she said. Danú placed her hand on Aideen's arm. "You don't need to be concerned. Cathal was here the whole night. You didn't miss a thing," she said and left.

Aideen stood still in the doorway looking at Elisa. She made no attempt to wake her from the dreamland or to offer any comfort to her as she slept. Nor did she call the doctor knowing that Elisa was slipping farther into the stillness as she lay on the bed. She scanned the bedroom to find what she was searching for earlier but didn't see it. Aideen turned and walked down the hallway.

In the dreamtime, the dark figures returned while Elisa lay immersed in the young fawn's light. Joachim crouched down when he saw them approach. Like all wolves before attack, he assumed an ambivalent facial expression in an attempt to stare down the dark figures. The strangers continued to approach. His ears tilted forward, and the hairs stood tall on his back. He curled his lips upwards and snarled. Donn laughed. Joachim then crouched backwards and cocked his tail. He showed his fangs and his eyes were wild. He snapped his jaws. His pack filed in behind him with bristled hair and snapping jaws. The dark hooded figures hesitated. Donn then removed his hood to reveal a black-eyed man with a fiery-red scar stretching the full length of his face. He looked at the others and then smiled. His teeth were liked pointed daggers in his mouth and black with rot. He lifted a gleaming silver sword from beneath his cloak and was certain that victory was his.

"The darkness will take her," said Micah. "It'll take her one way or another."
Rós did not answer him. She instead focussed on any sign of Iolar in the distance.
"They're preparing themselves for the time of fire," Micah said. "I never thought that I'd see it happen in my lifetime."
Rós couldn't think of anything other than Iolar and the fountain of youth. A red hue rested above the foggy hills as the sun began to rise. Rós' heart beat faster in her chest; the tension was almost unbearable. She searched the hillside and prayed for Iolar to appear from Dún Aonghusa.
"Hold on! Hold on!" said Micah, rising to his feet. "*I see her.* I see her!" he exclaimed. "Where?"
"There! Look! She's made it!"
Rós searched the far hillside and it was true. Iolar was on her return flight. There was no more welcome a sight on a Spring morning as this.

Elisa tossed and turned on her bed and slowly opened her eyes. She lifted her arm and caressed Joachim's side and he woke. "Joachim! You're *bleeding*," she said, lifting her blood-drenched fingers from his side. "I know what will heal you. *Don't move.*"

Elisa crept downstairs, passed her father sleeping on the armchair in the living room and stepped into the galley kitchen. She climbed up on the counter top and reached to the very back of the shelf to retrieve the jar of clear ointment. She quietly climbed down from the counter top and crept across the living room floor and tiptoed upstairs to Joachim. Danú smiled as she watched her from the chair in the corner. She stood up and left through the front door. "This will work, Joachim," said Elisa, unscrewing the lid of the clear glass jar.

She dipped her two fingers into the clear ointment and scooped out a big blob. Elisa lifted the black hair from around his wounded body and dabbed the ointment onto the puncture wound. The ointment soaked into the wound and began to heal Joachim internally layer by layer until it reached the surface of his skin and then his puncture wound closed. A small tuft of black hair grew in its place. Elisa applied the ointment to each of the five wounds while Joachim lay still.

"How are you feeling?" Joachim asked.

"I've a really bad headache."

"What do you remember?"

Elisa paused for a while. She remembered leaving the house, and she remembered cycling into town to meet Jamie. She remembered cycling, she was sure of that, and of feeling the cold fresh breeze on her skin. Beyond that, she struggled to think of anything else. "I don't know how I ended up in bed," she said.

"You bumped your head," Joachim said. "That's all. You just bumped your head and you needed to rest."

Elisa reached down and kissed Joachim. She pulled the blankets over him and he closed his eyes to rest. Elisa crept downstairs again to return the glass jar to the cupboard. She then decided to make some porridge. Elisa poured the oat flakes into the pot of water and stirred the oat flakes trying not to wake her sleeping father.

She couldn't find the bowls and couldn't remember where the spoons were kept.

"*Elisa,*" Cathal called, standing in the doorway. "How are you feeling?"

"I can't remember where the spoons are and I've a terrible headache. I wanted to make you porridge, because you were sleeping with your clothes on and..." said Elisa, becoming tearful.

"Shush, it's alright," Cathal said, hugging her.

"Dad, I've a *really bad headache.*"

I'm glad that's all you have," Cathal said. "Let me get your breakfast. Tell me what you'd like," he said, wiping the tears from her eyes.

"Hot chocolate and custard," Elisa said.

"Well, I'll definitely make you hot chocolate, and how about some porridge rather than custard?" he asked. "I promise I'll make you custard later. We can have it for dessert after dinner. Is that a deal?" he asked, and Elisa nodded her head.

"I think it would be good for you to rest again after breakfast," he said, placing his hand on her head.

"After you've eaten breakfast," Sinann said, handing Feehul a bowl of porridge, "you can go wherever you like then." "You're looking a lot better now."

"Go raibh maith agat," said Feehul. "Tá tinneas cinn orm anois."

"Well, I'm sure your headache will go soon," said Sinann. "Elisa is well again thanks to the phoenix."

"What happened?"

"The phoenix combusted with the stone that hit Elisa's head in her mouth. She has risen from the ashes and poor Éataín has been given the task of caring for her," said Sinann.

"Hahaha! Ahahaha!" Feehul laughed. "I'm sure she'll love that," he said. They both laughed heartily thinking of a robin rearing a phoenix.

On the hillside, Éataín took one final look over her shoulder as she pressed down the latch to open the front door of her cottage.

"All is well," she said in a low voice, stepping inside. "Fiona, we have a new fledgling to nurture," she said, pulling the phoenix from her coat pocket. "It's a good thing they grow fast."

Chapter 5

The Time of Fire

Elisa sat on her bed caressing the sleeping Joachim. Her head ached, and she felt a little fuzzy and very tired. To think of how Joachim ended up injured on her bed or anything else beyond allowing her hand to move along Joachim's body was too much to ask of her brain. Those soothing strokes soothed her too as she sat there. Elisa allowed her fingers to pass under the outer layer of his fur and she felt the warm, soft and delicately fine fur beneath. Elisa watched his lungs rise and fall in a smooth and regular motion and she felt completely relaxed.

"Elisa!" Jamie called, and he entered her room. "What's *he* doing here?"

Elisa looked at her brother in surprise.

"*What are you doing with that stick?*" Elisa asked, horrified.

Jamie made his way to Elisa's bed to strike Joachim. Elisa saw the fire in his eyes and stood in front of him. They both struggled for a few seconds until Jamie's anger got the better of him and he threw Elisa to the floor. Elisa began to cry.

"I'm *your sister*," she cried.

Joachim quickly stood up and placed himself squarely in front of Jamie. The hairs stood on his back and he snarled.

"You think you're *better than me*, but you're *not!*" Jamie shouted, holding the stick in his two hands.

"Jamie!" Elisa yelled.

Suddenly, a sliotar came flying through the air and struck Jamie on the shoulder, forcing him to drop the stick.

"Pleidhce!" said the voice from Kapheus.

Setanta stepped through the drawing and faced Jamie. The giant boy looked at him unflinchingly. For a short while, there was a stand-off between Setanta, the giant boy of Kapheus, and Jamie. In the end, Jamie withdrew and Setanta reached down to help Elisa to her feet.

"Did he hurt you, Elisa?" Setanta asked.

"I'm alright," said Elisa, and she blushed.

"I heard you were hit on the head. Ruan and Lir told me. *Are you alright?*"

Setanta swiftly reached out his hand to block Jamie from striking out at Joachim.

"*What's your problem?*"

"I don't *have one!*" Jamie snapped. "And I *didn't* invite *you* into *my house.*"

"What's the deal, Joachim?"

"He has a bee in his bonnet about something, Setanta," said Ruan, opening the door of the wardrobe. "And that's one thing for sure," he said, awkwardly climbing out of the wardrobe and then helping his brother Lir out.

Lir shoved two hot water bottles into Jamie's arms.

"*What am I supposed* to do with *these?*" Jamie growled.

"Boil the kettle and fill them again," said Ruan.

"I'm *not* doing that!"

"Be on your way now, that's a good lad," said Ruan, ushering Jamie from the room and closing the door shut behind him.

Ruan turned around immediately, and with both arms outstretched he held the door shut to block Jamie's return, and he exhaled deeply.

"Do *you know* what's hidden inside *that wardrobe?*" he asked.

"To be honest, I was really wondering what you two were doing in Elisa's wardrobe," said Setanta.

"Oh, that's easily told," said Lir, "we came back late last night to tell Joachim about the night stars, but he was asleep on Elisa's bed. We shook him a few times and he mumbled something about the wardrobe and kept saying 'keep warm'. So, we thought we were to keep warm in the wardrobe. I climbed in and then Ruan followed me," he said, demonstrating what he had done.

"*Get out of the wardrobe, Lir,*" Ruan scolded.

"I was only trying to tell the story," Lir said.

"Oh! Tell your story then! Finish it!"

"Well, I sat in," said Lir, about to sit into the wardrobe. He re-adjusted quickly and stood up straight. "...*there,*" he said, pointing to the base of the wardrobe, "and I felt something wobbly and warm, and well, I put my hand down and it was a hot water bottle.

And I thought *that was really nice of Joachim* to think of us, so I lifted
my hot water bottle and then I found another one for Ruan, and
then…" he said, becoming a bit confused as to where he actually
was in the story.

"And then we found the egg!" declared Ruan, placing his hands to
his head. "And *then* we found *the egg!*"

"Yeah, and then we found the egg," said Lir, proudly.

"And what did you do then?" Setanta asked.

"Well, my boy, we wrapped it up in the hot water bottles again and
well, we kept it warm," said Ruan.

"Elisa, would it be alright if I sit down?" Setanta asked. "It's quite
uncomfortable being bent over like this."

"Do, please," said Elisa.

The giant boy sat on the bedroom floor with his back leaning
against the wall and his legs stretching across the room and under
Elisa's bed.

"I remembered to wash my clothes this time, Elisa," Setanta said,
proudly fixing his cream woollen sweater. "Since I fell into the
fountain of youth my Mam says I'm a new boy. I don't grow as
much now… only as much as a regular boy grows… and *all* my
clothes fit me now, Elisa," Setanta said, ironing the creases on his
green cotton trousers.

Ruan looked at Setanta and lifted his hands to the air in
desperation.

"*It's not the time for wooing,*" Ruan remonstrated.

"Yeah, we were in the middle of a story," said Lir.

"Sorry," said Setanta.

"Well, we reached down and picked it up and examined it and *am
I wrong,* Joachim? Tell me if I'm wrong," he insisted. Ruan
scratched his head and took a breath. "The egg is the fiery red
colour. *Fiery red,*" he said, and then took a more anxious breath.

"It is," said Joachim, hopping down from the bed. He walked to
the wardrobe and grabbed hold of the handle of Fódla's satchel
with his teeth and pulled it out from beneath the clothes in Elisa's
wardrobe. Joachim then walked to Elisa for her to take the satchel
from his grasp, which she did.

"This is the dragon of great fortune. It's the dragon for the ages. One such egg is laid on the twelfth millennium and on no other," said Joachim.

Elisa removed it from the satchel and held it in her hands. The dragon egg was similar in shape to any egg she had ever seen, but much larger and was a lot heavier. She rubbed her thumb against the smooth surface and it transformed from a fiery red colour to the red and orange colour of molten lava.

"Ouch!" Elisa exclaimed. Elisa dropped the red-hot egg onto the bed.

"Let me see!" said Setanta.

He pulled his legs from under Elisa's bed and tucked his knees under him. Setanta stared down at the egg in awe. The egg didn't seem to hold the rigidity of its hard shell anymore, but rather appeared soft with a molten lava type substance flowing around its egg-shaped surface.

"Wow! I've never seen an egg like *that*," Setanta whispered.

"I was right! I knew I was right! *I just knew it*," said Ruan.

"What do we do with it?" Lir asked, shyly.

"We wait," said Joachim.

He rolled the egg with his snout and it returned to the fiery red colour and cooled down again to a hard-shelled egg.

"You can lift it now," said Joachim, grabbing the satchel in his mouth to open it.

"Um… *not you*," said Ruan, stepping between Joachim and Elisa. "*I* was assigned as Joachim's helper", he said, "and I take my duties *very seriously*," Ruan continued, helping Joachim place the egg back into the satchel.

Ruan returned the satchel to the base of the wardrobe and covered it again in the pile of clothes. Ruan's head was still in the wardrobe when Jamie walked into the room with the two hot water bottles. Jamie had a disgruntled look on his face like a boy who had been asked to do something that he clearly felt aggrieved about.

"*Here*," he said, dumping the two hot water bottles into Lir's arms. Lir looked at him and smiled, however, Ruan had a more dissatisfied look on his face. Either way, Lir tucked the hot water bottles around the dragon egg and was delighted to have had the honour of doing it.

Ruan scrutinised Jamie to see if there was any implement that he may have been concealing in one of his front pockets, he stretched to see if Jamie was carrying a sling shot in his back pocket and then looked squarely at Jamie again.

"*What are you looking at?*" Jamie snapped.

"Nothing, my boy," said Ruan.

"*I'm not your boy.*"

"There's truth in that. I'd hope that no boy of mine would behave like that… and *that's for sure*," said Ruan, looking away in disdain.

"*What* were *you* doing with *that egg*, Lir? It wasn't given to you! It was given to *my sister* Elisa," Jamie snapped.

"Jamie, don't be so rude!" Elisa retorted. Jamie ignored his sister. Lir smiled at Jamie. He was so proud of his find and so proud that he had been the one allowed to wrap the hot water bottles around the dragon egg. He couldn't contain his pride and smiled even more broadly at Jamie, showing his perfect set of teeth. Jamie had no answer to Lir's unfaltering happiness. He looked away from him in anger.

"You're *nothing but trouble*," he said to Elisa.

Elisa dropped onto her bed. She was deeply hurt by his words. She believed he was different to her mother. Jamie knew how much it hurt her when their mother said those same words. The tears rolled down her cheeks. Setanta looked at Jamie, but in his shock, he was unable to find the words to reproach him. Jamie in turn looked to all those faces looking right back at him, and though knowing how hurtful his words had been, he didn't care. He left the room.

"As it grows strong inside its shell it will bring your darkness into the light of day, and so it is doing it with Jamie," Joachim said. "It's bringing all the anger he holds deep inside him to the surface."

Jamie stomped downstairs towards the front door.

"Have you seen Eve and Danú?" Cathal asked Jamie.

"Ask Elisa!" Jamie snapped, and he slammed the front door behind him.

"That lad! I'll have to have another word with him this evening," Cathal said, putting his cap on. "I'm going into town to check on Eve. I'll stop by at Danú's on the way to thank her," he said.

"Wait! Bring this loaf of bread to Danú," said Aideen, making her way from the kitchen. "It's still warm, so be careful with it," she said, wrapping the loaf of bread in a tea towel. She kissed Cathal on the cheek.

"I wasn't expecting that. Is there another loaf of bread you'd like to hand me? My other cheek is feeling lonely," Cathal said with a smile.

"You'll have to wait until later," Aideen said, already half-way across the living room.

Cathal closed the door behind him.

In the Kaphien woodland, Cillian was busy securing and waterproofing his shelter that morning. The campfire was warm and inviting and kept the cold from his back while he worked. He felt a shiver every now and again and looked across the woodland to the meadow with a feeling of nervous anticipation. Since the great fire, he had taken it upon himself to be the guardian of the woodlands. The roots of a fallen ash tree had provided the base for this shelter to which he had added long and sturdy branches to create the roof apex joined together like ribs on a boat and secured by thinner and more pliable branches and green vines. By the time Cillian had noticed Feehul, he was in the process of weaving smaller branches in an alternating fashion, in and out of the roof ribs like a seamstress sewing a piece of fabric until he was convinced that the shelter was completely secure and strong. Every once in a while he would look over to see Feehul wandering aimlessly and seemingly lost to his thoughts and wondered what was wrong.

Cillian reached down and took from the pile of woodland debris he had gathered nearby. He added wet earth to it and then heaped it onto the shelter roof to make it waterproof. He looked over at Feehul again and this time he scanned the woodland to see if anyone would join him, but no one did. Cillian shook his head and added another layer of branches to his roof for good measure.

Inside the shelter, he had a thick base of dried leaves on the ground that helped insulate it from the dampness beneath his feet. All in all, it was as secure a shelter as any elf could have constructed. Cillian gave his hands a wash and then sat on his stool peeling a potato with his sharp knife.

"Did you burn your hand?" Cillian asked, seeing Feehul rubbing his hand.

Feehul looked across the woodland.

"It's probably nothing, Cillian," Feehul said, placing his hands down by his side.

Cillian pulled his large brown coat tighter against his body.

"Pass me that log," Cillian said, directing Feehul to the fire. Cillian reached to quench a spark that had escaped from the fire with his brown leather boot.

Feehul walked towards him and lifted the log from the ground and placed it on the fire.

"Sit down beside me. I've plenty of food," said Cillian.

"Are you cold? I can bring you my warm brown woollen jumper and woollen trousers if you want," Feehul said. An elf watched from a tree branch as Feehul sat next to Cillian.

"Get this into you," Cillian said, handing Feehul a bowl of his vegetable stew. "Here, you'll need a spoon," he said, handing him a wooden spoon. "I'm fine for clothes. I feel a chill coming from the east and nothing more."

"Go raibh maith agat," said Feehul. "Thank you," he said, lifting a spoonful of stew to his mouth.

They both sat at the campfire eating in silence until their bowls were empty. Feehul was glad of the silence. He needed to be alone for quite some time now to be in the silence of his mind. Cillian took the bowl from Feehul and filled him another portion of stew. He then added another half portion of stew to his own bowl and sat back down on his stool. The elf continued to watch them from the tree. Cillian waited although every part of him wanted to speak. He hadn't had a conversation with anyone in at least a week, but despite this drive in him to speak, he remained still. The fire needed another log, but Cillian didn't dare to move.

"Fódla is dead," Feehul said. Cillian didn't speak. "Lug almost died and my sister... she... I nearly lost her to the Dark One too... and all the Sanctuary of Lugh is empty... they have all gone to spirit... and the fire... so many died in the woodland... the trees... and Grandmother Oak..."

Cillian remained still. He could see the toll that this had all taken on the greatest medicine elf of all time. He could see how Feehul was expected to heal those around him, and how this expectation negated the fact that he was merely an elf the same as all the others. "I can't do this anymore," Feehul said. "I don't want to see anyone else die." Feehul brushed the dried leaves under his foot. "Do I sound weak?" he asked.

"No. You sound over-burdened. You need time and space," said Cillian. Feehul nodded in agreement.

"The time of fire is here," said Feehul.

"The phoenix has flown?" Cillian asked.

"Yeah."

"The time of fire is not altogether a bad thing. It's a time of wondrous possibility. It all depends on how you view it," said Cillian. He stood up to add another log to the fire. "What do you need?" he asked, fetching more logs from his pile nearby.

"I need to be with my sister."

"Then *go*. Spend time with Sinann, and make sure to tell her that I said hello." Cillian looked at the motionless Feehul. "You are not beholding to anyone. Go!" he said.

"Go raibh maith agat," said Feehul.

"You don't need to thank me. You came up with that idea yourself," he said, watching him walk away. "And *don't* worry about or take on the responsibility of Elisa either. The Children of Light have their own parents to take care of them."

On that particular night, the Children of Light were summoned by their father to sit around the fire. He wished to impart on them a valuable piece of his history, so he thought.

"Gather around now," Cathal said, carrying four mugs of hot chocolate from the kitchen. "Oh, Jamie, will you grab the plate of biscuits. I left it inside," he said.

Jamie rose from his chair with an annoyed look on his face and reluctantly went to the kitchen to get the plate of biscuits.

"Come on, Jamie," Cathal said, handing him a cup of hot chocolate. "I need to tell you a story about Eve and I. Something that happened to us when we were children," he said.

"*We don't* need to hear *another story,*" said Aideen.

"But I'd like to tell it," Cathal said, making himself comfortable on the chair. "Well, when I was a boy my Dad told me the story of the black dog who stood at the crossroads down at Ó Ceallaigh's field. It was the *hound of darkness,*" he said. "The hound would run across the fields in search of the man or woman, girl or boy he sought. He'd run all through the day and all through the night without tiring and without growing hungry or thirsty," Cathal said.

Elisa and Jamie hung on their father's every word. They were both scared but curious and could barely breathe. They desperately wanted to know what happened next.

"Well, that dog, the *hound of darkness,* when it found its next victim, would follow that adult or child home... He'd wait until darkness had fallen and the moon was high in the sky. Under the light of the moon, he would change into the figure of a man and sound three heavy knocks on the front door of the home of his victim," he said. Cathal struck his foot against the floor three times. Elisa and Jamie could barely breathe. "Three knocks," Cathal said. "When his victim opened the door, a dark figure draped in a black hooded cloak greeted that victim. He would reach out his hand and curl his finger towards himself calling forth *the soul* of the person he sought." Elisa looked over at the door.

"*What happened?*" Elisa asked.

"The victim dropped to the ground. Dead!" Cathal said.

"Cathal, *do you really need to tell ghost stories* to them before bedtime?" asked Aideen.

"But I do!" Cathal took another sip from his hot chocolate. "Well, wait until I tell you this," he said. "When Eve and I were children, we saw that black dog down at Ó Ceallaigh's crossroad and we saw him turn into the figure of a hooded man," he said, placing his cup down next to him. Cathal leaned forward. "The hound saw us watching him, and ever since then, he has chased Eve," said Cathal.

"Cathal, *would you stop making up yarns.* The children *don't need to hear your ghost stories,*" Aideen said.

She sat her cup back down on the coaster and did her utmost to avoid listening to the story as she flicked through the pages of the newspaper on the living room table.

"I saw the hound!" Jamie exclaimed. "*I saw it* when I was in the car with Elisa. *I saw the man and I saw the hound.*"

"I didn't see him," said Elisa, curiously.

"He hit you in the..."

"Jamie! Not another word out of you! *Go straight to your room* and I don't want to hear another word about this!" Aideen scolded. "Cathal, *I'm not having* this talk in *my home! What are you waiting for, Jamie? I told you* to go to your room! Go to your room *now!*"

Jamie looked at his mother with rage in his eyes.

"Go to *your room!*" Aideen snapped.

Jamie stamped his foot on each step he climbed until he reached the top of the stairs and then slammed his bedroom door behind him.

"Is Eve alright?" Elisa whispered.

"I think so," Cathal whispered. "I called to see her today, but she wasn't at the shop. I feel it in my heart that she's fine though and that's good enough for me," he said. "Are *you* alright? I hope I didn't scare you too much before bedtime," he said in a low voice. "You go on to bed now, Elisa. I'll see you in the morning," he said, and Elisa left for her bedroom.

"*I don't know why you thought* you needed to tell them *that ghost story. Do you not think* they've been through enough?" Aideen asked, turning the page of her newspaper.

"They needed to know. There are a lot of things that happen in the world that are beyond the seeing eye," Cathal said, collecting the empty cups. "You didn't need to snap at Jamie. He didn't mean any harm. She is going to find out anyway," he said, placing his hand on Aideen's shoulder. "Everything comes out in the end," he said, walking into the kitchen.

Aideen sat at the living room table for another few minutes flicking through the pages of the newspaper, but wasn't able to read a thing.

"*Do you have to* make so much noise when you're washing the dishes?" she complained. Aideen closed over the pages of the newspaper and walked to the stairs. "I'm going to bed," she said. "I won't be long after you," said Cathal.

It wasn't long before Cathal climbed the stairs. He took one final look into Elisa's room, and on seeing her sleeping, he gently closed her room door before turning off the landing light. Elisa wasn't asleep though. She lay on her bed for some time that night looking at the night stars in Kapheus until her eyelids grew heavy and shut. All across the land of Kapheus the lights grew dim as each Kaphien retired to their beds for the night. There was only one home wherein an extra light was lit and that was La Petite Maison Le Fèvre. Rós sat at her workstation designing her wooden masterpiece in the silence of the night with only the sounds of the ticking clocks to keep her company. She passed her hand along the smooth surface of wood she had prepared from Grandmother Oak's branch. She looked down at her pencil sketches on its surface one more time. Rós closed her eyes for a few seconds and then she began. She carved the shape of a strong warrior. Firstly, Rós carved the outline of a hurley hanging across his back, and then the sliotar in one hand and the shield in the other. The sound of the mallet and chisel echoed through that cottage for the rest of the night and was a sound that Micah was so used to hearing that it no longer disturbed him from his sleep.

Micah woke very early the next morning. He placed his two feet on the floor of his bedroom and in the darkness, he searched for his dressing gown and slippers. He yawned while pulling his arm into the sleeve of his dressing gown. Slowly he made his way to the bedroom door, half asleep and half awake and walked into the front room.

"You're up awful early, Rós. Did you *even* go to bed at all?" he asked.

Rós didn't lift her head from her tapping. Micah noticed a piece of splintered wood on the floor and picked it up. He was just about to throw it onto the embers when the tapping sound ceased. He placed the splinter on the mantelpiece above the fire place. The tapping sound of the mallet and chisel resumed. While deep in her

creative work, Rós was unable to speak or to engage with the outside world without an enormous amount of effort. The draw to the wood was far greater than the draw to the natural world around her at that time. Micah placed kindling onto the dying embers to reinvigorate the worn out fire.

"It'll be warm in here in no time," Micah said, adding three logs. "I'll make you something to eat," he said, and left.

Rós focussed sharply on the Spiral of Life she carved into the seam of Éiriú's dress with such incredible detail. Each spiral interlocked perfectly with the next and when it was complete, she lifted her head to examine the whole piece. Then Rós noticed the hair wasn't quite right on the wolfhound's large paws and added the finishing touches to them while he lay proudly on the grass in front of Éiriú, Banbha and Fódla, the three goddesses of Éire. The wolfhound's head looked into the distance as if watching for danger while simultaneously commanding obedience. Rós carved the final touches to his shaggy eyebrows. She blew away dust and shavings and looked at the timepiece again.

"Rós, do you need anything?" Micah asked. She shook her head. Micah's curiosity drew him closer to the timepiece and he looked over Rós' shoulder. He saw the warrior standing in his short trousers and bare feet.

"He reminds me of Setanta," he said and chuckled. "What'll you have there?" he asked, pointing to the empty space on the right hand side, but he heard no reply.

His wife stuck to the task of carving the Celtic symbols onto Setanta's shield and didn't break her concentration in case she would make a mistake.

"It's exquisite, Rós," he said. "It *definitely is* the timepiece for all the ages. You're almost there," he said, fixated on the carved detail of the clock.

"I think I'll have my breakfast now," Rós said. "Will I boil the kettle?" she asked.

"The breakfast is on the table," said Micah, unable to take his eyes from her work. He ran his fingers along the Celtic weave that wove around the whole timepiece.

"You're nearly there," he said. "Will I begin to make the clock?"

"No. We need Iolar first," she said.

Rós closed her eyes for a few seconds while she sat at the table and called to Iolar. The golden eagle heard her from her perch high in the far hills. She spread her wings and took flight.

"Are you not eating?" Rós asked.

"Oh, yeah, sorry," Micah said, returning to the table. "I'll go in search of Iolar after breakfast," he said.

Micah sat down and poured his cup of tea from the white tea pot and then added milk. He picked up his knife and skimmed it across the golden butter and then spread it across his slice of brown bread. He looked at his scrambled eggs, smoked salmon and tomato on his plate with delight. He took one sip from his tea and then lifted his fork and knife in anticipation of a scrumptious feast. Micah lifted a fork full of scrambled egg and was about to place it into his mouth when he heard a commotion outside. He placed his fork down in utter disappointment.

"I'll go," said Rós. She smiled at Micah. She knew how much he loved his food and breakfast was always his favourite meal of the day. "It's for me anyway," she said.

Iolar stood and waited on the rock outside.

"Take this to Joachim," Rós said, handing her something small enough to fit in the palm of one's hand. It was wrapped in a piece of cream coloured cloth and tied with a piece of twine. Iolar grasped the object in her talon and took flight into the meadow. She glided across the meadow scanning the whole area like a predator looking for her prey. Her eyesight was above and beyond that of any other Kaphien and her speed in flight meant that few survived her attack. Iolar's head looked to the left and then to the right, looking over and back along the valley in search of Joachim's messengers. Then she saw the two elfin brothers walking briskly a good distance away and sped towards them.

"*Where are we going*, Ruan?" Lir asked, impatiently.

"*I told you* I had to get away from that boy!" Ruan exclaimed, walking at a faster pace.

"How far away do you need to be?" Lir asked, struggling to keep up.

"I don't know. Far enough away to calm down. I... aargh!" Ruan yelled, tumbling to the ground. *"Why* did you knock me over, Lir?" he asked, picking himself up off the ground, but as he did, Iolar nudged his bottom with her beak and knocked him over again.

"Hahaha!" Lir laughed, holding his stomach it hurt so much. "Hahaha!"

"Lir, I could do without being knocked over by *yoouuu,"* he exclaimed, seeing Iolar standing on the meadow grass. "Run!" he shouted, tripping over. Iolar picked him up and then dropped him down onto his backside.

"I'm not planning on eating *an elf,"* Iolar said. "I learned in my youth that elves really taste *horrid,"* she said.

"Don't eat me either," said Lir, stepping closer. The eagle's golden yellow eyes pierced through him, and Lir took a step back.

"Well, if you're not going to *eat me,* then what?" Ruan asked, pulling himself to his feet once more.

Iolar scanned the meadow, which was something that unsettled Lir, who himself began to nervously look around him. Iolar then opened her talons and placed the small parcel from Rós on the meadow floor.

"Bring this to Joachim," she said.

Ruan slowly and steadily reached down to pick up the small parcel all the while Iolar watched him with her piercing eyes. Ruan shoved it deep into his pocket. Iolar then spread her wings and ran for a few short strides in synchronicity with her wing flap and soon she was in flight.

"What is it?" Lir asked.

"I don't know," said Ruan, "but there's one thing for sure, we need to get a move on."

Chapter 6

The Hatchling

Aideen lay asleep in her bed that morning and in her dreams, she saw a golden eagle glide high above a wide and expansive valley. She saw two elves hurrying along and then smoke billowing from a cottage. It wasn't yet dawn in her dream, and neither was it dawn in Éire, and it was this that caused Aideen to stir. The eagle doesn't fly before dawn and elves hurrying in a meadow and a fire lit in a cottage on the hill. All these things aroused Aideen from her sleeping state. She tossed and turned in her bed.

"Joachim!" a voice whispered from the drawing. Joachim climbed out from the wardrobe. "*Joachim*, we have something from Iolar," Ruan whispered, stepping through the boundary with his brother. Aideen woke. She looked at her sleeping husband next to her. Then she turned to see that it was dark outside her bedroom window. 'Who's calling?' she thought. She heard Cathal mutter something in his sleep.

"*What did you say*, Cathal?" she asked.

"Black wolf… there's a black wolf in the…" he said, and drifted into a deeper sleep.

"*A black wolf*," she said, rolling her eyes. Aideen laid back down on her bed and closed her eyes.

However, not too far from Aideen in Elisa's bedroom the black wolf stood next to Ruan.

"Joachim, Iolar gave me this for you," Ruan said. Joachim took the parcel in his mouth and then laid it on Elisa's bedroom floor. He tore open the twine and then pulled the cloth away to reveal the deep green emerald gemstone.

"*Wake Jamie*," Joachim whispered. "We must go. She'll have seen you. Tell him to get dressed."

Aideen saw the golden eagle in the sky and the smoke billowing from the chimney of La Petite Maison Le Fèvre. She searched for the elves in the valley but could not see them. Aideen became more agitated in her dream. Then she saw the jacket tail of one elf before it disappeared from sight. She tossed and turned and then woke from her dreams.

"Jamie hurry!" Lir whispered. Half asleep, Jamie did what Lir told him. "Here!" said Lir, handing him his stockings. Lir then pulled Jamie's green jumper from the dresser and tossed it onto his lap. "Am I dreaming?" Jamie asked, and his eyelids drifted shut again. Lir pulled him to his feet, snatched the imperial topaz from his bedside locker and escorted Jamie to the bedroom door. He looked up and down the hallway and then heard the floorboard creak in Aideen's room when Aideen placed her feet into her slippers. Lir hurriedly pulled Jamie across the hallway. Aideen thought that she heard something outside her room and quickly turned around. She reached over to get her dressing gown on the chair, but it wasn't there. She looked on the floor behind the chair and couldn't find it. Then she heard Elisa's room door close.

"I have him," Lir whispered, stepping into Elisa's room.

"What are we doing?" Elisa asked, tying the laces of her brown leather boots. She already had her red jacket put on her and was just about ready to cross the boundary between the two worlds.

"Here! Put on your boots," whispered Ruan.

"I'm not doing *anything* for you!" Jamie retorted, now awake.

Aideen looked around the room and saw her dressing gown draped across the end of her bed. She quickly put it on and rushed from her bedroom. She hurried down the hall to Elisa's room.

"I'm going *back to bed*," Jamie said.

"She's coming!" Joachim exclaimed. "Jump through!" he whispered, and Elisa and the two elves quickly crossed the boundary.

Joachim grabbed Jamie and tossed him into the drawing and jumped through himself the second Aideen turned the handle on Elisa's room door. Joachim snarled at Jamie lying on the meadow floor. Jamie immediately clambered to his feet and ran to the safety of Elisa.

"You might need these," said Ruan, handing Jamie his brown leather boots.

Aideen, seeing that Elisa was not in her bed, left Elisa's room and crossed the hallway to Jamie's bedroom. She ran downstairs, and then to the yard outside. Aideen stepped back into the house and closed the front door behind her. She placed her back against the door and looked to the hallway landing. Aideen marched back upstairs and entered Elisa's room one more time. She pulled the blankets and sheets off Elisa's bed and then pulled open the drawers of her bedside locker to search them. Aideen made her way to the wardrobe, threw open the doors and pulled out all the clothes, first shaking them, before throwing them to the floor. She checked all the pockets of Elisa's jackets and jeans but found nothing in them. Aideen was about to give up when she looked down at the base of the wardrobe. She saw the clothes in a dishevelled heap, something so out of character for Elisa, and so she bent down and began to feel between the clothes. In her frustration, she eventually decided to pull everything out. She found the two hot water bottles. She searched deeper into the closet, but there was nothing. Aideen held the hot water bottles in her hands. She shook her head, stood up and walked out of the room in a rage.

"*Where are we going?*" Jamie asked.

"Aroooooo," Joachim howled, "arooooooooo."

"Not this again!" moaned Jamie.

His pack heard his howl and came running from the hills.

"Where are we going, Joachim?" Elisa asked.

"We are going to visit an old friend in the hills," said Joachim.

"Éataín?" Elisa asked.

"Aroooo!" he howled, and then Joachim and his wolf pack ran deeper into the meadow.

Elisa watched them leave and knew they were completely exposed on the meadow without a single Kaphien they knew to help them. She scanned the area.

"Oh great! *I'm going home,*" said Jamie, lifting his hands to the air. Jamie turned to walk back to the boundary between the two worlds, but he didn't get too far, because Ruan put out his leg and tripped him.

"Shh... Stay down!" Ruan whispered.

Elisa continued to scan the meadow. She merged her heartbeat to the earth and felt its vibration. She felt the cold fresh breeze touch her face and the smell of the scents carried in it. Elisa pulled the satchel down from her shoulder and placed it at her feet. She waited. A sliotar came flying through the air and 'thud'. The gnome fell over and became visible.

"Reveal yourselves," Elisa called. "Reveal yourselves! Reveal yourselves!"

Elisa, Jamie, Ruan and Lir were surrounded by hundreds of gnomes.

"Does that apply to us too?" said Setanta, sitting on Banbha's back high above them.

"Banbha!" Jamie called to the green dragon.

The crowd of gnomes separated to make room for Banbha to land and Banbha gently placed her feet upon the Kaphien meadow. Elisa, however, remained still and alert to any danger among the crowd of gnomes.

"You have in your possession the lost dragon egg of Kapheus," one gnome said, stepping closer. He leaned down to grab hold of the satchel's strap.

Elisa stood in front of the satchel to block his attempt. She then picked it up and placed it onto her back. Elisa looked intensely at the gnome.

"It's the lost dragon egg of Kapheus," he said. Elisa said nothing.

"We are here to protect you on your journey to Rós," the gnome said.

"*Kubera?*" Elisa asked.

"Yes," Kubera replied. He bowed his head.

"You don't need to bow your head to *my sister,*" Jamie said.

"Has jealousy caught you in its grip?" Kubera asked, curiously. Jamie turned away. "Have you found many more riches of the world since we last spoke, Elisa?"

Elisa smiled.

"A few," she said. "Why are you here?" Elisa asked.

One by one the crowd of gnomes disappeared in front of Elisa's eyes.

"It's Feehul!" Jamie called.

They all watched Feehul walking towards them from the meadow. Elisa looked to Kubera, but he had vanished.

"Hi Feehul," Elisa said, hugging him.

"I heard you have something belonging to me," Feehul said. Elisa shook her head in denial. "A gnome visited me only a short while ago," Feehul continued, "he told me that I was to bring my emerald gemstone to Rós, but I already gave it to Rós for safe-keeping, so I don't really know what this is about," Feehul said.

"None of us do," Ruan interjected, "but at least we know where we are going," he said, walking in the direction of La Petite Maison Le Fèvre. Lir raced to catch up.

At La Petite Maison Le Fèvre, Rós saw a robin resting on her window ledge. She smiled when the robin sang her sweet tune, and as soon as it had ended, the robin flew away.

"We've guests coming today, Micah," Rós said.

"*We do?*" Micah asked, lifting his head from his moulds. "I'll need to make something nice for them to eat," he said, standing up. "How many will there be?"

"Probably thousands," Rós said, and she laughed.

"Thousands! How am I to feed *thousands*?"

"You'll need to finish those moulds before they arrive."

"I'm almost there," Micah said.

Micah lifted the bell jar from over the metal bowl on the shaking table, a table he manufactured himself when he arrived in Kapheus to be able to make the delicate clockworks for Rós' clocks. He began to pour the white investment compound into each of the metal flasks. Within each flask on the workstation was contained the wax patterns of the delicate internal clock parts he was yet to create.

"Thousands *of what* exactly?" he asked Rós, continuing to carefully pour the compound.

"Gnomes!"

"*Gnomes?*" Micah asked. He stepped into the living room. "I've never seen a gnome."

"You will very soon," Rós said without lifting her head from her work.

Micah scratched his head and then returned to his work. He placed a number of flasks onto his shaking table and covered it with the bell jar again. Micah slowly turned the large handle on the shaker table to gently remove the air bubbles without damaging the wax patterns inside the flasks.

"Gnomes… *What* do you think they might like to eat?"

"The same things as you," Rós said and smiled.

"The same things as me… *but aren't they small?*" Micah asked. He lifted the bell jar and placed the flasks back onto his workstation again.

"They may be small, but they're known for their big appetites. There's a reason they're all a little plump."

"You could make hot chocolate too," Rós said.

"Hot chocolate!" Micah said, entering the front room. "Are there *children* coming to visit?"

"Yes."

"*The Children of Light?*" he asked.

"Yes."

"It'll take the moulds another hour to harden," he muttered to himself. "I think a casserole would be nice for the children. It'll fill their bellies and help them grow strong," he said to Rós. "I'll have it done while I'm waiting for the moulds to set."

Micah removed his work apron, washed his hands and his vegetable rack for the perfect combination of vegetables for his casserole and then looked for herbs.

"Do you think a vegetable stew would be better?" he asked, approaching Rós with potatoes in his hands.

"I think whatever you choose will be great," Rós said without even looking up from her wooden carving.

"You're *no help*."

"Elves only eat vegetables if that's any help," she said.

"Elves!" Micah said, becoming a little flustered. "I'll make a casserole… and… I'll think of something," he said, entering the pantry.

In the meadow, nobody knew of the stress Micah was under in preparing a meal for them all. They were preoccupied by their own feelings and thoughts. For on that particular morning, the band of friends was less one, and for a short while, they didn't know what to do. Jamie and Elisa both looked around at different times in hope that they would see Fódla, but there was no little pink dragon calling *boo, boo.*

"I suppose this is it," Feehul said, not knowing what else to say. In the silence they felt their grief intensely, but none wished to speak of it in case they would not be able to stem their flow of tears. Elisa thought her chest would explode with the sorrow she tried to hold inside, and Jamie just wanted to go home to his sketchbook of drawings and leave Kapheus behind for good. After all, what good was a place that brought so many sorrowful memories and so much grief and pain. Jamie turned to walk away.

"Climb on my back," Banbha said, bending down. "Our team isn't complete without Éataín and word has it that she could do with a visit from her friends right now."

"What about Ruan and Lir?" Feehul asked. "You know we elves are happy enough to keep our feet on the ground. We…"

Banbha snatched Feehul and tossed him onto her back.

"You'll be alright, Feehul. I haven't let an elf fall yet," Banbha said. "Sometimes it's about putting one foot in front of the other no matter how sad you feel," said Banbha. "It's our turn to help lift Éataín from her sorrow, Elisa and Jamie. We need to stay together."

Elisa and Jamie climbed onto Banbha's back and were soon airborne. Banbha made a quick swoop down to snatch Ruan and Lir in her talons to the sound of screams from the terrified elves, and they were on their way to visit Éataín at her cottage high in the hills.

"Could you *please stop wriggling?*" Banbha asked.

"*Are you going to eat us?*" Ruan yelled.

"No!"

"I don't think we taste very nice," said Lir.

"Lir!" Ruan yelled.

"Don't worry Ruan, we're almost there," Elisa called.

"Look straight ahead! It helps!" Feehul shouted.

Fiona and Fiachra were unaware of the imminent arrival of their guests. Fiona placed a log on the fire in the living room and returned to the kitchen.

"Oh no! Not again!" Fiona yelled, walking into the kitchen.

The phoenix stood on the worktop with her head in the pot. When she heard Fiona, she lifted her head and looked blankly at her. She belched loudly and then twisted her head from side to side with a continued blank look on her face.

"Get out! Get out! Get out! I've had enough!" Fiona shouted, waving the dish cloth in the air.

The phoenix jumped from the counter, and as she dropped to the kitchen floor, she caught flight. She flew all about the kitchen, knocking over the drum of flour and tipping over the sack of oats on the floor. She lifted her body into the air and trying to avoid the dish cloth, she crashed against the clothes horse, knocking it and all the clothes hanging from it onto the floor. She flew over and back, this way and that and then squeezed by Fiona and into the living room.

"Open the door!" she shouted. Fiachra ran to the door.

"Don't open it!" Éataín shouted.

She transmuted into a robin and began to sing a sweet tune. She flew to the window ledge and sang an even sweeter tune. It was the Song of Éire. The phoenix turned her attention to the red robin sitting on the window ledge. She hovered for a moment and just before Fiona could hit her with the dish cloth, she flew to the ledge and sat down. The robin continued to sing the Song of Éire as the young phoenix watched.

"Red plumage is coming through her ashen fledgling plumage," said Fiachra, looking over his shoulder. "Had you noticed, Fiona?" he asked.

"There are plenty of things that I've *noticed,* but *that's not one of them,"* Fiona snapped, and she returned to the kitchen.

Three knocks sounded on the front door.

"Is it safe to open the door, Éataín?" Fiachra asked. The robin nodded.

"Dia duit, Fiachra," said Feehul.

"Dia is Muire dhiadh," Fiachra said.

"Oh, come in! It's wonderful to see you," said Éataín. "Come in, come in. How many of you are there?" she asked, approaching the door. "Ruan, Lir, you're welcome," she said, carefully holding the door, so that there was barely enough room for each of them to squeeze through.

"Come in Elisa and Jamie," she said. Éataín then gave Banbha a quick wave and closed the door shut.

Ruan looked around the cottage and then look questioningly to his brother. He reached his head around to see the mess in the kitchen.

"I'd say you wouldn't be the most house proud," said Ruan.

"Oh, a minor upset," said Éataín, ushering them to the centre of the room.

"A minor upset!" Fiona shouted from the kitchen.

"What's *that?*" Jamie asked, pointing to the phoenix on the window ledge. She looked blankly back at him.

"It's a phoenix," said Feehul.

"I saw a phoenix before and it *definitely didn't look as ugly as that,*" said Jamie.

"When did *you* see a phoenix, Jamie?" Elisa asked.

"When you were asleep in *your bed,*" he said, discounting Elisa.

Éataín approached the phoenix and when she did, the bird settled onto her hand. Éataín stroked her plumage.

"Her fire is coming through. She's maturing fast… She flew for the first time only a few minutes ago," Éataín said.

"And *we all rejoiced,*" said Fiachra, raising his eyebrows. He picked up the chair that had fallen awkwardly onto the living room floor and stood it next to the fireplace.

"We are on our way to Rós, and Banbha wanted to know if you'd like to join us," Feehul said.

"Oh, that *would be lovely*. What a *wonderful suggestion,*" said Fiona, emerging from the kitchen, "and maybe you'd take *that bird* with you. I'm sick of her!" Fiona remonstrated, waving her dish cloth in the air.

"Squawk! Squawk!" the phoenix sounded and she was in flight again, hitting off walls and chairs and almost falling into the fire.

Éataín immediately transmuted into a robin and sang the Song of Éire. The phoenix was transfixed by the robin's song. She hovered in the air for a while. Fiachra slowly and quietly walked to the front door and opened it.

"I think this is our exit call," said Feehul and they all ran outside to the waiting Banbha.

"Squak! Squak!" sounded the phoenix, following the robin in flight. "Squawk! Squawk!"

On seeing the phoenix following the robin, Banbha laughed before spreading her wings to fly.

"Squawk! Squawk!" the phoenix called, catching up to the robin.

The robin flew as fast as she could, but she was only a tiny bird compared to the already large fledgling phoenix. The robin continued to flap her wings as fast and as hard as she could. She was becoming breathless yet persisted in her quest to sing as loudly as she could and to fly as fast as she ever had to La Petite Maison Le Fèvre.

"Éataín, you'll never do this alone," Iolar called from a height. "Land on my back and sing. You are *far too small*. She'll pass you out by the time she reaches the valley."

The robin looked back at the phoenix and saw how fast she was losing her ashen plumage to the fiery red feathers bursting through. With each flap-flap-glide, the phoenix grew bigger and stronger. The robin flew onto the golden eagle's back and Iolar took her the rest of the way. She sang the Song of Éire to hold the phoenix's attention and it worked. The phoenix' entire plumage was replaced by the fiery red plumage she had before her brush with death by the time they reached the valley. The robin watched her large and majestic tail feather grew to full length seconds before they landed gracefully at the door of La Petite Maison Le Fèvre. The phoenix was back to her magnificent self.

"What's that outside?" Micah asked. He opened the door to see the phoenix standing straight in front of him and looking blankly at him. "*Not you again.*"

"That's not a nice way to greet a guest, Micah," Rós said and laughed. She wheeled her chair to the front door. "I see you've reached your full height again," she said to the phoenix and smiled, "and not without the help of a worn out robin and eagle."

"Elisa! Jamie! You're welcome. I'm Rós," she said, "and this is my husband Micah."

"You got my message then, Feehul," she said, returning to her living room.

"Fuair mé í," Feehul said, following her into the house.

"Micah has prepared something for you to eat. You must be hungry by now," said Rós.

"I'm a bit concerned about *that* phoenix," said Micah, looking peculiarly at the bird of fire.

"Don't worry! We're here to help Banbha," said Ruan, "and I take my responsibilities very seriously. Rest assured, we will mind *that* phoenix. Isn't *that right*, Lir," Ruan said, giving him a dig.

"I'd like some food too," said Lir.

"You go on inside," said Banbha. "Nothing's going to happen out here."

With that, Ruan and Lir joined the others and walked inside. Elisa, Jamie, Ruan and Lir were in awe of La Petite Maison Le Fèvre. They looked at the walls lined with clocks and couldn't believe their eyes. Micah signalled to Feehul and he followed him to his workshop.

"How many clocks do you have?" Jamie asked.

"More than I care to count," Rós replied.

Jamie stepped back to look high up onto cottage walls that seemed to go on forever and almost fell over a piece of wood. He looked down and picked it up. Then he saw it. The three goddesses at the top, the wolfhound, the man with the shield and sliotar. He took a step closer.

"What's going to be carved into the blank space?" Jamie asked.

He looked more carefully at the detail along its base and saw the inscription written in ogham and touched it with his fingers.

"For every word there is a meaning," Rós said.

"What does *that* mean?" Jamie asked.

"It means that you must be careful with your words. Words are powerful. They can create or destroy. Choose wisely," she said. "Every word has a different meaning depending on how it is carried by your voice and with whose ears it's heard." Rós brushed her hand along the inscription. "Words are one of the riches of the world," she said.

"Elisa, you might want to look at this," Jamie said. "It's the riches of the world," he said, and walked away from the table.

"What do you see, Elisa?" Rós asked.

"The Spiral of Life. *It's everywhere,*" Elisa said, brushing her fingers along the goddess' dress. "What do you think is missing?" Rós asked.

"A dragon," Elisa said, assuredly. Rós nodded.

"The clock will go there," Rós said, pointing to the centre of the wood carving.

"How do you know how much space to give the clock?" Elisa asked. "Like, how do you know that it will fit exactly into that hole? I think I'd be scared I'd get the size wrong," Elisa said.

Rós smiled and nodded her head.

"You know you're not wrong there, but I suppose, Micah and I have been doing this so long now that we have an understanding between us. He knows exactly the right measurements when he looks at the clock I'm carving, and I think I know exactly the right measurements of that space I have to leave free," Rós said. "We are a team like you and Jamie."

In the workshop, Feehul helped Micah place the metal flasks into the hot kiln, but before he did, Micah was careful to examine the surface of the plaster in each flask for cracks. Micah pulled away the soft rubber base from each flask and again he was scrupulous about making sure there were no plaster flakes in the funnel into which he would cast his gold. Every internal mechanism of a clock including springs, gears, pinions and bearings along with the clock hands were being made from moulds Micah had carefully shaped with the utmost precision. As soon as each metal flask was checked, he passed it to Feehul to place in the oven.

"It'll take about five and a half hours for these to set. Then I can pour the gold," said Micah, closing the oven door.

They both left the workshop and returned to the main living room.

"Do you have it?" Micah asked Elisa.

"*And what, may I ask,* is your *reason for seeking it?*" Kubera asked, appearing in front of Elisa with his hands on his hips and looking cross.

"Reveal yourselves!" Rós called.

Every corner of the room was filled with gnomes. Once they were identified in the act of observation they froze in front of clocks, ornaments and everything you could imagine. There were even gnomes seated at the living room table and one was sitting on Micah's armchair warming his feet by the fire.

"Good work," said a gnome, coming from the workshop, "*I like your style*," he said with a smile.

Micah was in shock.

"I can't feed *all of you!*" he exclaimed.

"What is your reason for seeking it?" Kubera asked again.

Kubera stood square with Micah, gnome to man, and although he barely reached Micah's waist in height, he looked formidable. Micah looked at Rós for support and then looked back down at the gnome.

"He doesn't know what you have, so your scrutiny is lost on him," said Rós. "He's not from around here. He hasn't grown up in the woodlands, the meadow *or* the hills. He doesn't know the history of this place. He came here by boat from the south," Rós said, wheeling her chair around.

"Elisa, you're carrying the lost dragon egg of Kapheus," Rós explained. "I called you all here, so that you could be a witness to what's to come."

Elisa looked to Feehul and he nodded. She pulled Fódla's satchel from her shoulder and opened it.

"Could you close the window shutters and light the candles?" Rós asked, and the gnomes obliged.

"I've a place prepared for your egg by the fireside. Would you like to lay it there?" Rós asked, pointing to the piece of black slate lying next the fire.

Elisa walked to where the slate lay and then removed the dragon egg from the satchel. She placed it onto the slate. The fiery red dragon egg shell changed to the flowing red and orange lava colour it had earlier.

"Wow! That's cool!" Jamie exclaimed.

"Yeah I thought so too," said Setanta.

"Do you *not have to be at home* with *your Mammy?*" Jamie mocked, and Setanta grew silent.

Jamie's words cut to his heart and he was deeply hurt by them. Setanta looked at Jamie but he simply couldn't find the words to say something to him. He became upset yet he didn't want Jamie to see him like that and so he held his wounded feelings inside.

"Setanta, I'd love if you could help me out with all these gnomes. Could you put some order on them?" Rós asked.

"No problem. Gnomes, who wants food?"

"Me!" they all said in unison, all but Kubera who remained close to the dragon egg.

"Everyone needs to line up then, and we will be able to sort something out," said Setanta.

Setanta felt proud to be from Kapheus in that moment and he knew that in Kapheus he was liked and appreciated and this place was home.

"Is that good enough?" Setanta asked.

"Yes, that'll do," Rós said and smiled.

Micah on the other hand felt under severe pressure now and returned to his casserole in a fluster. When Micah returned with the casserole the gnomes eyes tracked his movements. Their mouths watered and their stomachs rumbled. One by one they lined up for their dinner until the casserole dish was empty. The last seven gnomes who had waited patiently for their food looked at Micah. There was nothing left.

"Don't worry, boys. I made you a ratatouille," said the gnome, exiting the kitchen with a large dish. "Could I borrow your cook book sometime?" he asked Micah.

He placed the dish on the table and served his friends. The gnomes recycled their dishes seamlessly with each gnome washing their dish and spoon, and then passing them onto the gnome that was without.

"Ratatouille?" asked Jamie. "*What's that?*"

"*It's French,*" the gnome said, nonchalantly. "Try some. You might like it."

"It's delicious!" Feehul said, scraping every last morsel of vegetable from his plate.

Once their food was eaten there was nothing for them to do other than to wait for the dragon egg to hatch. It felt like it would never hatch and the only thing they could do was to fill the hours with stories and songs to pass the time. Ruan and Lir focussed their time on playing from the beautifully carved chess table, but not knowing how to play it became as big a challenge as the actual game itself.

"Does your mother know where you are this evening?" Rós asked Setanta.

"No. I told her I was going to visit Elisa but I didn't think I'd be gone this long… I'd kinda like to stay to make sure Elisa's alright," Setanta said.

"I'll send a message to let your mother know that you're here and that you're alright. In the morning, you will need to go home, so she won't worry," Rós said. Setanta nodded in agreement.

"Rós… how long more do we have to wait for the egg to hatch?" Setanta asked.

"It won't be much longer now, Rós," said Kubera, leaning forward. They all jumped up to get a look at the egg. The flowing lava on the shell returned to the fiery red hardened shell. The egg rocked over and back, and then stillness. They waited, but there was no movement. The egg grew cold and turned a bluish-white colour.

"*It's dying*, Rós. The dragon is dying," Micah said.

"Well, I'm here to ensure that doesn't happen," said Kubera. "Feehul have you the emerald?" Kubera asked.

"*No*. I left it with Rós."

"I gave it to Iolar to pass to Joachim," said Rós.

"Joachim ran off with the wolves," said Jamie, and he sat down. "It looks like this egg is going to die," he said, and in that moment everyone saw that Jamie, the leader of the dragons, didn't care.

Ruan pushed his way through the crowd of gnomes.

"I take my responsibilities *very seriously,*" Ruan said, and he handed the green emerald gemstone to Kubera.

"Jamie may I have your imperial topaz?" Kubera asked.

"I didn't bring it with me," said Jamie, uncaring.

Lir pushed forward and handed the bright yellow imperial topaz gemstone to Kubera.

"Here! *Where did you get that?*" Jamie asked.

"Good lad, Lir," Ruan said, patting his brother on the back.
Kubera carefully placed the emerald at the base of the egg and it
was absorbed inside. He then placed the imperial topaz at its apex,
and it too was absorbed. The hard shell of the dragon egg became
translucent with the thinning and weakening of the shell.
"Just one more to go," Kubera said.
"Elisa, do you have your fire opal?" he asked.
"Yes," said Elisa, handing him her fiery red opal.
By now the shell was transparent and the dragon could clearly be
seen inside. The little dragon appeared pink in the fiery red
amniotic fluid surrounding it. Its eyes opened and then its mouth.
"It's gasping for breath. Quick Kubera!" Rós said.
Kubera placed the fire opal onto the egg shell, immediately above
the dragon's heart. The gemstone was absorbed.
"This should be it," Kubera said.
The dragon continued to gasp for breath and couldn't break free
from its shell. The struggle was unbearable to watch. The dragon
gasped again and struggled to break free.
"There's something wrong!" Kubera cried.
"Break open the shell!" Micah called out.
"No. It has to break free or it will die," said Rós. "Banbha! *Open
the door*! Banbha!" she called.
Banbha reached her head inside.
"Bring the egg to me," she asked.
Banbha looked at the dragon near death inside the shell.
"I placed all the stones given by Taragon," said Kubera.
"Elisa, throw me Fódla's satchel," Banbha said. Banbha then lifted
the satchel and shook it out. The stone dropped out of the front
pocket and onto the delicate egg shell and was absorbed. "You
forgot the stone that was treasured by the smallest among us,"
Banbha said.
The dragon broke free and breathed the Kaphien air for the first
time. Micah hurried towards the dragon to collect the delicate
fragments of egg shell. He quickly made his way to the workshop
and removed the metal flasks from the hot kiln. He wound the
spinning handle to three turns inside the metal basin and set the
pin. He placed it into the bracket with the funnel end against the

crucible and lit the gas torch to melt his gold to a smooth flowing liquid. He then added a few egg fragments and allowed them to absorb into the liquid gold. He released the pin and raised the torch, released the arm and the handle spun at a rapid pace in the metal basin. The liquid gold with the egg shell infused in it was forced into the mould centrifugally. The process had begun.

"How long does it take?" Feehul asked.

"Oh, I'll just let it come to a stop in its own time. I'll let it cool a little and then I'll quench it in water," Micah said.

"How long does that take?" Feehul asked.

"Not too long. How is the dragon doing? I'll be as quick as I can."

Suddenly, three gnomes appeared next to Micah and he took fright. "We've tracked your movements now, and we understand fully the mechanism of your work. We are here to assist you," said one of the gnomes.

"Could you grab the thong and dip this flask in the bucket of water?" he asked.

He had no sooner uttered those words than it was done, and another gnome stood in front of him holding a hot flask from the kiln ready to be placed on the bracket. Feehul stepped away to give them space to do their work and walked back into the living room.

In the living room, the Kaphiens watched in awe as Banbha licked the little dragon clean and with every stroke of her tongue she expelled the remaining fluid from his lungs. He was breathing more easily now. The newly born dragon opened his deep brown eyes, lifted his head and looked around. The tiny creature was as white as snow and as small as the common lizard often seen in the hills. The only difference was that he had little wings on the surface of his back that with every lick from Banbha's tongue were set free. Banbha took a second to examine the little dragon. She nuzzled him to urge him to spread his wings and to stand. She nuzzled him again and then again and with jelly legs beneath him the newly born dragon shakily found his feet and stood. Everyone watched and willed the dragon to stand for a little longer, but those jelly legs hadn't yet found their strength and he plopped down on the floor. Banbha, however, wasn't willing to let him rest. She nuzzled him again and flicked his wings outwards and the little dragon stretched those transparent wings, which were as delicate as those of the dragonfly, and then flapped them.

"There is... yes..." said Kubera, searching the amniotic fluid. "There you have it," he said, lifting the deep green gemstone covered in thick clear fluid. "The emerald, the stone of healing," he said, reaching out his hand to return it to Feehul.

"Go raibh maith agat," said Feehul, catching hold of it with his handkerchief.

Kubera searched again through the slimy viscous amniotic fluid and found the bright yellow imperial topaz.

"The imperial topaz," he said, pulling it free. "The stone of divine origin and of spiritual alignment belongs to you," he said, passing it to Jamie.

Jamie searched his pockets but didn't have a handkerchief. Kubera held Jamie's hand and forced the slimy gemstone into it. Jamie squirmed as the fluid dripped through the gaps in his fingers.

Elisa, knowing what was to come, had already taken the initiative. She searched through the amniotic fluid, but eventually found her fire opal held tightly in the little dragon's arms. She tickled his belly and he wriggled and gurgled and released his grip on the gemstone. Elisa lifted the dragon into her arms and caressed him.

"The gemstone that awakens your inner fire and protects you against danger," said Kubera. He cleaned the stone and placed it into Elisa's hand.

"Thank you," she said.

Kubera reached down to pick up Fódla's stone, but was impeded by Banbha.

"*Fág í,*" she commanded. "This is my stone to lift."

Banbha lovingly licked the stone clean as if it was Fódla herself that she was cleaning, and when she was ready, Banbha shoved it back into Fódla's satchel.

From the moment when the baby dragon opened his eyes, Rós had worked frantically to carve the little dragon into the empty space on her wooden carving. She hadn't heard a sound from Micah, and Rós was beginning to become a little agitated at this stage. She left her workstation and made her way to Micah to see how far he was progressing. He worked diligently at his own workstation cutting the sprues off all the pieces and hadn't noticed Rós at the doorway. She watched Micah carefully file and sand the clock's internal gold pieces and left him be. One by one, Micah handed them to the gnomes to polish on his polishing barrel. They worked together with one gnome turning the handle while the other brushed the gold pieces against the fast moving barrel. It wasn't long before they gleamed and were set down next to the others on the polishing cloth.

Suddenly, they heard what sounded like a rumble of thunder coming from inside the mountain.

"I'm nearly there!" Micah shouted from his work station. "Is the frame ready?" he asked Rós.

The gnomes ran from the cottage and disappeared from sight. Banbha merged her heartbeat to that of the earth and she too was no longer visible. The golden eagle flew high into the evening sky and disappeared. The mountain rumbled again.

"Is it an earthquake?" Feehul asked, shutting the front door.

"It's sixty seconds. That's all the time we have before the darkness reaches us. Sixty seconds to save *this dragon's life,"* said Rós, hurriedly engraving the image of the newly born dragon onto the blank space on her sculpture.

Inside the mountain, the clocks chimed in unison to ring in the birth of this dragon and it shook the mountain. Again they rang out, and again the mountain shook.

"Main spring and power assembly done! *Are you ready, Rós?"* Micah shouted through the ear shattering chimes.

"Sanding!" Rós called out.

"Balance wheel and hairspring assembly done!" Micah shouted.

Feehul ran to the window and looked out at the dark clouds rolling towards them at a ferocious speed.

"Squawk!" sounded the phoenix outside. Feehul immediately opened the door and the robin flew over his head and into the cottage. The phoenix thundered along behind the robin and bowled Feehul over on route. Feehul pulled himself to his feet again, shut the door and dropped the large wooden door latch.

"Pallet jewel pin in place. Escape wheel in!" Micah shouted as the clocks chimed again.

Feehul ran to close the window shutters with the help of Ruan and Lir.

"Both pallet jewels in place! Gears and wheels sitting into place!"

"Twenty- five seconds!" Rós called out.

"Indicating hand in place! Gear train working. Dial in place. *We have the seconds.*"

He then attached a dial and fastened a pointer to the next gear wheel.

"We have minutes!" he shouted, and within no time, he had a dial attached, and then fastened a pointer to the next gear wheel for the measure of hours.

Micah worked at immense speed and precision. With all the bearings, pinions, screws, shafts, plates and bridges in place, he jumped from this workstation and ran to the front room.

"Will the wood hold the vibration?" he asked.

"Get it in!" Ruan yelled.

Micah set the clock mechanism into the wooden sculpture as the last chime sounded in the mountain.

"It's in!" he rejoiced.

"Guím gach rath ort! *May* you live a long life!" Rós exulted and turned to the little dragon.

The dragon, however, was clueless to the commotion around her and was happily curled up in the warmth of Elisa's arms.

"The clock for all ages," Micah said in a tone of relief.

"I'm sorry to interrupt your celebration, but the *darkness is upon us,*" Ruan declared.

Chapter 7

Clocks

Grandmother Oak felt the rumbling mountain beneath her roots and it sent a shiver through her bark as it did to all the trees in the Kaphien woodland. The vibration of the mountain's rumble shook the animals beneath the earth and those who lived in the trees. That vibration brought all those who slept below the ground to the surface. Mother Badger left her sett and raced to the edge of the woodland followed by her family who rarely left her side. She stood close to the bark of a tree and watched her dream unfold.

"Any second now," she whispered, and there it was.

Lightning struck and lit up the night sky. She turned around and saw the woodland trees glow white from base to tip. She watched Ogma fly from the woodland to the hills. His large black wings filled the night sky.

"*Oh no,*" she whispered.

The dark clouds blocked the night stars as they passed overhead and all of Kapheus, frozen with fear, grew silent. The elves held tightly to the light of the tree branches and the dragons stayed low in their nests in the tree tops. No one could take their eyes off the scene that played out in front of their eyes.

'Stay close to me,' Grandmother Oak whispered to the all who inhabited Kapheus. 'Remain in the light of your heart,' she whispered, and all of Kapheus heard her words in their minds.

The dark clouds rapidly passed over the valley and burst into heavy rain. The thunder rumbled loudly and lightning struck with increasing frequency as those dark clouds rolled towards the high hills.

"Grandmother Oak is calling to us!" Ruan said, anxiously. "*This is serious. This is serious!*"

Micah looked through the crack in his window shutter.

"He's right," he said, and packed the crack with a splinter of wood he saw on the floor. "Stay down everyone! Stay down!"

Elisa tucked the little dragon inside her jacket and held him close to her heart. She followed Jamie and they hid beneath the living room table. It wasn't long before Ruan and Lir followed them. La

Petite Maison Le Fèvre grew silent and Lir began to shake with
fear underneath the table. He huddled tighter to his brother. With
each second that passed, they heard the thunder rumble ever
closer. Then suddenly, a flash of lightning struck the cottage and
filled it with light.

"Squaaaawk!" cried the phoenix, and she ran under the table with
the robin following close behind. She landed on Jamie's lap and
shuffled her rump a few times until she found the perfect nesting
position. Jamie, now squashed against the wall and hidden in the
plumage of feathers, could barely breathe.

The wind howled loudly and with one fierce strike of lightning the
thatched roof caught fire. They huddled even more tightly under
the table. Lightning struck again and yet again and it was on the
fifth strike that the lightning tore through the roof with a stream
of white light that struck the oak floor with a loud crack.

"Squawk! Squaaaawk!" the phoenix cried. She stood up and tossed
the table into the air, and in an attempt to get away from the
frightening lightning, she ran straight into the armchair and fell
over.

"Grab the table!" Ruan shouted and they quickly placed it back on
its four legs.

The phoenix ran back to the table and shoved her head under it
and like an ostrich hiding in the sand, unbeknown to the phoenix,
the rest of her body was playing chicken with the lightning as she
danced this way, missing the streak of lightning by millimetres
while trying to push her body farther under the table.

"Feehul!" Rós called. Feehul crawled across to Rós. "We hurt
without moving! We poison without touching!" she said.

"Don't do this, Rós! We'll *figure a way out*," said Feehul.

The elf looked all around him but there was no way out. Rós leaned
closer to Feehul and held his jacket tightly.

"You need to listen! We hurt without moving. We poison without
touching. We bear the truth and the lies. We are not to be judged
by our size," she said. Rós released her grip on Feehul. "Take this
with you. Go!" she shouted, handing him the clock. "Place it where
it can't be found."

Feehul held the clock in his hands and scampered across the room to the others.

"Come with me!" he shouted, and they crawled out to follow him. The phoenix lifted the table high above her head and chased after them to the back door of the cottage. They waited for Feehul who nervously stood in front of the large wooden door. He faced the figures on the Spiral of Life that comprised the lock.

'We hurt without moving. We poison without touching. We bear the truth and the lies. We are not to be judged by our size,' he thought.

"We hurt without moving. We poison without touching. We bear the truth and the lies. We are not to be judged by our size," he whispered. "We hurt without moving… we…"

The front door blew in and the rain forced its way onto the floor.

"*We hurt without moving…*" Feehul said, panicking.

The phoenix pecked on the ogham inscribed on the door with ferocious speed. She then stopped and looked blankly at Feehul and tilted her head to one side. Feehul looked into her blank expression.

"We are not to be judged by our size. That's it!" Feehul exclaimed. "Words! *The answer is words.*"

He quickly focused on the Spiral of Life again. He looked at the image of the mother holding her newly born baby in her arms.

"She's singing to her baby," he whispered, and touched her mouth, 'click'.

He looked at the image of the children playing ball and saw that a child was crying. He tracked the boy's gaze to an older boy standing with his hands on his hips.

"His words wounded his own soul," he whispered. Feehul touched the boy's chest and 'click'.

The lovers were next. Feehul saw the man's hand close to the woman.

"He's asking her to marry him," he remarked, and moved the lover's hand to hers, 'click'.

He looked at the sick man lying on his death bed with his wife sitting next to him.

"She's saying goodbye," he muttered.

He moved the wooden figure to lean close to her dying husband to whisper goodbye and 'click'. Feehul became anxious. There were no more moves left on the Spiral of Life.

"I made a mistake," he said, anxiously. *"There is another* and *I can't find it."*

He scanned the Spiral of Life again but nothing. Then the phoenix pecked at the Ogham. Feehul looked up and read *Tír Gan Teanga Tír Gan Anam.* He quickly reached up to the word *Teanga.* He pressed the letter 'T' and the door opened to the tunnel. They hurriedly made their way into the heart of the mountain and the second they were inside, the door closed solidly behind them and then locked.

Feehul and his friends stood in the tunnel, but they were not alone in the darkness. The gnomes who had disappeared from sight earlier had not abandoned them. They indeed foresaw what was to come for they knew better than anyone the prophecies of Kapheus. They studied them their whole lives. The gnomes lifted their jars containing the fireflies they had harvested for this moment.

"You're a sight for sore eyes," Feehul said. "I'm glad you're here."

Feehul looked around him but didn't understand why there were so many clocks.

"What is this place?" Feehul asked.

"This is the place where you were born and will die," Kubera said. "This is your whole life playing out to the rhythm of a clock like the beating of a heart," Kubera said, pointing to all the clocks lining the tunnels. "Some are giants and some… well… like myself… are not so tall, but each tells the birth, the life and ultimately the death of every living thing."

Kubera stepped forward and chose a specific clock to examine.

"Elisa, would you like to take a look?" he asked. Elisa, Jamie and their friends looked closely at the clock face. "You'll see the pattern of this person's life here and to the trained eye, the moment of death," he said. Kubera noticed Jamie scrutinising the clock. "You know, Jamie, it is not for us to play with death or to decide when we will die. Death will come in its own time and it goes against all the laws of nature for us to interfere with it."

They looked at the clock face and saw the Kaphien's birth in water, they saw books, candlelight and the death of a dragon. They saw the loneliness and then the companionship of others. They saw the death by a fall when climbing a dragon's lair.

"*Whose life is this?*" Jamie asked.

"Indeed," Kubera remarked. Ruan smiled knowingly at Kubera and he nodded back.

"We cannot escape it, but we are bound to live each day and make a life for ourselves that brings us joy and love," Kubera said.

Then they heard a loud crash on the other side of the door and Kubera and the others quickly walked onward through the tunnel with the gnomes lighting the way.

"Where are we *going?*" Lir asked.

"As far away from *that door* as possible," Ruan remarked.

As Feehul walked through the tunnel with the others he couldn't find one crevasse that he deemed safe enough to hide the clock Rós had given him, for as long as that clocked ticked, the lost dragon lived. The weight of responsibility weighed heavily on him. He threw open the flap of his satchel and placed the clock into it for safe keeping. They heard another loud crash from the other side of the door and imagined what could have happened in La Petite Maison Le Fèvre.

On the other side of that door, the cottage was practically unrecognisable. The roof had almost completely fallen in and large wooden rafters had fallen onto the oak floor. Clocks barely clung to the walls and those that were not able to cling to their hooks had crashed and broken into pieces on the floor. The front door had been flung across the living room and beyond that door a ferocious wind howled, and the rain pelted down on a chasing pack of wolves.

"Aroooooo," Joachim howled, negotiating the treacherous mountainous terrain to La Petite Maison Le Fèvre.

Joachim looked up and saw the serfs of darkness fly through the gaps that appeared in the breaking black clouds and drop to earth. He then saw the hounds of darkness emerge from the clouds.

"*Arooooo,*" Joachim howled, knowing that time was running out to save those inside.

The wolves chased hard towards the house, yet the hounds were ignorant to their approach. With snapping jaws and salivating mouths, the hounds thought only of gorging on that which was born inside La Petite Maison Le Fèvre. Their powerful shoulders and large bodies could overpower even the strongest wolf and they feared nothing and no one. Joachim ran as fast as he had ever run in his life. By now, he and his pack could hear the screeching howls and high-pitched barks of the salivating hounds. The hooded figures whose faces were hidden beneath their black cloaks walked toward the cottage in the distance. The leader pulled the gleaming silver sword from beneath his cape and the hood from over his head and laughed.

Donn stepped inside the cottage. He saw the wheelchair lying on its side on the living room floor, the table turned over and the clocks barely clinging to their hooks on the walls, but the cottage seemed to be devoid of life. Donn became agitated and signalled to his serfs and hounds to search everywhere. He kicked the papers beneath his feet and cursed the floor on which he stood. Then something caught his eye a few feet away and he walked towards it and picked up the fiery red feather. Donn scanned the whole room until he was distracted by the hounds screeching in elation at the black slab on which the dragon was born.

"Get away!" Donn shouted, kicking them with his foot. He bent down to examine the slate and then took another look around. "Gnomes!" he yelled.

Donn walked to the door of La Petite Maison Le Fèvre and unleashed a harrowing cry. He summoned his serfs and hounds from the cottage and re-entered the dark clouds. In the distance, Ogma, the black warrior dragon, flew high above the valley and returned to the woods of Kapheus by the light of the moon. The thunder rolled over the hills and the dark clouds were soon gone from sight.

Joachim and his pack reached La Petite Maison Le Fèvre at the moment the Dark One's serfs had left. He ran inside and searched everywhere for a sign of life but there was none. His pack sniffed the air and soon all became clear to the wolves. Joachim hovered around the back door, sniffing at the floor.

"Aroooo! *Arooooo!*" he howled.

"*Did you hear that?*" Feehul asked.

"It's Joachim," Éataín said. "I think we're safe."

There was a dead pan silence in the tunnel for a few seconds. Everyone wondered if it was true. Were they actually safe and were their friends on the other side of that door safe? They were soon jolted from their thoughts when the phoenix barged her way through Feehul and Éataín in an attempt to squeeze her way between them and to catch up with Elisa.

"She *clearly* thinks she's slimmer than she is," said Ruan.

When the phoenix reached Elisa, she looked blankly at the bulge in Elisa's jacket. She tilted her head from side to side. In response to this, Elisa pulled down the zipper a little and showed the phoenix the sleeping dragon under her jacket. The little white dragon looked so content in the warmth of the jacket and slept soundly.

"I don't know what to feed him," Elisa said. "I'm not sure what they eat when they're babies." She turned to Jamie. "Do you know, Jamie?" she asked, but Jamie simply huffed and walked on.

"I've his food in my satchel. I'll have it ready for him for when he wakes," a gnome whispered.

Elisa smiled. She pulled the zipper back up on her jacket and continued to walk through the vast mountain tunnel in the green glow of fireflies. Not for a second were they not in awe of all those clocks crammed into the tunnel like spectators in a sports stadium, and for a long time these fascinating masterpieces, each with their own character, took them from all their worries. Jamie scrutinised the clocks in search for the one that symbolised his life, but rather than being in awe of the incredible workmanship all around him, he became obsessed with knowing more about his life and nothing else.

"It's nice," Elisa commented, and all except Jamie nodded.

For some reason, the tick tock sound of the pendulums swinging over and back and the ringing chimes seemed to resonate with their souls. Even Jamie didn't feel the sound as a never-ending, ear wrenching tick tock. They walked for several more hours through the mountain rock with the clocks as their companions and by now even the fireflies were growing tired. They eventually reached a point in the tunnel where there were no clocks and they strangely missed the company of those swinging pendulums.

"I felt alright when I had the company of those clocks. I felt close to Kapheus," said Ruan. Lir nodded.

"I haven't heard Grandmother Oak call to us since we entered the mountain. Do you think the elves are alright in the valley?" Ruan asked Éataín.

"Yes, I do," Éataín replied. "Grandmother Oak knows where we are and I'm sure Banbha's somewhere above this mountain rock. Now is not the time to worry."

It wasn't long after they spoke that the light of the fireflies died and the tunnel became a very lonely place in the darkness.

"There are only three fireflies that have any strength left in them," said Kubera, "we must be close."

"*Close to what?*" Jamie asked. He had had enough. He kicked the ground and then sat down. "I don't want to go any farther! *This tunnel* is going on *forever*, and…" he said.

"*And what, Jamie?*" Elisa asked. "Do *you think* that *I want to be here?* None of us want to be here but it's better than being dead!" Elisa argued.

"*Since when* did you become so grumpy?" Jamie asked.

"Since *you started treating me* the way you do," Elisa snapped.

Jamie shivered and looked over his shoulder. He pulled the collar of his jacket close to his neck and then pulled the zip to the very top.

"Why did you do that?" Kubera asked, curiously approaching him.

"Why did I do *what?*"

Kubera walked passed Jamie and felt a shiver.

"Do you feel a cold breeze?" he asked. "Do *you*, Éataín?"

"It's written that there is a hidden door in the mountain, a door that will set us free," Kubera said, feeling the wall of the tunnel.

Neither Feehul nor Éataín were aware of this, but knowing that the gnomes were the keepers of the ancient scripts and spent their whole lives studying them, they were sure that Kubera was right. Kubera placed his ear against the wall of the tunnel.

"Can you hear the ocean?" he asked.

The gnomes quickly lined the walls of the tunnel searching for the sound. They listened, but the only thing they heard was the tapping sound of the phoenix pecking the wall.

"Shhh…" Kubera said, and then all the gnomes in unison said, "shhh", but the phoenix did not listen.

Feehul grew curious. It wasn't the first time that this phoenix had helped him when he really needed it. He slowly walked towards her. As he approached, the phoenix stopped pecking and looked blankly at him. She tilted her head from side to side, and then resumed pecking the wall of the tunnel. Feehul looked to where she pecked and there in front of his eyes etched into the granite rock was row upon row of the ancient script.

"Kubera!" Feehul called.

Kubera stood next to Feehul. He scratched his head and then signalled to the other gnomes.

"We could do with a bit of light here," Kubera said.

"They've dropped to the bottom of the jars," a gnome commented.

"Are there *any* fireflies omitting light?" Kubera asked.

Three gnomes shuffled through the crowd towards Kubera with their jars, and those last three fireflies made all the difference. They shone a light on what was to be one of the most memorable scripts Feehul would ever read in his life.

"Is mise an Ghaeilge, Is mise do theanga," said Kubera. "It's been eroded by time," he said, trying to make sense of the worn inscription.

"Anois táim lag. Ach táim théith, Ach fós táim libh. Is beidh mé… go deo," said Feehul.

Elisa bent down to read the inscription at the very end.

"Tóg suas mo cheann. Cuir áthas ar mo chroí. Labhraigí mé! Ó labhraigí mé!" she read aloud.

"I didn't think you could read the old script," Kubera commented. "Where did you learn it?"

"I don't know. It just came into my head," Elisa said.

"What does it mean?" Jamie asked.

"I am Irish, I am your language. Now I am weak. Now I am feeble. But I am still with you. I will be… forever. Lift up your head. Put joy in my heart. Speak me! Oh, speak me!" said Kubera.

Kubera questioned the script he had just read.

"We have spoken Irish and nothing has happened," said Kubera.

"Well, maybe the door is a riddle. Maybe we need to figure it out," said Ruan.

"Well, there's nothing *up there* when we lift up our heads apart from the ceiling," said Jamie.

"Words," said Lir, proudly.

"Yes, Lir, we are looking for words," said Ruan.

"Words,, Lir said, putting his hands in his pocket in a state of relaxed delight.

Feehul looked at Lir a little peculiarly to begin and then he looked at the etching on the wall. Feehul brushed his fingertips along the letters until he found the letter F. He pressed it, and 'click'. He then found O in the same way and 'click'. He continued to brush his fingertips along the lines of words finding C – A – I, and with each 'click' a lock opened.

"L," Feehul said, pressing the letter 'L' and the door in the tunnel unlocked. "Focail, words," he said, and smiled broadly at Lir.

"Good lad, Lir," Ruan said, patting his brother on the back. "Come on, lads! Put your backs into it," Ruan said, and with their shoulders to the granite door, they heaved. "Again lads!" Ruan called. With one final push the rock broke free. "Arghhh!" Ruan shouted.

Ruan along with several others fell from the mountain face and tumbled down to the sea. Éataín transmuted into a robin, and along with the phoenix, they safely took flight. Several gnomes halted their forward momentum just in time and held on tightly to the wall of the tunnel. They watched in horror as their companions plummeted to the sea. Ruan and Lir were the first to be rescued by Iolar who with Banbha followed their heartbeats as they navigated the tunnel. Elisa and Feehul were saved by Méabh, the dragon with the golden scales, whilst the gnomes, holding one another's hands, landed safely on Ogma's back. Jamie was already safe and was helping the gnomes who had held on tightly to the ledge.

"That was a close one," Jamie commented when they were all onboard.

"Look!" a gnome called, pointing out to sea.

They turned to look at large grey clouds rolling threateningly across the sea. With every inch of ocean those clouds passed, the ocean froze beneath them. They all watched in a mixture of awe and fear, all that is except for the little robin who already felt her body becoming too cold to fly.

"An torathar ón oirthear, the beast from the east," Kubera said.

Éataín felt her muscles tighten and with all her strength she called out to the golden eagle and then lost her fight and fell through the air. Iolar flew to her and caught her in her talons. She then flew the robin to Elisa and urged her to place her next to the little dragon inside her warm jacket, which she duly did.

"Will she be *alright?*" Elisa asked, worryingly, but Iolar didn't respond.

Elisa did her best to nestle the robin next to the dragon and gently rubbed her to warm her body. In a short time, the robin slowly opened her little brown eyes and chirped. Although Elisa tried to keep her still and in the warmth of her jacket, that little robin fluttered and wriggled and did everything to escape and there was nothing Elisa could do to prevent it. The robin flew to Iolar to warm her body in the eagle's plumage. As soon as she was warm enough, the robin sang the Song of Éire, which pulled the others from their fixation on the incoming storm clouds. The dragons immediately altered their course and returned home. Iolar flew her cargo to the valley and dropped Ruan and Lir close to their home. She then changed direction and flew to the hills with the robin and the phoenix while all the others made their way to the woods of Kapheus.

"Light the fires!" Feehul said, climbing down from Méabh.

"How many?" the elves asked, from the tree branches.

"As many as you can! Light them *everywhere,*" Feehul instructed. Feehul ran to gather broken tree branches, dead leaves and twigs. "There's a storm coming! As fast as you can!" he called to his fellow elves.

Méabh carried Elisa to her nest in the treetop, eager to meet the new arrival.

"Let me see the little one," Méabh asked.

"The little one?" another dragon questioned, having overheard Méabh, and soon the word had spread throughout the woodland that there was a newly born among them.

"What does the little mite look like?" a dragon asked.

"She's opening the zip now," another said, watching every move Elisa made.

Elisa pulled down her jacket zip to half-way. She reached in and carefully lifted the sleeping dragon out.

"Oh, my dear. He is *so* beautiful!" Méabh exclaimed. She stood tall with outstretched golden wings in a stance of joy before coming to rest again.

"Look love," she said, turning to Ogma, "isn't he the *most beautiful little dragon.*"

Ogma looked at the defenceless dragon held in Elisa's arms and delighted. There had been so much sorrow in the woodlands since the loss of Fódla and to see a newly born was a small remedy to their sorrow.

"He's *white,*" a dragon whispered. Those words were carried through the woodlands like wild fire.

"The dragon *for all the ages,*" another whispered.

Méabh looked around and saw the enquiring looks on the dragons. She worried for the newly born and her maternal instincts wanted to take him under her wing and protect him but this little dragon was not hers to protect.

"Is this my baby brother, Mam?" Dara asked.

This was not the most outlandish question for Dara to ask. After all, Fódla had arrived into his life under similar circumstances. Méabh looked at Dara and then searched the dragons for a certain face in the crowd. She looked down below her to see if she was there and then above. Méabh searched again but the face was not there.

'How could his mother not have been a witness to his birth?' she thought. 'She felt his birth in her heart. She would have known that his birth had been imminent, and she would have felt him breaking free from his shell,' Méabh thought.

"Méabh!" Ogma called, but Méabh didn't hear him.

'Where is she?' Méabh questioned in her mind. She searched her surrounds again.

"What do you think, Méabh? Will you take him in?" Ogma asked.

"What?" Méabh asked.

"Will you take him in?" Ogma repeated.

"No. Not when his own mother is alive."

There was a loud gasp among the dragons and then silence. Méabh searched for the face that would reveal itself to her. She tried even harder to find the dragon's mother but again she failed to see her. The dragons tracked Méabh's vision and wondered who among them laid the egg to the dragon for all the ages. They did not know. The dragons watched Méabh and stretched to hear every syllable that dropped from her mouth.

"He's shivering. Tá an torrathar ón oirthear ag teacht," Méabh said. "He needs his mother. He'll die when the beast arrives from the east … all the weak and vulnerable will succumb to the beast," Méabh said. She reached forward and licked the dragon's head.

"What do you mean?" Elisa asked, but her question fell on deaf ears.

"What will we name him?" Ogma asked.

"Ahem!" Kubera said, having made his way to the tree top. He sat down carefully on the nest. The gaps between the branches were big enough for his whole body to fall through and he took one look down and gulped. "I hope you don't mind my intrusion in your home," Kubera said, tidying himself. "This dragon's name has already been given. It's written in the constellations."

"Well then, Kubera, be the first to pass your blessings onto him and to give him his name," said Ogma.

Méabh lifted him from Elisa's arms and with the little dragon held safely in her mouth, she raised him up for all to see. The little white dragon cried out and all the dragons cried out in return. Méabh placed the newly born into Kubera's hands. She blew a warm breath upon his shivering body and then bowed her head to Kubera who graciously bowed and then took one petrified glance down. The gnome took a deep breath, he took one nervous step towards them and then stood upright and proud. Kubera placed his left hand on the dragon's head.

"It is written that you will be given the name Geaspar," he said.
"May the blessings of all that be, rest upon you."
All the dragons bowed.
"Take him with you now. Keep him warm," Méabh said. "The
beast is coming. He knows the one for all the ages has been born.
He'll kill every newly born in search of the enlightened one. Bring
him to Éire," she said.
Kubera turned to Elisa and handed Geaspar to her.
"The beast doesn't know that it's a dragon that has been born. He
will try to kill all the young," Kubera said to Elisa.
Elisa placed the shivering Geaspar back inside her jacket and pulled
up the zip. Méabh nodded to Banbha.
"But what about *all the others?*" Elisa asked.
"Elisa, we need to go," said Banbha, and she snatched both Elisa
and Kubera from the nest.
"But…" Elisa said. Banbha didn't listen.
She flapped her wings and took them back to their home and no
word from Elisa would change her direction. Elisa looked back and
saw the elves and the woodland creatures scurrying about in search
of broken branches and anything at all that would start a fire. She
saw Madra Rua look up at her for a few seconds and then turn on
her heels and disappear into the woodland.
"You'll need to learn about the history of Éire and Kapheus.
Kubera will visit your house at six o'clock in the morning to teach
you what is written in the ancient text," said Banbha.
"Six o'clock!" Jamie remonstrated from Banbha's back.
"I'll toss *you* in the ocean if *you complain one more time*," Banbha
retorted.
Jamie kept quiet. He knew when he had crossed the line with
Banbha and he also knew that she would fulfil that promise.
It wasn't long before the siblings dismounted at the boundary
between the two worlds.
"Will they be alright?" Elisa asked.
"The time of fire is the time of power. Knowledge is power, Elisa,"
Kubera said before leaving them at the boundary between the
worlds. "There's a lot that can be done when you know things in

advance," he said, "you make your way home now." Kubera disappeared.

"Elisa!" he called. "It's one of the riches of the world," he said, watching them step through and then they were gone.

"You know they've survived a lot of things," Banbha said. Kubera's head was dipped when he reappeared to Banbha.

"Fire will bend even the strongest metal," Kubera said.

"You haven't seen her strength. I've seen it. She will stand her ground against any force of darkness. Jamie may be behaving badly at the moment, but that boy loves his sister and has risked his own life to save her in Kapheus. I've been there. I've seen it with my own eyes," Banbha said.

Kubera felt a little more hopeful.

"Will the others succumb? Are they equally as strong?" Kubera asked.

"Well, I'm not sure about *that* phoenix," Banbha said, and laughed.

Kubera smiled. Banbha reached down to toss him onto her back.

"I'll teach them everything I know," Kubera said, but we'll need Setanta.

"To woo her or to protect her?" Banbha asked. She laughed and took flight.

Joachim stood outside La Petite Maison Le Fèvre while the elves worked diligently to repair the roof. They came from the lowlands carrying bundles of golden water reeds three feet in length that had been seasoned over the winter months and laid them down in front of the house. The timber frame had to be almost completely replaced save for the heavy rain that quenched the fire before everything was destroyed. Eight elves laid the under-thatch layer of scraw. The scraw was cut in rolls two and a half feet wide and twenty feet in length and it took all their skill and strength to work with it, yet despite the heavy work, the elves never took a minute's break. The beast from the east was fast approaching and the elves rushed to tie the scraw to the roof with súgán, the long rope of straw.

"Arooooo," Joachim howled.

On hearing Joachim's howl, several more elves climbed ladders and began to thatch the outer layer of reeds. The efficiency of their work was to be admired. Inside La Petite Maison Le Fèvre, several other elves worked to tidy and make the little cottage on the hill homely again. Elves were not known for their mastery of clocks but they did their best to restore them to their rightful places on the walls of this wondrous place. There was one thing the elves did master, however, and that was the knowledge of wood. Three elves gathered all the shavings and wood splinters that were Grandmother Oak's and placed them into a basket for safe-keeping. Any other pieces of splintered wood were thrown into the fire and were set alight. The door hinges and window shutters were being carefully repaired and before long everything was hanging as it should.

"Aroooo," Joachim howled, "aroooooo."

The elves looked across the sky and worked against time to finish the ridge on the roof.

"Isteach libh!" an elf shouted from the roof ridge. Any elf that didn't need to be outside quickly ran inside.

"*Arooooo*," Joachim howled, and with that, he ran to lower ground. The elf tied the last piece of ridge down just as the beast was upon him. He skidded down the ladder and raced inside the door, shutting it behind him with a loud slam of the wooden latch.

The beast rolled over the mountain with bitterly cold winds sweeping a dense snowfall over the hills with a brutal force. The beast picked up speed as he swept through the valley leaving the Kaphiens blind to their surroundings in the snowstorm. The beast roared loudly in search of the newly born and swept through the dens and setts on the lower ground and then the wind whipped upwards to the trees, sweeping bitterly cold wind and snow through the nests. The beast roared again and changed direction.

"Hold onto the earth!" Grandmother Oak called to her fellow trees. The tree barks were being bent so forcefully that their roots were being peeled from the ground.

The sound of the wind and the blizzard conditions scared Mother Badger's family.

"Wait it out. We only need to wait it out," she said to her young.

"But what if we can't get out of our sett?" Timothy asked.

"I've never known a badger not to dig… *I'll hear none of this talk*," said Mother Badger.

Yet, there was fear etched on Mother Badger's face. No creature beneath the ground really knew what they would face if and when the beast would leave.

Cillian picked up the pale brown body of the jay and hurriedly carried it to his makeshift tent. He ran the back of his finger along the black stripe that stretched from the base of her bill to her neck. "Come on!" he pleaded.

He ran his hand down along her black wing and blew warm air into her bill. Nothing. Cillian then placed the jay onto his blanket and wrapped it around her. He blew warm air into her bill again. "Come on!" he pleaded.

He thought he saw her white throat move as if she breathed on her own. He blew warm air into her bill again and the jay opened her eyes. She shuffled her rump beneath the blanket to stand and to set her wings free.

"You're staying here," said Cillian, "until that beast leaves us alone."

The jay took one look out from the makeshift tent and decided stay.

"He's not after you. He's looking for Geaspar and I doubt that beast will find him where he's hiding," Cillian said.

Geaspar was safely nestled in Elisa's jacket when she and Jamie ran from the cold of Kapheus and straight downstairs to their living room fire.

"*Where were you two?* I was worried sick!" said Aideen, adding another log to the fire. "*Your father is out in the wood.* He's gone gathering timber, and *there isn't an animal fed*," she scolded.

Elisa and Jamie didn't say a word. They simply made their way to the door to go outside to feed the animals. "Hats, scarves and gloves!" Aideen shouted.

Aideen was about to lift another log from the basket when she paused. She slowly turned around. She looked her children up and down as they pulled their hats and scarves on them.

"Elisa, are you feeling cold?" Aideen asked.

Elisa froze.

"No, Mam," she said without turning around.

"I think you should take your jacket off and sit down here by the fire," Aideen said.

Elisa didn't know what to do.

"Can *I?*" Jamie asked. Aideen gave Jamie a scolding look and he knew not to challenge her any further.

"Turn around *and look at me when I'm speaking to you,*" Aideen said.

Elisa tucked her scarf deep into her jacket next to Geaspar and turned around.

"Aideen, put the kettle on there, love. The water is frozen in the pipes," Cathal said, entering the house. "I'll need to free the tap for the animals."

Elisa stood frozen to the spot and unable to speak. Seeing the tension between his mother and Elisa, Jamie decided it was best if he left the room to boil the kettle. Cathal looked at Elisa and then at how Aideen stared straight at their daughter.

"You stay here, Elisa. Help your mother," Cathal said. He closed the door quietly behind him.

It wasn't very long before Jamie came from the kitchen and quickly made his way to the front door.

"Slow down! You'll *scald* yourself," Aideen snapped.

The sound of the door closing behind Jamie was possibly the scariest sound Elisa had heard all day. She was alone with her mother and knew she was in serious trouble without an escape route. She thought of all the things she could do to get out of this situation, but she knew none would work. The only option she had left was to stand her ground.

"Take off your boots. You're not going outside," Aideen said.

This was Elisa's chance. She sat down on the stairs and turned her back to her mother as she reached over to untie her shoe lace on the stairs. She removed her woollen hat and zipped her jacket down to half way. Elisa untied the lace of her other boot, and while she was bent over, she lifted Geaspar into her woollen hat and placed the scarf around him.

"Are you ready?" Aideen asked.

"Yeah, nearly there," said Elisa. She placed her boots by the door and took her jacket off and hung it up, leaving her woollen hat and scarf on the step.

"You can leave those next to the fire. They could do with a bit of airing," Aideen said.

"No. They're actually fine, Mam," said Elisa, holding her hat and scarf in one hand.

"*By the fire,*" Aideen said, firmly.

Elisa had no choice. She placed her hat and scarf on top of the logs in the basket.

"Go upstairs and wash," Aideen instructed.

Elisa hesitantly left Geaspar behind.

Chapter 8

The Beast from the East

The beast continued to unleash his fury across the land and Kaphiens were losing their struggle to keep their young alive. The temperatures plummeted and the wind howled bitter cold. Mothers cried next to their perished young and their wails could be heard through the woodlands. The rabbits quickly began to despair. They wrapped up their furless young in their own fur, but it wasn't enough to save them. The deadly cold perished the young fledglings in their nests and Cillian could not save even the adult birds who desperately clung to life. Hopelessness gripped the woodlands and the elves could do nothing to save the animals and birds. They looked to the fire dragons to save them. The dragons blew flames across the floor of the woods from their nests in the tress in an attempt to warm the earth for the badgers and rabbits and every other small animal who needed it. The guardians took to the sky and cast flames of fire over the meadow to fight the plummeting temperatures, but they were no match for the beast. The beast grew furious at the sight of the fire dragons, the winds strengthened and he cast blizzard conditions upon them. The dragons were forced to retreat to the island.

A mother hare scratched on the door of La Petite Maison Le Fèvre with her leveret in her mouth. The leveret was cold and limp when the elf opened the door. The hare hopped inside, by-passing the elf and laid her young close to the fire.

"Rub her chest… Don't frighten her mother," said one elf.

The elf removed the red woollen stole from Rós' chair and wrapped the leveret in it. He rubbed his body to warm him, but there was nothing. He lifted him and held him up by his hind legs and rubbed his chest and back.

"Come on little leveret," he said.

He rubbed him again and then swung him gently from side to side. The leveret opened its mouth to take a breath.

"Here!" said another elf coming from the kitchen with a hot water bottle in his hand.

The elf placed the hot water bottle on a cushion and then placed the stole over it with the leveret on top. The little leveret breathed faintly. Another elf placed a warm towel over the leveret.

"She'll be fine," the elf said to the mother hare. The hare approached her leveret. She tucked the towel around her and willed her little one to survive.

"It looks like this hare knows Rós and Micah. I see Micah's handy work," the elf remarked, pointing to the splint on the leveret's leg.

Kubera trudged through the blizzard conditions with a satchel slung over his shoulder bursting with ancient scrolls determined to fulfil his promise to the Children of Light. The ground was heavy underfoot and the gnome's legs felt like they had lead weights attached to them by the time he reached the mid-way point. His freezing cold arms carried an additional pile of scrolls that were almost impossible for him to hold, and unfortunately, every now and then, one dropped onto the snow. The act of reaching down to pick up the scroll that dropped was never easy as another three or four scrolls often fell from his arms when he bent down and his numb fingers were not readily able to grasp them.

This was an arduous journey for a gnome of such small stature. Kubera muttered some pattern of words to himself over and over again as he walked. He had mapped out in his mind exactly how he would teach Elisa and Jamie and in what order he would unravel the mystery of the ancient scripts. He walked all the way to the boundary reciting his method for fear he would forget a single pattern in his mind. It was approximately twenty minutes to six that morning when Kubera reached the boundary between the two worlds and crept into Elisa's bedroom.

Kubera saw Elisa sleeping and as quietly as he could, he laid his bundle of scrolls down on the floor and then emptied the satchel. He lifted each scroll, examined it and then placed it down in the particular order that appealed most to his method of teaching. Once he was sure they were in the correct order and no further switching around was needed, he sat down and waited.

Kubera rested his back against the wardrobe and watched Elisa sleeping. Soon his eyelids became heavy and he struggled to keep himself awake. He stretched his body in an attempt to wake himself up. He rubbed his eyelids and then suddenly Kubera startled at the sound of footsteps coming towards the room. The handle turned on the door and he froze, and as all gnomes do when they are scared, he disappeared. He watched as the door slowly opened and then carefully shut behind.

"We have him," said Lir, pulling a bleary-eyed Jamie along.

"What time is it?" Jamie whined.

"It's time you were up, me lad," said Ruan. "Now, *sit down there,*" Ruan said.

"Elisa! Elisa!" Lir whispered. He poked her on the shoulder. "Elisa, are you getting up? It's six o'clock," Lir said.

Elisa rubbed her eyes and stretched in her bed. Then she suddenly remembered whose voice she had heard.

"*What* are you doing *in my room?*" she asked, startled. The visitors quickly left the room and stood outside. "*You too, Jamie. I'm not getting changed with you in my room,*" Elisa said.

"Sorry," Jamie said. He stood up and left the room.

"I'll call you when I'm dressed," Elisa said.

The four stood in the hallway looking at each other while they waited for Elisa to get ready.

"Heavy snow last night, Kubera," said Ruan. "The worst I've seen in my lifetime."

"The Beast from the East," said Kubera.

"A *beast?*" Jamie inquired. Kubera nodded.

They stood looking at each other and then at their shoes. They tucked their hands into their pockets, because they simply didn't know what else to do.

"There'll be plenty of snow drifts in the valley," Ruan said, searching for something to say.

"Plenty," said Kubera.

They looked around them again and then looked at the door of Elisa's bedroom, hoping that she would call them in and release them from their very awkward conversation.

"You can come back in!" Elisa called.

Now fully dressed, Elisa was ready for her lessons.

"I think it'd probably be best if you ate breakfast," said Kubera.

"That's for sure. I always say that an empty sack can't stand," said Ruan, walking downstairs.

"Yeah, and you always say that a full sack can't bend," said Lir.

"That's right!"

Elisa overtook Ruan and Lir on the stairs and ran to Geaspar. She lifted the scarf from her woollen hat and there he was sleeping. Elisa lifted him into her arms, and when she did, he opened his little brown eyes and looked up at her. Kubera came to look.

"And a fully belly too," he said. "You're doing a great job. Wait 'til he starts moving around. You'll have a job to keep him down," he said, rubbing Geaspar under his chin.

"I can make scrambled eggs on brown bread if that's alright," said Jamie.

"Banbha was right. You're not such a bad boy after all," said Kubera. "That'd be delicious."

Lir stood in front of Jamie.

"Are you alright, Lir?" Jamie asked. Lir nodded and then blinked. "Are you looking for something, Lir?"

"Hot chocolate."

"Oh, good lad Jamie! You make the hot chocolate and I'll make the scrambled eggs. I might toast that brown bread if that's alright with everyone," Ruan said, passing them by and walking into the kitchen.

Jamie tried to get around Lir. Every time he moved to the left or right, Lir accidentally stepped in that direction too. Jamie held onto Lir for a second and moved to Lir's right and then entered the kitchen. Despite all the commotion in the kitchen, no one seemed to be concerned about the sleeping parents in the room at the back of the house. Egg shells and splashed milk adorned the counter top. Jamie added the cocoa powder to the milk in his pot, careful to ensure that he added the exact amount for perfect hot chocolate. Ruan scrambled the eggs on the large black frying pan and Lir watched the bread in the toaster. They worked incredibly well together and for once Ruan and Jamie didn't need space from each other to cool down.

Elisa placed the dragon back into her woollen hat and covered him with her scarf.

"He's a content little thing. You must've been up all night feeding him," said Kubera.

Elisa looked at the little dragon with the full belly and wondered how he was so full. She thought he might have left the comfort of her hat and found food somewhere in the house, but he was so small. How could he possibly have been able to do that?

"Expectation is a good thing," Kubera said.

"Huh?"

"You can live your life hoping for things to improve or you can expect it. When we expect things to go our way, they often do. Expect to receive and you will. The time of fire is here. It's a time of great abundance…oh, they're here," said Kubera.

Elisa felt even more confused by what Kubera said. What was she supposed to expect? She sat with the others at the table eager to start on her lessons with Kubera. Lir took his first sip from his cup of hot chocolate and smiled with a frothed lip. Food was the one thing that the elves and Jamie had in common and despite Jamie's obvious bad manners before the dragon egg hatched, it was clear that his bad mood had lifted in the presence of food. He took a bite into his scrambled eggs on toasted brown bread and closed his eyes in complete satisfaction.

"Oh, Elisa. We don't have any school today. The weather is too bad, and Dad said he doesn't think we'll have any for the rest of the week," Jamie said. "Do you want to build a snowman later?" he asked, reaching down for another piece of scrambled egg on toast.

"I'm making his face," said Elisa.

"Alright."

The thought of building a snowman was far from Kaphien minds that morning. Mother Badger left her badger family drinking their cups of hawthorn tea and made her way to the entrance of her sett.

"Wrap up warm. No one is going out today. I won't be long," said Mother Badger to her family.

She burrowed her way through the snow at the entrance to her sett and saw the elves gathering around the campfires in the woods as the snow continued to fall. She saw birds fly to Cillian who offered them food and as much warmth as he could beneath his shelter. Mother Badger watched them huddle against each other and fluff their feathers to keep warm and then Cillian pulled the heavy blanket back over the shelter opening. The blizzard conditions became too much for Mother Badger and she retreated to her sett. The animals were cold and hungry and Madra Rua was no exception. The fox slowly approached the campfire in search of warmth.

"Madra Rua, come sit with me," Rós called.

The fox came closer. She observed the movements of those around her and when she felt it was safe, she accepted Rós' invitation. Lug offered her a piece of food.

"You might as well. She froze to death in the snow," Lug said. He laid the rabbit on the ground next to the fire. "Don't let her life be in vain," Lug said, tempting the fox to eat.

Madra Rua crept closer and then hungrily tore at the rabbit's flesh and ate. When she had finished eating, she then climbed onto Rós' lap and curled her body into a tight ball.

"You made this sled for me at the perfect time," Rós said to Lug. She pulled the waxed coat tighter against her body and placed the heavy rug over Madra Rua.

Lug was too distracted to really hear Rós speak. He looked over his shoulder and saw Joachim standing between the trees and then looked back at Rós. He returned his gaze to Joachim but he was gone.

"The beast won't be happy until all the young are dead," Lug said. He prodded the potatoes in the pot over the campfire. "There is nowhere for us to hide."

"They were all perished by the time I got to them," Micah said, sitting down next to them.

Lug needed to get Rós out of this cold before she succumbed to it herself. He watched her body shiver and her lips were already blue. He added another log to the fire but knew that it was hopeless against these freezing temperatures with a body so still.

"Are you warm enough, Rós? We'll perish in this snow if these conditions don't ease," Lug said. Lug's eyes searched for Joachim and his pack.

"The wolves will bring you home, Rós," said Feehul, approaching them. Lug breathed a sigh of relief. "We need this blizzard to ease first and then we can safely get you home," Feehul said, and Lug's anxiety rose once again.

"I've no home to go to," Rose said.

"You do."

"*I do?*"

"Yes. Everything is waiting for you and the fire is on," said Feehul.

"How can we thank you?" Micah interjected.

"You'll be there for us one day," said Lug.

Rós longed to spend one more day in the woods that she had called home, but she knew she had to leave. La Petite Maison Le Fèvre had everything she needed and the terrain of the woodland was too undulating for a wheelchair to negotiate. '*One more day,*' she thought.

"Have you seen my mother?" Rós asked, longingly. "Do you know if she is alright?"

"I met her the other day. She's doing well. She's in Éire, so this blizzard hasn't affected her," Feehul said.

"She's getting too old to come to me and I'm not able to come down to the valley unless Micah carries me in the Summer months," Rós said.

She longed to meet any member of the Tuatha Dé Danann yet she knew she was running out of time. She couldn't believe that none of them had come to see her. She rarely if ever came to the woodland.

"*And Dagda?*" Rós asked. "Have you seen him?"

"I'm here," her brother said, stepping from behind a tree.

Dagda didn't know how Rós would receive him and was filled with remorse. It was he who had thrown the stone that hit his sister. Donn threw the stone at Dagda, and when he missed, without hesitating, Dagda picked the stone from the ground and flung it in the direction from which it came. He struck his sister in the back as she stood ready to shoot an arrow from her bow. That was the blow that left Rós in a wheelchair and Dagda struggled to live with what he had done every day since then.

"Will you play to me?" Rós asked.

"I'm so sorry, Rós," Dagda said.

"Play to me," she said, "I've missed the sound of your harp... Play!"

"But, I haven't played it in a long time. I probably wouldn't know how to sing to the harp now," he said.

Rós refused to accept this for an answer and it wasn't long before the Tuatha Dé Danann came from the hidden parts of the woods with Dagda's harp. They placed it on the snow next to him. Dagda was bewildered by the sudden appearance of his harp and the anticipation on the faces of family and friends. He didn't know what else to do other than to sit on the wooden stool close to Rós as the snow fell. He looked at those around him again and his heart began to beat fast in his chest. It had been so long since he had sung to his harp. Dagda rubbed his freezing cold fingers and blew into his hands. Dagda took a nervous breath. He barely touched the strings of his harp, but that delicate touch was enough to place him at peace in his heart and mind. His heart slowed and his breath was easy.

Dagda sang the *Song of Dreams* to his harp while gently caressing its strings. He sang so softly yet the sound of his voice was transformed as the harp strings carried the melody to the hearts and souls of Dagda's family and friends that morning. The Kaphiens listened and forgot about the snow, the cold, and the worries of the world. They were completely transfixed by the *Song of Dreams* and nothing could pull them from that beautiful melody. The sound drifted through the whole of the woodland and into the valley. The notes floated through the cold air and fell upon the ears of all the creatures that hid in their homes from the perishing cold. The *Song of Dreams* carried a message of hope, of unity and of love, and the beast itself was silenced. The sharp winds ceased howling and as the winds died, stillness fell upon Kapheus. The ferocious beast who had ripped through the valley and torn through the dens, setts, nests and Kaphien cottages with devasting results, laid down on his blanket of snow and felt unable to move as those floating notes consumed him. The Kaphiens looked out from their homes and felt the stillness in their souls with every note Dagda sang. Feehul stood with his fellow elves in the woodland and looked into the valley.

"Keep playing," Feehul said. "The beast has fallen asleep."
Dagda continued to sing to his harp and the elves joined him in
low, soothing voice. They sang to the dreamland and Geaspar
woke. The little dragon wriggled inside Elisa's woollen hat and then
poked his head out. He pricked his little dragon ears and listened
to the sound until he was pulled from the lullaby with Elisa lifting
him into her arms. Geaspar reached his head around and looked
into the drawing again to listen to the song while Elisa sat listening
to all Kubera had to teach her in her room that morning.

The notes floated so gracefully into Elisa's bedroom from Dagda's
harp and that peaceful feeling brought her to a place of easy
learning. Elisa stroked Geaspar's body while she looked at those
visually impressive ancient scripts with margins adorned with
intricate scroll work. She was mesmerised by the colourful initials
at the beginning of paragraphs that were depicted by animals
alongside the black interior text written. Elisa held the vellum
script to see more closely the image of a chained dragon referring
to the text in which was written 'free me'. She read of a fire that
could not be quenched with the symbol of a dragon flaming a
furnace next to it.

Kubera spoke to Elisa all the while the sound of the *Song of Dreams*
whispered to her. Elisa listened to Kubera's every word and drifted
to those places Kubera wished to bring her in the ancient texts as
if she had spent her whole life reading and learning with the
gnomes. Kubera showed her the large scroll of the choir book. The
notes were beautifully displayed on the scroll as if it was written
today with all the tools of typing rather than one thousand years
before Elisa was even born. The songs told of fire and water, of
war and peace. The songs told of struggle and power, and of hope
and love. Kubera read on. The *Song of Dreams* had long since lulled
Jamie to sleep and Ruan and Lir had followed him into the
dreamland, and for once it didn't matter. For all that Kubera was
teaching could still be heard through the notes of that song and
those words floated deep into Jamie's mind as he lay sleeping.

Then it happened. Geaspar coughed and spurted out a clear gel-
like mucus from his mouth. Kubera lifted the little dragon into the
air in delight. He held him close to him and taught the ancient texts

to him as if the newly-born understood every word. Geaspar couldn't stay with Kubera's words, but instead stretched to listen to the notes of that song as they floated through Kapheus. He was transfixed by the song and so too was the phoenix in Éataín's cottage. She fell in love with those notes in a way she had never loved before. The phoenix lifted the latch on the cottage door and took flight. She floated through the vast valley, spun in loops and danced to the sound of that song. The majesty of her flight and the vibrancy of her fiery red plumage were a beauty that one could only hope to ever witness in life, but never believe possible. The Kaphiens looked up to watch her flight. They tracked her movements all the way to the veil of the Meadow of Discovery and watched her seamlessly pass through. The phoenix soon came to rest on Grandmother Oak's branch, but couldn't resist the lure of the harp and soon left the branch and stood on the woodland floor next to Dagda. The elves and all who dwelled in the woodlands of Kapheus came from their homes to view the magnificent bird who was so captivated by the music that she was oblivious to their presence.

The Dark One stood at the entrance to Cormac's Cave and listened to those same notes floating through the air. He watched the dark earth turn brown and the burnt grass die away to green shoots before his eyes as the notes travelled through the Woods of Dé Danann. Then he felt the floor of the cave crack beneath his feet. He grew afraid and looked at his precious jars on the shelves. He quickly turned to retrieve them but he heard the walls begin to crack. He fled before they collapsed on top of him. The clock dial split into eight pieces and screams cried out until the walls fell on top of it and Cormac's Cave was no more. The Dark One transformed into a dark cloud and left.

In that woodland, tree barks, diseased for so many years, began to lose their blackness and were restored to their original brown, golden or silver colour. The water transformed from silted, dirty, undrinkable water to clear water, through which one could see the riverbed beneath the ice. The animals whose sores had plagued them and whose minds had tortured them lifted their heads to hear the notes float through the sky. Their minds were healed by the beauty of that sound and as they licked their open sores they healed and the sores closed for the first time.

The more Dagda played, the healthier the Woods of Dé Danann became. He sang to his harp all that day and late into the night and it was as if time passed without anyone noticing. The sound was so captivating. Elisa had continued to absorb all Kubera taught her that day, and Jamie too in his sleeping state. In the end, Kubera rolled up his scrolls and bid Elisa good night.

"It is one of the riches of the world, Elisa… Taragon taught you that. *Play,*" he said, "it dissipates all darkness. When there is joy in your heart there is no room for anything else." He looked at the sleeping Jamie and the elfin brothers and smiled. "You learned so much today. I think my job is done," he said. "Good luck on your travels."

Kubera crossed the boundary between the two worlds and blissfully carried his heavy load with him across the snow-laden valley. Many of his fellow gnomes appeared in the snow to help lighten his load. They held their jars of fireflies to light the way and filed across the dark night in a stream of green light. Kubera was happy to return to Taragon and his home in the Wood of Illusion. He took one last look back to the boundary between the two worlds before he disappeared. Elisa watched Kubera and waved from the drawing. She observed the stream of green light until it disappeared from sight. She waved one last time to Kubera and then slowly turned around.

Elisa looked at Jamie and the elves sleeping in her room and decided not to wake them. Instead, she carried Geaspar downstairs and laid him in his basket by the fireside.

"You're beautiful," Elisa said, caressing him. "Maybe one day I'll be able to tell you about Fódla. She was the best dragon ever." Geaspar looked at Elisa with heavy eyelids and soon fell asleep. "One day I'll tell you," she said.

Elisa quietly walked upstairs to her room. She hesitated to turn her bedroom door handle and decided to cross the hallway to Jamie's room instead and climbed into his bed. Elisa immediately fell into a deep sleep and didn't hear the footsteps outside the room door and neither did anyone else. Those same footsteps crept

downstairs to the living room and gently walked across the room
to the basket by the fire. The sleeping dragon was carefully lifted
from the woollen hat and caressed and then those same footsteps
crept into the kitchen to prepare food for the hungry Geaspar. The
music floated through her whole being while she prepared the food
for Geaspar who silently waited for her on the countertop. He
watched as she stirred the pot and began humming the tune of the
Song of Dreams. His stomach rumbled as the aroma of her cooking
filled the air and soon his food was ready. She added a little cold
water to cool it for him and then the dragon opened his mouth and
swallowed the soft food he was fed.

"Tá ocras ort anocht," the voice said. Geaspar didn't understand,
he simply continued to eat his fill. "I'm sure you're not the only
little Kaphien who's hungry tonight," she said.

As soon as Geaspar finished his meal, she carried him to the living
room and sat on the chair by the fireside. She sang the *Song of
Dreams* and her voice filled the house and no one stirred.

The two elfin brothers were in such a deep sleep that they didn't
realise whose room they were sleeping in that night. Kapheus
called to them and they were unable to stir.

One little creature stirred, however, when he heard the *Song of
Dreams* drift beneath the door of La Petite Maison Le Fèvre. The
young leveret twitched his ears just like Geaspar had done and
when he listened to the song he began to feel a little better. The
little one crept out from beneath the towel and huddled against his
sleeping mother.

"She'll be alright," the elf said, and fell back to sleep.

Dagda played all through the night until the sun rose the next
morning. When he stepped away from his harp, the Kaphiens
woke. They saw that the wind had ceased and that it had stopped
snowing. They watched the sun rise over the hills and knew that
the beast was gone.

"You can take this back to wherever you found it," Dagda said to
his warriors, and they duly did as he asked. Dagda sat down next
to Rós.

"Go raibh maith agat… thank you for last night. Thank you for
everything," Dagda said.

"Dagda, I love you," Rós said, "I always will."

"The wolves will be here soon," said Dagda. Rós nodded.

"I wish I could stay in the woods forever."

"There is no forever... not in anything. We only have now and nothing else."

Rós nodded, she reached out and hugged Dagda, and as she did, she saw the wolves from the corner of her eye.

"It's time to go," she whispered.

Micah harnessed the wolves to the sled and it wasn't long before Rós was leaving the woodlands for her home in the hills.

Dagda watched his sister leave, but this time it was different. She wasn't the wounded and vulnerable sister who had left all those years before. He saw her courage and her strength and no longer felt afraid. He seized some of the courage for himself and knew that his own days of hiding had ended. He did not yet know it but the Dark One had left the Woods of Dé Danann. The warriors came running towards him, and as close to the dreamland as he will ever be while awake, he watched them rejoice around him as if in a dream. Dagda returned his gaze to his sister until she disappeared from sight. He left the woods of Kapheus and walked into the snow-laden meadow.

"From darkness to light," Grandmother Oak said. "The time of fire is truly here."

"Will he be alright?" Feehul asked.

"Yes, he will. He'll come back in his own time," she said, admiring Dagda for dropping the darkness of his shame and sorrow and stepping into his true light.

"What is the time of fire about?"

"You'll soon see," she said.

The leprechauns had heard the music float through the air the evening before and it tormented them. They returned indoors and closed all their window shutters to block out the sound. By now, they could venture outside if they so wished, but didn't dare for at least another few hours. The *Song of Dreams* unsettled them, and they were not ready to be transported to a place of hope. It was still early when Seán put sods of turf on the fire. He had tossed and turned in his bed all night, and there was no point in him trying to stay in his bed any longer. He sat down by the fireside and drifted in his thoughts. He wondered how Dagda got hold of his harp. He thought that one of his fellow leprechauns had stolen it and hidden it near the fountain of hope, a place where no one would suspect. Dagda's harp was the most valuable musical instrument in all of Kapheus and Éire. He began to wonder how safe his own pile of treasure now was and thought of other places that he could possibly hide his treasure trove.

Suddenly, three dull knocks sounded on Seán's door. Curiously, he left the fireside to see who stood at his door on such a cold and snow-laden morning. He looked through the crack in his shutter but saw no footprints in the snow. He tried the window shutter on the other side of his cottage, but again there were no footprints in the snow. Three dull knocks sounded once again. Seán took his fire poker in his hand.

"*Cé atá ann?*" he asked. The visitor did not answer. "You are in Kapheus. *Why* do you *not know the language of your kin?*" he asked. "*Who's there?*"

"Open the door," the voice said.

Seán took a second before nervously opening the door. The figure of a man stood in front of him in a black hooded cloak. The phoenix stood a distance away and watched the cloaked figure hand a money purse to the leprechaun and swiftly enter the home without legs to carry him. The phoenix watched Seán step outside to look around him before the leprechaun withdrew inside and closed the door. The phoenix returned to the woods of Kapheus. When the phoenix returned to the woods, she stood in front of Cillian.

"Whatever you're looking for, I don't have it," Cillian said, stoking the fire. He turned to feed the birds beneath his shelter. When he turned back the phoenix was looking blankly at him. "Unless it's food you're looking for," he said, reaching out his hand filled with grain, "I don't have it." The phoenix continued to look blankly at him.

Cillian gave up and reached his hand into his inner pocket. He pulled out the silver coin.

"Is it this coin you're after?" Cillian asked.

The phoenix reached out to snatch it but Cillian pulled his arm back in time.

"Look at the coin and be sure it's this coin you want," he said.

The phoenix looked at the coin and then tilted her head from side to side.

"That's good enough for me," said Cillian, and he handed the coin to her.

The bird of fire picked it up in her beak and flew away. Cillian returned to feeding the birds beneath his shelter. The phoenix flew to the Wood of Illusion and entered the earth dragon's lair. She tapped her beak against the wall until Kubera came from the stairway to greet her. She looked at him blankly.

"Well, are you going to give it to me?" Kubera asked, reaching out his open hand. The phoenix dropped the silver coin into the palm of his hand. "How many coins were needed to buy him?" Kubera asked. "Thirty, I suspect," he said, shaking his head. "It's already written in the ancient text."

Kubera examined the coin in his hand. He felt its weight and knew that it was genuine.

"It doesn't seem to be possible to stop this now. The momentum is building like a snowball rolling down a hill," Kubera said.

The phoenix looked blankly at him. She then tilted her head to one side and then the other.

"I've taught her all that is possible for a child so young to absorb. She is on her own now," Kubera said. "There's no stopping this. The time of fire brings everything into the light."

"Squawk!"

"*There is nothing else* for me to do," said Kubera. "*Why are you even asking me?* You know I can't stop time or turn back the clock!"

"Squawk! Squawk!" the phoenix reiterated.

"Your squaking won't change anything."

"Squawk! Squawk!"

"*Alright…* I'll talk to Taragon," Kubera said. With that, the phoenix flew away.

There was one other thing that phoenix needed to do in Kapheus that morning, and on her way, she stopped at the boundary between the two worlds. She had the vision to see the sleeping Jamie on the other side and the two brothers with their heads resting close to each other. She then saw the handle turn on the bedroom door and saw it open. The phoenix then caught her reflection in the boundary and saw Iolar flying overhead and decided to join her.

The footsteps crept inside Elisa's room. She saw the two sleeping elves huddled together and saw that they were as close to each other as the day Lir was born into Ruan's world. She pulled the blankets over Jamie while he slept on Elisa's bed and then took the throw from the base of Elisa's bed and placed it around the sleeping elves. The footsteps then walked from the room.

"Achoo!" said Lir. He scratched his nose and woke. "Ruan, are you alright?" he asked. Ruan rubbed his eyes.

"Yes. I fell asleep, Lir. Do you need me?" he asked, sleepily.

"I'm hungry," Lir said.

"Well, then I *will make you* something nice to eat," said Ruan. "You are my favourite brother after all."

"I'm your *only* brother."

"That may be the case and that's what makes you all the more special. You're the only brother I have."

Ruan pulled the throw away and stood up. He folded it and placed it at the end of Elisa's bed.

"Maybe it's our turn to make the hot chocolate," he said, looking at the sleeping Jamie.

"Come on, Lir. We'll cook something nice for this family. I'd love a scone this morning. How about it?"

"*Yes,*" said Lir.

The two elves then left the room.

"You know, Lir. When I was small I fell into a badger sett and Mother Badger picked me up. She brought me to her home and applied ointment to my wounds. She baked scones for me and they tasted delicious. I *will never* forget the smell of her freshly baked scones," Ruan said, walking downstairs.

"Where was I?" Lir asked.

"You were still in our mother's arms."

The two elves made hot chocolate together and baked scones. They each brought a fresh baked scone to the living room table with golden butter and blackberry jam. They laid them on the table and as they ate, they talked about all the things they loved as elfin children. They spoke of their mother and father and of all the tricks they played. They laughed and never once felt that they could disturb anyone in the house from their sleep. The time the elves spent together that morning would be a memory they would both cherish for the rest of their lives.

"Moments make memories," Lir said. Ruan nodded and then took another sip from his hot chocolate.

"I wonder how he's doing over there," Ruan said. Lir shrugged his shoulders. "The dragon for all the ages," Ruan said, looking at the woollen hat. "That'll be a tough road for the little fella."

Chapter 9

The Blood Moon

"I've an eye for precious things," said Caoilte, observing the phoenix in flight.

He had followed the beast from the east with great interest to see his wrath upon the Kaphien plains. He landed his fire dragon on the eastern hilltop and clad in his coat of silver and gold armoury, Caoilte stepped down from his mount. He removed his golden helmet to watch the phoenix in flight.

"The magnificence! Do-chreidte," Caoilte said.

The phoenix flew as if dancing a spring waltz with Iolar. The smoothness of their wing flaps; the synchronicity of their movements. It was as if they were floating on clouds and they were. The sky was their ballroom and they were the masters of the dance floor. They glided along that floor as if no one was watching. They held each person who observed their effortless flight captivated. Caoilte was mesmerised by the dance. He had never seen anything more beautiful in all his life and he prided himself on having an eye for precious things. This, however, was more precious than anything he had every acquired, and yet its beauty was only visible when it was free. To hold the phoenix in a cage of gold would steal its beauty away. He thought of how he would catch her, but in a split second, he thought against it. This was one that he could allow to get away from him.

The phoenix was suddenly distracted by something shiny on the eastern hilltop. The golden breastplate of the fire dragon distracted her as the morning light reflected from it. The phoenix broke from her dance and flew to the hilltop. She landed in front of Caoilte and looked blankly at him. She tilted her head from side to side.

"Um… umm…" he said, very flustered.

The phoenix looked at the fire dragon with his golden breastplate and helmet and saw the bit in his mouth and then the long reins and saddle on his back. She looked at Caoilte again and he looked as blankly at her as she did at him on this occasion.

"I don't know what you're looking for from me," he said. The phoenix tilted her head. *"I don't have anything to give you,"* Caoilte argued.

She looked into his eyes more deeply, and then Caoilte handed her his golden helmet. The phoenix bowed and Caoilte placed it aloft her fiery red head. The phoenix then blinked and flew away.

"The lost dragon egg has hatched. The dragon for all ages lives," Caoilte said to his dragon. He happily mounted him again.

The phoenix flew to the boundary between the two worlds and stood there waiting for Ruan and Lir to pass through. She sat there for what seemed an eternity but never faltered on the cold snow beneath her talons.

"Well, I think we'll leave them to their lives," said Ruan, standing up from the living room table. "I've a funny feeling we're needed in Kapheus anyway," he said.

They washed their dishes and then placed a large plate of scones on the living room table.

"There's plenty of hot chocolate left in the pot for them," he said and then joined Lir up the stairs to Elisa's room.

They crept across the bedroom floor, so not to wake Jamie, and then took one look at each other before stepping through the drawing. Ruan had no sooner stepped into Kapheus when he fell over, tripped by the helmet laying on the blanket of snow.

"What's this?" he asked the phoenix, growing more concerned by the second.

Ruan lifted the golden helmet and examined it. He then looked all about him, but everything was still as the beast lay sleeping.

"Bring me to where you found it," he instructed. The phoenix shook her head. "You *didn't* find it! Bring me to where Caoilte gave it to you," Ruan said.

"Caoilte *our cousin?"* Lir asked.

"Not a word to anyone, Lir, until we're sure."

Just then Iolar swooped down and snatched the two elves. The phoenix dipped her head in the snow and shuffled around a bit until she had the helmet back on her head. It wasn't long before she too was airborne and leading them all to the eastern hilltop. The two elves came tumbling to the ground when Iolar released

them from the grip of her talons. Ruan looked to the east and saw
Caoilte flying away in the distance.

"Can you take me farther?" he asked Iolar.

The eagle took flight and passed over the valley, releasing a number
of loud cries. Ogma heard her call, left his nest in the treetop and
flew to them. He reached the eastern hilltop before anyone knew
he was gone.

"Climb upon my back. I'll take you there," Ogma said.

"Maybe you should stay here in case anything happens," Ruan said.

"I'm coming with you," said Lir.

"Alright so."

The two elves climbed onto the black warrior dragon's back and
flew to the billowing furnaces.

"Merge your heartbeats to the earth," Ogma instructed, and they
disappeared.

The phoenix took flight and as she closed in on the boundary
between the two worlds, she threw the golden helmet into Elisa's
room and flew away. Jamie woke to the sound and jumped out of
his bed immediately to grab hold of the helmet.

"I can have *anything I want,*" Jamie said. "I'm getting a new bike…
I won't have to go *to school anymore.*"

He rubbed it with the sleeve of his sweater. He looked around and
then pulled Elisa's throw from the base of her bed and hid the
helmet beneath it.

"This is mine and no one's getting it," he said.

Jamie crept across the hallway and opened the door of his room
but Elisa was there. He slowly closed the door again and made his
way downstairs and outside to the shed. He climbed the ladder that
lead to the loft and hid the helmet behind the straw at the very
back of the loft. He climbed down the ladder again and crept into
the house without waking anyone. Jamie was about to walk upstairs
when he smelt the fresh baked scones. He grabbed one from the
living room table and just as he was about to turn around to go
upstairs, he smelt the aroma of hot chocolate. Jamie left his scone
on the table to fetch a cup of hot chocolate.

On his return, he noticed that his scone had vanished. He stepped
back into the kitchen, but it wasn't there either. Jamie reached

down to lift another scone from the plate and he felt a tug. Jamie
pulled the scone a little harder and found Geaspar dangling from
it. The little dragon held on tightly and Jamie grew frustrated with
him. He shook the scone and Geaspar fell and struck his body
against the bowl as he landed. Geaspar released a high pitched shrill
and within seconds the room door opened at the back of the house
and Jamie's mother came running down the hallway.

"Look! You got me *into trouble* now!" snapped Jamie, lifting him up.
He ran to put him into the woollen hat before his mother reached
the halfway point on the stairs.

"Are you *alright?*" she asked, anxiously.

"Yeah, I was just adding logs to the basket," Jamie said.

"*What* was the shriek?"

Jamie shrugged his shoulders.

"Jamie, go out and bring in more logs for the fire. This cold snap
is here for another few days," Aideen said.

"Will I have no school?"

"No school this week," said Aideen. "Just bring in a few logs…
and have a quick look in the shed to see if the animals are alright.
Your father will be down shortly to feed them."

Elisa came to the surface of her dreamtime with a stretch of her
body. She opened her eyes and saw the phoenix standing straight
in front of her. She sat up and rubbed her eyes and the phoenix
was gone.

"Elisa, will you help your father with the animals this morning.
Jamie has gone missing," Aideen said at the doorway.

"Okay Mam."

Jamie did not return with logs for the fire basket as his mother had
asked, but instead sat on the straw high up on the loft where he
couldn't be seen. He caressed his golden helmet and thought about
all he would do with the money he'd get for it. Down below him
he watched his father and sister tend to the animals and he didn't
offer to help.

"I'll get another jug of hot water, Dad," Elisa said.

"Oh, good on ya," said Cathal, forking out the manure from
Buddy's stable. "*Elisa.*"

"Yeah!"

"Will you hand me the sweeping brush before you go?"

Elisa picked up the sweeping brush from its resting place next to the door. She turned around quickly, and for some reason, she saw Jamie trying to hide from her in the loft. Elisa gave her father the sweeping brush and left to fetch a jug of hot water. As she walked heavy-footed across the snow laden yard, she wondered why Jamie was trying to hide from sight. She thought that it was very peculiar that Jamie would hide from her of all people and mulled it over as she filled the jug of hot water. She hadn't noticed Geaspar who had climbed out from her woollen hat and scampered across the living room floor in search of a raisin that had fallen from the table.

Far away in Kapheus, Ogma flew towards the billowing smoke. The journey was long, and night closed in as they approached the outskirts of the town of Fodar. It was a place of little beauty with rows of large mills lining the town. The furnaces roared and the smoked billowed from tall chimney stacks that reached to the clouds. The place looked sickly with smog filling the air and the lungs of all who inhabited it.

"Can you bring me down?" Ruan asked.

Ogma landed gently on the flat roof of a building. They watched another elf walking down the street wearing a dark suit and bowler hat. He coughed incessantly and drew the attention of youths hiding around a corner. As soon as the man passed that corner, the youths knocked him to the ground, stole his wallet and ran off.

"Will we help him?" Lir asked.

"No," whispered Ruan. "He isn't badly injured."

The man pulled himself from the cold and wet street and continued his walk home.

"He seems to have lost hope," Ogma said.

They were suddenly distracted by a rowdy group of elves exiting the door of a public house, laughing and falling to the street.

"*What's wrong* with them?" Lir asked.

"They're drunk," said Ruan.

Lir had never seen this before and thought that it was the most tragic thing to happen to an elf. His heart filled with pain and his

mind was torn by thoughts of wanting to help them but not knowing how.

"They have lost their way, Lir," said Ogma.

"There he is," said Ruan, pointing to Caoilte below.

They saw Caoilte dismount from his dragon and then hand the reins to another elf in tarnished clothes. They withdrew into the courtyard.

"Where is he going?" Ruan asked. He turned to his brother. "Lir, I need you to stay here to signal to me when it's time to leave. I'll go down to see what Caoilte's doing," he said.

"I want to go with you."

"I need you here, Lir," said Caoilte.

He climbed down the metal fire exit stairs traversing the length of the building to the street below. Ruan crossed the street and into the courtyard. He heard the sounds of people talking and tracked the sound to a narrow wooden doorway. He stood against the wall and saw Caoilte inside speaking to a number of men seated at a table.

"We strike on the blood moon. The dragon has hatched. We can't wait any longer than that. He'll be too strong for us," said Caoilte. The men laughed.

"How could a *defenceless newly born dragon* be too much for us?" a man asked. He lifted the pocket watch from his waistcoat and looked at the time.

"*This is the dragon for all the ages,*" Caoilte insisted, leaning across the table.

"Elf! Take *your mucky hands* off my table!" the man retorted. Caoilte stood upright. "Apologies, Mr. Adley," Caoilte said.

"We will go, but only because you have brought me much wealth. You're my lucky elf," Mr. Adley remarked. He looked at Caoilte. "Well, *what are you doing standing here?*" he shouted. "*Do you want lashes from my cane?*"

Caoilte ran from the room, passing Ruan by as he ran from the courtyard and onto the street.

It wasn't long before Ruan was airborne again and leaving the eastern shore. He was silenced by what he saw, but Ogma could read his thoughts and saw all that had happened in the courtyard while Ruan mulled his thoughts over in his mind.

"What did you find out?" Lir asked.

"Fodar is no place for an elf."

Ruan called to Grandmother Oak in his thoughts. He didn't know what else to do. He told her everything he had seen in Fodar and all that was to come. Grandmother Oak's branches shook and a shiver ran down her bark.

"Grandmother Oak? Are you alright?" asked Méabh. She had been woken in her nest by the shiver.

"Yes, I'm fine. You get your rest," she said. Grandmother Oak whispered to all the creatures of Kapheus. 'Sleep well. Rest easy in your bed tonight,' she whispered to them in their dreams.

Ruan didn't know what to do. Who would he tell beyond Grandmother Oak? Who would be the leader among them?

"Ogma, I'd like to wait outside Rós' cottage until they wake," Ruan said. "Would you mind dropping us off there on your way to the woodlands?"

"That's no problem," Ogma said.

Ogma flew through the night air all the while thinking of what was to come in Kapheus. He thought of the army of fire dragons that were bound to the will of the humans in Fodar. What match would the Kaphien dragons be to these metal armoured dragons? Ogma swooped to the earth and gently placed his feet on the hilltop. Ruan and Lir climbed down from his back.

"We elves are not accustomed to flying on dragons' backs, but *I have to say* that it was *a pleasure* to fly with you tonight," Ruan said. "We'll rest here for a little while if you don't mind," he said, sitting on the rock outside La Petite Maison Le Fèvre. Lir sat next to him. "I'm partial to watching the sunrise and today is no different to any other."

Ogma nodded, and without hesitation, he took flight in the direction of the woods of Kapheus. Ogma glanced towards the boundary as he flew home and thought about the little white dragon in Éire. He wondered who was caring for Geaspar and if Méabh would ever have another dragon of her own to rear. He remembered Fódla and how she brought so much joy to his family and got up to so much mischief along the way. He thought about the fate of the goddesses of Éire and wondered if their lives were doomed from the beginning. He worried for Geaspar's future.

Beyond the boundary in Éire, the footsteps crept downstairs to the living room and found the little dragon asleep in Cathal's boot at the door. She lifted Geaspar who had now become accustomed to her touch. She carried him to the kitchen, and like every other night, she made food for him. This time, however, he was able to eat from the saucer. She caressed his body while he ate and as her fingers glided down his silky skin, the fiery letters appeared along the length of his body. Over and over again she stroked him while he ate and those same words reappeared.

"Am neamhbhuan," she said. "Time ephemeral… Our time together will only be brief," she said.

Geaspar ate his fill and he grew visibly stronger by the day. His little wings stretched a little farther and the length of his body grew such that he could now wrap his tail around the sugar bowl as he licked the saucer on the worktop.

"I think I'll need to find a more comfortable home for you," she said, lifting him into her arms. She searched the living room but could find no safe place to lay him down. The footsteps crept upstairs and entered Elisa's room. She walked towards the sleeping Elisa and tucked Geaspar under Elisa's blankets close to her pillow. The footsteps then walked from the room. Elisa opened her eyes and saw Geaspar's little brown eyes looking back at her. She pulled him close to her and drifted back to sleep.

As Ruan and Lir sat on that cold rock outside La Petite Maison Le Fèvre on that bitterly cold morning, the two brothers were a million miles apart in their thoughts. Lir shuffled and blew warm air into his hands while Ruan thought about all he saw in Fodar.

"*I'm really cold, Ruan.* Do you think Rós would let us in if we knocked?" Lir asked.

"It's almost sunrise," Ruan said, huddling closer to Lir. "Then Rós will welcome us in."

Rós saw the two elves from the window of the cottage and didn't hesitate to open the door.

"Maybe I'd like to join you to watch the sunrise," Rós said.

"Rós, it's good to see you," said Ruan.

"Ruan, you look like you've seen a ghost," Rós said, approaching them. "Lir you go on inside and add another log to the fire. I'll be in in a minute."

"Oh, *thanks Rós.*"

Rós sat next to Ruan for a few seconds until she was sure Lir was safely inside.

"It must be big if you haven't confided in your brother," she said. Ruan nodded. "Lift the burden of silence off your shoulders."

"We're going to war," Ruan said, he lifted his head and looked into Rós' eyes. "I was in Fodar. They're going to attack on the night of the blood moon."

Rós was afraid to speak in case she would miss a word of Ruan's story. He told her everything and she listened as the sun rose behind them. For once, the sunrise was a distant thought in their minds as Ruan's story unfolded. While Ruan spoke, Rós called to Iolar who sat on her ledge in the hills, and then to Éataín who slept soundly in her bed and to the phoenix who stared blankly at the sunrise from the front door of Éataín's cottage. Finally, Rós called to Grandmother Oak and she too heard her in her mind's ear.

"He's my cousin. He grew up in the valley. We grew up together," Ruan said in distress.

Rós listened all the while concocting a strategy in her mind, one which she shared with those she called.

"Where's his helmet now?" she asked, fearing that it may have fallen into the hands of the leprechauns.

"I don't know. Umm… it was on the head of the phoenix the last time I saw it," Ruan said.

"Are you coming in?" Micah asked.

Without saying a word, they both entered La Petite Maison Le Fèvre and the door closed behind them.

Éataín woke from her dreamtime to those thoughts that floated from Rós' mind to hers and on hearing them she needed to get out of bed. She sat at the living room table and lifted the lid off the butter and took a slice of bread from beneath the cloth on the bread board and placed it onto her plate. Éataín silently ate her breakfast and didn't notice Fiachra setting the fire in the living room. He looked over at Éataín every once in a while with concern. It wasn't long before Fiona joined them in the living room. Fiachra simply directed his gaze towards Éataín. Fiona looked over and saw Éataín lost to her thoughts. She sat down beside her and placed her hand on Éataín's. There were no words spoken between the two and Éataín's gaze did not shift from that point in the middle of the room. Eventually, Fiona lifted her hand away and walked into the kitchen.

Iolar who had also heard Rós' words, watched and waited from her ledge. This was the place in which she was born. These were her hills and valleys. She stretched her wings and took flight. The phoenix saw Iolar in the sky and she too took flight. They met and spun together in the air for a short time before parting company. Iolar flew westward to the Kaphien woods. She passed through the veil and soon landed on the branch of Grandmother Oak at the very same time that the phoenix came to rest outside La Petite Maison Le Fèvre. The bird of fire looked blankly at Micah when he opened the door. Micah called to Rós, and the phoenix entered the cottage.

There was a heaviness in the lives of those Kaphiens that morning and there was a heaviness too in the lives of Aideen and Cathal's family for a very different reason. Cathal turned the handle on the front door and walked inside.

"Jamie!" Cathal said. "*Where were you* this morning?"

"Nowhere," Jamie remarked.

"I *really* could have done with your help," Cathal said, hanging his cap up.

Jamie shrugged.

"What are you reading?" Cathal asked, tossing Jamie's hair as he passed him by on his way to the kitchen.

Jamie looked at his father dismissively and tidied his hair again. Cathal soon returned with a bowl of hot porridge.

"Have you eaten?" he asked, laying the bowl on the table. "It's *freezing* out there."

Jamie didn't respond. He instead looked down at his book.

"You must be glad that you've no school this week," Cathal commented. Jamie didn't speak. His father's voice was now a source of annoyance and Jamie found it hard to even tolerate his presence at this point.

"What are you planning to do with your day?" Cathal asked but was ignored.

Jamie was so angry that his father was disturbing him right now and he could barely hide it.

"That book must be very good. You can't take your eyes off it."

There was no response from Jamie. Aideen walked to the table and looked over Jamie's shoulder.

"Why don't you get yourself another book from the bookshelf? I'm sure they're a bit more interesting than that one," Aideen said, taking the book away from Jamie. "This one is beyond your years," she said, snapping it shut.

Jamie squinted his eyes in anger and stood up from the table. He searched through his mother's books and although Jamie had always loved to pick one of them up to read, today they meant very little to him. He pulled the smallest one he could find from the shelf. It had a tarnished red hardback cover, with an unrecognisable title on the worn material. He wiped it clean with his hand, but the golden lettering was still unrecognisable. He returned to his seat at the table and turned his back to his father.

"Come on, Elisa. You can help me. I need to pull another bale of straw down from the loft," Cathal said, standing up and walking to the kitchen with his empty bowl.

By the time he had returned from the kitchen, Jamie had his boots and jacket on and was halfway out the door. Cathal stood and wondered what was going on. He looked at the little book Jamie had left behind him. Cathal flicked through the blank pages and then closed the cover.

Sometimes we choose the wrong path. We let anger or greed have the advantage over our moral being, and when that happens, and we walk the wrong path, finding our way back can be the biggest challenge of our lives. Seán sat next to the fire rubbing his sore leg. The varicose veins bulged out of his calves and he already had an ulcer breaking through his increasingly sickening skin. His hair had already begun to fall out and he couldn't help but notice blemishes appearing on his face whenever he looked in the mirror. The Dark One passed over and back, pacing the floor, and yet had no feet. *"Tell me everything* you know about the Tuatha Dé Danann," he demanded. "I want to know *everything*, Seán. I want to know *all their secrets,"* said the Dark One and then he struck Seán who came tumbling onto the floor. Seán writhed in pain. The Dark One transformed into the figure of a scar-faced old man and kicked Seán into the stomach. "You *good for nothing* leprechaun!" he yelled. Seán drifted in his thoughts to the bog of Kapheus, to the fountain of hope and to the meadow. He closed his eyes.

"Get up *you fool!"* the Dark One shouted, but there was no response. The Dark One left.

The Kaphiens felt a heavy feeling in their hearts and minds when they woke that morning. They didn't know what it was that caused them to feel so low. Some looked at the clouds and blamed them for how they felt, others thought it was their food that wasn't quite right. However, there was one elf who knew exactly what it was that caused his heaviness. Ruan had seen enough in Fodar to know he had seen more than he ever desired to see in his life.

"Lir, I think you should go to our cousins in the wood of illusion. I think that would be the safest place for you," Ruan said, placing his cup of tea back down on the table.

Micah looked at Rós in surprise.

"You said they were a little crazy. *You said* I wasn't to go there," Lir insisted.

"I know I said that then, but it's different now."

"I'm *not going*, Ruan. I'm staying with you!"

Micah became even more unsettled in his chair and scrutinised the faces at his table to find out what was going on. The weight of the burden Ruan carried was clear to see. His face was ashen grey and he had no interest in his food. Micah looked at his wife who had barely touched her breakfast and to Lir who had been carefree up to the point of his brother asking him to leave him.

"*What's going on here?*" Micah asked. Just then he heard a knock on the door and stood up to answer it. "Come in, Éataín. Maybe you could make sense of what's going on in this cottage this morning," said Micah, closing the door behind her.

"What will we do?" Éataín asked.

"We'll come up with a strategy," Rós said.

"We're no match to their power," said Ruan, placing his hand to his forehead.

"As spoken by an elf," Rós said with a smirk. "Intelligence beats brawn every time. We'll outsmart them... and we'll work together," she said.

"*Who? What's happening?*" Micah asked.

"We are going to war, love," said Rós.

"*War! With whom?*"

"Ruan?" Lir asked.

"It's the truth. Caoilte is gathering an army. They're coming after *that defenceless dragon.* The poor mite... They'll destroy everything in their path to get a hold of him."

"Éataín?" Lir asked.

"We're not going to let that happen, Lir. Don't you worry," Éataín said, but in her heart, she felt afraid.

"Wait a second! *How* do you *know this?*" Micah asked. "*When* is this battle due to commence?"

"On the night of the blood moon," said Ruan.

"*The blood moon...* but, *that's only* three nights from now," Micah said. "*How are we* to get an army together by then? We don't *even* have soldiers!"

Micah looked at his discontented wife and rephrased his sentence. "We've plenty of soldiers. The Tuatha Dé Danann and the elves and... I need to get some air," Micah said, stepping outside.

"Ní neart go cur le chéile. Together we are strong, Ruan," Rós said. "Now, I want you to listen carefully to what I have to say..."

"He's not listening *to anything* I have to say. It's as if I'm a piece of dirt on the ground!" Cathal argued, sitting at the living room table.

With that, a knock sounded on the door. "Jamie, get that," Cathal called to the kitchen, but was again ignored. Cathal sighed. "Here, I'll get it myself."

"Danú come in. Tá fáilte romhat," Cathal said.

"Oh, I won't annoy you two. I only want to see Elisa. Is she in her room?"

"I don't know… *Jamie*, check to see if Elisa's upstairs," Cathal said. Jamie instead sat at the living room table.

"Don't worry about a thing! I'll run up myself," said Danú, already on the third step.

Cathal returned to the living room table and sat directly across from Jamie. However, Jamie had no interest in sitting with his father and decided to leave.

"*Sit back down,*" Cathal said in a firm voice. Jamie took no heed and left the table. "If I have to *physically* place you in *that chair*, Jamie, I will! *Don't* test me." Jamie looked at his father.

"You don't control me! I can do *what I want*. I can live my own life!" Jamie shouted.

"You can do what you like when you're eighteen, but until then, you'll do *as I say*. Sit down!"

"No!" Jamie shouted and turned to run upstairs.

"No, you don't!" Cathal said, reaching out his hand and pulling Jamie back. Cathal sat Jamie down on the chair.

In the Kaphien wood, Cillian got to his feet quickly and looked to the oak tree. The blood drained from his face when he saw the golden eagle sitting aloft Grandmother Oak's branch. He grabbed an empty sack lying on the ground and tore it open with his knife. "Don't go on me," he said, looking over his shoulder.

Cillian tore a second sack and then hung both from the door of his shelter to give an extra layer of protection to the birds inside. He snatched a few garlic bulbs and spread them across the entrance and looked over his shoulder again. The snow was still heavy on the ground as he trudged. His eyes were fixated on the golden eagle. When he reached her, Cillian stood in fear, but it was not the fear of seeing a sublime aerial predator. Cillian was afraid, because the supreme and fearless predator herself tightened her talons on Grandmother Oak's branch and shook with fear.

"Grandmother Oak, have you seen this?" Cillian asked.

"I can feel her fear shiver through my bark," Grandmother Oak replied.

"*What can we do?*" Cillian asked.

"Could you find Lugh? I feel his footsteps in the Woods of Dé Danann. Maybe you could ask him to come," Grandmother Oak said.

Lugh stood at what remained of the entrance to Cormac's Cave. The walls had cracked and fallen and the cave sat as a ruin on the landscape. He climbed onto one of the boulder rocks and saw the clock dial broken beneath him.

"He can't hurt another child now," Lug said.

Lug walked across the boulders looking through the crevasses in the ruins to see the broken glass jars. He saw a girl's red ribbon and a boy's conker.

"He has no control over you now," Lug said.

Lug stood tall and looked around. The birds flew freely across the sky. The trees were healthy and strong. He could hear the water splash over the rocks in the river as it thawed. He saw a robin land on the boulder beside him. The robin sang a celebratory tune and then flew away.

"It's over!" Lug shouted in delight. "It's over!"

His years of torture at the hands of the Dark One had ended. Cormac's Cave was gone and with it the Dark One. Lug climbed down from the boulder and walked to a nearby tree. He did what every elf does, he climbed it and sat on its branch. Lug leaned against the bark and struggled to absorb the magnitude of his years of torture and now his freedom. He breathed deeply and drifted in his thoughts to the secret garden, the leprechauns in the wasteland, and Banbha. He thought about how Feehul carried him when he was close to death.

"Bhí mé i mbaol bháis," he said and then he noticed his brother approaching him. "Feehul!" he exclaimed.

"You called," said Feehul with a smile. "I thought I'd come to see it myself."

"Clear blue skies!" Lug rejoiced, raising his hands to the air.

Those clear blue skies spread all the way east to Fodar.
"Ogma, the skies are clear blue. Are you sure they can't see you?
Have you merged your heartbeat to the earth?" Ruan asked.
"Yes."
"You can't stay on my back forever. Climb down," Ogma said.
Ruan nervously climbed down from Ogma's back and onto the flat
roof of the apartment block with Lir following close behind.
"Do I look alright?" Ruan asked.
Ruan wore the clothes of his fellow elves in Kapheus, an earthy
brown and caramel herringbone tweed suit with its baggy trousers
and fitted waistcoat and jacket above his strong brown leather
boots.
"Your cap," said Ogma, "the city elves wear them."
"Oh, yeah," Ruan said, fixing the cap onto his head. "Here, Lir.
Put yours on," said Ruan, pulling another cap from his pocket.
"I hope Rós is right about this," Ruan said, walking towards the
metal fire escape ladder.
"I won't be too far away," Ogma said. "Go n-éirí libh. Good luck."
They swiftly climbed down that fire escape and were soon at street
level. The two elfin brothers looked up and down the street and
then Ruan signalled to Lir to follow him.
"Don't look suspicious," Ruan whispered.
They walked briskly through a narrow street lined on both sides by
terraced houses. They saw a woman look suspiciously at them for
a few seconds from a second floor window before she drew the
curtain shut. The brothers walked on. The small terraced houses
seemed to run forever and with every step the brothers took they
grew more anxious. Lir looked back a number of times to see if
anyone followed them whilst Ruan stayed focussed on reaching the
cobblestone square.
"It's around this bend," Ruan said. "Keep to yourself, Lir," he
advised.
Finally, the narrow street opened onto a cobblestone square. In the
centre of the square was a large fountain with a unicorn rearing to
the sky. They briskly made their way passed the fountain and across

to the street on the opposite side. Lir saw an elf on the other side of that street sitting on a stool and playing a fiddle.

"He's drunk," Lir whispered.

The elf sang a song about the good old days of plenty. He sang of meadows green and elves who were free. He sang of the waterfall that thundered down from the mountain and the elf that seduced the fish at her feet. He sang of the golden eagle high in the sky and woodlands so clean.

"He's singing about our home," Lir said in a low voice.

"Shh…" whispered Ruan.

Lir watched the fiddler being approached by other elves. One elf bent down and stole the money from his cap while the other knocked him to the ground. He cried out for help, but no one took notice. Lir ran across to help. Ruan raced to catch up with Lir while desperately hoping that their cover wasn't blown. By the time Ruan reached them, Lir had already helped the fiddler to his feet.

"Kapheus!" the elf whispered.

"Not a word," said Ruan.

The fiddler held tightly to Ruan's arm.

"Take me back there," he said.

"Who are you?" Ruan asked.

"Pádraig Ó Briain," the fiddler said.

"I'll take you home to the meadow," Ruan said, "but we've something else to do first. Keep playing your fiddle."

Ruan and Lir passed down the busy cobblestone street that lead to the metal mills. The street was lined with jewellery stores, shoe shops and clothes boutiques. They couldn't believe their eyes. They noticed the elves had painted their faces with shades of colour that appeared to darken their own skin and they coloured their eyelids and wore clothes that did not even compare in quality or beauty to the handmade clothes of the meadow elves.

In the middle of the street stood an elf singing and playing the guitar. He was taller than average for an elf with dark brown hair that was tied in a short ponytail. He wore a magnificent navy woollen overcoat, dark trousers and shiny black shoes. He looked completely wrong for this environment, but nonetheless was at home on the street. He had placed his cap about two feet in front of him on the pavement in the hope those passing by would part with their coins for a song.

"You would stand in your bare feet in the snow to listen to a voice like his," Ruan said, mesmerised by the smoothness of his voice.

He watched the people and the elves hurrying by as they approached and Ruan couldn't understand it. He even saw a woman walking with a small child on either hand. She danced with her children as she walked but still she didn't stop to give money to the singer.

"Why don't they recognise it?" Ruan asked. Ruan and Lir stopped for a short while to listen.

The elf finished his song and rubbed his fingers that by now pained him due to the freezing cold. The elf then sang another song and both Ruan and Lir were transported to another world as he sang in their native tongue.

"There's years of training in that voice. He's minding his chords," said Ruan, rubbing his throat. "His timing is perfect."

Two elderly elves came walking up the street. They linked each other as they fought the bitterly cold easterly breeze. One elf threw a silver coin into the cap and then held the other elf steady so that she could do the same. Ruan searched his own pocket for a silver coin. He and Lir walked towards the elf and tossed the coin into his cap.

"Thank you," he said, between the notes of his song.

"Tá fáilte romhat," said Lir.

"Be careful speaking your native tongue around here. It's not well taken," said the elf. "Where have you come from?" he asked, breaking from his singing.

"Kapheus," said Lir.

"*Shh...* Don't mention that place around here," whispered the elf, holding tightly to Lir's arm.

He watched a man looking slightly suspicious of them as he walked by. The elf strummed his guitar and sang out loud and the man forgot what drove his suspicion.

"Where are you from yourself?" asked Ruan.

"Tara, but I've been to many places."

"And why are you here now?"

"I'm in search of a child called Elisa. I've a message for her," the elf said. "I heard that there is a portal between Éire and here and that the child Elisa is on the other side of it. I've been searching for the boundary between the two worlds for years."

"What's your name?" Ruan asked, feeling a little suspicious.

"Tim," said the elf. Ruan looked him straight in the eyes.

"Tim is not a name of yours," he said.

"It's my nickname. It's easier around here. My real name is Finn Ó Conchobhair," he said.

"What do you want with such a child?" Ruan asked.

"Let's walk," Finn said.

"Where we are walking, you may not follow," said Ruan.

"I know about the war that's looming," Finn said. "I need to get to the child called Elisa."

"*What war?*" Ruan asked.

"Come with me. I'll show you," said Finn.

He swung his guitar across his back and escorted the brothers down the street towards the mills. High above them, Ogma tracked their movements, and as soon as they passed through the streets laden with mills, Ogma retreated to the apartment block.

"Follow me," Finn whispered.

"The *only reason* we're following *you* is that my heart is sure you are to be trusted, but my head is saying *something very different*," said Ruan.

They turned down a dark alleyway and then climbed an old metal fire escape ladder. They had almost climbed the entire height of the large red-brick building behind Finn when the elf stopped at one of the mill's small metal framed windows. Finn pulled hard on the stiff metal frame and then climbed inside with Ruan and Lir following him. They were on a loft and it seemed to the elfin brothers that this loft was where Finn had been calling home. There in front of them on the floor of the loft was a potato sack to sleep in with a pillow at its head made from a combination of Finn's satchel and a cotton shirt. This makeshift bed was close enough to the window for a quick escape but far enough away too that the cold breeze didn't cut through him as he slept. Finn crouched down and Ruan and Lir did the same.

"There's no need for electricity here," whispered Finn. "The dragons can turn the turbine for free."

Down below them on the factory floor were powerful dragons harnessed and tied to large wheels. They had chains on their wings to keep them from trying to escape and were lashed consistently to keep them moving the heavy wooden wheel around. Finn scurried across the loft.

"Why use coal when you can have fire dragons?" asked Finn, sarcastically. He pointed to the large furnaces that were fuelled by the flames of the dragons' breath.

"Why are you *showing us all this?*" Ruan asked.

"Come with me," Finn said.

He climbed out of the window and onto the metal stairs that transported him to the roof.

"Keep down," he said.

Finn brought them to the edge of the roof and pointed to the factory across from them.

"*Look,*" he said.

Ruan and Lir watched the workers through the factory windows. There were rows of tables where elves were assembling armoury.

"Gold breastplates, so spears won't penetrate dragon hearts and gold and silver helmets, so they cannot hear the voice of Grandmother Oak. They can only abide by their master's words," Finn said.

"How do you know of Grandmother Oak?"

"My father is Cian Ó Conchobhair. He grew up in the woods of Kapheus. He was sent by Grandmother Oak to the east. I was born and he told me that I would finish the work Grandmother Oak sent him to do," said Finn.

Ruan couldn't believe what he heard. He knew Cian Ó Conchobhair, but he thought he abandoned Kapheus for the treasures of the east. At least that's what everyone had said, everyone, except his son, and Ruan believed his son. Ruan wondered what had happened to Cian, where Finn's mother lived or if they had both gone to meet their ancestors.

"My father died from the disease of the lung that comes from these furnaces," Finn said. "He died for Kapheus… Come on, I want to show you something else," Finn said.

"Wait! *When* did he die? *Why* did Grandmother Oak send him away?" Ruan quizzed.

"He was sent with seven other elves. One was called Lugh. My father spoke about him a lot. He said that he was not more than a boy when they left. The rest of them were grown men and women," Finn said, scurrying ahead of them. "My father died last winter," he said.

They followed him to the other side of the mill's roof and looked through the windows of the adjacent mill to see elves and dragons practicing combat drills. They were wearing armoury of gold and silver and using spears. Several elves practiced with their bow and arrows against both stationary and moving wooden targets and had a skillset that was rarely seen amongst elves.

"It's all been done away from the public eye," said Finn. "They're preparing for *war*," he said.

"I think I've seen enough," said Ruan, feeling unwell.

They returned to the metal stairs that lead to the street below them. "*Wait*," said Finn.

He climbed through the window of the loft to collect his satchel. They continued to climb down the ladder to street level. The people on the street seemed to be oblivious to what was taking place behind the factory doors in their very own city. They merely went about their business in the same carefree nature as they had always done.

"Will you take me to Elisa now?" Finn asked.

"You'll need to get us out of here alive first," said Ruan.

Finn walked back through the streets with his two new companions. He stopped every once in a while to sing a song and to entertain with his fast wit and his jovial manner. Finn knew something about this place that Ruan and Lir didn't. He shielded the two brothers from suspicion every once in a while without the elves even knowing it was happening. Finn noticed a man speaking to an elf and pointing to the three of them mid-way up the street.

"Cross to the other side and look in the shop window," Finn said.

He sang a song of love and hope and as he did the man and the elf
stopped speaking. They were transported to another world by the
sound of Finn's voice. They walked towards him and stood less
than three feet away from him. Finn grew nervous, but his song
played on. The song lulled the two far away from Fodar to a world
where love was pure and hope alive. The man tossed a coin into
Finn's cap, smiled and moved on. Finn sang another two songs
and then bid the elf farewell.

"It's time for me to have soup to soothe my throat," he said,
rubbing his throat. The elf moved on.

Lir and Ruan watched his reflection in the shop window. Lir was
just about to follow him when Ruan pulled him back.

"Wait Lir," Ruan whispered.

They waited to see if someone would follow Finn and no one did.

"Now, we can go," Ruan said.

The town square was busy when they passed through it. Lir looked
over to where the elf had sat but he was gone. He nudged Ruan.

"Keep moving," said Ruan.

They walked down the terraced street and paused before they
climbed the metal stairs to the roof. Ogma was gone. Ruan started
to breathe more heavily and his heart began to race.

"*We're trapped,*" Ruan whispered.nn

They were suddenly distracted by the sound of a scuffle on the
street below them and saw teenage elves fighting. Ruan looked
high above him and scanned as much of the skyline as he could.
Then he looked across all the other rooftops. He looked in the
direction of home thinking that Ogma may have abandoned him
and then suddenly he felt a warm breath on his neck.

"I'm right behind you," Ogma whispered.

He appeared, caught Finn in his teeth and tossed him onto his
back.

"It's alright I can climb," Ruan said, but it was too late.

Ogma snatched the brothers and tossed them onto his back and
disappeared. They were airborne.

"Where did the fiddler go?" Lir asked.

"He may have been too afraid to return to the land of his birth. It's hard when you feel that you can only return if your life has been a huge success," Ruan said.

Onward Ogma flew and the journey home didn't seem half as long to them that day.

"Where would you like me to take you?" Ogma asked.

"You can drop us on the eastern hilltop close to La Petite Maison Le Fèvre. We'll make our own way to Rós," Ruan said. Ogma released his grip and the three elves came tumbling to the ground. "Finn has a pure heart, but can he fight?" asked Ogma, and he flew away.

"Can you?" Lir asked. Finn shrugged.

"That's not what bothers *me*," Ruan said. "I'll need to ask Rós if you can be permitted to see Elisa," he said, walking towards La Petite Maison Le Fèvre, "she is the goddess of Éire you know, *the goddess of Éire*," he continued. Ruan muttered something unrecognisable under his breath and lifted his hand to the air. "*You have to speak to Elisa*. You're asking a lot for a *stranger…*"

Chapter 10

Fire's Folly

Elisa opened her wardrobe door and briefly expected to find Joachim huddled in the bottom of it but remembered that he was in Kapheus. She wondered if Joachim would ever return to Éire. Elisa worried that Geaspar would leave her soon too and she didn't want to let him go. She had made a decision. Elisa pulled down her old navy down feather jacket from the hanger and then reached down and picked up Fódla's satchel and stuffed her soft jacket into the bottom of it. Without saying a word, Elisa lifted her teddy bear from her pillow with Geaspar clinging to it like an infant to his mother and hugged them both before carefully placing Geaspar and the teddy bear into the satchel. Elisa closed the straps and gently pulled Fódla's satchel over both her shoulders and ran downstairs and out of the house.

"Elisa!" Aideen called, running to the door, but Elisa was already gone.

Elisa ran into the woods by her house to catch up with her father. "Dad!" she called.

"Come on, Elisa," Cathal called from his cart.

Elisa ran to catch up and her father stopped to help her on board. "Jamie's farther up the track. I asked him to gather another pile of wood. One of the trees has fallen," he said.

When they reached Jamie he was sitting on a pile of wood. He had done nothing since his father had left him to return to the yard with a load of timber. Elisa jumped down from the cart and immediately began to gather wood to load onto the cart. It was a crisp morning and it felt very cold as the snow thawed.

"Jamie, come over here and give me a hand," Cathal said, preparing to cut a large piece of bark. Jamie reluctantly made his way to his father to help.

"Spurt! Spurt!" Elisa heard from the satchel. The little dragon was squeezing his way to freedom through the gap in the flap. "Spurt! Spurt!" he said and climbed onto Elisa's shoulder. Geaspar tucked his body close to her neck and watched.

"Dad?"

"Yeah, Elisa!" Cathal said.

"Nothing."

Cathal lifted a piece of bark and carried it to the cart before dropping it in.

"*Useless horse,*" Jamie said, tossing his pieces of timber onto the cart next to his father.

"*What's wrong with you,* Jamie?" Elisa said, annoyed.

"It's *so embarrassing,*" Jamie whispered. "Everyone else's Dad does cool stuff and they don't go around on a *horse and cart,*" Jamie said. Elisa was shocked.

"Dad?" Elisa called. "Why do you bring a horse and cart to the woods?"

"Because the distance between the trees is too tight for a tractor and trailer. The horse will not damage the plantation and the tree roots when he walks. Machinery will, and I could run the risk of a tractor toppling over on the hilly parts," Cathal said. He stood up. "*Why* are you asking me this?"

"Jamie wanted to know," Elisa said, bending down.

"If horses are *so great* then *why didn't you* bring the horse to town to collect Elisa and me?" Jamie asked.

"Cars don't spook," Cathal said. "*What's this about?* I bring the horse and cart to town on Saturdays, because I craft pieces of furniture from wood and I build horse carriages and carts for sale. *What's the point* in taking a car if I want to sell a carriage?" Cathal looked at his son with discontent. "*What's this about?*" he asked.

"Everyone else's Dads work in offices and *you* work in the woods," said Jamie. "When *I grow up* I'm getting a *really good job,* and I'm *never* coming back."

"Well, I hope it works out for you, Jamie. I wish you well in whatever you do," Cathal said, and returned to his work.

Elisa looked crossly at Jamie, but Jamie ignored her and walked back to the large tree bark. Suddenly, the sky went dark and a large black cloud hung over the wood. Cathal stood up and scanned the woodland.

"Do ye see anything?" he asked. The children grew concerned.

"*Get out of here!*" Cathal shouted and threw a stone at the large black dog.

The dog whimpered and ran away. Jamie watched the black dog transmute into the black figure of a man wearing a hooded cloak. He tried to see where he was going but lost sight of him between the trees. Suddenly, they saw a flash of lightning, heard a loud crack and with it the tree next to them exploded, sending splinters of wood in all directions. Buddy reared into the sky, he bolted and then stumbled and fell, turning the cart over.

"Quick!" Cathal shouted, "take his harness off!"

"What will I untie?" Jamie asked.

"Everything!" Cathal shouted. He opened the buckle on the breeches. "We need to get him out from under this cart!" Cathal opened the belly band. "Get the traces, Elisa!" Elisa reached down and unclipped the traces to release Buddy. "Come on! Gid up! Giddy up!" Cathal called. Buddy tried to pull himself to his feet. "Gid up! Giddy up!" Cathal shouted, running across to see if any part of the harness was caught under Buddy. "Gid up! Giddy up!" he called. Buddy lifted himself from the ground. Cathal pulled Buddy forward. "Giddy up! Giddy up!" he encouraged.

Buddy stepped forward from the cart shafts. He stood while Cathal removed the loose harness and collar.

"That's the good lad," Cathal said, having noticed the puncture wounds in Buddy's lung and flank. "Good lad," Cathal said, though distraught.

Cathal couldn't help but remember all the good days with Buddy. His mind was so confused in the bath of emotion that washed over him. Buddy shook like a leaf as Cathal's hand drifted down his neck to his shoulder and onto the large splinter of wood lodged in his lung.

"It's too deep," said Cathal.

The blood poured from the wound and Cathal had no way to control it. He passed his hand down Buddy's loin to his flank and saw the other splinter had penetrated very deeply into his flesh. Buddy breathed heavily and then dropped.

"Good lad, Buddy," Cathal said. "That'a boy," he said, rubbing his neck. "Elisa, stay at his head. Talk to him," Cathal said, and left.

"What *am* I supposed to do?" Jamie called.

"I need to get the gun!" Cathal shouted.

"The gun!" Jamie cried. He looked at Elisa. "We need to do *something. He can't shoot him*, Elisa!" With each second that passed, Buddy breathed more heavily. Jamie looked at their horse suffering. "What will I do?" he asked.

"Talk to him," Elisa said.

Geaspar climbed down from Elisa's shoulder and onto Buddy's neck. He scampered down along his shoulder to his wounded lung. He watched the blood pour from this wound and began to lick it.

"*Get away* from him you *stupid dragon!*" Jamie shouted. Elisa pushed Jamie over before he could strike Geaspar.

"Take the timber off the cart, Jamie!" Elisa shouted. Jamie walked away.

Elisa watched Geaspar lick the wound and for some reason, she stood up. Elisa reached down to the large wood splinter lodged in Buddy's lung, and with a strong pull and an enormous roar from Buddy, she removed the splinter.

Cathal came to a sudden halt in the woodland. He looked back and thought that might have been the last breath Buddy took. He almost choked on his breath but continued his run to the house.

"Spurt! Spurt!" sounded Geaspar. A clear mucus expelled from his mouth and into the pumping wound. The rate of blood loss slowed down. "Spurt! Spurt!" he sounded again.

Elisa looked down into the gaping hole in Buddy's lung and saw the tissue close up, layer by layer before her eyes. Buddy snorted.

"That a good boy," Elisa said, softly. "That a boy," she said again, rubbing Buddy's neck.

She looked back and saw Geaspar playfully roll onto his back.

"*Geaspar,*" she said. He looked up.

Elisa lifted up Geaspar and carried him to Buddy's flank. She laid him down next to the wound and Geaspar did as before. Elisa pulled the splinter to a roar from Buddy who tried to get to his feet. Seeing what was happening, Jamie rushed to Buddy to keep him still.

"Shh, Buddy," Jamie said, kneeling down on the ground next to his head. "Stay down, Buddy," Jamie said, softly.

Cathal was close to the crest of the hill carrying the gun in his hand when Geaspar climbed into Fódla's satchel to sleep.

"Step away," Cathal said, approaching them.

Buddy stood to his feet and turned to face Cathal.

"There's no death in those eyes," Cathal said to Buddy. He looked to his lung and his flank and then he walked around Buddy. "There *isn't a mark on him,*" Cathal said. He scratched the back of his head and walked around Buddy again. "*Nothing,*" he remarked, rubbing his chin. "Did you see the fairies?" Cathal asked. Both Elisa and Jamie shook their heads. "The fairies have strange powers," he said. "They're all over these woods."

Aideen stood at the doorway as Cathal, Elisa and Jamie returned from the woods. She was surprised when she saw Buddy pulling an empty cart with the others walking alongside.

"What happened?" Aideen asked.

"I think the fairies had a role to play in this," said Cathal, returning Buddy to his stable. "Some things can't be explained," he said.

"Elisa come inside quickly," Aideen called. "Jamie come inside."

Aideen ushered her children inside while scanning her surroundings for any signs of disturbance. She looked at the clouds in the sky and then returned to scanning the wood.

"What did you two see in that wood?" she asked before closing the front door shut.

Micah closed the front door to La Petite Maison Le Fèvre and walked with his bundle of wood to the basket next to the fireplace.

"*What do ya mean* they don't know?" Finn asked.

"They don't know!" Ruan reiterated. He shook his head.

"*Well, someone needs to tell them,*" Finn remonstrated.

Ruan stood up and walked to the fireplace. He stared into the flames but there were no answers hidden in them.

"They're only children," Ruan said.

The logs fell out of Micah's hands and landed with a crash onto the floor next to the basket. Ruan reached down to help him to gather the logs.

"I'm sorry Ruan. This is all a bit too much for me. I've lived through war before and I've seen terrible bloodshed," Micah said in a low voice.

"Micah, what do we need?" Ruan asked.

"Armour, and lots of it," Micah said.

Beyond what Jamie had told his mother, he could not think of anything else that he had seen in the woods that morning. As far as he was aware, he saw a dog and then a man in a black cloak and when he was about to tell his mother about Geaspar, Elisa stood on his foot. Jamie decided to let Elisa finish the story. He left the kitchen and sat at the living room table flicking through the small book with the tarnished red cover.

Unbeknownst to Jamie, Geaspar had climbed out of the satchel resting on the chair and onto the living room table. He approached Jamie, and it was then that Jamie had seen him from the corner of his eye. Geaspar sat looking at Jamie for a few seconds and then took another step closer. He sat again to watch Jamie and Jamie pretended he hadn't noticed. Geaspar then crawled a little closer and then closer and finally he was next to Jamie's hand. All of a sudden, he began breathing quite rapidly. Jamie had a look of irritation and just as quickly as it started it had ended. Jamie turned back to his book and to staring into space. Then Geaspar took a fit of spurting. He spurted a clear thick mucus onto the page of the book and then another and another.

"Get off!" Jamie snapped and pushed him away. "*That's disgusting,*" he said.

Jamie pulled some kitchen towel from the roll hanging on the kitchen wall and returned to the living room. By now Geaspar had found a cosy spot in the fruit bowl to rest. Jamie gave Geaspar a displeased look before rubbing the mucus off with the kitchen towel. As he rubbed, Jamie noticed something. The helmet he had hidden in the shed appeared on the page in bright gold and silver colour. Then the elf appeared clad in the armoury of battle and Jamie could also see the dragon.

"Spurt!" Jamie commanded, placing the kitchen towel in front of Geaspar's mouth. Geaspar gladly obliged.

Jamie turned the page of the book and saw the spears and the bows and arrows with details of their weights and dimensions sketched next to them.

Jamie lifted Geaspar, put on his jacket and boots and left for the loft in the shed. He climbed up to where he had secretly hidden the gold and silver helmet to see if this was identical to the one in the book. He flicked through the pages to find it.

"Yes!" said Jamie. "I'm going to be rich!" He lay back on the straw and thought of all the things he would do with all the money he would have. "Wait!" he said. He flicked onto the next page. "Spurt," he said, and Geaspar did so.

Jamie wiped the mucus across the page and saw what looked like doorways. He rubbed the page again with the mucus and soon saw a brown wooden doorway shaped in an arch. He then saw the door knocker in the shape of a closed fist. He read on.

"Ní mar a shíltear a bhítear," Jamie read aloud.

"Nothing is as it seems," Elisa said, climbing onto the loft. Jamie snapped the book shut. "Are you learning your Irish homework?" Elisa asked.

"No,", said Jamie, nonchalantly. He stuffed the book into his back pocket. He reached behind him to make sure the helmet was well hidden beneath the straw. "What do you want?" he asked.

"I thought I'd go to Kapheus, and I was wondering if you wanted to come?" Elisa said, sitting down beside him.

"Umm… yeah… sure. Why do you want to go?"

"I want to ask Méabh about feeding a baby dragon." Elisa lifted Geaspar into her arms. She stroked his body. "Geaspar seems to always have a full belly but I've never fed him," said Elisa.

"Elisa, there's something on his body," said Jamie.

"*What?*" she asked. She lifted Geaspar up and pulled a strand of straw from his belly. Elisa resumed stroking him.

"Elisa, *I'm telling you* there's something on him."

Elisa looked down again and this time she saw the fiery red letters along the length of his body as she stroked Geaspar. Elisa read the words *fealltóir i bhur measc.*

"What does it say?" Jamie asked.

"It says that there is a traitor among us," Elisa said.

"Here! I wouldn't believe *that crap,*" said Jamie, standing up. "When are we going to Kapheus?" he asked, climbing onto the ladder.

"Umm…"

"I'll see you later. I've things to do before we go," said Jamie and he left the shed through the wicket door.

Elisa stroked Geaspar's body again and *filleann an feall ar an bhfeallaire* appeared in fiery red.

"Treachery returns to the traitor," she said.

Jamie ran upstairs to his room. He had just about enough of the mucus left on his tissue to wipe another four pages of the book. He saw what was hidden behind the arched doorways. He rubbed again and the page shone gold and silver.

"There is *so much treasure* hidden in Kapheus," Jamie enthused.

He turned over the page and saw the map leading to the hidden doors in Kapheus. Jamie jumped up and pulled his school bag out from the end of his wardrobe. He dumped the contents onto the base of the wardrobe and then opened the drawer of his bedside locker. He took out his flash light, slingshot, penknife and then shut the drawer. He grabbed an extra jumper hanging from his bedpost and an extra pair of socks from the second drawer of his locker. Jamie snatched the gemstone and turned to leave.

"Where are you going?" Aideen asked.

"*I'm*... nowhere," Jamie said, dropping his bag.

"Where's Elisa?"

"She was in the shed the last time I saw her," Jamie said.

"And did you help her clean a few stables?" Aideen asked. Jamie didn't answer. "It might be a good idea to give her a hand."

Jamie shrugged his shoulders and left. Aideen stood in the doorway until she heard the front door close behind Jamie. She walked to his desk and picked up the tarnished red book. She opened it, but as she did, the images faded and disappeared. Aideen closed the book again.

It seemed that those elves who were clueless to imminent war were also the elves that had influenced Elisa and Jamie's lives the most. Feehul and Lug walked back along the same path they had taken since they were elfin children from the Wood of Dé Danann to the roots of Grandmother Oak. They talked about all the good times they had had as children, swimming in the river and chasing squirrels up the tress. They laughed as they recalled the first time they found a dragon egg on the woodland floor only to feel a warm breath on their necks before turning around to see a massive dragon looking angrily at them. They laughed again when they remembered how polite Sinann was to the dragon and handed back the egg before they were eaten. Lug and Feehul loved every moment of the freedom that was now theirs. Sinann soon joined them.

"News travels fast," Lug said.

"Is cinnte."

"Táim chomh sásta," Lug said. "*I'm so happy*, Sinann."

"Mise freisin. I couldn't be happier for you," Sinann said and hugged Lug.

The three siblings walked shoulder-to-shoulder laughing and chatting all the way to Grandmother Oak.

"It's as if we have stepped back in time," Cillian said, watching the siblings approach.

The red fox joined them and then Mother Badger and her family of badgers followed.

"It's good to see you," said Cillian.

"We wanted to share our news with Grandmother Oak," Feehul said. "The Dark One has left the Wood of Dé Danann forever. My brother is free!" Feehul rejoiced.

"Comhghairdeas Lugh! Congratulations my dear elf," said Grandmother Oak. "Words cannot express my happiness for you."

In all that joy, something wasn't right. Feehul looked at the golden eagle shaking on Grandmother Oak's tree branch. He climbed up to her to discover it was Iolar.

"Iolar, why are you shaking?" he asked, but Iolar could not speak.

"*Why* is she shaking? Does anyone know what happened to her?"

"She's terrified of what's to come," said Grandmother Oak.

Feehul looked beyond the meadow but there were no storm clouds in the sky. He smelled the breeze but there was nothing unusual. Feehul placed his hand on Iolar's heart. The fear shook him to the root of his being. Then he saw what Iolar feared.

"Ní neart go cur le chéile," he said, looking into Iolar's eyes. "Together we are strong."

"What is it?" Lug asked.

"There's a war coming. They're coming for Geaspar," said Feehul, climbing down from the oak tree.

"But they can't have him. He's in Éire," Lug said.

"They don't know that. Fodar is preparing to attack us with fire and weaponry on the night of the blood moon," Feehul said.

"That's only two nights from now!" Sinann remarked.

"Together we're strong. Mother Badger call the badgers from their setts. Lug send a whisper through the trees," Feehul instructed. From the corner of his eye, Feehul saw Madra Rua run away. "She'll have her own plan," he remarked. "Great, you're here," Feehul said to the dragons.

Feehul climbed onto Grandmother Oak's branches again.

"Iolar take me to the boundary," he said. Iolar looked into Feehul's eyes. Her fear began to dissipate, and she breathed a little more easily. "I need your help," Feehul said.

Iolar spread her wings, and when she did, Feehul jumped from Grandmother Oak's branch and was caught in mid-air by the golden eagle. They flew from the woodland through the veil of the meadow towards the boundary between the two worlds to Elisa and Jamie's home.

The window slammed shut in the kitchen and startled Aideen as she stood at the worktop rubbing the butter into the flour in her mixing bowl. She heard the front door close.

"Elisa is that you?" she called from the kitchen. Aideen waited for an answer. "Elisa!" she called. Aideen briskly rubbed her hands together to remove the excess flour and butter from her fingers. "Elisa is that you?" she called, wiping her hands on her apron. There in the centre of the living room stood Aideen's Uncle Davin. "The dead arose and appeared to many," Aideen said. "What brings you here?" she asked.

"I'm here to see the children," said Davin.

Aideen looked at him, but said nothing for a short while.

"You've changed. I've never known you to wear black," she said, having noticed his normally bright and colourful suit jacket replaced for a long black trench coat.

"I don't want people to know I'm here."

"Why?" Aideen asked. "Oh... I don't want to know," she said, returning to the kitchen. "I'm baking scones for us. I... I wanted our family to have time together this afternoon."

Aideen returned to rubbing the butter into the flour. She cracked the egg shells against the side of the bowl and added the eggs to the mixture. Aideen placed the egg shells to one side and paused.

"Why don't you want people to know you're here?" she asked Davin.

"A lot of things have changed," he said, standing at the kitchen doorway.

Davin removed his coat and then fixed his red suede jacket and tucked his white shirt into his dark trousers. He buttoned his bloodstained shirt a little higher to cover up the cuts on his skin. The red stripe along the centre of his shirt where the buttons met was now torn in places. Davin reached over to place his coat on the back of a chair.

"The coat hanger is by the front door," Aideen said. She looked down to see Davin's peculiar well-polished leather shoes and noticed a significant scratch on the side of one of them.

"Here, you'll need this," Aideen said, reaching for the ointment jar in the back of her kitchen press.

"Would you prefer if I stayed somewhere else?" Davin asked, hanging his coat on the hanger.

"Yes, I would, but that's not going to happen. Danú won't take you in," said Aideen.

Aideen took a glass from the cupboard, and turning it upside down, she began to cut out the shapes of her scones on the countertop. One by one she placed the scones onto the baking tray. She suddenly stopped what she was doing, placed her two hands on the countertop and took a deep breath.

"What are you looking for?" she asked Davin.

Davin turned around with a book in his hand, but didn't see Aideen, so he returned to searching through the books on her bookshelf in the living room. Aideen closed the door of the oven and then stepped into the living room.

"Go upstairs and wash yourself in the bathroom. You can have one of Cathal's shirts and take one of his trousers from the wardrobe," Aideen said. "I'll wash those clothes and do my best to mend them."

"How did you injure that leg?" she asked. The bloodied trouser leg was visible from even that distance across the room.

"Everything is different now," said Davin, returning a book to the shelf, "and no one is safe."

Aideen stepped back into the kitchen.

"I could do without any more visitors," Aideen said.

Davin slowly made his way upstairs to the landing and stopped at Elisa's bedroom door. He slowly turned the handle and stepped inside. Davin stood in front of the drawing and watched every movement in Kapheus. As soon as he saw Iolar flying towards the boundary with Feehul, he stepped back from the drawing. Davin swiftly left the room.

"There's Ruan and Lir!" Feehul said, pointing to the small figures below them on the ground.

Iolar swooped to the ground and dislodged Feehul before she landed herself. Feehul came tumbling onto the meadow and stopped at the feet of Finn. He caught sight of the polished black leather shoes, the dark trousers and navy woollen overcoat as he stood and was a little mistrusting.

"Dia duit!" Feehul said, reaching out his hand to shake Finn's.

"My sincere apologies, Feehul. Finn this is Feehul the greatest medicine elf in all of Kapheus. Feehul this is Finn the most beautiful of all the singers I've ever heard. Well, apart from Sinann of course. We're taking him to Elisa," said Ruan.

"Elisa?" Feehul asked.

"Yes. He's from Fodar and he has a message for her and he won't tell us what it is."

"That must be *some* message," said Feehul. "I'll walk the rest of the way with you if you like."

"It'd be a pleasure," said Ruan, and with that, Iolar flew away.

"She's finding it a bit tough at the moment," Feehul said, pointing to Iolar.

"Aren't we all," Ruan remarked and walked ahead of them.

Feehul continued to observe this stranger and scrutinised everything about the elf.

"Ní neart go cur le chéile," Feehul said to Finn.

He was testing Finn to find out if Finn could speak the language of his kin. After all, it was rarely if ever spoken in Fodar. Finn nodded but Feehul was not satisfied. Feehul was Elisa's guardian in Kapheus, and he needed to be sure.

"That's *not your satchel,*" Feehul remarked. "*That* was made by my father. His stamp is on its side."

Finn looked down at the mark on his satchel. "Mac Dara," Feehul said. "He only made them by request. They were *never sold* in Fodar."

"Finn Ó Conchobhair is ainm dom," Finn said, shaking Feehul's hand again, "I am the son of Cian Ó Conchobhair. He was born in the woods of Kapheus. I was born in Tara and my father worked in Fodar," he said.

"He was sent there by Grandmother Oak," said Lir.

Feehul sighed deeply. When they had walked another few metres Feehul looked at Finn again.

"What do you know about the battle?" Feehul asked.

"I know that it's two nights away and Kapheus seems to be paralysed with fear and this *blooming snow,*" Ruan interjected, feeling the sludge of thawing snow under his feet.

"Why do they want Geaspar?" Feehul asked Finn, but again Ruan answered.

"There are always those who want to take what doesn't belong to them. They're hungry for wealth and power. This is the most powerful dragon they've ever known," Ruan said.

"How well they found out," said Feehul. He looked intensely at Finn and the elf felt very uncomfortable.

"They'd always find out. Those who are hungry for power search out power and steal it or quench it," Ruan said.

"You seem to know a lot about war," said Finn, feeling uneasy.

"I know a lot about my cousin and that's enough," said Ruan.

He picked up the pace to avoid any further questions. There is a point when one doesn't want to speak about anything and he had reached that point.

Iolar flew back towards her nest, but was spotted in the sky by Rós before she reached her home. Rós called to her from her front door and the eagle flew across the sky and landed on the rock in front of her.

"Could you give this to Dagda?" she asked, handing the eagle a piece of cloth tied with string. "Nobody seems to know where he is."

Iolar took it in her talons and flew away.

"Squawk! Squawk!" the phoenix sounded. She flew from inside La Petite Maison Le Fèvre and over Rós' head.

"Good luck!"

The phoenix flew across the meadow to the base of Grandmother Oak.

"Squawk, squawk!" she sounded, passing over Ruan and his friends.

"You! If *you* do that to me again!" Ruan shouted.

"It's only a phoenix, Ruan," Lir said.

"You seem a bit edgy, Ruan," Feehul remarked, "are you alright?"

"I'll be a lot better when I know *that dragon* is safe," Ruan said.

The phoenix soon landed at the feet of Grandmother Oak.

"I was waiting for you," said Sinann.

The phoenix looked at Sinann blankly.

"You'd want to steer clear of her. She'd rob you blind," said Cillian.

Sinann laughed.

"It's for that reason that I want her," said Sinann.

"Since when have you taken to becoming a robber?" Cillian asked.

Sinann laughed. She walked with the phoenix through the woodland.

"Where have you been?" Sinann asked the phoenix. "I've already called Setanta. He'll meet us there," she said, hurrying.

The phoenix kept stride with Sinann for a few steps before she became distracted by something in a tree.

"Come on!" Sinann called and the phoenix followed her again.

Then the phoenix saw a bird fly by and chased after it.

"Come back!" Sinann called, diving onto her tail and holding on tightly. The phoenix returned her attention to Sinann.

"Are you *with me?*" Sinann asked. The phoenix looked blankly at her. "Keep your focus… *alright?*"

By the time they had reached Setanta, Sinann was worn out trying to hold the phoenix' attention.

"*What took you so long?*" Setanta asked.

"A distracted phoenix took us so long," Sinann said.

"Shh… here he comes," said Setanta.

They watched Seán step outside to fill the bucket of water at the well close to his house. His body was wracked in pain and there was no cessation from the pounding headaches. The light reflecting from the water in the bucket burned his eyes as he lifted the bucket from the well. He placed the bucket back down on the ground and rubbed the bulging varicose vein.

"What do you want from me?" Seán asked.

"*Everything,*" the Dark One croaked.

Seán's legs started to buckle under the weight of his bucket. He stumbled and fell, spilling the water.

"*How* are you *so weak?*" the Dark One asked. "Lug was never so weak," he commented.

The Dark One reached down and with the pointed nails on this decaying hand he touched Seán on the shoulder. The leprechaun cried out in pain. The Dark One gave up. He returned to the cottage and slammed the door shut. Seán lay on the cold earth for some time before he could find the energy to stand.

"Is it time?" Setanta asked.

"Not yet," said Sinann.

Seán pulled himself to his knees and then slowly and with great effort lifted himself off the ground. He hobbled to the cottage and entered it.

"Give him another second or two," said Sinann. They waited. "Alright. Go!" she whispered.

Setanta stood up and tossed his sliotar into the air and drew on it with his hurley. He struck it with such force that it flew across the air faster than the phoenix could fly. The sliotar struck the door.

"Who's that?" said the Dark One. "Send them away," he commanded.

Seán opened the door to the phoenix. He was mesmerised by her magnificence. The phoenix looked blankly into Seán's brown eyes. She tilted her head to one side. Seán stepped inside the cottage and closed the door.

"Don't forget the sliotar," Setanta called in a voice low enough to be heard by the phoenix, but hopefully not by the Dark One.

The phoenix looked at the sliotar, then caught it in her beak and burped. The sliotar disintegrated in a ball of flames.

"Aww, great. I'm going to have to do a lot of work for Mam before she'll buy me a new one," said Setanta.

"*Who was at the door?*" the Dark One yelled.

"Ní raibh éinne ann," said Seán, walking across the room. He entered his own bedroom at the back of the cottage.

"*And what does that mean?*"

"No one. No one for you," he said.

Seán reached under his mattress and pulled out the purse of silver given to him by the Dark One. He struggled to stand up with the pain of his aching muscles and joints.

"*Do you take me for a fool?*" the Dark One yelled, and then he saw the purse of silver in the leprechaun's hand. "*What are you doing?*" the Dark One asked, panicking. "A leprechaun never parts with his wealth. *Where are you going?*"

"My treasure is mine to do with as I wish," Seán said.

"*Where are you going?*"

"A leprechaun never reveals where his treasure is hidden."

"You'd better not be *playing me for a fool*, leprechaun," the Dark One said and made his way to his new cauldron hanging above Seán's fire.

Seán reached out his hand and with great pain turned the handle on his door. He stood in front of the phoenix and looked into her clear blue eyes.

"*What? What's this?*" the Dark One said on seeing the image of Seán standing in front of the phoenix in his cauldron. "*No!*" he shouted. He turned around and raced to the door. Seán handed the purse of silver to the phoenix. "Arghhh!" the Dark One roared.

The spell was broken.

"Arghhh!" the Dark One yelled. He stumbled in the room and fell against the door frame. He began to choke and held his throat. Seán stood back from him and the Dark One fell onto the ground outside the cottage. Weakened, he transformed into a dark cloud and fled.

Immediately, Seán's body began to heal. He reached down to the aching varicose veins bulging from his legs and they disappeared. The open sores closed. He felt the strength return to his body and the pain release. His health was restored.

"We're looking for your help," Setanta said, approaching him.

Chapter 11

An Claíomh Solais

They all sat at the table that afternoon for tea or hot chocolate and scones. There was so much that Aideen had planned to say to the children but didn't wish to do so in the presence of Davin. Aideen reached out and picked up a freshly baked scone. Before she could even slice it with her knife she had crushed the scone with her hand and it now resembled the remnants of a collapsed building after an earthquake on her plate. She reached to get another. Elisa saw all this and watched her mother grow more tense with every passing second. She looked at her father and saw him fixated on both Davin and Aideen. Jamie, however, seemed to be oblivious to all that was happening and was immersed in the world inside his mind, which was bursting to capacity with all the things he would do with his new wealth. The hot chocolate and scones never tasted so good to him. Jamie reached out to take another scone from the plate in front of him. He reached over for the butter, but his father had already seen his happiness and passed him the butter. Jamie looked at his mother and Davin too, and saw them in turn watching him. He looked at Elisa from the corner of his eye and she looked back. Jamie buttered his scone and then added a layer of blackberry jam.

"You look particularly pleased with yourself," Cathal said, watching Jamie bite into the scone. "Considering all that we could have lost today," Cathal said.

"*It's not his fault,*" Aideen scolded. "He *wasn't to know* that lightning would strike that tree."

Silence returned to the living room table.

"I was searching through your bookshelf earlier, Aideen, and I noticed that a book was missing. One that I'd seen on every other occasion I've visited," Davin said.

"Which one?" Elisa asked.

"It's a small book with a tarnished red cover," said Davin.

Jamie stopped chewing his food and stared at Davin.

"There's nothing in that book. I saw Jamie trying to read it the other day," said Cathal. "It's more of a notebook than anything else."

"Maybe I was wrong. Maybe it has no drawings on it or secret maps," said Davin, looking in the direction of Jamie. "My mind can get the better of me sometimes." Davin reached across the table for the blackberry jam. "Some people want to take what doesn't belong to them," he said.

Elisa looked at Jamie and knew for sure that he was up to something. Geaspar couldn't even speak and yet he could tell her that, and now Uncle Davin.

"May I be excused?" Jamie asked.

"No," said Cathal. "Your mother wanted us to sit at the table today to talk about things."

Jamie said nothing. He instead kept his head down.

"Elisa," Cathal said, pulling a note from his pocket, "this is for you."

"*Why?*"

"You gave me a great helping hand," said Cathal.

"Thank you!" said Elisa.

"Jamie, what would you like to get in the shop? Mam, mint or honeycomb chocolates this time?" Elisa thought for a second. "Umm... is it alright to go to the shop, Dad?" she asked.

"I'll take you when the roads clear if you like," Cathal said.

"What would you like Dad? Uncle Davin you're getting sherbet fizz bombs. You always make funny faces when you eat them."

"That would be lovely, Elisa," Cathal said and smiled.

"Oh, Jamie. Here you go," Cathal said, handing Jamie another note from his pocket.

"But Elisa got the *same as me!*" Jamie remonstrated, looking down at the note. "I'm *older* than Elisa." Cathal looked sternly at Jamie.

"This is *not fair* Dad. Here! You can have it! I *don't need your money* anyway," Jamie said, getting up from the table.

"Sit down at the table, Jamie. We've a guest," Aideen said. Jamie sat back down.

"Davin would you like to explain what's going on inside *that skull?*" Cathal asked, directing his attention to Jamie.

"Power, I suspect. He's hungry for power," said Davin.

"At the cost of his own and everyone else's happiness," said Cathal. He placed the note back into his pocket. Elisa reached across the table and gave her note back to her Dad. "I don't want it back, it's alright, Elisa," he said.

"You can have it, Dad."

Cathal stood up and put the note into the brown jug on the dresser. "We'll get sweets with it when the roads clear," Cathal said.

Power and greed are strange elements that can take hold of the mind and body and make anyone do things they wouldn't ordinarily do. There was none so aware of this as Caoilte. Caoilte stood at the factory door watching the human and elfin children skating up and down the street on their skateboards. He watched them hopping off pavements, stumbling and falling and then getting back up and trying it all over again. He watched elfin children run to place their rolled up jackets on the street to make goalposts on either end of their makeshift soccer pitch. A young boy cruised passed the opposition and struck the ball hard into the goalmouth and down the street. Caoilte stopped the ball as it rolled and awkwardly sent it back up the street to rapturous laughter and applause. Caoilte remembered his time in the woods of Kapheus and in the meadow as a young elf and all the fun he too had.

"Get back to work!" a man shouted at an elf who bent down to tie his lace. "I'm not paying you to tie your laces!" he shouted, and Caoilte was pulled back to the reality of factory labour and warfare. The elf looked worn out from the hard labour. His face was filthy from the furnace and his hands were as black as coal. He rolled up his sleeve another turn to buy himself some time before having to return to striking the gold on the anvil with his hammer.

"*Goal!*" an elfin child shouted.

Caoilte looked around and saw the elf being pushed to the street by a boy. He saw the boy scold him and mock him and then turn his back. The elfin child stood up and ran down the street crying. Caoilte reached out his hand and grabbed hold of him.

"Let me go! Let me go!" the elfin child cried. Caoilte released his grip and the elf ran home.

"He's jealous of you," Caoilte whispered. "I wanted to tell you…"

A large and overweight grey-haired man in a grey pin-striped suit approached Caoilte from behind.

"How close are you to being ready by the blood moon?" Mr. Adley asked.

"I'm making the final touches," Caoilte said. "It's only the poison left to be added to the arrow tips and we are there," he said.

"That's why you're my lucky elf," said Mr. Adley, placing his hand on Caoilte's shoulder. "You're willing to kill everyone you've ever known for a few pieces of silver," he said and laughed out loud. Mr. Adley walked down the street laughing as he went. He noticed a straying football and kicked it back up the street and laughed again. He pulled the handkerchief from his pocket and dusted off his shiny black shoe and walked on.

Finn looked down at the boots he wore made of fine leather and questioned why he had purchased such flimsy footwear in Fodar. "How much farther do we need to walk?" asked Finn. "These shoes really don't suit walking through a water-logged meadow."

"It's here," said Ruan.

"*Where?*" Finn asked.

"Take a leap of faith," said Lir. Finn looked confused.

"Here! Come on!" said Ruan, catching hold of Finn's hand.

They took the next step forward and landed in Elisa's room. Aideen stood up from the table and walked to the end of the stairs. "There's someone in our house, Cathal," she said, concerned.

Cathal ran upstairs to the landing. He looked down the hallway and then back at Aideen, who pointed to Elisa's room. Cathal turned the handle on the door and stepped inside. He looked all around but saw no one.

"*Why* hasn't he said something? *Why* can't he see us?" Finn asked, trying to tip toe around Cathal.

Cathal reached down to check under Elisa's bed for a small animal that may have crawled underneath. Nothing.

"*What is this place?*" asked Finn, anxiously.

"This is Éire," said Ruan. "He'll only see you if your destinies are shared, and *yours are obviously* not."

Cathal stood up and took another look around the room. He placed his hand on the door handle and stepped into the hallway.

"*Nothing in there*, Aideen. I'll try the other rooms," said Cathal, closing the door shut behind him.

Feehul then crossed the boundary between the two worlds.

"*What am I doing in a child's bedroom?*" Finn asked.

"This is Elisa's bedroom. *You are* looking for Elisa?" asked Ruan. With that the black wolf roared through the drawing and dived on top of Finn knocking him to the bedroom floor.

"*Who are you* to have entered Elisa's room *without my permission?*" he growled.

"There's someone up in that room. *Do I have to go up myself to sort this out?*" Aideen asked, placing her foot on the first step of the stairs.

"Aideen, sit down here with your children. I'll go," said Davin. He passed Cathal on the stairs and entered Elisa's bedroom. "And *I thought my life* was tough at the moment," Davin remarked. He had a quick look back downstairs and closed Elisa's door firmly shut. "What's going on here?" he asked.

"Help!" Finn yelled.

"What's the problem, Joachim?" Davin asked.

"He entered Éire without my permission," Joachim said, salivating. Finn watched as a long drip of saliva broke away from Joachim's mouth and landed on his face despite all his resistance. "Who are the *fools* who let him enter?" Joachim said, staring right at Ruan and Lir.

"Umm… well…" said Ruan.

"You might as well eat him," said Davin, pulling a chair up beside them.

"*What? Does nobody care about me?*" Finn asked.

"Not really," said Davin, brushing a fleck of dust from his sleeve.

"*Help!*" Finn shouted.

"For the sake of knowing before you pass to the next world and for no other reason," Davin said, "would you like to tell me your name?"

"Finn," said Lir.

"What's your name?" Davin asked.

"I'm Finn Ó Conchobhair the son of Cian Ó Conchobhair from the woods of Kapheus," he said.

Davin stood up and walked to the door.

"You can have him," Davin said.

Feehul watched with great interest to see what would happen next. He too was very wary of this elf.

"*Where* are you going?" Finn asked, anxiously.

"It's alright, Aideen. I'm sorting out that intrusion for you," Davin called down.

Aideen nodded from the bottom of the stairs.

"I'm going to help!" enthused Jamie, jumping from his chair.

"Me too!" said Elisa. She snatched Fódla's satchel from the bottom of the stairs and raced up after Jamie.

The two burst through the door with youthful enthusiasm. Feehul immediately caught hold of Elisa's arm and pulled her behind him. They stepped backward to the wall. On seeing this, Ruan caught hold of Jamie's arm and pulled him over to where he and his brother stood. Davin closed the door and sat back down on the chair next to Joachim and the stranger.

"*Who* did you say you were?" Davin asked.

"Finn Ó Conchobhair," said Finn.

"The son of *whom*?"

"Cian Ó Conchobhair."

Davin sat back on his chair and took a deep breath. He glanced over at Feehul before turning his attention back to the elf.

"I happened to know Cian Finn Ó Conchobhair," Davin said, "and he had *no son*."

They were all amazed and no one dared speak in case they'd miss what was to come next.

"He married someone I cared very deeply about. They lived in Tara until her death and then Cian moved to Fodar. He lost his way for quite a while and ended up on the streets singing for food," Davin said. "He lost his way, the poor lad." Davin's head dipped, and his sadness filled the room. "I don't know what became of his daughter."

"I'm his daughter, Tara," Finn said. Joachim released her from his grip.

Tara gathered herself and sat with her back against the wardrobe with the staring eyes of everyone examining every inch of her.

"You know I'd never have survived on the streets of Fodar if anyone thought that I was a female elf. They'd have taken me. Men have the power in Fodar and they use the women and elves for their pleasure. Girls and women are taken from the streets and abused. Some are dumped back on the streets; some are never seen again," Tara said. "I've seen things happen to boys too, but at least as a boy, you stand a better chance and definitely as a man you're safe," she said.

Elisa stepped out from behind Feehul to take a better look at Tara. "Would you like some of my hot chocolate?" Jamie asked. Tara smiled.

"Stay for a little while longer, Jamie. There may be things you need to hear," Davin said. He leaned towards Tara. "I still don't know what you're doing here," Davin said.

"Grandmother Oak gave my Dad a job to do. She asked him to find the emerald encased in An Claíomh Solais and to remove it. My Dad found it in Tara and did as she asked," Tara said. She reached into her pocket for her handkerchief and wiped Joachim's saliva from her face. "He sold everything for whiskey. Everything he owned he lost but he never sold the emerald. Tara reached into her satchel and pulled out a piece of cloth tied with twine. She opened the twine and removed the cloth around the emerald encased in silver.

"Aroooo," Joachim howled, and his pack stood to defend the boundary between the worlds.

Feehul moved closer. The clasp's workmanship was as intricate in detail as the Celtic weave on the ancient scripts, and he was in awe. It was absolutely exquisite in its complexity. There was layer upon layer of symbolism contained in it.

"Do you mind?" Feehul asked.

Feehul held the piece in his hand and saw a small otter with a fish in its mouth, the dragon breathing fire, and the wolf howling, all moulded into the silver clasp holding the emerald.

"An Claíomh Solais nár fhág riamh fuíoll buille," said Feehul. "The Sword of Light, whose stroke never failed," he whispered. Feehul handed the clasp back to her.

"Grandmother Oak sent my Dad to find the sword and to remove the emerald from it," Tara said. "Donn has been searching for years for the sword. He wants to overtake his father as the ultimate symbol of darkness," she said.

"Donn's searching for Geaspar," Joachim said. "I saw him. He has An Claíomh Solais and its blade glows green," said Joachim.

"The blade glows green while it searches for its love," said Tara. "As long as it glows green, it only has the same power as any other sword."

Unbeknownst to anyone in Éire, there was something else at play in Kapheus while Tara sat in Elisa's room. Iolar found Dagda and gave him the small parcel from Rós and flew away. Dagda crouched down and looked across the rugged mountain ranges. He saw no fleck of light and no coat of armoury. He looked to the skies and they were blue. He lifted the end of his trouser leg, pushed the key deep into his stocking and pulled the trouser over his boot. Dagda watched Iolar until she had reached her home on the ledge. He rolled open the piece of leather cloth and read it carefully. Dagda continued on the path set out for him by Rós.

"The sword is useless without the emerald," Tara said. "Once the two are united, the holder of the sword has more power than any other warrior. The sword has never failed."

"Are you sure?" Jamie asked.

"Yes, or else my father's whole life was in vein," Tara remarked.

"Sure, I'll mind it for you if you like," Jamie said.

"I think we'll let Tara choose," Davin interjected, holding back Jamie's outstretched arm.

"The message I've carried my whole life is only to be said to Elisa," Tara said.

"In that case, we'll leave you two alone. I think we'll bring tea and scones to the room for our visitors," Davin said, standing up. "Are you coming, Jamie?"

Jamie reluctantly followed Davin from the room.

"If you need us, we're on the other side of this drawing," Ruan said, and he and the others including Joachim stepped through.

Alone in the room, Tara told Elisa all the knowledge that her father had imparted onto her. She told her of his battles with the darkness inside him and how the Sword of Light will bring all the darkness that rests inside you into the light of day.

"It is a very powerful sword. It can bring you wondrous joy or untold sorrow. It'll pull you deeper into the darkness if you let it," Tara said. She placed the emerald into Elisa's hand and closed her palm. "When you unite the emerald with the sword, your heart must be aligned to your inner light and above all else you must expect it to have the strength to transcend any darkness. If you don't have this expectation An Claíomh Solais will fail," she said.

"But it's the sword that has never failed!" Elisa remarked.

"It has never failed, because the only warriors who ever held it in their hands were those who expected to always win. They were the ones who believed in the light inside their hearts and trusted in themselves. Their expectation was of victory. You need to have that expectation," she said.

Elisa nodded. Tara looked into Elisa's eyes and then embraced her. "You have to expect it to be and it will be," she said. "It's not about hoping or even believing that something will happen someday. You have to expect it to happen now and it will," she said. "That's the power fire holds," Tara said. "It will give you everything you desire for good or ill. Keep it safe, Elisa," Tara said. She looked into Elisa's eyes again. "You'll know what to do when the time comes."

Elisa placed the clasp into the side pocket of Fódla's satchel, and as she did, Geaspar peeped out from the satchel and then squeezed out from under the flap to climb onto Elisa's shoulder.

"You've *a dragon* on your shoulder," Tara said, in awe.

"His name is Geaspar," said Elisa, and smiled.

Tara reached out and tickled him under his chin.

"How old is he?" she asked.

"Only a few days."

"Why do I have to bring the scones?" Jamie complained, entering the room ahead of Davin.

"We're having afternoon tea in Elisa's room!" Davin called from the landing. "The door is open if you wish to join us!"

Cathal and Aideen heard him call but decided to stay put.

"I know what I'd like to do," Cathal said. Aideen furled her eyebrows. "I'd like to sit with my beautiful wife for afternoon tea," Cathal said, and smirked. "You're a hard nut to crack, Aideen," he said, pouring her another cup of tea.

"Thank you for your kind offer of afternoon tea, but if you don't mind, Lir and I have a few things to do in Kapheus," Ruan said. "Would that be alright with you Joachim?"

"Yes."

Joachim sat with his back to all of them. He could not take his eyes off something he was watching in the drawing.

"I'll need to introduce you to your cousins in Kapheus, Tara," said Feehul. "We might tag along with you, Ruan," he said. "I won't be too far away, Elisa. If you need me just call," he said and stepped through the boundary between the two worlds with Tara.

"It's just us," said Davin, placing his cup down on the tray.

"And Joachim," mumbled Jamie, annoyed.

"I've a puzzle that you may be able to solve," said Davin, "and this is it," he said, pulling his chair closer to them. "It's clear to me that you've not wanted to enter Kapheus since Fódla's death... The time you spent there recently was only short-lived... I've tried to figure this all out in my mind, but I'm lost."

Elisa tried her best not to cry but she could not stop the tears bathing her eyes.

"Is it that you don't want to be there or is it that... I really don't know what it is," Davin continued.

"I plan to go soon," said Jamie. "I've things to do in Kapheus."

"What kind of things?" Davin asked.

"Just stuff."

Well, there's the drawing. Step through," Davin said.

"I need to organise a few things first," Jamie said.

Davin looked at Jamie and thought about the choices he was making. Davin was disappointed that Jamie wanted to keep something from him when he was the one who had introduced Jamie to the fantastical world of light. There was no inch of ground on Kapheus that Davin did not know and no creature that he had not met. He wondered if Jamie had even read the letter he had sent to the children. He could not understand the reason for them still being in Éire.

"You know, I really don't understand what's happening here. You two are on the cusp of greatness and you are floundering about in Éire when Kapheus awaits you," Davin said, frustrated.

"It's none of your business," Jamie said.

"It is my business. I've waited your whole lives to see you succeed beyond all you dreamed possible. I've seen your struggles. I won't deny that there have been many," he said, lifting the cup from the tray. "Elisa, I've seen you cry and laugh together. I have seen so much!"

"How?" Jamie asked. "It's not as if you've been around."

"I've never been too far away," said Davin, softly.

Davin's head bowed and he wondered if these children would ever be able to take up the mantles of goddess of Éire and leader of the dragons, and help to reawaken Éire to the fantastical world of light. He believed his only hope rested with Elisa now.

"Elisa, I want you to know this," he said, leaning closer, "this is the time of fire, so your power will now come to the fore and it is possible for you to achieve more than you ever thought possible."

Elisa stroked Geaspar. Everything she thought about power was filled with hurt and pain. She didn't want any more hurt and she didn't want power. Geaspar looked up at her and smiled as she stroked his belly. He took her finger in his mouth and sucked it.

"You have struggled, you have sacrificed… you have worked so hard. Now, expect the rewards for all that you've learned along the way," Davin said. He leaned back on his chair. "It's there! You're touching it. Step into your power, Elisa," he said in absolute frustration.

Elisa struggled with her thoughts. She felt she was suffocating inside but didn't want anyone to notice. 'I can't be powerful,' she thought, 'Mam would kill me.' Elisa looked down at Geaspar as she stroked her fingers along his body. The fiery red letters appeared along his side and Elisa read the words bí chomh cróga le Fódla.

"Be as brave as Fódla," Davin said, softly. Elisa nodded her head.

Davin rose from his chair and gathered the last of the cups. He carried the tray to the room door and took one last look at the two children.

"There is a battle looming. They'll come over the eastern hills in two nights. Fodar wants Geaspar," he said, standing at the doorway. "Geaspar isn't safe in Éire," he said, and left the room.

"That guy has serious issues," said Jamie. "A battle in Kapheus. Right!"

Jamie watched Elisa stand up, open Fódla's satchel and place Geaspar inside.

"Elisa, what are you doing?" Jamie asked, nervously. "They're the boots you got for your Birthday," said Jamie, watching Elisa open the cardboard box containing her new boots. "*Elisa,*" he said, but Elisa didn't answer.

Jamie ran from the room and crossed the hallway into his bedroom. He grabbed his school bag and then raced out. He held onto the banister with his two hands and slid to the end of the stairs, landing with a thump. Jamie reached down for his boots and then snatched his jacket from the hook.

"Hats, scarves and gloves," Davin instructed, while standing next to the bookshelf perusing Aideen's books.

Jamie grabbed them from the table and ran upstairs fast before Elisa had gone without him. He reached Elisa's room the second she passed through the boundary between the two worlds.

"Wait for me!" Jamie called, and he jumped through to catch up with her.

"Elisa you know there's no one here. You're on your own. This is a really bad idea," Jamie said.

"You're never alone in Kapheus," said Elisa. They stood still. "Reveal yourselves!" she called, and they were surrounded by gnomes.

"Call Banbha," Elisa said to Jamie.

"Call her *yourself!*" Jamie retorted.

Elisa rolled her eyes and then called Banbha from deep inside her heart. Within seconds Feehul spotted Banbha in the sky above him. He turned around to see where she was going and wondered if Elisa was alright. He was her guardian and the one who had escorted her through all the dangers in Kapheus every time Elisa had placed her feet upon its earth.

"Banbha will call us when she needs us," said Ruan, "Elisa will be safe with Banbha." Feehul nodded and continued with Tara and the others in the direction of the woods.

It wasn't long before Banbha gently placed her feet on the Kaphien meadow and leaned forward for Elisa and Jamie to climb onto her back.

"Will you take us to Rós?" Elisa asked.

"Elisa, I would certainly take you to Rós, but I know what's in your heart and it's Éataín you need right now," said Banbha.

Elisa knew Banbha was right but did not want to admit to herself that it was Éataín in which she yearned to confide.

"I'll leave you to it," said Jamie, pulling the satchel from Elisa's back. "I'll take Geaspar with me. *I am* the leader of the dragons after all," he said.

"Elisa," Banbha asked, "where is your fire now?"

Jamie removed the satchel from Elisa's shoulders and placed it on his own.

"He expects to be able to take what you've nurtured. What's your response?"

Elisa looked at Jamie who seemed to be oblivious to what Banbha had said. His only thoughts were on finding his treasure and using Geaspar to help him do it. Elisa did not want to take from Jamie. He always took what he wanted. She was always second place in her family. Her mother made that clear to her. Jamie was more important than Elisa and that's the way it was. Her mother always idolised Jamie and if she would ask for what was rightfully hers then Jamie could say something to their mother and Elisa would end up in serious trouble.

"You're not in Éire now, Elisa," Banbha said. "Be as brave as Fódla. I think you know what Fódla would do."

Elisa *did* know what Fódla would do. She would never let anyone have her satchel. It was the one thing that she slept with every night and it was the bag that contained all her favourite things. She knew that if Fódla was in Kapheus at this moment, she would not let Jamie leave with it.

"Jamie," Elisa called, but Jamie didn't listen. "Jamie!" she called, and Jamie turned around.

"*What is it, Elisa?*"

"Jamie, I want the satchel back. I'm minding Geaspar. I've been minding him all the time he was in Éire and you didn't care about him. I'm taking care of him in Kapheus," Elisa said.

"I think you've forgotten that *I* am the leader of the dragons, Elisa," Jamie said, dismissively.

"And I *am* the goddess of Éire," Elisa said.

The brother and sister looked at each other and in that time, Jamie knew that he could not overpower his sister. He knew that she would not accept no for an answer. Jamie took the satchel down from his back and threw it on the ground to the sound of a loud cry from Geaspar inside.

"*You can have it!*" he said, angrily. "I *don't need you* or that *stupid dragon* anyway!" he shouted and walked away from them.

Elisa picked up the satchel and opened it to comfort Geaspar inside. She lifted out her teddy bear to which the frightened little dragon clinged. Elisa looked at Jamie. She felt guilty about speaking up and felt that she had hurt him and had done something terrible.

"You only feel that way, because your mother has made you feel that you are less than Jamie. It's not the truth. You are equals and he needs to learn that," said Banbha.

Elisa hugged Geaspar and the teddy warmly.

"It's alright, Geaspar. I'm here now," said Elisa, comforting the little dragon.

"Climb on my back. I'll take you to Éataín," Banbha said.

"But what about Jamie?" Elisa asked.

"Jamie's made his own decision. He'll have to work this one out himself," said Banbha.

Elisa climbed onto Banbha's back and looked back a number of times to see if Jamie was alright. She felt terrible about challenging him.

"The time of fire is not always about war and fighting. It is about standing your ground, expecting others to treat you with dignity and respect, and stepping into your own power," said Banbha.

"You've a lot to do in a very short time… Jamie's choosing his own path and you can't do anything about it."

Before long, Banbha gently placed her feet upon the earth outside Éataín's cottage and Elisa climbed down.

"Do you want to mind Geaspar, Banbha?" Elisa asked.

"No, take him with you."

Elisa knocked on Éataín's front door and was soon ushered inside. Banbha watched as the door closed behind her and then left.

When Elisa stood in her power at that moment of confrontation with Jamie, so too did Feehul feel empowered. He stepped into the woodland with a new elf that none of his friends or family had seen before. He told her about the woodland and about the medicines that can be made from the plants and the herbs and then he felt uncertain.

"What is it?" Tara asked.

"I don't… Elisa…" Feehul said, looking over his shoulder. He pulled his thoughts together again and walked on.

"I must introduce you to Jeremiah," said Feehul, "but he won't be out of hibernation for another few weeks. He sleeps at the base of Grandmother Oak, so be careful where you step."

Tara was in awe of the woodland. She saw elves living freely in the trees, and others feeding birds and squirrels who were suffering from the cold. Tara stood for a moment and watched an elf check a hedgehog to make sure he wasn't too cold. The elf gently placed an extra few leaves on the hibernaculum.

"Who's that?" Tara asked.

"Oh, that's my brother, Lug," he said.

"*Lug?*" Tara asked, confused. "I've never heard that name before," she said.

"It's Lugh," said Lug. "My name is Lugh. I was born Lugh. I was named Lug when the Dark One took me," Lug said, and he reached out his hand to shake Tara's.

"It seems your name has travelled far, my dear Lugh," Grandmother Oak said.

The spirit of Grandmother Oak stepped out from the tree bark. Tara marvelled at the white glow that emanated from the old woman. She wore a dress of white that reached down to her bare feet and had long, flowing white hair. Her face was so beautiful with eyes of emerald green.

"Grandmother Oak," Ruan said, dropping to his knees.

He reached out his hand to pull his brother Lir down too. They both bowed. Grandmother Oak smiled. She gently placed her hand on Ruan's head and he felt the light of such powerful love fill his whole being. Grandmother Oak spoke to him through his mind's ear and having heard her voice, Ruan nodded and then stood up with his brother and walked into the wood.

Tara couldn't believe what she was seeing.

"Ó, tá brón orm," Lugh said. "I'm very sorry…I'd like to introduce you to Grandmother Oak," he said, and the spirit of the great oak tree stepped back into her bark.

"I think it is you she desires more than me, my dear Lugh," said Grandmother Oak. "She has waited her whole life to meet you."

It was true. Tara had waited her whole life to meet this elf. She dreamt about him and wondered at how an elf so young could have been selected by Grandmother Oak to take on the responsibility of safeguarding Kapheus' light.

"I… I need to find Sinann," said Feehul. "Umm… I'll see you later," he said, and soon was out of sight.

Tara and Lugh stood in the woodland as if nothing else existed in this world other than each other. They didn't notice the dragons in the treetops or the elves or the animals, or even the bird songs or the cold air against their skin. They didn't notice the world about them and every creature in that world did their utmost to ensure they went unnoticed for fear that they would take from Tara and Lugh's moment together.

"Umm… your feet are wet. Would you like me to have new boots made for you?" Lugh asked.

"Thank you. I'd love that," said Tara.

Lugh held her hand and they walked to the cobbler who lived by the stream.

Far away on the plains, Jamie searched through the blank pages of the tarnished red book to find the map again. There were certain landmarks he remembered.

"I know I've seen that lake before," he said, recalling all the time he spent on Banbha's back. Jamie shoved the book into his back pocket and looked up again but was startled by Prometheus standing in front of him. "What are you doing here?" Jamie asked. "You're supposed to be in the waterfall. I saw you go through myself with Pyrrha and Deucalion," he said.

As instantaneously as Prometheus appeared, the young unicorn foal disappeared again.

Chapter 12

Heroes are Born

"*What's eating you?*" Cathal asked, sitting at the living room table.

"Nothing," said Aideen, staring into the fire.

Cathal placed his cup back down on the table and looked at the fire.

"I don't see what you see," he said.

"And you probably never will," said Davin, flicking through the pages of a book.

"You're not going to find what you're looking for on that shelf," Aideen said.

"Probably not,", said Davin, returning the book to the shelf. He sat back down at the table. "You're not likely to find what you're looking for in the embers either," he said.

"You're speaking in code now, because *I haven't a clue* what you're talking about," Cathal said.

"You never feel so alive until the moment you're closest to death," Davin said.

"Who's dying?" Cathal asked.

Cathal looked at them both. The uncle who rarely visited seemed to know so much more about his wife than he ever could, and his wife who seemed hopelessly tied to this man. He, in some way had some power over her, yet he knew no one else who had power over his wife. Cathal became more confused with each second that passed. He saw this man almost play with his wife's emotions like a puppeteer dangling his puppet on a string. The longer he watched the dynamic between the two, the angrier he became. The fire rose inside him to the point that he could no longer remain quiet.

"Leave," Cathal uttered. They both looked at him. "*Leave,*" Cathal repeated in a firm voice. "Leave my wife in peace. *Whatever* decision you're pressing on her to make, it ends now." Cathal looked directly into Davin's eyes. "My wife is a powerful woman beyond measure. She'll do the right thing and you *will not force her* against her will. Not while *I'm* her husband," he said. "*Leave my home.*"

Davin stood up and left. He closed the door behind him. Davin reached his hand across the table and placed it on Aideen's.

"You're my wife and I love you," he said. Cathal then stood up and walked into the kitchen.

"*Aideen*," Danú called, entering the house. "Aideen," she said, approaching her. "Are you alright, my love?"

"I don't know," Aideen said with a sigh.

Caoilte stood on the eastern hilltop looking down into the Kaphien meadow. Standing at the highest point in the mountain he felt like he was standing on the top of the world. The elf recalled the first occasion he left the lush green meadow and the Kaphien valley for the eastern hilltop. He struggled to climb those narrow trails that appeared and disappeared in the scree. On the mountain trail as wide only as his two feet, he merely had large boulders of rocks and dried out grass as his companions for long stretches of his journey. Yet, as time passed he began to notice the four broad lilac pink petals of the biolar gréagháin whose little flower grew in clusters across the craggy landscape as well as the deep yellow peaflowers of the aiteann galida with its rigid leaves and furrowed thorns.

Caoilte recalled some of the winding paths and steep passages and the strong glare from the exposed rock of the hillside. He remembered climbing around big boulders that fell onto the narrow trails and laughed as he remembered the goats that bleated loudly at him when he landed awkwardly. Caoilte looked across at the point in the hillside where he sat such a long time ago to view the valley. He remembered that he so desperately wanted to hold that view in his mind forever.

"And here I am again," Caoilte whispered.

A well of emotion rose up inside him and Caoilte distracted himself by gazing at the magnificence of the mountain ranges reaching into the skyline and enclosing the treasure that was Kapheus and its inhabitants like a secret world hidden from the rest of civilisation. His eyes glanced across at the lushness of the Kaphien valley, the lakes and the river and then the waterfall and it was as if he had never left. He removed his helmet and did as he had done so many times as a very young elf, he watched the birds glide across the sky and drifted in his thoughts. He remembered his elfin childhood of climbing trees and playing games in the woods of Kapheus. He thought of his mother picking wildflowers in the meadow and his father waving to him as he cut the long summer grass with his scythe. He watched the eagle fly from her nest on the mountain ledge.

"Flap-flap-glide," he whispered. "Flap-flap-glide," he said more loudly. "Flap-flap-glide!" he shouted, forgetting himself and waving his hand in the air.

The phoenix stood behind him, and realising this, Caoilte looked over his shoulder.

"I don't have what you are looking for," he said.

Yet, the phoenix unflinchingly stood staring into his eyes. She tilted her head to one side and then the other. Caoilte's eyes slowly filled with tears. He sat down on a rock and buried his head in his hands.

"Tá an galar orm," Caoilte cried. "There's no cure," he said, shaking his head.

"Squawk!" the phoenix sounded. "Squawk! Squawk!" she sounded more loudly.

"For such a beautiful creature, you have the most abominable voice," Caoilte said without lifting his head.

"Squawk! Squawk!" she sounded and the door of La Petite Maison Le Fèvre opened. Rós appeared at the door and waved to the phoenix to come join her.

"Squawk!" she sounded and pecked at Caoilte's head. "Squak!"

"Stop!"

"Squawk!" she sounded again, and this time, she bowled Caoilte over.

Caoilte gathered his body beneath him and when he stood he noticed the cottage door open.

"It's Rós," he whispered.

He saw her signal to him to join her at her home. He hesitated. He knew he would go to his death with eyes wide open after spending time with Rós. He saw her smile and smiled back. Despite the depth of his sorrow, Caoilte climbed onto his dragon, and knowing what lay ahead, he flew to La Petite Maison Le Fèvre. For it is said that at the moment of greatest sorrow one is carried by that speck of light inside the heart like a lighthouse on a dark and stormy sea.

There was no speck of light presenting itself to Jamie, however. The boy who had abandoned his sister for a life of wealth was alone on the open plains.

"*This stupid map,*" Jamie moaned, sitting on a rock. "I know I saw that rock somewhere," he said, looking across the bleak landscape of wild heather, bog and granite outcrops. He watched the large red damselfly on the black bog rush for a little while and thought about the time Feehul had released the damselfly from the glass jar in the Wood of Allurement. Jamie sighed and looked away. His legs had grown tired and his mind weary from climbing the hills and he was now at the end of his tether.

"The silver hawk… It'd be nice to be able to fly right now," Jamie said. He admired the Hen Harrier with its sleek pale grey body, white underbelly and black wing tips for a short while.

Jamie reached into his pocket for the last piece of chocolate he had. His mouth watered as he slowly tore the wrapper away. He was about to bite into his bar of chocolate when he heard the hen harrier's call and lifted his head. It was then that he saw the wild bush next to the boulder rock. He dropped the bar of chocolate, jumped up and ran towards the boulder.

For all the time they spent together, Elisa didn't truly know the inner workings of Jamie's mind. She had spent her whole life by his side and yet in the past few days she realised that he was not the brother she thought him to be. So is the nature of life that we never truly know ourselves or anyone else until the moment of plight and in that moment, everything comes into the light. The leprechauns were no different.

"You ask a lot of a leprechaun," said Seán, reaching into the jug on his kitchen dresser. He pulled out a key and then reached down to his wooden chest on the floor. He opened it and searched through the bundles of neatly folded shirts and trousers. He dug deeper until he found what he was looking for.

"Go raibh maith agat," he said. "Thank you."

His body had healed and his pain had gone, and for this, Seán was immeasurably grateful. He unfolded the cloth wrapped around a small metal tin with a red lid and silver base. Seán took a quick look around him to see if any leprechaun was spying through his windows. He then slowly opened the lid and pulled out the small leather cloth.

"I have it," he said, and left the house with Setanta and Sinann following close behind.

With another quick look around, Seán turned the key on his front door and left with the elf and the giant boy.

"Why isn't Jamie with you?" Éataín asked, lifting Geaspar from the satchel.

Éataín sat down and placed the bowl filled with soft food on her lap. She held Geaspar next to the bowl and the little dragon ate his fill while she gently stroked him. Having heard nothing from Elisa, Éataín looked up from the dragon to see a girl a million miles away in her thoughts. She watched Elisa look worryingly towards the window.

"Did he come with you to Kapheus?" Éataín asked. Elisa nodded. "But he's not here?" Éataín queried. Elisa shook her head. "And he's in the meadow?" Éataín asked. Elisa shrugged her shoulders, and then the sound of Geaspar burping was heard.

"I think you need to wind him," said Elisa.

"So, you *do* have a tongue," said Éataín, "and if I was a betting woman, *which I'm not*, I would say that you and Jamie had a falling out over this little dragon," she said, stroking him. Elisa nodded. "What happened?"

"He wanted to take Geaspar with him and I told him he couldn't," said Elisa.

"And what's wrong with that?" Éataín asked.

"He got really angry with me and he threw Geaspar on the ground... I think he wanted to hurt him, so that he could hurt me," Elisa said.

"And you didn't let him take Geaspar."

"No."

"Well, you did the right thing, Elisa," said Éataín. She took the empty bowl away from the dragon. "Why do you feel so bad?"

"He got really angry," Elisa said.

"He got really angry, because he was trying to get his own way...
and he didn't care who he hurt to get what he wanted."

"But, I'm not sure if he's alright," said Elisa.

"He needs to work this one out. *You are not* responsible for his
thoughts, emotions or actions," said Éataín.

Éataín rocked over and back on her chair while caressing Geaspar.
Heavy eyelids fell on weary eyes, and although the little dragon
fought against the sleep, it soon took him over and his eyelids shut.

"I'm sure you didn't come here to tell me about Jamie," said Éataín.

"No."

"Then why did you come?"

"Well, Uncle Davin came to our house and he said that Geaspar
wasn't safe in Éire or Kapheus and that people are coming to get
him," said Elisa. "How do I save him?" she asked.

"I don't know," Éataín said. "*You'll have to tell me* the answer to that
one."

"What did Kubera tell you?" Éataín asked.

Fiona and Fiachra sat down next to them and listened. Elisa
struggled.

"I told her that she doesn't have to know all the answers right
now," said Kubera, appearing with his fellow gnomes. "I told her
that she'll need to be strong. I told you, Elisa, that you need to trust
that you will know what the right thing is to do when the time
comes." Kubera took a step closer and placed his hand on Elisa's
arm. "Don't anticipate the future, because it's not here. Make the
most of this moment," he said. "There's no pressure on you,
Elisa," Kubera said. "All the answers will appear when you need
them the most."

"Fódla died," Elisa said. "What if that happens to Geaspar?"

"That's out of your hands as it was with Fódla. If his life is to end,
all the battles in the world won't change that," Kubera said, looking
across the valley to La Petite Maison Le Fèvre on the far hillside.

In La Petite Maison Le Fèvre, Caoilte sat patiently waiting for Rós
to come from the back of her home. He tried his utmost to stop
his leg shaking, but to no avail. Caoilte's eyes drifted to all the
clocks on the walls, but he wasn't able to focus on any one clock.

His eyes shifted their attention to anything he could find in the room on which he could focus his thoughts, but it was no use. He clasped his hands together and tightened his grip so tightly that the whites of his knuckles appeared.

"Umm… she won't be long," said Micah.

Caoilte nodded. His eyes glanced to the backdoor and he took a deep breath. He remembered his childhood of playing in the woodland trees. He remembered the sun streaming through the tree branches in summertime and even the time he caught falling leaves in autumn.

Micah looked at the elf and wondered what could possibly be going through his mind. He saw his anxiety and couldn't imagine what it would be like if faced with this.

"I'll make a cup of tea for you," Micah said in a low voice. He then left the living room.

Caoilte looked down at the polished oak floor. He remembered helping his father tend to the trees in Kapheus and remembered his father teaching him how to make the paste to bring the diseased branches back to health. He thought of disease. There was never very much of it in Kapheus. It was a thing of old age or a misadventure of youth like when the poisoned mushrooms were mistakenly eaten.

"Here it is," said Rós, interrupting Caoilte's thoughts. She handed him the clock.

"When is its time up?" Caoilte asked.

"It's hard to know but…"

"How long?"

"Maybe three weeks," Rós said. She saw the despair on Caoilte's face. "Maybe longer. It's hard to say in certain terms."

Micah entered the living room and saw Caoilte in distress. He left the tray on the table, took his coat from the hanger and closed the door behind him.

"What now?" Caoilte asked. Rós had no words for him. "What now, Rós?"

"The clock has not stopped ticking. You still have a life to live," she said.

Caoilte removed his gold chest protector and laid it on the floor beside him. He lifted the cup of tea from the tray and took a sip.

"I've missed this, you know. I've missed the taste of the tea that's made from the fresh water of the stream... I've missed the company of friends."

Rós continued to listen. She rolled her chair closer to the table and lifted her own cup of tea.

"You can ask if you want. I know you want to ask," Caoilte said.

"I didn't want power and wealth. It was a façade. I was one of eight sent from Kapheus," Caoilte continued.

Rós was barely able to breathe. She couldn't believe the words that were dropping from Caoilte's mouth.

"Grandmother Oak summoned us. There were eight of us in total. We were told never to tell a soul of..."

The sky was turning grey and the wind swept across the open bog and by now Jamie's body was cold and very hungry. Jamie reached the tree and searched the boulder next to it for a clue.

"In the drawing there was an elf sitting on the ground with his back to the rock," Jamie said, searching. "*Here,*" he said.

Jamie crouched down on the wet bog with his back to the boulder at the exact point as in the map on the book. The only clue he could see in the landscape was not a clue at all, but the rain teaming down from a cloud burst a mile away. Jamie thought better than to sit waiting to be soaked by the rain. He placed his right hand on the ground next to him and leaned on it to help him stand. As he did, he noticed his hand balancing on a flat outcrop of rock, the surface of which was decorated in beautifully engraved circular motifs.

"The spirals must be a clue," he said.

Jamie looked down at the next flagstone and saw more spirals. It was as if there was a map laid on the ground to follow all the way to the treasure. Jamie forgot about the impending rain shower and continued to trek across bog, boulders and streams following the stony outcrops that rose from the boggy soil.

"He doesn't get it," Banbha said, watching him from above. She merged her heartbeat to the earth and flew in the direction from which she came.

As Banbha flew back along the valley she saw the fire dragon outside La Petite Maison Le Fèvre. She waited to see who came from the cottage.

"Goodbye Rós. Maybe we'll meet again one day… in a better place," Caoilte said.

Caoilte climbed onto his dragon's back and left Kapheus for Fodar. Rós watched him leave and despite doing her utmost to appear as if unaffected by his story, Rós was left reeling from the shock of what she had been told.

Banbha watched the dragon fly back to Fodar and thought that it was the right time to speak to Ogma the warrior dragon of Kapheus. Banbha flew to the woodland and soon came to rest upon Méabh and Ogma's nest.

"When?" Ogma asked.

"We need to wait for Elisa," said Banbha.

"Well, then *go to her*. Keep her safe," said Ogma, becoming more anxious. "I'll do what I can here."

Ogma stood tall on his nest with outstretched wings, and by this simple act, the dragons left their nests in the treetops and flew to the island. Ogma nodded to Feehul on the branch of Grandmother Oak. He then took flight and followed the others. Feehul whispered through the trees and the elves heard him. They climbed up to the dragons' nests and stood tall and looked to the western coastline. Feehul was the last to reach the nest high up on Grandmother Oak's branches. He whistled three floating whistles and waited. He heard three floating whistles return from the western woodland, then another three from the east, then the north and then the south. The elves then laid low in the dragons' nests and watched as the veil of darkness slowly placed its blanket of stars on the night sky.

"It'll be dark soon," said Éataín, looking out her window. "The stars will soon fill the sky."

"Do you think Jamie will be alright?" Elisa asked.

"There's a point in your life, Elisa, when you are going to *have to put yourself first*," said Éataín. "If you *do not* find your power and *seize your moment*, destiny will never fall to you."

"Go easy on her, Éataín," Fiachra said.

"Go easy on her! The blood moon is tomorrow night!" Éataín complained.

Éataín opened the door, transmuted into a robin and took flight.

"Where are you going, Elisa?" Fiona asked.

"I need time to think," said Elisa. She grabbed hold of the satchel and gently placed Geaspar inside, and she too left.

Elisa walked down the hillside with the satchel carrying the most precious cargo in all of Kapheus on her back. To the naked eye, she was unprotected and vulnerable and a very easy target, but that could not have been further from the truth. With each step Elisa took, the fire rose inside her, and as it did, the fire rose within the beating heart of the little dragon cuddled up asleep on her teddy bear. Banbha watched Elisa from the sky, Iolar from the ledge, and the Dark One hidden in the long grass writhing in pain. His power had almost forsaken him, and he was merely a shadow of the creature that tormented Lugh in Cormac's cave. The Dark One watched Elisa as she approached. He summoned all the energy inside him and reached out to grab hold of her ankle, but Elisa saw him at the last minute and escaped his grip.

"*You're mine,*" the Dark One whispered.

He struggled to breathe and struggled to lift his head from the ground, yet the Dark One could not let go of the obsession he had with Elisa, the child of light. Hatred filled his heart and rage rose up inside him giving him one last cry of strength. He roared to the night sky and his call was heard. The dark clouds rolled across the sky and lightning struck a short distance away. Elisa stepped farther from the Dark One and looked at the rolling clouds. They soon opened and with them came Donn, the serf of death.

Far away in the woods of Kapheus, Feehul felt Elisa in his heart. He froze. Then he saw the dark clouds in the distance. Feehul stood tall and called the dragons from the island.

"An Claíomh Solais nár fhág riamh fuíoll buille," said Feehul. "The Sword of Light, whose stroke never failed!" he shouted. "Ogma! Ogma!"

Elisa stood still as the Dark One's serfs came from the clouds and landed in front of her. Behind them came the hounds of darkness, salivating from their mouths and snapping their jaws. Elisa didn't flinch.

"*Not afraid?*" Donn asked. "What gives you such courage?" he asked, walking around her.

"My light," said Elisa.

Donn looked Elisa up and down and smiled.

"How did you get your scar?" she asked.

Donn continued to leer at Elisa. He stood so close to her that she could feel his cold breath on her face.

"Not even a shimmer," he said. "Why do you not fear me, *child of light?*" he asked.

"Get on with it," the Dark One gasped.

Donn walked towards the Dark One lying helplessly on the ground. He bent down.

"*Don't tell me* what to do," he whispered. "Your time is up old man," Donn said and spat on his face.

He stood up and approached Elisa again. The hounds snarled and barked eerily.

"Shut them up!" Donn yelled. The serfs struck the hounds and they whimpered.

"How did you get your scar?" Elisa asked.

"*Don't,*" Donn said, lifting his hand to strike Elisa. He readjusted and wrenched his neck a little, "ask me that again," he said. Joachim and his pack encroached. "It's dark now, and you see, Elisa, darkness is my friend," said Donn. "I'm powerful beyond measure. If you come with me, I'll give you everything you need and you too will be more powerful than any other girl in all of Kapheus or Éire," Donn said.

He raised both his hands to the sky and lightning struck. Donn then turned around in hope that Elisa would be in awe of his power, but she was not.

"I have An Claíomh Solais," he said, removing the shiny silver sword from beneath his cloak.

Donn caressed its gleaming blade. "It glows green when it is in search of its love," said Donn.

Elisa saw the hole in the hilt that ordinarily housed the emerald she stored in her satchel.

"*You fool!*" the Dark One gasped.

"*Why is it not glowing green?*" he asked, shaking the sword in his hand. The sword's light grew stronger and it glowed perfectly white. "Argh!" he yelled as the light shot a piercing pain through his hand. He dropped the sword.

"An Claíomh Solais tar chugam," Elisa said, and the sword of light dropped at her feet. Elisa bent down to pick it up.

"*What* kind of *magic is this?*" Donn asked. "There's no magic in Kapheus, only true love," said Elisa, holding the sword in her hand.

"*What sorcery* do you possess? *Why is the blade not green?*" Donn asked. He lunged forward to snatch it back, but he was too late. Elisa had already reached to the side pocket of Fódla's satchel and pulled the emerald stone from it. She took one step back and quickly snapped the emerald into its position on the hilt. A large green light shot into the sky with a loud crack. Elisa held tightly to the sword with both hands.

Jamie looked up and saw the green light. He knew it must have been Elisa. He thought for a moment that he would go to see if she was alright. He could call the dragons to fly him to her, but the draw to gold was far stronger at that moment than the draw that pulled him to help his sister. He hurried to find his secret treasure.

"You won't do it," Donn said. "A child of light won't take a life," he said, taking a step closer.

Elisa grew nervous. She remembered all that Jeremiah had taught her in the woods of Kapheus. She breathed calmly and felt her heart beat slowly. Elisa became one with her surroundings. She felt the cold air on her face and heard the sounds carried in the wind. Her stillness unnerved Donn. Elisa allowed her thoughts and emotions to flow and her muscles relaxed. She listened to her heart.

"The biggest mistake anyone has ever made is to underestimate me," Elisa said. "This is An Claíomh Solais, the sword that has never failed, and we will be victorious."

Then Elisa felt Iolar a short distance away watching and waiting like the predator hunting her prey. She heard the sound of a wolf's breath the way she had heard Joachim breathing so many times in her room each night. Elisa felt Feehul in her heart. She briefly looked up and saw him in the sky aboard Ogma. Elisa grew stronger and more confident.

"There is no one here to save you *now*," said Donn. He signalled to his serfs to attack.

Elisa stood in stillness as the attacking mob approached. She raised her sword the moment the hound came flying through the air to tear at her neck. She struck him, and the sword sliced through him and he vanished into a cloud of ashes, which floated to the ground. Three more hounds ran in unison to overpower her, and Elisa struck out again. Their ashes fell to the earth. The serfs were furious at the sight of their trained hounds succumbing to a girl. They flicked their hands to allow a knife to drop from their sleeves. Elisa remained still. She was in complete flow with her surroundings. Donn saw that serenity and in fear withdrew into the cloud. One by one the serfs attacked Elisa and the sword that never failed stood the test. One-by-one it sliced through the hooded figures each of whom turned to ash until there was only one left.

"What's your choice?" Elisa asked. The serf panicked and ran back into the cloud.

Elisa was enveloped in the light of the sword and didn't notice the Dark One reaching out his hand to trip Elisa until it was too late. She came tumbling to the ground, rolled and quickly returned to her feet. She turned to face the Dark One but that touch was enough. She watched the light scorch the Dark One's hand turning it to ash on the ground. The light flowed through his arm and onto his shoulder turning them to ash. The Dark One screamed in pain with every inch of his body the light touched until he had completely turned to ash.

Elisa heard thunder roll and looked around to see the cloud disappear from sight. She dropped her body onto a nearby outcrop in exhaustion. Joachim withdrew from the hillside along with his pack. Iolar flew back to her ledge on the mountain and Ogma returned to the woodland. Elisa was left alone in the silence of her thoughts. She couldn't actually believe that she had fought the serfs and hounds and that the Dark One was gone. She looked around for her friends, but they too were gone.

"It is said that you enter this world alone and you leave it alone. Maybe it is that you are alone all the time you're here too," a voice said from behind her. Elisa looked around.

"I didn't think I'd ever *see you* again," Elisa said in delight.

"Do you mind if I sit next to you?"

"Oh, yes, please do."

The centaur tucked his four legs tightly underneath him and then dropped to his knees and laid his body down onto one side with his legs tucked underneath him. Elisa never ceased to be in awe of the centaur with the body of a horse and the torso of a man. She tried not to stare at him but there was a point where it was almost impossible.

"I've been watching you from up there," he said, pointing to the stars. "I've admired you."

Elisa nodded. She looked up at the star-filled sky and wondered what it would be like to live there. She remembered when she first met the centaur in the Wood of Anguish and how they became good friends even though they had only spent a short time together.

"How is your knee?" she asked.

"It's all better now," the centaur said, and smiled. "You know they call me Chiron up there now. I spent so much time in the Wood of Anguish that I had forgotten my name. *It's Chiron.*"

"Hi Chiron," said Elisa.

"Hi Elisa," he said and smiled. He placed his hand on her shoulder. They both sat in the silence of the night as a little robin watched from a nearby bush. Feehul had almost reached Elisa now and could see the bright silhouette of the centaur by her side. He crouched down and waited.

"Jamie didn't come," Elisa said.

"No."

"Everyone left me. They were here," Elisa said, looking around her.

"You're carrying An Claíomh Solais, the most powerful sword ever made," he said, admiring the detail of the engravings along the length of the blade. "They are the letters of Ogham," he noted but Elisa wasn't interested in the sword at that moment. "They didn't run away from you. They retreated from the sword. You held in your hand the power to kill anything that came in contact with you. Do you not think they would take a step backwards?"

"But *I would never hurt anyone,*" said Elisa.

"No, but you're powerful, and power scares people. Even when it is for good."

Elisa pulled her satchel from her back to check on Geaspar. She opened it and he climbed out and onto her shoulder.

"And all along, Donn didn't know that you had the dragon he has been crazily trying to find," said Chiron. He laughed. "The world is a peculiar place."

"Do you know about Geaspar?"

"Who doesn't!"

"People want to take him to Fodar," said Elisa.

"There's nothing new in that, Elisa. Since the beginning of time there have been many and there will be others in the future who want what doesn't belong to them. They've a feeling of entitlement," said Chiron. "*You don't have that, do you?*" Elisa shrugged her shoulders. "I didn't think so."

"Davin said that I am touching it, but I am afraid to take it," Elisa said.

"I'm sure you're talking about power," said Chiron.

"Yeah."

"Well, answer your own question. Are you afraid of power?"

"Yes," Elisa said without hesitation.

"What part of power are you afraid of?"

"I don't want to hurt people. I don't want to be like..."

"I get it. You don't have to say who they are."

"And power means abuse of power to you, not fire and light and hope and abundance," Chiron said, raising his hands to the night sky.

A star shot across the sky in an arc of streaming light.

"What do you mean?" Elisa asked.

"Power is what you want it to be, Elisa. If you want the time of fire to be about war and violence and abuse and manipulation and so much more, then it will," said Chiron, getting to his feet. "But if you want the time of fire to be about abundance and hope and life and joy then it will be that too," he said, and smiled. "I think I remember you telling me about something a wise man once said to you. How you believe the world to be is how the world will be. If you believe you are no good then you will fulfil that destiny, but if you believe that you can have abundance and light and joy, then you will have that."

"I believe these things," said Elisa. "Jamie gets them all the time."

"Oh, you believe them for others, but you don't expect them for yourself. This is the time of fire, believing is not enough. Expect that you too can have abundance and light and joy. If *you believe you'll lose Geaspar* to this battle then it is likely you will, but..." Chiron said.

He looked up to the night sky and reached his hands to the air like a child wishing to be lifted into his mother's arms.

"You had the power to save me, Elisa, when I believed it wasn't possible," he said.

He sped in a shooting star to his home in the night sky. "You risked everything for me!" he said and disappeared.

"Hi Elisa!" Feehul said, approaching her.

"I thought you'd gone," Elisa said.

"*Not likely.* You know I'm afraid of the heights dragons reach. It's *completely unnecessary* for him to do those loops too. He *knows* I don't like flying," said Feehul. Feehul lifted Geaspar from Elisa's shoulder. "Come on. It's too late to have this little fella up. I'm sure he'll need a bath and another belly full of food," Feehul said, making his way to Éataín's cottage. "Well, are you coming?"

Elisa picked up her satchel and followed him.

"I've brought some herbs for Fiona. She loves them for her soup," said Feehul.

The robin flew from the bush and onwards to La Petite Maison Le Fèvre where she found rest on the window ledge. She watched Rós as she pencilled on her large white paper. She saw Micah sitting by the fireside and was about to fly away when Rós opened the window latch.

"What's troubling you tonight, Éataín?" Rós asked. Micah looked peculiarly at his wife. He didn't see the robin and was convinced she was talking to herself. "Love, would you make a cup of tea for Éataín?" Rós asked.

Micah looked out the front window and looked a little confused. He saw no one at the door. He scratched his head and rather than say anything that would make him sound like a fool, he left the room.

"Sit by the fireside. You must be cold," Rós said.

"Not too bad," said Éataín, sitting down.

"We're both troubled by the same thing, but only Elisa has the solution," said Rós, continuing to pencil.

"And she can't make it without Jamie," said Éataín.

Éataín took a deep breath. She felt there was nothing she could do to make either child see sense. Jamie was consumed by greed and Elisa was too afraid to be powerful. The more she thought about it, the more frustrated she became.

"Where is the lad now?" Rós asked.

"*Oh, he's gone off* looking for *some treasure.*"

"*Treasure,*" Rós said, dropping her pencil. "*You mean the Kaphien armoury.*"

"Yes."

"Oh, we might have a problem," said Rós.

She pulled her chair back from the desk and made her way to the front door.

"What kind of a problem?" Éataín asked.

"Does Iolar know?" Rós asked, opening the door.

"Not that I know of," said Éataín.

"Or Grandmother Oak?"

"No. *Why?*"

Chapter 13

The Thief

"At least the roads have thawed," Cathal said, closing the door behind him. "I'll bring Elisa to town tomorrow to get her sweets. I want to call in to see Eve anyway."

Cathal hung up his coat and then his cap. He heard nothing from Aideen and turned around. Cathal quietly stepped across the living room floor to the fireside. He picked up the throw from the armchair next to him and gently placed it over his sleeping wife. He kissed her on the cheek and quietly made his way upstairs. When Cathal reached the final step on the stairs Kubera appeared on the armchair across from Aideen. He waited to hear Cathal leave the bathroom and walk down the hall. He listened to him closing his bedroom door and then breathed more easily. Kubera lifted the small, red, tarnished book into his hands to read. As he read, the words floated like musical notes through the air to Aideen in her dreamtime. Aideen soon woke. She looked at Kubera and the tarnished red book.

"It's strange the books you'll find on that shelf," Kubera said.

"But no one can read it," said Aideen. She pulled the throw away from her body and leaned forward on the chair to retrieve it.

"You do remember me," said Kubera. Aideen nodded. "Then you'll know that I've no difficulty reading from this book or any of the ancient texts of Kapheus."

He handed the book to Aideen, who herself flicked through the pages, but the drawings and writing faded and disappeared.

"*You* on the other hand," Kubera said, "it is *you* whom I've the most difficulty reading."

Aideen closed the cover of the book and brushed her hand across the title. The tarnished gold sparkled and read *Slí na Fírinne*.

"It reads both ways," Kubera said, "the *Way to Glory* or the *Way to Death*. It was dropped in the bog by a young boy. It seems he has also hidden an item from these drawings somewhere in Éire."

"*He couldn't have,*" Aideen said with a gasp. "I would've known."

"Aw, Aideen, my dear Aideen, none of us know the ways of our children until it's often too late." Kubera placed his hand on

Aideen's. "Remember all I taught you. Open the book again and read the passages... Find the way, Aideen," Kubera said.

He then left Aideen alone with the book, walked upstairs and closed Elisa's room door behind him.

Jamie hit the handle of his torch a couple of times, but apart from a few dim flashes, the battery was completely dead. He threw it back into his bag and continued to walk. By now, he could see the lake and no longer needed the stony outcrops to guide his way. He started walking briskly now and reached the lake very quickly. Jamie stood at the edge of the lake and looked all around him. He did his utmost to recall every clue on his map. He reached into his pocket to pull out the little red book and it was gone. He checked his other pocket and then looked all around him. The book was gone and there was no way that he could retrace his steps. It was far too late in the evening and he would have to wait until dawn. Jamie looked around him again and saw the cluster of hawthorn trees and ran along the boundary of the lake to the other side. In his hurry, he tripped over a rock and landed heavily on his knee. He winced in pain, clutching tightly to his leg. He opened his eyes and standing above him was the unicorn foal, Prometheus.

"*What do you want?*" Jamie snapped.

The foal pawed the ground in front of him.

"*What?*"

The foal whinnied.

"*What? What do you want?*" he yelled, pounding the ground with his fist.

The foal stepped back and then whinnied once more. It was then that Jamie saw the marking on the outcrop under the light of the moon. It was the Spiral of Life and Jamie knew that only good came from anything associated with it. He also knew that the treasure was on the other side of the lake and he could have anything he wanted once he had that treasure.

Elisa couldn't sleep thinking about Jamie and wondering if he was alright. She tossed and turned in her makeshift bed and then finally got up and stepped outside of Éataín's cottage. She walked to the gate and searched for Jamie, but she couldn't see any trace of him. She stayed there for a while hoping to see her brother. Elisa searched the valley and the hills and every place she thought he might be, but in the end, she released herself from the worry and the longing and decided to let him go.

"Could you take me to the eastern hills?" she asked.

"How did you know I was here?" Banbha asked.

"You're always here," said Elisa.

"Well, if *you're* going, *we're* going," said Setanta, approaching her.

"Hi Elisa," said Sinann.

"Squawk! Squawk!" sounded the phoenix, and the only thing Elisa could do was to laugh.

Feehul woke and saw that Elisa wasn't there. He quickly pulled on his boots and went outside.

"Wait for me!" he whispered, shutting the door quietly behind him.

"I'd love some scones," Elisa said, climbing onto Banbha's back.

"That's normally Jamie's request," said Banbha, thinking peculiarly of it. "Your brother must be on your mind."

By now, Caoilte had returned to Fodar, and when he did, Fodar felt his wrath.

"I want every dragon armed and ready!" Caoilte shouted.

"*But* what about the young?" asked an elf.

"I don't care! Dragon eggs, hatchlings, young dragons, old dragons we're taking them all!"

"That's my boy!" said Mr. Adley. "Hahaha! I'll leave it all to you, Caoilte. You've always been my lucky elf," he said, and delighted. He left the warehouse.

"Bhuel, ar chuala tú mé? *Did you hear me?*" Caoilte yelled.

The elf ran off to follow orders.

"*I will* hand pick *my own* warriors. *Who's ready?*" he asked.

"They're training in the battle yard," said another elf.

Caoilte left the warehouse and walked down the street to the compound guarded by walls built so high that they blocked out the sun from the street. He knocked on the wicket door at a large grey double gate and an elf opened the latch. When he saw who was standing at the other side, the elf quickly closed the latch again and opened the door to Caoilte.

Inside the compound were simulated battle scenes. Fire dragons shot flames from their mouths onto synthetic elf targets. The reins were pulled tight on young dragons to temper their enthusiasm. Elves and people were clad in gold and silver armoury shooting at targets with bow and arrows and long spears. Some were aboard dragons while others were foot soldiers. The training ground was undulated similar to the hills and valleys of Kapheus.

"Tell every elfin warrior who wants to fight to be here at six o'clock, and *as that sun rises, I will choose the elves to fight*," Caoilte shouted.

"What about the men and women?" the elf asked.

"Where we're going, laddie, is no place for men or women. I'll have elves and dragons and not another creature," said Caoilte. "I'll be back *here at 5.55am* and *not a minute* later. *Make sure everything* is in order."

Caoilte left through the wicket door and walked down the empty street to the courtyard. He removed his helmet and walked through the small door and across the cobblestones to his home on the other side. He switched on the light and stood looking at the home he had created for himself in Fodar. At that moment, all the things he had accomplished meant nothing to him. He looked at the wooden clock on the mantelpiece above the empty fireplace and listened to its ticking sound. He glanced across at the large wooden dresser against the wall and the polished table in the centre of the room with the vase of wildflowers. He switched off the light and walked to the back room to rest.

In contrast, Jamie walked between the wind swept and weather beaten hawthorn trees. He was cold and wet, and his stomach rumbled with hunger, but none of that mattered. He wanted his treasure. Within that small hawthorn woodland with its uneven and often unstable surface, Jamie stumbled across a small low-built stonewall. It wasn't much higher than his ankles. He crouched down and placed his hand on the wall and traced its design. It didn't seem to have any purpose in this place. He looked behind him and noticed the wall increase in height as it passed along the higher ground. He turned back again and something inside him told him that he needed to follow it to lower ground. Jamie walked along the wall until it disappeared into the ground. Jamie stood up. At this point, he had had almost enough. He threw his bag on the ground. The ground beneath him opened up and down he fell into the shaft with a crash.

"*Who is he?*" a voice asked among the hawthorn trees.

"I don't know. It's too dark to see *anything* here," said the other voice.

The two strangers moved on. Jamie, however, didn't feel like he could move anywhere. He looked up to the opening of the shaft. It was too far for him to climb and he was now feeling very afraid. What if no one would ever find him? He looked up at the moonlight and called Elisa from the top of his voice, but she could not hear him.

"Elisa!" he shouted again, but he had left her.

Jamie pulled the matches from the pocket of his school bag. He took his extra pair of socks and tried his best to set them alight, but they only burned for a few seconds. He searched in his box and there were only four matches left. He lit one and looked down the shaft.

"Left or right," he said. He closed his eyes tightly. "What would Elisa do?"

Jamie picked up his bag and crawled down the shaft. The farther he crawled, the larger it became until he could stand. He lit another match and saw a torch hanging on the wall. He picked it up and lit it.

"There isn't much here. I really hope it lasts," Jamie said. "Elisa find me," he pleaded, and continued down the narrow passageway. It was cold, damp and mouldy in the passageway and Jamie began to cough. He reached into this bag in search of another bar of chocolate or anything to eat, but there was nothing. Jamie started to cry. He felt he had ruined everything and he was lost forever in Kapheus. He believed he should have listened to Prometheus and now it was too late. Jamie placed his bag on his back again and then stumbled, having tripped over something on the ground. The ground opened again and this time he fell head first down a long, deep and winding shaft all the way to its end.

"Aarghhh!" Jamie shouted.

Jamie landed in a heap on the ground and every bone in his body ached. He tried to stand up but couldn't. There were too many pieces of metal underneath him. Jamie sat back down and pulled out his box of matches.

"I've only two left," he said, feeling his way to striking the match along the length of the box.

The match lit, and when it did, Jamie was in awe. He was sitting on a mountain of gold and silver armoury. Everywhere he looked there was treasure. He spotted a torch hanging on a nearby pillar and stretched to reach it. Jamie slipped and slid down the mountain of gold armoury.

"Arghh!" he shouted until he finally came to rest at the bottom of the pile. He stumbled and slipped until he was able to get to his feet.

"Only one left," he said.

He struck the match and this time could reach a torch on a nearby pillar. Jamie lit the torch and saw clearly the vast store of gold and silver armoury housed inside this gigantic mine. He looked down at the polished marble floor that seemed to reach to the end of the world. There were large granite stone columns connected to each other by domes. Jamie walked beneath the rib vaulted ceiling and through the portal adorned with the ancient carvings of Kapheus to the next room. This room was again filled with gold armoury of all kind. He even saw gold tipped arrows and spears. He couldn't believe his eyes.

Jamie tripped and looked down and saw what he thought were horse reins. He picked them up and saw they were made of finely threaded strands of gold. Jamie looked at the portals that lead to other rooms and they seemed to go on forever. He quickly opened his school bag to fill it with gold and silver. Suddenly, the torch blew out.

"In ainm Dé!" he complained.

Jamie reached down to stuff more items into this bag as quickly as possible while now standing in complete darkness. He zipped his school bag shut and with great effort lifted it onto his shoulders. He felt his back heave under the weight of the gold and silver. Jamie walked to where he remembered leaving the torch down. He bent down to pick it up and a foot stood on the torch, preventing him from lifting it.

"Tóg é!" the voice said. "Quickly!"

Suddenly, Jamie's mouth was gagged, and then a sack was pulled over his head and it was tied tightly at his neck. His hands were tied before he knew what was going on and he was dumped to the floor.

"Grandmother Oak will have a word or two to say about this," said Ruan. "I take my responsibilities *very seriously*," he said.

"You take his legs and I'll take his torso," he said.

"*If there wasn't enough going on in Kapheus*, without this *thief* causing problems for me," said Ruan.

The two elves carried Jamie through the chambers of the gigantic store room to the door that lead to the bog of Kapheus.

"He's doing enough wriggling anyway," said Ruan.

"Yeah! I wish *he'd stop* trying to *kick me*," said Lir.

As they approached the entrance, Ruan and Lir were confronted by a band of leprechauns.

"*Who dares steal* from a leprechaun's treasure chest?" Seán asked. "Hand over your cargo!"

"*Indeed and I will not!*" Ruan retorted. "*Your treasure!* I've never in *all my life* heard the likes." He pulled his thief closer to his body. "*Did the leprechauns steal it* from the dead warriors and dragons as they *lay in the valley? Did those same leprechauns steal* the shirt from the *back* of *my dear father* who *fought and died*, so that *you* may live free, leprechauns? *Do not dare to insult me* with your words!" Ruan shouted.

"You *can't* take him," said Seán.

"*No*. It is *you* who *cannot take him* or *anything else* from these chambers that does not belong to you. *Cast open* these doors, so that all Kaphiens may protect themselves from the atrocity that is about to unfold."

Ruan passed the leprechauns only to find Dagda waiting at the entrance.

"*What now?*" Ruan snapped.

"Umm… my brother is a bit upset, Dagda," Lir said, squirming.

"It's alright, Lir. I heard it all, and you don't need to worry, Ruan. I've the key to all the chambers. Every door will be cast open. Kaphiens *will have* the opportunity to protect themselves."

"*So be it,*" said Ruan, and he passed Dagda by. "I've business to attend to that I would prefer I didn't have to deal with, but I take my responsibilities *very seriously,*" Ruan said.

Dagda looked at the boots of the thief as the light of the moon shone down on them and the elves carried him beyond the entrance. He smiled a wry smile.

"Well, lads. It looks like we've plenty to get on with. There are warriors that need protecting," said Dagda.

"And that's the very reason *I'm here,*" Seán retorted.

Outside, there seemed to be no space for Ruan and Lir to walk. They nodded to the dragons as they tried to navigate their way between dragon legs and tails.

"Do you wish me to take your thief to Grandmother Oak," Ogma asked.

"Yes, well. I would Ogma, but you know us elves and the whole flying thing," said Ruan.

Lir dropped Jamie from his grip and the force threw him out of Ruan's hands and onto the cold bog.

"*Ruan! How am I* going to be able to carry *this thief all the way* to Grandmother Oak? *Do you know how far that is?*" Lir whined.

Ogma laughed. He snatched the thief from the ground and threw him onto his back with a thump.

"Climb on board my friends," he said, and reluctantly Ruan followed Lir onto the back of the black warrior dragon.

It wasn't long before they were airborne and flying over the lake and in the direction of the woods of Kapheus.

"Hold on tight to that thief! We don't want him slipping off my back," Ogma said.

"What brought you all here?" Ruan asked.

"*Who* would be more appropriate, and in answer to your question, Seán brought us all to the treasure trove," said Ogma.

"*Seán did,*" Ruan remarked in surprise. "Did the leopard *change his spots?*"

"Beidh lá eile ag an bPaorach," Ogma said. "No leprechaun hands over his treasure as you well know. I'm sure there was a deal done whatever it was."

While Jamie was lying helpless on the back of Ogma on his way to Grandmother Oak, Elisa and her friends were being taken to the eastern hillside at her request by Banbha. Their experiences were worlds apart. Jamie was now feeling scared, cold and hungry, whereas Elisa was beginning to step into her power surrounded by her friends. By the light of the moon she and her friends saw all they needed to see. The guardians flew overhead as they always did. The sea breeze blew strongly from the western coastline and the hills were dotted with lookouts and hiding spots.

"Call to the guardians, Banbha," Elisa said.

"Before you do, let me down out of here," Feehul requested, and Banbha gladly obliged.

Elisa and Setanta remained aloft the green dragon as she lifted her body high into the sky and opened her heart centre. A ray of light shone brightly from the Spiral of Life at her heart. She screeched into the night and her screech shook the whole of Kapheus. The dragons waiting in the bog heard it and startled. The elves felt that vibration to the heart of their being and rose from their slumber in their homes in the hills and the valley. They opened their doors and looked out their windows. Banbha screeched again and the guardians encircled her.

"You know every inch of this land," Elisa said, pointing to Kapheus beneath them. "There's a battle coming. Fodar wants to take Geaspar and we can't let that happen," she said.

The elves stepped outside of their homes to marvel at the sight above them. The dragons continued to encircle Banbha as the Spiral of Life shone as bright as the moon itself.

"The elves will be waiting for you. Banbha will give you the signal. Decide where they need to be, so that they can best protect Kapheus," Elisa said.

The elves watched as Banbha's light dimmed and the dragons broke from their nightly flight and returned to the island.

"It doesn't look like anyone in Kapheus is sleeping tonight," Éataín said, standing at the door of La Petite Maison Le Fèvre, "and it'll be dawn before we know it."

Éataín saw Banbha come to rest on the hilltop and watched Elisa and Setanta dismount. She saw Elisa stand on the boulder on the hilltop and look into the valley, and point to places in the landscape. She saw her friends take on board everything Elisa had to say. Éataín didn't move from the door.

"You can't hide it, Éataín," said Rós, approaching her from behind. Éataín looked at Rós and smiled.

"No, I can't… The world is her oyster now," Éataín said. "I wish her well."

"You have a lot more to teach her yet. Fly to her. Give her this message and be careful."

Éataín transmuted to a robin and flew to Elisa with the small piece of cloth in her mouth. She landed on the outstretched arm of Sinann.

"Go raibh maith agat," Sinann said. She handed the message to Elisa.

Elisa read it carefully and thought. She looked behind her in the direction from where the dragons would come from Fodar.

"How many sliotars can you buy with that purse of silver?" Elisa asked.

"*How did you know* we had a purse of silver?... Never mind… Ummm… umm… maybe two hundred, but I'm not sure if I'm allowed to spend it on sliotars," said Setanta.

"Banbha will you take Setanta with you to buy them?"

"Should I not ask if it's alright first?" Setanta asked.

"It's alright," said Banbha, snatching Setanta with her teeth and launching him into the air and onto her back. "We'll be back shortly," she said, and flew away.

"What do you need from me?" Éataín asked. Elisa handed the message to Éataín. She read it carefully. "I'll talk to her," she said. Éataín transmuted to a robin once again.

As the piece of cloth carrying the message dropped from Éataín's hand and floated through the air the phoenix caught it in her beak and swallowed it. She belched, and a plume of ashes burst free from her mouth.

"That's the end of the message," said Feehul.

Elisa looked down at the river and then high onto the waterfall. She looked to the far coastline and the island.

"I know what to do," said Sinann.

"Good, because I don't," said Feehul. "I don't understand war. I *haven't a clue* what to do."

"We'll figure it out. Leave the water to me," Sinann said.

"We'll need dummy elves," said Elisa.

"What do you mean?" Feehul asked.

"We'll need to set traps. If we have elves that are dummies in the valley... there... there... and there. We could draw in the dragons and the warriors and then we could ambush them. What do you think?" she asked. Sinann nodded. "Reveal yourselves," Elisa said. There were three gnomes standing on each other's shoulders trying to see where Elisa had pointed. They stretched as far as their bodies could stretch and nodded. They climbed down from each other's shoulders and ran down the hillside.

Sinann signalled to Iolar. The golden eagle left her nest and flew towards her.

"I'll go. I'm sure we'll meet again before the blood moon, but if not, stay safe," Sinann said. She hugged Feehul and was then snatched by Iolar who flew with her to the waterfall.

"There's Banbha! I wonder where she's going," said Ruan.

On hearing this, Jamie tried to kick himself free and attempted to shout for Banbha, but Banbha continued on her path.

"That's enough of that *thief!*" Ruan snapped. "Daylight will soon be here, and Grandmother Oak *won't be happy* when she sees your face."

Ogma flew through the valley with the speed and force of the warrior dragon he was. Few questioned his power and leadership and none in Kapheus ever challenged him. Suddenly, Ruan and Lir heard an almighty screech coming from their left. Ogma diverted his path, tucked his wings into this body and sped like a bullet through the air.

"Arghhhh!" Ruan and Lir yelled. "Arghhhhhh!"

They were convinced they would come crashing to the valley floor. At the point of crashing head first into the valley, Ogma slowed and gently placed his feet upon the ground.

"Get me down from here!" Ruan shouted.

"Ruan, I'm going to be sick," Lir cried. He then spontaneously vomited all over the thief.

"I'll take your cargo the rest of the way," said Éiriú, the great white dragon, when she landed.

"Happily," said Ogma.

"*Not happily, not happily at all,*" said Lir, terrified.

"What my brother means to say is that, well, I take my responsibilities *very seriously* and I've my own cargo to deliver to Grandmother Oak," Ruan said, pointing to his thief. "It's *my responsibility* to deliver this cargo…"

"And we don't want to be eaten by *you,*" Lir added.

Ogma reached back, caught hold of Ruan and tossed him onto Éiriú's back and then did the same with Lir.

"And you can have your *thief too,*" said Ogma. He then took to the skies.

"Goddess of Éire, I know you have a *slight* anger issue, one might say that you're *a bit* temperamental…" said Ruan, "Arghh!"

"I don't want to *die* today!" yelled Ruan.

"Mairfidh thú," Éiriú replied.

"Are you sure I'll survive?" Ruan cried.

Éiriú flew to the woods. She gently placed her feet upon the earth and unloaded her cargo.

"Steady now, Éiriú. I'm very well able to climb down from a dragon," Ruan said, nervously.

Cillian stood up. He had seen the white dragon land and slowly walked towards Grandmother Oak with immense curiosity. He watched as Éiriú caught the thief in her teeth and dropped him onto the ground with a thump.

"If you'll allow me," said Ruan, nervously.

"Lean ort," said Éiriú.

"Well, Éiriú, goddess of Éire." He took a deep breath. "Grandmother Oak," Ruan said, "I found this thief in the gold mines."

As Ruan spoke, the sun began to rise, and light streamed into the woodland.

"Continue," said Éiriú, "*a thief is a thief* and there is no need for you to fear. *You've a responsibility* after all."

"Yes, I do. Grandmother Oak, you imparted on me a *serious responsibility* and I found this *thief* stealing from the gold and silver armoury in the mines."

"Let me see the thief," she said. "Cillian will you help them to untie him."

Cillian bent down and untied the thief's legs, and as he did, he realised the identity of that very thief. He helped to untie his hands and the moment Ruan pulled the sack from over his head, the sunlight streamed into the wood and onto the face of Jamie. Ruan and Lir were horrified. Cillian remained silent. He nervously looked at Éiriú and then Grandmother Oak. Cillian looked around the wood and saw the Tuatha Dé Danann and his fellow elves watching them. Mother Badger bounded across the woodland and ripped the cloth that tied Jamie's mouth. Her family raced behind her and jumped on Jamie to hold him down.

"How *dare you steal* from Kapheus!" Mother Badger scolded. "I *risked my life* and the *life of my family* to save *you* from the Dark One. My husband is dead!" she scolded.

Éiriú's eyes began to fill with tears. She couldn't believe what she was seeing. Éiriú took a deep breath and gathered herself again for fear that anyone would notice her tears.

"This reminds me of the boy, who on his first few minutes in Kapheus wanted to tie a rope around my branch. I asked him if he thought that it wouldn't hurt me. It seems *he didn't think at all*," said Grandmother Oak.

Ruan opened Jamie's school bag, pulled out the pieces of gold and silver he had stolen and laid them on the woodland floor. Jamie frantically looked around. There was no possibility of escape.

"Only a coward thinks to escape," said Lugh. "A boy owns up to his wrongful action and takes responsibility for what he has done."

Jamie looked at Éiriú.

"What are you going to do to me?" he asked.

Éiriú didn't answer. She had no words for this act only an overwhelming feeling of shame.

"You've been brought to *me*, Jamie. It is for *me* to decide your fate," said Grandmother Oak. The spirit of the great oak tree stood in front of him. "This cannot go unpunished," she said, and she pondered. "I could exile you from Kapheus forever," she said, "or I could summon your sister to straighten this mess out, but why would I call Elisa? I would only act to punish her with the burden of you who has committed the crime"

"I…" Jamie said.

"*Shush!* Don't speak!" said Grandmother Oak. "Your presence is a disturbance to me right now… Lugh, take him back to Éire," she said. "Jamie, get yourself washed and into some clean clothes… *Oh, eat something healthy* and be back here by midday," she said, irritated.

"Dara, are you able to carry an elf and a boy?"

"Yes, Grandmother Oak," Dara said, landing on the woodland floor next to Jamie.

"You can let him go, Mother Badger, and I'm very sorry for your distress."

Lugh pulled Jamie to his feet but not before Jamie rescued his school bag. Lugh helped him onto Dara's back.

"*Lugh*, don't let him out of your sight. Be back here by midday," Grandmother Oak said. Jamie tightened his school bag straps to his shoulders. "Be careful Dara. Call Ogma if you need help," Grandmother Oak said, and Dara left.

Dara had no sooner taken flight than the little red robin flew over Cillian's head and came to rest on Grandmother Oak's branch.

"I don't think we could handle any more surprises today," Cillian said.

The spirit of Grandmother Oak withdrew to the bark. The robin sang a sweet tune, tilted her head from side to side while remaining focussed on Éiriú, and then flew away.

Chapter 14

Éiriú's Secret

The sound of the water spraying down on Jamie in the shower was the only thing that could be heard in the house at sunrise. The steam escaped from under the bathroom door all the while Lugh sat on the floor waiting for him to finish. Half awake, Lugh yawned and looked down the hallway to the top of the stairs and thought of eating something nice for his breakfast. He thought of the really good hot chocolate Jamie made the last time he was in the house, but then hot chocolate is not always the best thing to have for breakfast.

"Dia duit," Cathal said.

"Dia is Muire Duit," Lugh responded.

Cathal stopped in the hallway and looked around. Lugh on the other hand was still dreaming of hot chocolate and thought nothing of this encounter. Then he noticed someone looking right at him. He looked up and saw Cathal and startled.

"There's nothing to be startled about," said Cathal. "Are you waiting for Jamie or Elisa?"

"Jamie," said Lugh.

"Well, I can breathe a sigh of relief in that case. Do you go to school together? I haven't seen you before."

Lugh did his best to pull his hair over his pointed ears without Cathal noticing.

"Hi Dad," said Jamie, leaving the bathroom with a towel wrapped around him.

"*You're* up early. I didn't know you were having a friend stay."

"Yeah, Dad," said Jamie, holding his filthy vomit splattered clothes in his hands.

"Here, give them to me. They'll need to go straight into the wash. Get dressed I'll make some breakfast for us," Cathal said, walking towards the stairs. "Sorry, I didn't get your name."

"Oh, it's Lugh."

"Come on then, Lugh."

"Well, I'd like to but I think I'll wait for Jamie."

"Don't worry. He's not going to run away."

"Well, Grandmother O… my grandmother asked me not to leave his side."

"Suit yourself. I'll be downstairs. Jamie, hurry up. Don't leave your guest sitting on the floor waiting for you. It's not good manners," said Cathal and he walked downstairs to the kitchen.

Jamie ran into his room and shut the door firmly behind him. He pulled open his dresser and hurriedly put on his clothes. Lugh, on the other hand, stood at the top of the stairs fascinated by the fact that Cathal could see him. Jamie pulled on his socks as quickly as possible.

"I'm almost ready!" he called to Lugh outside.

Jamie laid down on the bedroom floor and reached under his bed for his school bag. He pulled it out and opened the large front zipper. He stuffed the imperial topaz into his pocket and then reached in to pull out something far more substantial.

"Are you ready?" Lugh called.

He didn't hear a reply. Lugh opened the door and saw Jamie stuffing something back into his bag in a hurry.

"*I'm ready,*" said Jamie, "I need to get my boots," he said, passing Lugh by.

Lugh looked into the bedroom and then back to the stairs. He closed the door of Jamie's room.

"Lugh are you coming?" Cathal called. "I've a hot pancake here. Do you like blueberries?"

"Umm… yes… go raibh maith agat," he said and walked downstairs.

Far away in Kapheus, the aroma of hot scones floated through the morning air to where Elisa and Feehul stood on the eastern hilltop.

"Squawk! Squawk!" the phoenix sounded and took flight.

"It's time for breakfast," said Banbha, landing beside them.

"How many did you get?" Elisa asked.

"Two hundred and five… I think my mother would *kill me* if she saw me coming home with *two hundred and five sliotars,*" Setanta enthused. He smiled in perfect delight. Banbha bent down for them to climb on board. "We had to go to *five houses.* It's not usual to sell that many sliotars in one go," Setanta said, delighted. He couldn't contain his excitement.

"Here we are," said Banbha.

"Hi Rós!"

"Come in for breakfast. Micah has scones baking in the oven," she said.

"They're ready!" Micah announced from the kitchen.

"Rós!" Setanta said.

"Yes."

"My Mam says that I'm not allowed to eat in other people's houses. She says I'll eat them out of house and home," said Setanta.

"Ha! I wouldn't worry about that. Micah loves to bake and will have more than enough scones for everyone. Tar isteach," Rós said.

"Rós," said Banbha.

"Yes."

"I'm needed in the woods. Éiriú is there," Banbha said, anxiously.

"*Oh*, I wish you well," Rós said, and Banbha was gone.

Banbha screeched loudly above Grandmother Oak's branches. Down below her, Cillian stood with his back against Grandmother Oak's bark watching Éiriú. He was completely in awe of this magnificent white dragon. Yet, he could not understand why her eyes were filled with such sadness.

"She'll wait for you," Cillian said.

Éiriú looked around the woodlands with a feeling of shame and under-achievement. The Tuatha Dé Danann were hidden behind trees watching and listening. She could feel their breath and hear their thoughts. Mother Badger looked at her and could understand her torment.

"She'll wait for you," Cillian said.

Vulnerability was something that Éiriú was not used to displaying, but she was completely vulnerable now. The elves stood and waited for her to do or say something but she had no words.

"*Go.* You'll work it out between you," said Mother Badger. "You'll find a way."

Éiriú looked at Grandmother Oak who in her silence left Éiriú feeling that she couldn't take the next step. Grandmother Oak knew Éiriú for many hundreds of years and knew that she could not tell her what to do. If she did, she would run the risk of losing Éiriú to the rage that burned inside the dragon. The silence was Éiriú's only hope.

Éiriú looked at Cillian again and in an instant she joined Banbha above the woodland. Banbha and Éiriú then flew together until they reached the coast. They crossed the sea to the island and soon Banbha came to rest on the courtyard. Within only a few seconds Éiriú had landed next to her sister and for a little while there was nothing said between the two of them.

"How are you?" Banbha eventually asked. This question only seemed to incite Éiriú's rage. She looked at Banbha angrily and then looked out to sea. "None of this is my fault," said Banbha. Éiriú said nothing. "I didn't *make Jamie* steal from Kapheus!"

"You didn't stop him either!" Éiriú snapped.

"*Éiriú* would you *listen to yourself? That boy* wanted only one thing and he *abandoned his sister* in Kapheus for it. *He even* wanted to *take Geaspar* so that he could use him to get his own way."

"That's not true!" Éiriú snapped, turning around.

"You don't want to hear it, because you know it's true," Banbha said, firmly.

Éiriú walked to the other side of the courtyard.

"Elisa has An Claíomh Solais and she's already fought the darkness with it. The Dark One has gone," said Banbha. "Donn is the only one who remains."

"What was in the father will soon come out in the son. Darkness is never too far away," said Éiriú.

"Elisa has the *Sword of Light*. She's organising *everyone around her* for this battle tonight. She's stepping into her power!"

Éiriú sat down. She looked out to sea and was lost to her thoughts for some time. Banbha had enough of waiting for her sister and in that moment, she realised that she had given her too much power her whole life. She stood directly in front of her.

"You have spent *your whole time* idolising Jamie and ridiculing Elisa, yet Elisa is the one who's your shining light. Despite *all you have thrown at her*, she is rising like a phoenix from the ashes."

"She always does," said Éiriú, dismissively.

"*Why then* do you *still try to put her down? Can you not* acknowledge her for the woman she will become?"

"*No,* I can't!"

"You're jealous. You're jealous of your own daughter," said Banbha, taking a step back. "You don't want her to outshine you."

The old scarred face grey dragon appeared from the shadows. He walked slowly towards them and then stood in the centre of the courtyard.

"Elisa will shine. I do believe that now, and I don't think it is too late for her. Jamie too will find his way. But, these children are not the reason you entered Kapheus, Éiriú. Are they?" he asked.

"No."

"Who told you?" the old dragon asked.

"No one needed to tell me. Every mother will recognise her own child."

"He has your colour, that's for sure," said the old dragon.

At that moment all the memories flashed through Banbha's mind connecting up the dots. The lost dragon egg of Kapheus stolen by Carman, given to Elisa, the newly appointed goddess of Éire and rightful heiress, the hatching was only complete with the final stone from Fódla, the deceased goddess of Éire, Méabh would not rear him, because she said that his mother still lived.

"Geaspar is your *son!*" Banbha exclaimed. Éiriú nodded. "A Dhia! Geaspar is *your son!*" Banbha repeated.

"Saying it over and over again won't change it," said Éiriú.

Banbha walked over and back along the courtyard trying to work this out in her own mind but couldn't.

"Where is he now?" Éiriú asked.

"He's with Elisa in La Petite Maison Le Fèvre. She's been carrying him in her satchel. He clings either to her teddy bear or to her all day long," Banbha said.

"Has Geaspar eaten?"

"He's a full belly. Everyone feeds him. Even Feehul bathed Geaspar last night and gave him a full belly of food," said Banbha. "You've so many who want to help," Banbha said.

Banbha couldn't stay next to her sister any longer and she withdrew from the courtyard. She stood high on her two hind legs, spread her wings and took flight. Éiriú watched Banbha leave and didn't know what to do.

"She'll be back," said the old dragon.

Banbha flew from the island and along the coastline until she finally came to rest on the Blascaoidí, the very place where she had helped rescue Deucalion. She sat on the marram grass and thought.

"A penny for them," said Turlough.

"I didn't know you were still here," said Banbha.

"I never left… I don't think I could find my way back to the woods now even if I wanted to."

Banbha looked out to sea. The water was dark and calm in comparison to her mind that was being ravaged by her thoughts.

"Spill," said Turlough.

"The problem with me telling you this is that once told I'll have to take you with me back to the woods of Kapheus. I couldn't leave you here with your links to pirates."

"No one can be trusted these days," said Turlough. "You know just the other day elves and a green dragon came here and stole *my unicorn. Could you believe that?*" he said.

Turlough then looked at Banbha peculiarly. He tracked her scales all the way to her tail, and then looked at her face.

"You're a green dragon," he said.

"Yes, and I'm the green dragon who helped free the unicorn."

"Well, *isn't that a good one,*" said Turlough.

Banbha nodded. Silence returned and they both sat looking at the sea.

"I've often thought of dragons. I wonder if dragons often think of elves," said Turlough.

"They do," Banbha replied, "but I doubt in the same way."

"I think I'd like to eat a dragon."

"You wouldn't. You're an elf and elves don't eat dragons."

"Is that what I am? *Isn't that a good one,*" said Turlough. "I only told my legs this morning that they were looking quite thin," he said, rubbing his cold and thin legs.

"Maybe this wasn't a good idea," said Banbha, looking back in the direction in which she came.

"Ideas never are," said Turlough.

Banbha raised herself high on her hind legs, spread her wings and took to the sky. She snatched Turlough on her way and carried him with her back to Éiriú. It wasn't long before Banbha gently placed her feet upon the courtyard. She gently dropped Turlough from her mouth.

"Thank you. I have to say that was a fascinating visit to the sea," he said. "Am I home now?" Turlough asked.

"Nearly," said Banbha.

"I'm not going to ask," Éiriú said.

"It's best not to."

"I'll leave you to it," said the old dragon and he left the courtyard. "Geaspar can't be reared in Éire. You're a woman there, and he needs his mother. Your husband is in Éire. I've been mulling this over in my head, but I can't find a solution," said Banbha. "If you come to Kapheus then you can rear him. He *is* the dragon for all the ages. He needs to be reared in the way of the dragons. But then, you are a dragon here and I don't think your other children recognise you. They will lose their mother if you stay here. But if you stay then Elisa will become a dragon when she comes of age. She is a goddess of Éire. Jamie will not. Cathal will lose his wife and you will lose both your son and your husband," said Banbha, trying to work out the best solution.

The more Banbha spoke the more despairing Éiriú became. She felt completely trapped by her circumstances. There seemed to be no way out.

"Oh, *I like riddles myself,*" said Turlough. "I can say on this occasion that I have the solution. *I do love* a riddle," he said.

Both Éiriú and Banbha looked at him. Turlough danced a gig in front of them and muttered something to himself. He smiled widely in the delight of his intellectual prowess.

"*And the solution is…*" Turlough said. The dragons waited. "And the solution is Banbha you will rear Geaspar and you being a goddess of Éire will be perfectly attuned to the needs of this dragon. You, Éiriú will return to Éire and rear your son in the way of people and when Elisa's time comes to decide, she will do so by her own free will," Turlough said and danced another gig. "Your husband will have his wife and you will leave and return to

Kapheus when he reaches old age and dies for you will not age the way he will and that is my solution. You will be here to rear Geaspar as a mother before long. *Time is relative.*"

The feeling of relief that came over Éiriú and Banbha was incalculable. An elf, whose mind had almost abandoned him, had spoken with the most clarity and had found the solution to a problem that had plagued Éiriú since before Geaspar was even born. The sleepless nights and the days filled with troubled thoughts were behind her.

"Will you do it?" Éiriú asked.

"The dragon will never be mine. I'll love him as a mother, but you'll take him with you whenever you decide. He'll never be mine. I don't think I can do that. *What* if something happens to him? Look at what happened to Fódla," Banbha replied, becoming more distressed with every word she spoke.

"Ní bhíonn in aon rud ach seal," said Turlough, stepping closer to offer his support.

"Sorry, Turlough?" Banbha asked.

"I said nothing lasts forever. Ní bhíonn in aon rud ach seal."

Banbha thought for a moment and took a deep breath before speaking.

"Alright, I'll do it," she said.

Banbha snatched Turlough from the courtyard and brought him across the sea to the woods of Kapheus. She gently placed her feet on the floor of the wood and dropped Turlough.

"This is my home, you know. This is where I was born," said Turlough.

"And this is where you will live," said Cillian.

"Hello. My name is Turlough."

The elves gathered around. Some brought clothes for him to wear while others saw his emaciated body and prepared food.

"Turlough will be cared for here, Banbha," said Cillian. "Where is Éiriú?"

"I don't know… On the island," Banbha said, distracted.

With that the great white dragon was seen flying over the woods of Kapheus and into the meadow. Éiriú flew across the meadow to the hills until she landed outside La Petite Maison Le Fèvre. Rós opened the door.

"I'd like to see Geaspar," Éiriú said.

In their home in Éire, Cathal poured the batter onto the frying pan and searched for the honey.

"*What are you looking at?*" Jamie snapped.

Cathal heard Jamie. He lowered the heat on the frying pan. Cathal then stood in the doorway between the kitchen and living room and without saying a word watched his son's interactions.

"I'm wondering what you have in your bag," Lugh said.

"*It's none of your business,*" Jamie retorted.

"Why are you so angry?" Lugh asked. "After all you're the one who has committed the crime."

Cathal eagerly awaited the answer to this question. He wondered what crime his son had committed and what had brought on Jamie's poor behaviour.

"It's because *of you*, because *of all of you*. I spent *all day and all night* looking for it. *I* had the *map* and *it's mine.*"

"*You think* you have the *right to something*, because you have *a map.* Do *you think* you have a right to *everything* I have too, because you're *my son?*" Cathal asked.

"Yeah!" Jamie snapped.

"I've worked hard for everything I have. I've sacrificed, *I have scrimped and saved! I've fought hard* to build this home and to raise you and Elisa, and *you think* you're entitled to have it all," Cathal said, furiously.

Cathal returned to the pan tossed the pancake and then placed it on a plate. He added blueberries and honey and brought the plate to the table and placed it in front of Lugh.

"You must think I'm an awful fool. *Go out* to the loft *and take down* what you're hiding up there."

Jamie looked shocked.

"It's mine!" he remonstrated.

"*I'll decide* whose it is. *Bring it here...*" he said, looking at the clock, "you have one minute to go out there, get it, and bring it back in here before I go out there after you."

Jamie ran outside and into the shed. Lugh sat at the table salivating. He had never known that pancakes could have had such a wonderful combination. Blueberries were something that were rarely seen and honey, sweet honey.

"Eat up," said Cathal.

Lugh didn't need to be told twice.

Jamie climbed onto the loft and reached to the very back bale of straw. He pulled out his gold and silver helmet and took one final adoring look at it. He polished the metal with the sleeve of his jacket and with a heavy heart made his way down the ladder and outside.

Cathal watched the second hand on the clock. There were only five seconds left before Jamie was due to arrive through the front door. He remained fixated on it for the final five seconds and just at the minute strike, Jamie ran into the house to his father. He handed Cathal the helmet.

Lugh couldn't help but look. This situation between father and son was becoming more interesting by the minute. He ate another forkful of pancake while he watched.

"*Where did you get this?*" Cathal quizzed.

"In Elisa's room."

"And *what was it doing* in *Elisa's room?*" Cathal asked. He looked at the helmet and marvelled at its beauty. "This is *real* gold and silver!"

"I know," said Jamie, feeling very disgruntled.

Lugh thought he'd enjoy his breakfast as much as he enjoyed this moment. He added another few blueberries from the bowl in front of him onto his plate.

"Do you have anything else you'd like to show me?" Cathal asked. Jamie shook his head. "*Now,* Jamie!"

Jamie pulled the zip down on the front pouch of his school bag and reached inside.

"*I haven't all day*, Jamie."

Jamie pulled out a very large gemstone. It was so large that he needed to hold it with both hands. It was a rich red colour and was mesmerising. Lugh was happily eating his pancake at this time, and just for a second looked up as a matter of interest. He almost choked when he saw the gemstone in Jamie's hand.

"I suppose you know who owns this," Cathal said. He placed his hand on his head, knowing the value of this stone was a million times more than all he possessed, and his son had stolen it.

"It belongs to Éiriú and Banbha."

"And the helmet?"

"That's Caoilte's," Lugh said.

"How much is this stone worth?" Cathal asked.

"That's a blood diamond. It's the most expensive gemstone in the world."

"*What?*" Cathal asked. "*Where did you get it?*"

Jamie didn't reply. Cathal shook his head. He sat down at the table.

"You cannot put a price on this stone," Lugh said. "It is the most valuable in all the world."

"And my son stole it," Cathal said in utter disappointment. He put his hand to his head. "Do *you* *know* what this *means?*" he asked Jamie. Jamie stood there unable to speak. "*Your life is over* if anyone finds out that *you've stolen* this!"

"Dad," Jamie said, but Cathal shook his head.

"Give the stone to Lugh," Cathal said. Jamie handed Lugh the red diamond. "Lugh, is there any possibility that you can return this to Éiriú and Banbha?"

"Yes," said Lugh.

"*And the helmet,* Jamie." Jamie handed Lugh the helmet.

"Lugh could you take both of these back to their rightful owners?" With a heavy heart, Cathal lifted his body from the chair. "Please convey to them my deepest apology for my son's behaviour." Cathal walked to the kitchen. "Jamie, you'll need to go with him… You need to take responsibility for what you've done. Your fate is in their hands. I can do nothing for you," Cathal said.

"*Dad.*"

"You'll need to eat a pancake before you leave," he said, unable to look at his son.

Far away in Fodar, Caoilte walked along the parade of elfin soldiers. Every now and then he stopped to stand in front of the elfin soldier and look carefully into his eyes. If he saw in that elf's eyes all he needed, then Caoilte tapped him or her on the shoulder. The soldier was allowed to leave the parade to choose weaponry.

"You have a wife," Caoilte said.

"Yes, but she isn't a warrior," the soldier said.

"And a child?" Caoilte asked.

"Yes, but..."

"*But what?*" Caoilte shouted. "Are *you telling me* that you are willing to commit *treason!*"

"*No, no,*" the elf replied in fear for his life.

"I'll take them. The boy can carry the dragon eggs and your wife can care for the hatchlings... Am I making *myself clear?*" Caoilte asked.

"Yes."

"*Yes what?*"

"Yes, sir," said the elf, shaking.

"Anyone else who does not do *as I say* will be trialled for treason!" he shouted.

Dara stood at the boundary between the two worlds to wait for Jamie and Lugh as instructed by Grandmother Oak. While he was waiting for them he watched the dragons fly over and back from the bog to the meadow and the hills carrying gold and silver armoury to the elves. He watched as the elves emptied the large sacks on the ground. The armoury was distributed in the flash of an eye and then the empty sacks were handed back to the dragons to refill. Dara counted eight drop-off points in all. He scanned the hills and the valley to see if he missed one.

"One...two... three.... *Argh! What's that?*" he asked.

Dara looked again and saw a flash of light in the northern hills. He scanned the meadow and the hills again to see who received the signal.

"*Leprechauns,*" he said. "*What* do *they* want?"

The light flashed again. Dara looked over his shoulder for a second distracted by seeing Lugh cross the boundary into Kapheus with Jamie. Dara returned his attention to the flash in the hills.

"It's not yet eleven o'clock," Lugh said, "we have time to return these."

Seeing that Dara was uninterested in them, Lugh thought to track Dara's line of vision. He stood in front of the dragon to get a better look.

"Do you *see it?*" Dara asked.

"Yeah, I do," said Lugh. He hurried to climb up on Dara and pulled Jamie's arm to help him up.

"I don't think I can go anywhere without my Dad knowing first," Dara said.

"Call him. He'll need to know about this," said Lugh, "but call him in your heart. Don't screech."

Ogma appeared over the hills and swiftly made his way to Dara.

"Dad, there's something flashing in the hills. I saw a leprechaun on the other side picking up the message," Dara said.

"Come with me," said Ogma, "we'll check this out together."

"Umm… Ogma. I don't think it's wise for us to go with you. I've the blood diamond."

Ogma called from his heart and Banbha and Méabh appeared. They flew to La Petite Maison Le Fèvre together with Ogma leading the way followed directly behind by Dara flanked on either side by his mother and Banbha. They landed on the earth in front of La Petite Maison Le Fèvre.

"Éiriú, we have a serious problem," Ogma said.

Elisa came to the door of the cottage. She was delighted to see Jamie.

"I was *so* worried about you, Jamie. I thought something might have happened," she said. "*Where were* you? *Why* didn't you come back?"

"Oh, Elisa," Jamie said, dismissively.

Éiriú looked at Jamie and then looked away. Her anger was too great and she feared that if she opened her mouth to speak to him that she would not be able to contain herself.

"What's the problem?" she asked Ogma.

Lugh lifted the flap of his satchel and Éiriú looked inside.

"*You stole* my *mother's heart!*" she roared.

The ground shook beneath them and Jamie fell over. All those inside La Petite Maison Le Fèvre came outside. The robin flew to the window ledge and then transmuted into Éataín.

"Did you feel that rumble?" Caoilte asked. He gazed across the skyline in the direction of Kapheus.

"No," said the guard, holding the wicket door.

Caoilte stepped onto the street again. He stood for a while watching the sky, but there were no other signs coming from Kapheus. He sighed and crossed the street towards his home again. He stopped to watch the children playing marbles on the street. The young elf raised his hands in delight to a loud cheer. Caoilte smiled and walked on. He saw the children playing hula hoop farther up the street and caught a wandering ball flying through the air. He kicked it back up the street before crossing over to the courtyard.

Outside La Petite Maison Le Fèvre, they watched and waited like a jury waiting for the defendant to proclaim his innocence and refute his involvement in a crime. Elisa stood close to Jamie in case he needed her support. However, when she stood shoulder to shoulder with him, he pushed her away with his elbow. Banbha looked at Éiriú and saw the pain in her eyes. She then looked at Jamie and wondered how he could stand so defiantly, knowing that he was in so much trouble.

"*How?*" Rós asked. "You could *never* have found that on your own," she said.

"The unicorn foal led me to it."

"But Prometheus is in the dreamtime now," said Éataín.

"I was looking for the treasure. I had *my map* and *Prometheus kept standing in front* of me. He showed me where the diamond was," said Jamie. "Can I have it?" he asked, enthusiastically.

"Bad move, Jamie," Elisa whispered.

Dara wanted out of there and he wanted out of there fast. He knew that this wasn't going to end well for Jamie, and Éiriú frightened him.

"*Dad*, what about the leprechauns?" Dara asked.

"Yes, we must go," Ogma said, and he and Dara left.

Jamie was face-to-face with Éiriú, who by now had done enough to contain her anger sufficiently to speak.

"What level of *stupidity* exists inside *that mind of yours?"* Éiriú remarked. *"I told you* that was *my mother's heart.* You have no right to it!"

"But goddesses go all the way to their ancestors," said Jamie, "Fódla did."

"Everyone leaves something of themselves behind when they die. Sometimes their legacy is left in their children, sometimes it's left in the earth," Méabh said. "For Ernmas, it was her heart. It was left as a reminder to us all that she gave her heart to her children, to this land, and to all those she met. In the end, she gave her heart to Kapheus."

"Well, *I'm* the *leader of the dragons,* and if I say *I want it,* then *I can have it!"* Jamie retorted.

"Take it," Banbha said. "Take my mother's heart from Lugh's satchel," she said.

Lugh couldn't believe his ears. He looked at Banbha to be fully sure that this was what she wanted, and then he opened the flap of his satchel. Jamie reached in for the red diamond. He held it in his hands and smiled gleefully.

"It's blood red," said Méabh.

Jamie looked at the diamond and saw something beating inside it. He saw blood flow. The beating grew stronger with every second that passed until Jamie's hands began to turn blood red as the blood leaked from the cracks in the diamond onto his hands and dripped down onto his boots. Within another few seconds he held a beating live heart in his hands with no trace of a diamond left.

"Make it stop!" Jamie shouted. "Elisa, make it stop! Elisa!"

Jamie dropped the heart from his hands when Elisa reached out her hands to help him. Elisa quickly saved the heart from falling onto the grass but came tumbling onto the ground herself. Elisa pulled the heart close to her chest, to prevent it being damaged in the fall.

"I'm sorry Banbha! I didn't drop it!" she insisted, doing her utmost to preserve Banbha's mother's heart. Elisa held on tightly to the heart and pulled herself to her feet. "I'm sorry Banbha. I'm sorry about your mother's heart. I hope it's alright," she said, reaching

out her hands to give it to her. *"I'm really sorry,"* Elisa repeated as
she felt the heart grow still. *"I didn't mean to..."*
"You did nothing wrong," said Éataín. "The heart grows still,
because it's returning to the form of a diamond."
Elisa looked at Éataín and then looked down at the heart and saw
it harden and return to diamond.
"My mother's heart bled for you, Jamie," said Éiriú.
"Could someone tell me what that means?" Setanta asked.
"A mother or father's heart bleeds with overwhelming sorrow. It
happens when their child dies in life or to the life their parents had
hoped they'd lead," said Lugh.
"I hope my Mam doesn't feel like that, Lugh," said Setanta. "I'd
feel awful if she felt like that. Do you think my Mam feels like that
Éataín? I've *a lot* of sliotars. She'd probably *kill me* if she knew I
spent *all my money* on sliotars."
"It wasn't your money. It was *our* money and we made that decision
for you," said Banbha. "Your mother knows you're a good lad,"
said Éataín, and she smiled.
Jamie thought about what Éiriú said. Maybe if he gave the stone to
Elisa to sell in Kapheus or Éire then she'd be able to get the money
for him. Banbha struck him with her tail and knocked him to the
ground.
"Jamie, you can have the blood diamond the day it doesn't bleed
for you," said Éiriú. "By then you won't want it."
Elisa left the company of the others and signalled to Iolar in the
hills. The golden eagle took flight and glided above the valley
before landing close to La Petite Maison Le Fèvre.
"Elisa, where are you going?" Jamie asked, but Elisa didn't reply.
Iolar lifted her high above the valley and flew through the meadow.

Cathal sat alone in the living room that morning. He lifted his cup
to his mouth and hadn't the heart to drink his tea. He pushed his
breakfast plate away from him. The only sound in the house was
from the Grandfather Clock as its pendulum swung over and back
to tick tock. A sound that always gave Cathal a feeling of safety and
stability now irritated him. He couldn't take any more of it. He
stood up to put on his coat and boots at the door, but a thought

crossed his mind. He rested his hand on the banister post and looked upstairs.

"He found it in *Elisa's room*," Cathal thought.

Cathal walked upstairs to Elisa's room. He stood outside for a moment battling with his thoughts and then he slowly turned the handle on Elisa's door and stepped inside. Cathal didn't know what he was looking for, but he had to find out if there were any other pieces of gold and silver in Elisa's room. He opened the large wardrobe and searched through the clothes. He then reached to the top of the wardrobe and skimmed his hand along the surface. Cathal laid down on the floor and looked beneath the wardrobe. There was nothing there. He looked under Elisa's bed and nothing. "Elisa has never stolen anything in her life," he said, sitting on her bed.

He glanced over his shoulder to the drawing and turned back again. He sat still for a second. Something had caught his eye in that brief backward glance. He looked again at the drawing and then turned around. He stood directly in front of it now.

"Wolves," he said.

Joachim raced through the meadow at top speed while Cathal stood frozen to the spot watching the pack of wolves run towards him. With each stride they took they seemed to gain more momentum in Cathal's mind. He tried to shake himself from his dream state. He dared to reach out his hand.

"They couldn't be moving," he said.

He felt the breeze from the meadow and the sounds of the birds in flight. Cathal looked to see if the room window was open but it wasn't. He turned back again and reached out his hand to touch the drawing. The chalk felt dusty to his fingers. He looked at his finger tips and rubbed his thumb along them, but there was no chalk, no dust, not even remnants of colour. Cathal reached out his hand to touch the drawing again and he could feel the breeze touch the palm of his hand. He reached in a little farther. The tips of his fingers were lost to the drawing.

Suddenly, he heard a wild and ferocious roar. Joachim rose high from the meadow and dived on Cathal as Cathal passed his hand through the boundary between the two worlds. Cathal landed heavily on the bedroom with Joachim pinning him to the ground. The black wolf snarled and clapped his jaws.

"Of all the days in your lifetime, *this is not* the one to enter Kapheus!" Joachim said.

"You… you *can talk*," Cathal said. He passed out on the bedroom floor.

Joachim dragged Cathal from the room to the stairs.

"Let me help," said Davin, lifting him up.

Davin carried Cathal as best he could downstairs to the living room. Cathal mumbled something and then grew silent again.

"You'll be alright. You had a bit of a fright that's all," said Davin, dropping Cathal into the armchair. "He'll be alright Joachim," he said, walking upstairs and into Elisa's room. The door shut behind him.

Chapter 15

The Heart of Ernmas

Elisa dropped to the woodland floor in front of Grandmother Oak. A short distance away, Mother Badger tidied the clothes on Turlough and then combed her claws through his hair while the elf sat eating. When she looked to see what the disturbance was, she saw Iolar land on the tree branch. She turned away, but then something caught her eye and when she looked again, she saw Elisa and wondered why she was in the woodland.

"Grandmother Oak!" Elisa called.

"Yes, Elisa."

"Grandmother Oak, I don't want anyone to die," Elisa said. Elisa reached out and hugged her bark. "I don't want anyone to die," she cried.

"Who's going to die?" Grandmother Oak asked.

"The elves and the wolves and the…"

Mother Badger slowly made her way to the bark of Grandmother Oak always fearful of the golden eagle. She saw the child upset and as a mother she longed to comfort her. Cillian too had seen this unusual scene and curiosity got the better of him. He met with Mother Badger and they both walked to the base of the oak tree. He nodded to Iolar, and the eagle then knew the badger would not be on her dinner plate on that particular day.

"My dear Elisa," said Mother Badger. "Why are you so upset?"

Elisa sat at the base of Grandmother Oak. Her heart was torn. She took a deep breath and tried her best to speak.

"I don't want any heart to bleed," Elisa said.

"My dear Elisa," said Mother Badger, comforting her. "Hearts bleed every day. It's out of your control." Mother Badger brushed the hair from Elisa's face and wiped her tears away. "Hearts bleed every day, my dear Elisa."

"There's a battle coming," said Elisa. "So many will die," she said. Éiriú gently placed her feet on the dragon nest atop Grandmother Oak's branches and looked down. The elves and all the animals and birds heard what Elisa said and silence fell upon the Kaphiens as their thoughts flew to those they loved. Mother Badger looked across the woodland at her family caring for Turlough. She saw their playfulness as the elf happily chased them around in circles in an attempt to retrieve his cap. Mother Badger looked at Cillian. She saw his ashen face and then looked at Iolar, the mighty predator, shaking in fear on the tree branch.

"I hope that everyone will be safe," said Grandmother Oak.

"They won't by virtue of the fact that it is a battle," a voice said from beneath a pile of leaves. Jeremiah's nose appeared from his hibernaculum. He sniffed the air and then stepped out. "Good morning," he said to Elisa. "It's been a long winter."

Elisa was delighted to see Jeremiah. She had longed to tell him everything that had been happening in her life, but he was so far away in the woods and then when she did reach him, he was equally as far away in the dreamtime. Jeremiah climbed onto Elisa's lap.

"You know Elisa, war doesn't always have to take place. You are the goddess of Éire now. You have power, and this is the time of fire."

Elisa looked at Jeremiah and hoped more than anything else in the world that he would be able to save everyone.

"Fire brings everything into the light. No matter how dark, fire will shine its light on it," said Jeremiah. "Please lift me up. I would like to look into your eyes, Elisa," he said. Elisa lifted Jeremiah. "Elisa, fire will shine a light on everything, but unless your eyes are open, you won't see it," he said.

Cillian sat down beside them. He earnestly wanted to learn from Jeremiah and listened carefully to every word.

"You need to be open and honest. That's what fire asks of you. Be honest and straight with everyone you meet, so that nothing is lost to the darkness of people's thoughts."

"What d'ya mean?" Elisa asked.

"Don't leave anything open to interpretation or misinterpretation for that matter."

Jeremiah then thought for a little while. He wondered how he'd be able to explain this to Elisa. It was such a complex thought for someone so young.

"Elisa, you don't know what is going on in another person's mind or life. You don't always know their challenges and their pain.

When you're honest about your thoughts and feelings then you
bring fire to your life. You open up your whole life to wonderful
possibilities," Jeremiah said.

Jeremiah looked at Elisa's blank face and struggled to explain
clearly what he meant.

"Have you learned from the ancient texts? Did Kubera teach you?
I've been asleep for so long..." he said.

"Yes," said Elisa.

"Oh, fantastic. Then you know that war is not inevitable. You
know that when we speak openly about our experiences, our
thoughts and our feelings that we allow the other person to do the
same. It doesn't have to lead to a fight, a battle or war," Jeremiah
said. Elisa nodded.

"Who's leading this battle, Grandmother Oak?" Jeremiah asked.

"Caoilte," she replied.

Jeremiah fell from Elisa's hands. He curled into a tight ball before
he landed onto the ground. He quickly gathered himself and
uncurled.

"*Caoilte's time has come?*" he asked in a mixture of surprise and
horror.

"Yes," said Grandmother Oak.

"I've been asleep *far too long,*" Jeremiah said, climbing back onto
Elisa's lap.

"Caoilte is not who you think he is, Elisa. Speak to him and work
together to change everything. Bring all the power and fire that is
in your belly to this battle tonight. Rise up and be all you were born
to be. Be the goddess of Éire! You don't need to fear what is to
come. You need to celebrate it! Kapheus will lead the way if you
stay open and honest in everything you do," Jeremiah said.

"*Did you hear me?* No tricks! Openness and honesty and Kapheus
will be triumphant. Go now! Go!" he said.

Iolar swooped down and snatched Elisa before she could say
goodbye. Éiriú watched as Elisa was carried back to the meadow,
and when she was safely out of sight, Éiriú placed her feet on the
earth of the woodland.

"It's almost time, Éiriú," said Grandmother Oak.

Jeremiah looked quite confused. He looked at Grandmother Oak and then at Éiriú. He couldn't understand why the great white dragon stood on the woodland floor and not in Éire. Jeremiah looked to Cillian for an explanation, but Cillian didn't offer anything. He knew Mother Badger would tell him.

"Time *for what?*" Jeremiah asked.

"Jamie stole from Kapheus. He stole the gold and silver armoury," Mother Badger explained.

"He stole my mother's heart," said Éiriú, trying her utmost to contain her anger.

"And *what are we doing here?*" Jeremiah asked. "Get it back! *All of Kapheus* depends on the heart of Ernmas!"

Jeremiah frantically searched for the gnomes to help him.

"Reveal yourselves!" he said, looking around but they were not there.

"Éiriú, *what are you doing here?*" he asked.

"*Waiting,*" said Éiriú.

Éiriú looked angrily in the direction of the meadow and with that Jeremiah tracked her gaze and saw Banbha flying towards them. It wasn't long before Banbha came to rest on the woodland soil next to them. Jeremiah watched as Lugh and Jamie climbed down from the dragon.

"I heard that you stole something other than gold and silver," Grandmother Oak said. "I estimate that you could not have stolen this since we last met. Lugh is far too smart to have left you out of his sight," she said. The spirit of the great oak tree stepped out from her bark. "In that case, you must have hidden it from us when we last spoke. Why?"

"Thief!" Mother Badger snapped.

Jamie looked down at his bloodstained boots. It was in Jamie's silence that Éiriú lost patience with him.

"Abair é!" she snapped.

Jamie looked up at her but still refused to speak. He kicked the dirt beneath his feet. He knew he had the upper hand if only for a short while. However, knowing Jamie as well as he did, Jeremiah saw the fire in the boy and saw how he now used it to frustrate those around him.

"I once knew a boy who risked his life to save his sister. I also knew a boy who didn't like that his sister seemed to hold more power than him at times. I recall *here in this wood* on a foggy night that…"

"It's *not* about *Elisa!*" Jamie shouted.

"It seems to me that it is indeed not about Elisa. It's about fire," said Jeremiah.

"What are *you talking* about!"

Jeremiah bowed to Cillian and he bent down and lifted him into his hands. The hedgehog stood face-to-face with Jamie now and looked firmly into his eyes.

"I'm speaking about the time of fire," he said. "Grandmother Oak, I hope you don't mind."

"No, not at all, Jeremiah."

"Jamie, I'm speaking of fire. Fire and power are one in the same," he said. "When the time of fire comes, *and it has*, then a boy has to choose the type of man he becomes."

Jamie rolled his eyes and looked away.

"I understand that you stole the armoury…" Jeremiah said. Jamie had no choice other than to nod in agreement. "And, I also understand that you stole the heart of Ernmas."

"I…"

"You," said Jeremiah.

"The unicorn told me where it was. It's not *my fault*," Jamie remonstrated.

"*Prometheus?*"

"Yeah, *and I wasn't* even looking for it."

"The heart of Ernmas! *Why* would Prometheus lead you to the heart of Ernmas?" Jeremiah questioned.

In those few seconds that Jeremiah tried to find the solution, Turlough became evermore restless. He danced over and back in front of them bursting to tell Jeremiah the answer. Jamie looked at him dismissively.

"*Why* would the young foal do that?" Jeremiah questioned again.

"*Oh*, I know! I know!" said Turlough.

Jeremiah looked at him but could scarcely recognise the elf.

"What's your name?" he asked.

"Turlough."

"*Turlough, is that you*? You've been gone a long time," said Jeremiah. "This is my home, you know."

"You're right. This *is* your home." Jeremiah watched the elf as he anxiously anticipated being asked the unsolvable question. "Tell me, Turlough, *why* did Prometheus lead Jamie to Ernmas' heart?"

"I have it! I have it! I have it!" he proclaimed, dancing a gig.

"I don't know *why we're even listening* to *him*," Jamie retorted.

"I'm Turlough," Turlough said, sadly. He stopped dancing.

His sadness filled the air and Banbha's heart almost broke for him. The elf looked down at his boots and cried.

"You are Turlough and *you* are an elf. *You* are the most valued elf in all of Kapheus at this moment," said Banbha. "*You* tell us the solution."

Éiriú swung her tail and struck Jamie, sweeping his legs from under him. He landed with a thump. Turlough smiled and felt proud. He stood tall and took a breath.

"Prometheus led Jamie to the heart of Ernmas to stop the battle and to save the elves," said Turlough.

Unfortunately, this made no sense to anyone. Cillian removed his hat and scratched his head.

"Elisa must carry the heart into battle. She has the power to stop the battle," said Turlough.

He smiled from ear to ear, revealing a mouth with only a few teeth left. His words made little sense to those gathered but they silently waited until Turlough did make sense.

"You must take the heart to Elisa, *but never touch it*," he said to Jamie.

Lugh lifted the flap of his satchel and Turlough reached for the diamond. Turlough removed his jacket. He laid the blood diamond on it and pulled off his shirt. He then wrapped the heart of Ernmas in his shirt.

"You must carry it in leather or linen, but no other material. You must do that," Turlough said to Jamie, handing the diamond back to him. "Your hands must not touch this or it will bleed," he said. Turlough held Jamie's hands and looked deep into his eyes for a few seconds.

"You've allowed fire to lure you into its illusion," Turlough said. "Out of the worst times often the best times come."

Turlough's words spoke the truth more clearly than anyone else. Jamie felt his words touch his heart and the tears rolled down Jamie's cheeks.

"You're sad," Turlough said. Jamie nodded.

"Are you sad, because you lost?"

Jamie shook his head.

"Then you must be sad,", said Turlough, looking inquisitively at Jamie's tears, "because you made a mistake?" Jamie nodded. "I've made a million myself," Turlough said, nonchalantly. "You must right the wrong. Right the wrong. Right the wrong. *That's* what you must do."

Turlough scratched his head. He knew he had seen leather some place. He looked around and Lugh reached out his hand to offer him his leather satchel. Turlough shook his head. He ran from them to get his own mix match of leather skins he had stitched together and worn like a dress for so long. He soon returned to Jamie.

"Please make a satchel from my cloth?" he asked.

"I don't know how," Jamie said, wiping away his tears.

"This is the redress for your crime. Cillian will show you and you'll carry the heart of Ernmas into battle," said Grandmother Oak.

Jamie looked down at the worn piece of cloth that had clothed Turlough for so many years.

"Jamie, to be given a satchel in Kapheus is a very significant event. Elves receive a satchel when they come of age. It's theirs for their lifetime. It's a sacred thing," Éiriú said. "You've been given a monumental gift. Appreciate it."

"Go raibh maith agat," Jamie said. "Thank you, Turlough."

"Come with me," Cillian said, putting his arm on Jamie's shoulder. They walked to his shelter to get the tools needed to make the leather satchel. Turlough smiled gleefully.

"Turlough is ainm dom," he told Lugh.

"Agus Lugh is ainm domsa," Lugh responded. "Would you like me to find you another shirt?"

"Yes please."

The two elves walked together through the woods as close to each other as the best of friends.

"Sometimes we don't need to fight," Banbha said to Éiriú.

A distance away, Ogma and Dara crouched down on the eastern hills and watched closely as the signal flashed across the valley.

"Are you ready?" Ogma whispered.

"Yeah," said Dara.

"Then let's see how fast you can fly."

Ogma and Dara took flight and sped through the valley. They swooped down, snatched the two leprechauns from the opposite hills and carried them to the centre of the meadow.

"Explain yourselves!" Ogma demanded.

The black warrior dragon breathed heavily and the warm air from his nostrils blew the hair on the leprechaun's head. The leprechaun crawled backward along the grass.

"There's no point in trying to run. *I will catch you* and *I will tear you to pieces.*"

"He didn't do anything!" the other leprechaun shouted.

"*What?*"

"He didn't do anything," he said, quivering.

"What were you doing in the hills?" Ogma asked. He placed his foot on the leprechaun's chest. Ogma gripped his talons and they tore into the leprechaun's clothes.

"We were only trying… we were only trying to…"

"*What?*" Ogma spread his wing and knocked the other leprechaun over as he tried to run. "You were only trying to *what?*"

"*Steal,*" the leprechaun said. He closed his eyes tightly and tried to defend himself with his arms.

"*Steal what?*" Ogma yelled.

"We thought that when they die, we'll take their armoury… My friend has sacks left under the heather bushes," he said, pointing, "and I've a few between those rocks," he said.

"Get up!" Ogma shouted. "*Be on your way.*"

The leprechauns scrambled to their feet and ran.

"*Dad*, are you *not* going to do anything about it?" Dara asked.

"No. Armoury is no good to an elf when he's dead. They only want to add to their pile of treasure," he said, watching them run away. "They're not plotting against us."

"But they're not fighting *with us* either," an elf said, walking by. He carried armoury in his arms and struggled to manage its weight. "Do you need my help?" Ogma asked.

"I have to carry it to the dummy point. Thank you," he said.

"Dara, I'll stay here for a while. Will you go to La Petite Maison Le Fèvre to see if Elisa needs help?"

"Yeah," Dara said, and he was gone.

Elisa poured sliotars from the sack into the shallow depression on the ground while Setanta looked for another good vantage point.

"Elisa, we can hide my sliotars over there and probably try there too," Setanta said, pointing.

He covered the sliotars with a thin layer of soil and grass and lifted the sack. They walked towards the next location.

"It'll be alright you know, Elisa. Your plan is really good. I'll be able to knock the helmets off the dragons and Grandmother Oak *will* call them."

"It's not my plan *at all*. I don't know the best spots for you and how fast you can run... Without you, I couldn't do this," Elisa said.

"Together we're strong, eh, Elisa," Setanta said, nudging her. They both laughed.

Cathal walked over and back along the living room floor thinking about the wolf and the world beyond the chalk drawing on Elisa's wall. He scratched his head. Cathal then decided that the only rational thing for him to do was to make a cup of tea, and so he walked into the kitchen. He opened the tin on the worktop and saw that the tea leaves were all gone and snapped the tin shut again. "Tea leaves," he said.

He reached up to the press and opened the door. His hand searched through boxes and packets until he eventually found the box of tea leaves at the back of the press. He pulled it out, but as he did, he knocked over a bag of flour. The bag flew through the air, desperately being chased down by Cathal, but despite all his effort to catch it the bag of flour burst open on the floor. Cathal hurriedly bent down to clean the mess. His hands touched the flour and he remembered. He brushed his thumb across his fingertips. "*The chalk,*" he whispered.

Cathal rubbed his hands into the flour on the floor and observed them turn snow white. In an almost trance like state, Cathal left the kitchen and walked upstairs to Elisa's room. With each step he took on the stairs he remembered a little more about the drawing on Elisa's wall and the possible world beyond it.

"Cathal!" Danú called. Cathal looked around. "I'd love a cup of tea," Danú said, closing the front door behind her. "How are you all keeping?" she asked. Cathal looked at Danú and then looked down at his hands. "Have you seen a ghost?"

"No. I… a wolf," he said.

"You must've been dreaming. There are no wolves in Éire. God be with the days when they roamed freely on this fair isle," she said, removing her scarf. "A cup of tea?" Danú asked. Cathal walked downstairs. "Aren't the lambs *lovely*? I saw a few in the fields on my way up here," Danú said.

Ruan, the elf who always took his responsibilities very seriously, piled his favourite childhood toys into his sack while Lir watched. He shook the rattle with its slip handle and bubble top one last time and recalled with fondness the times he dangled it over Lir in the cradle.

"Here Ruan," Lir said, handing him his own toys.

"Do you think we could get any more?"

Those words were no sooner spoken than small toys dropped from the sky and landed on them. They crouched down and covered their heads until the rain of toys finally ended.

"Do you have enough?" Méabh asked.

"Plenty!" Ruan replied.

He stood up and looked at the array of wooden toys decorating the woodland floor. It was like Christmas day in the woodland. He lifted the wooden rattle seahorse and shook the rings along its long, curved tail. He passed his hand over its beautifully carved head that gracefully bent downward as if bowing to him. There was so much work to do and Ruan knew he really didn't have the time for reminiscing. Ruan put the rattle into the sack and then picked up another. He rolled the wooden ball in the centre of the squirrel rattle.

"Go raibh maith agat," he said, looking up.

"You'll need another couple of sacks," Méabh said, and tossed them down onto the woodland floor.

Lir sat playing with a wooden clapper in the shape of three rabbit heads that knocked together with a clapping sound. He laughed out loud.

"Lir, into the sack with it," Ruan said. "We haven't much time to get this done."

Danú placed the cup of tea on the table next to Cathal who remained fixated on his flour covered hands.

"You look troubled," Danú said.

"Umm... do you think that drawing can move?" Cathal asked.

"*Move?*" Danú asked, sitting next to him. "Now, *where* would it be moving to?"

"*No.* Do you think there is something inside the drawing?"

"Like what?"

"I saw a pack of wolves. They were coming right at me," he said.

Cathal's hand began to shake and he spilled tea on his clothes. He placed his cup back down on the saucer. When he looked up, he saw Danú looking peculiarly at him. He tried to gather his thoughts and attempted to construct a clear sentence.

"I saw my hand go right through the drawing," he said, reaching out his hand. "It went right through and then... I saw it."

"What did you see?"

"*A wolf.*"

"*A wolf?*"

"A *wolf*," said Cathal, looking directly into Danú's eyes. Danú looked strangely at Cathal.

"And did it *eat you?*" she asked.

"No! If it had *eaten me* I wouldn't be here!"

"Well, thank goodness for that," said Danú. "I was beginning to worry." Danú brushed the crumbs from her skirt and returned to drinking her cup of tea. "You haven't touched your scone," she said.

Cathal was more confused than ever. The wolf raced towards him, pulled him down and pinned him to the floor, but didn't eat him. He thought that *maybe* he dreamt it. Maybe Danú was right. He was asleep on the armchair after all and there was no one in the house when he woke.

"I need to wash my hands," he said, standing up.

"Good idea," said Danú, "will you bring me a cloth on your way back. I'm dropping crumbs everywhere."

As the night drew in, the elves grew anxious. They huddled together at campfires in the meadow and looked at their family and friends, holding on tightly to the moment and the memory as if it would be their last time seeing each other in this world. Jamie walked through the crowd and sat next to Elisa. There were no words needed. Elisa loved her brother and she could see that he was sorry. They both sat together watching the sunset, and then they saw the guardians fly from the island and pass over the land of Kapheus. To anyone who didn't know, Kapheus seemed to be completely unaware of the fate that was about to befall it. Caoilte stood on the eastern hilltop and watched the guardians fly overhead. It had always been his desire to fly on a dragon's back, and in this lifetime, he had achieved that. There was nothing that brought him more joy than to fly high above the earth. Caoilte watched the guardians until they disappeared from sight before his attention returned to the home he once knew and the elves with whom he shared his youth.

'Sing to them,' Grandmother Oak whispered to Sinann.

Sinann stood by the bank of the river and sang the song of Éire. The elves listened to her sing the first verse and in unison they joined her in the chorus. The song lifted their spirits, and if only for a short while, they forgot about the battle that was about to commence. Elisa stood up and walked between them with Jamie by her side. Jamie grew scared for what was to come when he saw the faces of the elves, and sensing this, Elisa held his hand.

'Let them feel your courage,' Grandmother Oak whispered to Jamie. 'You *are* their leader.'

"Jamie," Banbha called. "Your time has come. Lead us in this battle."

Jamie looked up to see Banbha waiting. He gulped. He didn't know how he would do this.

"I'll see you on the other side," Elisa said, giving him a hug.

"Elisa, I'm sorry," Jamie said.

"I know."

Banbha snatched Jamie and tossed him onto her back and they left in the direction of the woodland. Elisa was on her own again. She scanned the whole meadow and saw the faces of elves, gnomes and leprechauns alike looking to her to save them. She looked up to the eastern hills and it was then that she saw Caoilte. Elisa sang, and with each note she sang, her voice grew stronger, and in that time, she remained focussed on Caoilte high in the hills.

For a second, Caoilte was distracted by the door opening in La Petite Maison Le Fèvre. He saw Rós at the doorway. She nodded to him. His time had come. This was the moment he had waited for his whole life and he was never more terrified. He felt the fire inside his heart and didn't know how he would contain it. He struggled to breathe.

"Take a deep breath," Kubera said, appearing next to him. "Breathe as Jeremiah taught you. This is your destiny and you are on the brink of greatness."

Kubera then disappeared. Caoilte remembered all Jeremiah had taught him. He felt his heart beating and slowly found his breath and a calmness within. The fire burned brightly, but for now, it was contained. He took another few breaths and then returned to his fire dragon and climbed on board. It was almost time. The blood moon would appear in only another hour. Caoilte flew to meet his oncoming army.

Chapter 16

The Battle

Elisa stood on the eastern hilltop holding An Claíomh Solais tightly in her left hand. Strapped to her back was Fódla's satchel with Geaspar cradled next to the soft teddy bear inside and unaware of the battle that lay ahead. Elisa felt the presence of the Kaphiens in the valley and the hills and stood tall as a mark of courage and leadership. They looked to her to save them and Kapheus from a terrible fate, and Elisa needed to stay focussed and confident. She breathed deeply into her soul and felt her heart beating. She sent a wish to Chiron, the centaur in the night sky and suddenly she saw a shooting star and then knew that Chiron was with her. She sent a message to Fódla asking for the little pink dragon to stay close to her in this battle. She thought of Fódla's bravery and knew if her spirit was next to her, she would feel safe.

Elisa took a deep breath before glancing across at Setanta bent down. She felt the heavy weight of expectation and tightened her grip once more on the sword of light. Then Elisa saw the guardians flying back from their watch far earlier than they would ordinarily. The large grey dragon at the head of the v-formation swooped low and screeched before returning to the group. This was the signal that Caoilte and his army were fast approaching. Elisa took another deep breath and looked across at Setanta again. He nodded to her. Feehul stood up from his watching station, approached Elisa and stood next to her. He nervously looked at Elisa and then looked back in the direction of Fodar.

"It's your time to go, Feehul," said Elisa.

"Go n-éirí leat. I wish you well, Elisa," he said, and then ran down the narrow path on the hillside.

Rós closed the door of La Petite Maison Le Fèvre and dropped the wooden latch. One by one, she closed the window shutters to a snapping sound. Kubera appeared at Elisa's side. He looked up at her reassuringly for a moment and then watched for any signs from the east.

"Remember, fire brings everything into the light. Be honest in your dealings," Kubera said. He disappeared again.

Elisa felt an enormous pressure on her. She didn't know how she was going to be able to do this. She felt her stomach tighten and thought she was going to be sick.

"I'm here, Elisa. It'll be alright. Beidh gach rud ceart go leor," Setanta reassured.

Elisa then heard a loud screech behind her and looked over her shoulder to see Éiriú flying towards her. Éiriú's very presence gave hope to Kaphiens. The sight alone of such a large and powerful white dragon would put fear into the hearts of their enemies. The elves tightened their armoury to their bodies, held their bows in their hands and checked their quivers. Those managing the catapults checked the fastened nets one more time. The leprechauns who were about to scurry away until the battle had ended, changed their minds on seeing Éiriú, and stayed in the hills. They crouched down next to their empty sacks in their rocky outposts to watch this battle play out.

Jamie saw Éiriú from Banbha's back and felt a shiver down his spine. She wasn't the dragon who filled him with even a morsel of excitement.

"*Seo linn,*" Éiriú called to Banbha, and Banbha followed her. It wasn't very long before Éiriú and Banbha came to rest on either side of Elisa.

"Jamie, climb down from her back," Éiriú instructed.

The three goddesses of Éire stood side by side waiting. Setanta whistled and signalled to Jamie who ran and crouched down next to him behind the boulder.

"Squawk! Squawk!" the phoenix cried and then the three goddesses saw them.

The phoenix took flight and with flap-flap-glide, flap-flap-glide, she announced to all Kaphiens that the warriors from Fodar were visible in the skyline. The phoenix danced in the sky with loops and spins and then she was gone. She passed through the veil and disappeared into the woodland. The leprechauns saw the clouds disperse and the blood moon shine brightly, and they shook with terror.

"Prepare yourselves, lads. They're coming," said an elf, crouched down.

Elisa watched what seemed like thousands of dragons fill the sky. She saw clusters of younger dragons in between the larger and more robust adults. The moon shone down on their armoury of silver and gold and Elisa became afraid. They looked so powerful and all the dragons, every single one, had a golden helmet on its head, and wore a gold and silver breastplate. She took a step backward.

"Beidh gach rud ceart go leor. Beidh gach rud ceart go leor," she uttered in a low voice.

"It will," said Kubera, appearing next to her, "everything *will* be alright. No matter what." He disappeared again.

Elisa then saw a shooting star and thought of Fódla and felt safe. She looked at Banbha and then Éiriú and they appeared unafraid. Elisa's strength was restored. She stepped forward.

"What are we waiting for?" Jamie whispered.

"The goddesses have sovereignty over the land of Kapheus and Éire. If there is a battle, then it is customary to speak to the goddesses before it commences. It's a way of trying to settle an argument before it becomes a fight," Setanta said.

"How do *you know* so much?" Jamie asked.

"Because I live here." Setanta moved another two steps and placed his hand on his hurley. "Jamie, if Fodar refuses to leave then get ready to run. You'll need to make it easy for Banbha to reach you." Jamie looked confused. "*Jump off the mountain,*" Setanta explained.

"*What?*"

"Have faith. She'll catch you... if she doesn't get struck beforehand... don't look so worried," said Setanta.

Jamie was worried beyond belief. He was expected to run and jump off the craggy mountain edge. If Banbha didn't make it in time he would fall to his death.

"Here they are," Setanta whispered.

Caoilte climbed down from his dragon and stood in front of Elisa.

"What are they saying?" Jamie whispered.

"I don't know."

They watched Caoilte closely trying their best to understand what was being said. Setanta looked up at the Fodar dragons hovering

in the sky and noticed a solid pattern of young dragons inside, older
ones at the periphery and a significant gap in between. He puzzled
over that gap and then looked higher in the sky and saw that a row
of dragons had left the periphery and were hovering above all the
others. Setanta slowly raised his hurley but was held back by the
hand of Kubera. He shook his head and Setanta placed the hurley
back down on the grass.

"Elisa, it's a pleasure to meet you, the daughter and goddess of
Éire," Caoilte said. "Éiriú… Banbha," he said, bowing his head to
each of them in turn.

"Be open and honest, be open and honest," Kubera willed Elisa.

"You have something belonging to us," Caoilte said.

"We have nothing belonging to you that we are aware," Éiriú
remarked.

"What is it you seek?" asked Banbha.

"I want the one who was born only a few days ago. I want the
dragon for the ages, the one that is white and has the power to heal
all wounds and cure all illness."

Elisa was surprised to hear this. She knew Geaspar could heal,
because he saved Buddy's life, but she didn't know he was that
powerful. How could he be? Geaspar was only a few days old.

"And what makes you think that dragon was born? *That*, as far as
I'm aware, is an old tale that has grown legs and wings. Does the
lost dragon egg of Kapheus *even exist?*" Éiriú asked.

"We believe it does, and we'll search all of Kapheus for it. I'll
ensure *that elves are slain* and *homes are burnt* until you hand over the
white dragon!" Caoilte said with immense force.

"What do you want to do with the dragon?" Elisa asked.

"We'll keep him and use his spittle to heal."

"*You mean* you'll tie him up and chain him down for the rest of his
days!" said Banbha, angrily.

"Well, everyone must make a sacrifice for the better good. We've
all done it," Caoilte said. "Will you hand him over or do we have
to slay elves to have him?" he asked. Caoilte looked inquisitively at
the satchel on Elisa's back. "What do you have in your satchel?"

"The dragon for all the ages," said Elisa.

She held An Claíomh Solais tightly in both hands. Caoilte raised his hands and backed away.

"The sword that has never failed," he said. "I'm no match for that, and I have to say that was a genius stroke to keep him in your satchel," he said, taking another step backwards. "How are we to get to him without killing you who holds the sword that has never failed?" Caoilte climbed onto his dragon's back. "You've made this an almost impossible task," he said, "but there are many ways to slay a dragon."

Setanta nudged Jamie.

"Get ready," he whispered.

Éiriú lifted her body high and roared from deep inside her soul. That battle cry shook the earth. The elves readied themselves in the meadows. They crouched down low in the long grass and tightened their grip on their weapons. The elves in the hills reached their hands over their shoulders ready to pull an arrow from their quiver.

"Now!" Setanta shouted.

Jamie ran to the mountain edge and jumped. Within a flash of an eye Banbha had flown to him and they flew at top speed across the valley. By the time Setanta looked back, Éiriú and Elisa were gone. Setanta's heart beat faster and faster in his chest.

"Stay calm, stay calm," he whispered to himself. Setanta watched Caoilte raise his hand. "*Come on* Grandmother Oak," Setanta said, lifting a sliotar.

Caoilte dropped his hand. The battle had begun. Setanta stood tall. He raised the sliotar into the air and struck it with the full force of his hurley. The sliotar sped through the air and struck a helmet dislodging it from the dragon.

"Only the young, the old and the defenceless, Setanta," Kubera instructed.

Setanta struck a sliotar and then another with the speed of a supreme athlete. A young dragon came so close he almost knocked Setanta over. He reached up and clipped the helmet with the tip of his hurley and it flew off the dragon's head and rolled off the mountain edge. Setanta turned around and grabbed another sliotar in his hand. He tossed it into the air and struck it hard against another helmet. Over and over he did this until the pile was empty. Setanta ran to the next pile and then the next, smashing helmet after helmet. In the end, sliotars came flying towards him, which he struck one after the other.

"More lads!" he shouted.

The gnomes appeared and then disappeared again in search of the fallen sliotars. The golden armoury fell to the ground like a hail shower in spring.

"Let the young and defenceless pass through!" Banbha called.

"*Don't strike any dragon* without a helmet," Lugh shouted to his fellow elves. "No helmet, no strike!" the elves shouted to each other as the message spread through Kapheus.

The Fodar dragons devoid of helmets passed through the hordes of waiting Kaphiens untouched. It was a surreal experience for the women and children on board. Their panic soon left them, and they found themselves nodding to the dragons in a gesture of thanks. A young elf held his overloaded sack of dragon eggs close to his body for fear that they would be destroyed by the Kaphiens but they were unharmed.

"You may pass through without harm," Ogma said. "Ruan and Lir are waiting for you."

A warrior pulled his arrow from his quiver and drew his bow, but his wife held his arm and he dropped his bow.

"Let them through!" Jamie shouted.

"Taraigí chugam! Come to me!" Grandmother Oak called to the dragons. They heard her call and flew to the veil of the Meadow of Discovery.

"Strike the helmets!" Lugh shouted from the hills.

The elves lifted their bows and arrows and struck the helmets of the dragons. The arrows flew through the air but bounced off the helmets. They drew bows again and struck the helmets of the dragons and again it was to no avail.

"Setanta!" Lugh called. Setanta looked down. He ran back a few feet and then took a deep breath and ran and jumped off the mountain edge. He landed on Banbha.

"Go raibh maith agaibh! Thanks lads!" he said.

"No problem," said Jamie.

Banbha swooped down, flew low and Setanta jumped from her back and onto the meadow floor. Setanta rolled and then quickly got to his feet and ran.

"The gnomes are coming!" he shouted.

With that sliotars were tossed through the air as Setanta ran and struck each one against the dragons' helmets. A horseback Kaphien came galloping towards Setanta.

"Here! Tóg í!" the fair-haired woman called, and threw a wooden shield adorned with the symbol of the Spiral of Life to Setanta as she galloped by. She drew her bow and struck the Fodar elf whose arrow was aimed towards Setanta. The woman turned and drew her arrow several more times until her fellow horseback archers reached her. When they arrived, she quickly dismounted, ran to a crevice on the hillside, crouched down and watched. She signalled to her companions through simple sign language and they dispersed into the several more crevices on the hillside. The speed with which their arrows flew through the air was no match for any enemy elf. Although they heard and saw the arrows flying towards them, the arrows had reached them before they could dive, duck or draw their bows, striking them and knocking them from the dragons backs. They came tumbling through the air, yelling and flailing their arms and legs as they fell. They were sure that they were about to meet their deaths only to be caught by the Kaphien elves' large nets on the meadow floor.

Jamie looked around and saw the hail of arrows beating down and called the guardians. Time after time, Setanta struck the sliotars and hit the helmets with absolute precision to disarm the dragons. His shield was laden with arrows at this stage and it was no longer of use to him. Setanta threw it away.

"Taraigí chugam! Come to me!" Grandmother Oak called to their minds' ear.

The dragons ignored the lashings of whips and the pulling of reins and instead passed through the horde of Kaphiens and onwards to the woodland, carrying their angry elfin soldiers on their backs.

Then the robin flew low and sounded her sharp tick, tick, tick warning call into the ear of the fair-haired woman. The woman looked over her shoulder and saw scores of Fodar foot soldiers streaming down through the hillside. She sounded a loud and looping whistle and ran up the hillside. While she was running, she heard Jamie shout and looked back over her shoulder.

"Setanta!" Jamie shouted. "Help Setanta! Guardians!"

By now, there were too many arrows hailing down on Setanta for him to escape injury.

The fair-haired archer scanned the battle scene.

"A h-aon... a dó... a trí... a ceathar... a cúig... a sé..." she muttered.

She thought about the sequence with which she would shoot, she calmly notched the arrow, held the tension on the bow string until the perfect moment and shot it 250 feet through the air. The arrow hit the first Fodar archer on dragon back. Then with absolute speed and precision, she struck the next five arrows before she herself heard an arrow shooting through the air in her direction and realised that she was the target of that arrow. She ducked, rolled and then ran to another crevice in the hillside. Her fellow archers traced the Fodar archers and one-by-one they fired bows in their direction, disabling them.

Jamie called out to the dragons again to save Setanta.

"Tá sé i mbaol! Tá sé i mbaol!" he cried out.

Suddenly, a white cloud rose from behind the far hilltop that under the light of the moon sparkled like diamonds at its exposed rocky peak. That white cloud blocked the light of the moon with its outstretched wings. The Fodar elves' hearts contracted in their chest when they heard the sound of the dragon's wing flap. They saw Éiriú appear over the diamond hilltop and they froze. She was the largest and most threatening dragon the Fodar elves had ever seen. Her brown eyes were fixed on them as if she was looking into their individual souls all at once. They felt the certainty of death in that moment. Immediately, they recognised her as the great white one, the goddess of Éire, the dragon they had heard about in stories of folklore as children, but never really believed could possibly exist. Éiriú roared in the night sky and by now there wasn't a single creature in Kapheus who did not know that the great white dragon had entered this battle.

Éiriú dived faster than they could register it in their minds and with a ferocious attacking force, she tossed dragons into the air like toys. She reached out her claws and tore the helmets off the Fodar dragons as they fell and tossed them in the direction of the passage between the hills. The guardians caught the falling elves and flew them from the valley to the woodland. Jamie, Dara and the earth dragons did their utmost to assist the guardians.

"Get them out of here!" Jamie shouted. The earth dragons followed the guardians to the woodland.

"Attack!" Caoilte roared. "Attack!"

Caoilte's troops were in disarray. The force of the Kaphien attacks was so powerful and so unpredictable. They simply couldn't get to grips with the chaos. They had never seen a dragon as powerful as Éiriú and were completely vulnerable to her attack and could not re-organise fast enough to recover.

"Cast your flames!" Caoilte shouted.

The Fodar dragons roared and then sprayed fire down on Kapheus, burning everything in sight. The Kaphiens searched for the Tuatha Dé Danann but they were nowhere to be seen. They called Éiriú for help, but she was doing everything she could in the sky. There was nowhere for them to go. The flames scorched the earth and the army of meadow elves were in complete disarray. Sinann sang to the river and it rose up and washed over the land. The elves cheered loudly.

Seán waited for the red moonlight to reappear between the clouds. The clouds obliged and slowly passed by the moon allowing a stream of fiery red moonlight to appear. Seán scanned the lower hillside where his fellow leprechauns hid beneath the over-hanging patches of bog. He looked to his left and then to the right and signalled to his companions to wait. They crouched down tightly against the large patches of exposed granite rock on the higher ground. The Fodar foot soldiers filed pass them as they ran down over the hilltop and down to the lower ground. They counted their enemies and waited. Seán looked down one last time and whistled.

"Anois!" Seán commanded.

The leprechauns came from every crevice in the hills and ambushed the foot soldiers. They dragged them down and tied their arms and legs. They then tied them to each other in bundles and with three sharp whistles the earth dragons swooped low, snatched the foot soldiers and took them to the woodland. Seán came from the granite outcrop and dived onto the last foot soldier. He fought relentlessly to subdue him, but the soldier was well-trained and knew the art of fighting. Seán's body weight was forced in the wrong direction and his feet slipped on the small loose rocks on the steep slope. Seán pulled the soldier with him and they both came speeding down the side of the mountain until finally Seán managed to turn the soldier over and slowed them both down. The leprechaun fought with the elf on the loose scree until Seán finally had him subdued. Seán tied his arms and while he was reaching behind him to get the rope to tie his feet, Seán noticed the lines of gold in the rock in the moonlight.

"There's gold in this mountain," he whispered, and looked a little closer at the rock.

The elfin soldier, seeing Seán distracted, got up and ran only to be chased down the mountain again and pulled down by his ankles.

"You don't make it easy," Seán said, tying his legs.

"Leprechauns and your gold!" a voice called from above and the dragon swooped down and snatched the elfin soldier and carried him away.

Seán looked around and saw that his fellow leprechauns had managed to reduce the number of foot soldiers reaching the meadow by about seventy percent, but their work was not without rewards. All but Seán had stripped the soldiers of their armoury before they whistled to the dragons to take the soldiers with them, and then heaped the gold and silver into their sacks.

Seán spotted the escapees, but his leprechauns were too distracted by the gold and silver armoury. The fair-haired woman then sounded a floating whistle and signalled to him to leave the hillside. She moved onwards with her fellow archers to find and to capture the remaining foot soldiers.

"Move on!" Seán commanded. The leprechauns hid their sacks beneath the purple and yellow heather bushes and followed him to the valley. Like hidden dragons, the leprechauns noticed the archers only briefly as they ran. The archers appeared when their arrows flew through the air and then they retreated into the darkness and swiftly moved on.

"Get them!" the Fodar warrior shouted from the sky and the Fodar dragons sprayed flames of fire onto the earth dragons who flew their foot soldiers away. The earth dragons screeched and recoiled in pain. These agonising cries were heard by Sinann and she sang to the waterfall. The river changed its course and broke its banks. The water roared across the land and wide across the mountain ridge and with an unbelievable force sprayed outwards and across the valley soaking the grateful earth dragons.

"Éalú! Éalú!" Seán shouted. He reached out to a dragon to pick him up. "Get out of here!" he shouted.

The earth dragons carried their elfin cargo through the mist and escaped.

"Get after them!" Caoilte shouted, and the Fodar dragons obeyed his command. They flew through the meadow chasing down their prey. They reached into the quills and pulled out their poisoned arrows. They drew their bows and aimed their arrows to the weakest point beneath the dragons' wings.

"Wait! Wait!" Lugh called. He waited for Seán.

The dragons raced to the pass between the hills, and at the moment Seán came into sight, Lugh gave the command.

"Anois!" he shouted.

The elves released the catapults and large nets flew into the air and onto the chasing dragons. The Fodar dragons tried to stretch their wings but were unable to break free from the heavy nets and came tumbling to the ground. The Kaphiens ran to grab the soldiers and to drag them from the dragons' backs.

"Quick! *Pull off the helmets*! They'll burn holes in these nets!" Seán shouted.

Joachim and his pack of wolves pounced on the dragons and wrestled their helmets off.

"Release the nets!" Lugh instructed.

Grandmother Oak called to the dragons, and without hesitation, they flew to her. Joachim watched them leave, and for some reason, he glanced upwards to Carman's home in the hills. Such a role this woman had played in the death of Fódla, the birth of

Geaspar and now this terrible battle. Carman came to the door of her home to see the disturbance below. She looked out at the burning flames and saw the Kaphiens strife. Joachim heard her laugh heartily before going back inside. He turned away.

"Take them with you," Joachim said to the elves.

The elves tied their hands with rope and pulled their captives along in a line towards the passage between the two hills.

"There's no place in Kapheus for poisoned arrows", Seán said. "I'm heading back to the hills. Will you be alright?" he asked.

"Yeah, *go*," said Lugh.

Seán signalled to a dragon to take him to the hills and in an instant he was gone.

"Arooooo," Joachim cried out, and he and his pack took chase.

"Distract them lads!" Feehul shouted.

The elves ran to the cluster of dummy elves. They reached down and lit the fireworks and within an instant the sky was lit with explosive colour of green and purple and yellow. The Fodar warriors lashed their whips against the dragons who reared in terror of the flashes of light. The warriors lashed them again even harder and forced the dragons to spray flames from their breaths onto the meadow. Those flames scorched the dummies.

"Split up!" Feehul shouted.

The elves split into three groups and lit the explosive fireworks of another three clusters of dummies. Their lightning power was, however, only short lived.

"Sinann, the dummies are used up!" Feehul called.

It was then that the large brown Fodar dragon cast his flames on Sinann. The river rose up and created a wall of water in front of Sinann when she sang to it, but the fire dragon did not give up. He took a deep breath and with all his might streamed an unquenching flame with unrivalled force at the wall of water.

"Sinann!" Feehul shouted, running as fast as he could to his sister. The flames grew stronger and the water could not withstand the force. Sinann tired, and seeing that she was about to collapse, Éiriú rose in the night sky and sped through the meadow as her body received blow after blow from the poisoned gold tipped arrows.

She reached the Fodar dragon and with all her power, she struck him on his side and threw him to the meadow floor. The gnomes ran to pull off his helmet before the dragon could get to his feet. Éiriú turned and faced the approaching Fodar dragons. She roared out as the arrows struck her and then took chase.

"Retreat!" the elfin warrior shouted.

"There'll be no retreat!" Caoilte yelled. He struck his dragon with his whip and pulled an arrow from his quiver.

Caoilte aimed and shot the gold tipped arrow from his bow. It flew through the air unhindered, penetrated the Spiral of Life beneath Éiriú's wing and travelled straight to the heart of the dragon. Éiriú released a high-pitched screech and fell through the air. Elisa held on as tightly as she could until she was finally catapulted from Éiriú's back when the dragon hit the ground. Elisa landed heavily on her shoulder and cried out in pain; she dropped the sword from her hand. Without a second thought, she scrambled to her feet to retrieve it, but as she reached it, Seán stood on its blade. For a moment, he thought to keep it for himself, but instead he lifted it up and handed An Claíomh Solais to Elisa.

"Make it count," Seán said. He whistled to the leprechauns and they came running from every crevice in the land.

Elisa stood at the wounded body of Éiriú and with the support of the leprechauns who stood with their backs to Éiriú they were ready to face the Fodar troops. The elves looked at their fallen goddess and knowing that the arrow had pierced her heart they felt hopeless. Their hearts sank. They believed there was no chance they could defeat the enemy without the great white dragon.

Jamie, however, was clueless to what had happened and continued to catch the fallen elves and was so consumed in the struggle to hold them down long enough before tossing them onto the backs of passing earth dragons that the cry from Éiriú had gone unnoticed to him. However, it wasn't long before the guardians knew of Éiriú's plight and they began to screech excessively. Jamie looked around him but couldn't find the reason for their screeching.

"Banbha!" he shouted. "*What's going on?*"

"Éiriú has been injured and the life is draining from her body," said Banbha. "Decide what you want *now*, Jamie. *You* are the leader of the dragons. They'll obey your word."

Below them on the meadow grass, they saw Fodar elves dismount from their dragons. They slowly approached Elisa.

"You can't save yourself against all of us," the elf said. "Your goddess is close to death. She can't save you either," he said, stepping closer.

"This is the sword that has never failed," said Elisa.

"That's true but it would be impossible for someone as inexperienced as you to be able to defend yourself on all sides," he said, "and maybe even from above."

"The leprechauns are on my side."

"Leprechauns are easily bribed. *Even you* must know that."

Setanta lifted a stone from the ground and flung it across the sky, dislodging the helmet from one of their dragons. The dragon heard Grandmother Oak's call and flew in the direction of the woodland. The elves grew nervous. Another stone flew through the air dislodging yet another helmet and the dragon flew away. The Fodar elves frantically climbed onto their dragons.

"*What are you doing?*" the Fodar elf asked. "Get down!"

The elves refused his order. Another stone flew through the air and struck one of their dragon's helmets and it flew off. The elf lost his mount and tumbled to the ground when the dragon heard Grandmother Oak's call.

"The dragon is only *two feet from me* and an *inexperienced child* is holding the sword," the Fodar elf remonstrated. "*Could you keep it together?*"

He saw the dragon taking flight and his fellow warrior in a heap on the ground.

"Let it go… You two, find the source of *that stone throwing,*" he commanded. They flew in search of Setanta.

Jamie looked down at the Fodar warriors swarming around Elisa and Éiriú.

"What's your move, Jamie?" Banbha asked.

"Jamie, *make up your mind!*" Banbha shouted. "I can't save *my sister,* but *you can save yours!*"

Jamie looked around. He saw the warriors closing on Setanta and then saw a weakened Sinann being helped from the river by Feehul. He looked to La Petite Maison Le Fèvre, but there was no sign of life inside. Jamie turned back and watched the few last Fodar foot warriors creeping along the hills to ambush the Kaphiens. He didn't know what to do. Iolar's frustration grew with every second Jamie hesitated and in the end, she took flight from her ledge and sped towards Banbha and Jamie.

"End this battle now!" Iolar shouted. "Give Elisa Ernmas' heart!" Caoilte saw Iolar circling Banbha and the wounded Éiriú on the ground and he knew that his troops would not now retreat and that he could end this battle. Caoilte flew to the meadow floor and dismounted.

"We need Feehul," Jamie said.

"You need more than Feehul!" Iolar exclaimed. "Give the *blood diamond* to Elisa!"

"*How important* is your sister to you, Jamie?" Banbha asked.

"She's everything to me!" Jamie snapped.

"Well then do something!"

"Get Feehul!" Jamie commanded.

Banbha flew to Feehul and Sinann and lifted them from the riverbank.

"What next?" Banbha asked.

"We need to get Feehul to Éiriú," Jamie said, and before long Sinann and Feehul landed on the meadow next to Éiriú with Jamie. "She'll be dead very soon," Caoilte said, "and your sword won't save her. Nothing can save her now apart from the spittle of the white dragon you hide in your satchel... *That arrow* pierced her heart," Caoilte said, "I shot it myself."

Feehul ran to Éiriú and desperately tried to stop the bleeding. Caoilte laughed.

"Not even the great medicine elf can save the goddess now," he said. "This battle has ended. I've conquered Kapheus," he said, gleefully.

The elves dropped their weapons.

"The heart of Ernmas. *Put an end to this battle!*" Iolar called, swooping low.

"The heart of Ernmas!" Caoilte said. *"Who has the heart?"* he asked, frantically looking around. He scanned the leprechauns and the elves, but he didn't notice them hiding anything.

"Bring everything into the light," Jamie said to Elisa, pulling the blood diamond wrapped in the linen shirt from his satchel and handing it to her.

Elisa stood her sword on the ground and opened the cloth.

"The heart of Ernmas," Caoilte said. He dropped to one knee and bowed.

"There are only about forty dragons left in the sky," Jamie said. "We can take them." Jamie placed his hand on Elisa's shoulder. "Elisa we can do this." He climbed onto Banbha's back.

"Tell the guardians to stay in the hills, Banbha, and ask the earth dragons to join them and to form a line to block all exits from Kapheus. We'll trap them in the meadow and they'll *have to surrender,"* he said, and they flew away.

Banbha screeched and Ogma heard the message.

"There's no need," Caoilte muttered, but Jamie had already left.

Two dragons pulled Setanta along the ground and dropped him at Elisa's feet. Caoilte's eyes were filled with tears. He looked at Setanta but didn't really see him. Caoilte climbed onto his dragon.

"Elisa, *be prepared,"* Caoilte said. "Fire brings *everything* into the light!" he shouted, pulling on his dragon's reins. "You've lost!" he shouted and then flew away.

Half way across the meadow, Caoilte pulled up his dragon and they hovered in the air to watch. "What did he mean?" Elisa asked Seán.

"I don't know but I doubt it's good," Seán said.

Caoilte waited and gradually the clouds dispersed and the blood moon shone brightly. The moonlight struck the blood diamond and its light radiated across the land and high into the night sky, revealing everything that was once hidden including the ancient knowledge. Kapheus revealed to them the ancient truth about leprechauns and elves and even gnomes. For the first time in countless generations the elves knew that the leprechauns were not their enemy, but that they had been trapped in the illusion of power. The leprechauns saw that the elves were not so pure and good but were flawed just like them, and that they too had fallen prey to power in different ways.

Seán saw in his mind's eye all that Lugh had experienced at the hands of the Dark One. He nodded to him in acknowledgement of his pain, and though some distance away, Lugh recognised him and nodded back. All Kaphiens saw each other's truth and grew in their deep understanding of each other. The spirits of their ancestors greeted them and stood next to them in the meadow and the hills and they were unafraid. The ancient animals came from the dreamland and emerged from beneath the waterfall. Pyrrha and Deucalion cantered towards them with their unicorn foal, Prometheus, until they stood in front of Elisa. The foal snorted and pawed the ground.

"Elisa, fire will bring all that is hidden into the light no matter how dark," Kubera said. "The heart of Ernmas has the power to end war, because it shows all of us that we are not very different from each other."

Elisa had already placed the heart of Ernmas onto the ground for fear it would bleed. She looked down at it again and wondered how a heart could have the power to end war.

"I didn't know that knowledge ended war," she said. "Kubera, you said that Kapheus would be triumphant if I was honest and straight."

"Yes, that's true. You need to be honest, so that the person next to you is allowed to be honest too and to reveal their thoughts and emotions without prejudice. This is the essence of fire," Kubera said.

Pyrrha, the unicorn, looked back at her foal and whinnied. Prometheus stepped forward and then leaned under her mother's belly and suckled.

"Prometheus brought fire to you in the form of Ernmas' heart. He has shown you, I hope, that the truth has the power to end war," Kubera said.

Deucalion whinnied to his foal and turned to walk back to the waterfall with Pyrrha and Prometheus.

"Fire brings everything into the light," Kubera said, and walked away. He sat down on a stone close to them and shook his head.

Many miles away in the city of Fodar, Mr. Adley saw the sky turn red from his bedroom window as he pulled his tie off and unbuttoned his shirt.

"It looks like my lucky elf isn't so lucky after all," he said.

"What's that my love?" his wife asked, climbing into bed.

"It's time to move on," Mr. Adley said, and switched off the light. He left the curtains open and sat on his chair to watch the night sky.

Caoilte was in awe of what he saw in Kapheus that night.

"The heart of Ernmas," he whispered.

It wasn't long before he shook himself into the reality of war and quickly looked around to see if anyone was watching him. A large and threatening black cloud rolled across the sky and Caoilte withdrew. The blood moon was hidden, and the blood diamond's light receded as darkness fell upon Kapheus.

"Pull the helmets off your dragons!" Jamie shouted. "Pull them off!"

The Fodar warriors refused until they looked around and saw the mere skeletons of the dragons of darkness with wings and hearts of fire approach.

"Take them off!" Jamie shouted. The Fodar elves pulled hard on the dragons' reins until they arched their heads backward and then they removed the helmets and freed them to hear Grandmother Oak's voice.

"Stay in the light of your heart! Merge your heartbeats to the earth!" Jamie commanded.

The elves looked at him in surprise. They couldn't believe that Jamie knew the ways of elves and yet he wasn't even one of them. In that moment of confusion, the Fodar warriors struggled to find their balance and to merge their heartbeats to the earth. After all, Jamie was the enemy, and they couldn't understand why he wanted to help them.

"Listen to your beating hearts," Ogma instructed. "Feel your hearts beating and merge to the beat of the earth."

The Fodar elves noticed their dragons grow still and at ease, and they listened to Ogma and did what he said. Down below on the meadow grass the Fodar elves were nervous. They thought that they had won this battle and now the balance seemed to have tilted in the direction of the Kaphiens.

"He's abandoned us!" the Fodar warrior said.

"We're trapped!" said another, panicking.

"*Take off* your dragons' helmets!" Lugh commanded.

"No. We can't, we…"

"*Take them off* or we'll be forced to do it!"

The warrior elves had no choice other than to remove the helmets and surrender. Grandmother Oak called to the dragons, and without warning, they flew to her.

'Be still,' she whispered to all Kaphiens. 'Listen to your beating heart. Breathe,' she instructed.

"You can stay with us," said Lugh. "Stay in the light of your hearts." The Fodar elves huddled close together. "We'll protect you."

Donn emerged from the clouds with his serfs and the dark hounds. The hounds snarled and salivated as they waited to be given the word to attack.

Elisa pulled An Claíomh Solais from the ground and held the sword of light in both hands.

"Bow to the Dark One," Donn commanded.

"You've a new position then, Donn. Have you taken over from your father?" Elisa asked.

Feehul could feel Elisa's fear and his heart beat fast in his chest. He began to panic as he desperately tried to stem the flow of blood from Éiriú's heart with his blood-drenched hands. The goddess of Éire's life was held in his hands and he knew he couldn't save her. No medicine could heal a punctured heart.

"Yes, my father was a *useless leader* and he was *weak… not like me,*" he snapped. Donn stepped forward. "I came prepared this time, Elisa. I brought my father's dragons. I command legions now," he said, proudly.

"Congratulations," Elisa said.

High above them, Jamie looked around and saw Caoilte leaving the meadow and flying toward Iolar's nest in the hills.

"Ogma, will you be alright?" he asked.

"Go after Caoilte!" Ogma shouted.

Caoilte, however, was close to Iolar's nest on the mountain ledge by now. He saw the eye of the mountain and passed through it.

"Go after him, Banbha!" Jamie directed, and within a few seconds Banbha and Jamie had passed through the mountain.

"Strike when you have the chance," Ogma instructed, and the Fodar elves listened.

Under the light of the blood moon they waited. They held tightly to the heartbeat of the earth and watched the dragons of darkness searching for them in the sky. The fiery red eyes pierced through them, but the skeleton dragons could not see them. The Fodar and Kaphien dragons gently glided by them avoiding their wings of fire. The Fodar warriors watched Ogma for the sign, and when he nodded, they reached out and shot an arrow through the fiery hearts of the dragons of darkness. They screeched into the night sky. Then blow after blow struck their skeletal bodies until the dragons of darkness could take no more.

"Merge your heartbeat to the earth!" Ogma shouted, seeing that a Fodar dragon had grown afraid and was now visible.

The dragon of darkness struck the Fodar dragon and he screeched loudly before coming tumbling down onto the meadow floor. Ogma caught the warrior and tossed him onto his back, but it was too late to save the dragon, who couldn't recover from the blow and skidded along the meadow grass as he landed.

Donn flicked his eyebrows and gave a wry smile.

"It doesn't look like you can win any battle today, Elisa," he said.

"*What do you want?* I've *far more important* things to deal with tonight."

"I want to kill the dragon, Geaspar, and I believe you're carrying him on your back," said Donn.

"Yes, I am," Elisa said, tightening the straps on her shoulders.

"Don't move," Lugh whispered, holding the Fodar warrior's arm back. "You'll lose."

With a flick of his head, Donn had signalled to his hounds to attack. A hurley came flying through the air and with it a sliotar. Setanta reached for his hurley and struck hard on his sliotar knocking the hound back with a yelp. The gnomes appeared and then disappeared again. Seán winked to his fellow leprechauns. They reached into their pockets and drew their slingshots. Sinann stretched her fingers and Éiriú's blood flowed along the meadow grass to where she stood.

"Get him! Get *that dragon!*" Donn yelled.

Sinann sang softly to the blood at her feet and it created a film along the surface of the ground. The serfs slipped and fell in their attempts to catch Elisa. In their struggle to stand they fell over again but their hounds broke free. Their wide paws pounded the ground   as   they   ran.

"Now lads!" Seán shouted.

The leprechauns pulled on their slingshots casting sharp stones into the air. The gnomes helped and tossed stones into Setanta's path and he struck them hard and low, puncturing the hearts of the dark hounds. They dropped dead instantly and turned to ash. The serfs then transmuted into miniature tornados and spun above them before landing back down on the ground to surround Elisa on all sides. They transmuted back into humanlike figures with black hooded cloaks and laughed loudly.

"Hahaha!" Donn laughed. He stepped into the centre of the enclosed circle. Donn removed the hood from his head and stood face-to-face with Elisa.

"You really should get that scar looked at," Elisa said.

"It's fiery red, because a *fire dragon cut me with his talon!*" he shouted. Donn did his utmost to temper his fiery anger and took an extra second before he spoke. "No one can save your precious parcel now," Donn said.

Elisa didn't know how she was going to get herself out of this heap of trouble she was in. The serfs spun into miniature tornados again and blocked anyone from reaching Elisa from outside their enclosed circle.

"*What do we do?*" Setanta asked.

"There's not a lot we can do," said Seán.

"The blood diamond," Sinann whispered. "Elisa! Lift the blood diamond!" Sinann shouted, but she couldn't be heard.

Suddenly, the robin flew over Sinann's head and through a tiny gap between the tornados. Éataín picked up the diamond and turned to face Donn.

"You seem to have forgotten a far more precious gift," Éataín said. Donn quickly turned around. "You're looking for the dragon of all the ages, so that you can kill it," she said, "and for *what*?" she asked. "So that you can stop anyone of us having more power *than you*? But *you* will end up with *nothing*."

Donn looked confused.

"If you steal the blood diamond, you will have everything you desire," said Éataín.

Donn stepped closer. He looked at the diamond. It was truly the largest he had ever seen.

"This couldn't be real," he said.

"This diamond is priceless. You could conquer the world with it, bit by bit," said Éataín.

"My father thought that I was worthless… this would make me worth more than anyone else in the world."

"All the wealth and riches you desire will be yours," said Éataín.

She handed the diamond to Cillian. Elisa noticed the serfs beginning to transmute into human-like figures. She gripped the sword's hilt tightly and then struck out with her sword, ripping through the hooded figures. They screeched in pain and fell to the ground in a plume of ash. Elisa looked at Éataín and took one step backwards.

Cillian held the diamond in his hands. He nodded and smiled. He didn't care that his serfs were dust at his feet, he was the most powerful of all. Not even his father could do this. He marvelled at the beauty and enormity of the diamond. Slowly, he felt the diamond soften in his hand and bleed. The heart started to beat strongly.

"Arghh!" he shouted, and dropped the heart of Ernmas onto the meadow. "You tricked me!"

Donn looked at the elves and leprechauns and An Claíomh Solais.

"*Finish him*, Elisa!" Setanta shouted.

Donn panicked. He spun into a dark cloud and fled.

"You could *have finished him,*" Setanta said.

"There is no light without dark," said Elisa. She dropped her sword.

Kubera appeared next to Setanta. He took pleasure in Elisa's words and nodded his approval to her.

"At least *that* fella's gone," said Setanta, sitting down on the grass.

"And the dragons with him," said Seán, noticing that the dragons of darkness had retreated.

At the fountain of youth, the otter swam to the bottom of the pool and pulled the ore in the shape of the Spiral of Life to the surface and into the waiting hand of Caoilte. The otter scurried down the river bank.

"Go raibh maith agat," he said. "Thank you very much my friend."

Suddenly, Elisa collapsed onto the meadow grass. Her face was ashen and her body cold.

"Elisa!" Feehul shouted, trying to arouse her from her sleep.

"Elisa!" He shook her again and again, but she was lost to this world.

"Only the dragon can save her," Feehul uttered.

Feehul opened the fasteners on Fódla's satchel and lifted Geaspar into his arms. The dragon released his grip on the teddy bear and instead clung to Feehul.

"Which one do I save?" he said, panicking. "Lugh! Sinann!" he called. "*Which one do I save?*"

Lugh ran through the crowd of elves to his brother. "The one Geaspar chooses!" Lugh answered, pushing his way to the front of the crowd. Lugh stood there in shock on seeing the two goddesses of Éire close to death.

"Tá siad i mbaol a mbáis," Lugh said.

"I know," said Feehul. He placed Geaspar on the meadow grass and the little dragon ran to Éiriú.

"Let me help you," said Lugh, lifting him onto Éiriú's side.

Geaspar ran along the length of Éiriú's body until he reached her bleeding heart. He licked her blood-drenched scales until he reached the large puncture wound.

"Pull it out!" Seán said. He climbed onto the dragon's side and slid down to her wing. "Lift it up!" he called. The elves and dragons lined up and with all their might they lifted the dragon's wing just enough for Seán to be able to reach in and pull the arrow out. He tossed the arrow onto the ground.

"Here, little fella," he said, lifting Geaspar, "don't fall in now," he said, placing him next to the gaping wound at the Spiral of Life.

Geaspar coughed and spurted and a lump of spittle came from his mouth and landed on her bleeding heart. Seán watched as the deep wound began to heal, layer by layer.

"The hole is sealing on her heart," Seán said, fascinated. "Do-chreidte," he said.

Geaspar spurted again and another lump of spittle came from his mouth and added to the healing process.

"You're a handy fella to have around," Seán said.

Layer by layer the wound healed until the wound closed. Éiriú screeched and lifted her wing into the air, tossing the elves and leprechauns who came tumbling down on top of each other. Seán grabbed Geaspar just in time before he was crushed by the dragon and rolled out of the way. She screeched again and tried to lift herself from the ground but was too weak and fell back down. Geaspar ran from Seán's grip towards Éiriú.

"*Come back here you*. You're going to get yourself *killed*," Seán said, grabbing a hold of his tail. "I'll lift you up," he said.

Geaspar ran down the length of Éiriú's body to the next wound. With each place he stopped to heal, either Feehul or Lugh pulled the poisoned arrow from her body.

"He'll be a hungry fella at the end of all this," Seán said.

Feehul nodded. He couldn't help but wonder if Elisa's time was up. Geaspar could go to her now and Feehul thought that he could nearly heal the rest of Éiriú's wounds himself without the need for Geaspar. He looked over at Elisa again and he felt completely helpless. He didn't know how to heal this wound of the mind.

"Feehul, I think you should sit down and rest," Sinann said.

"No, I've just a headache. I feel her pain. We're linked you…" he said.

"Sit down, Feehul. We can do the rest," Lugh said.

Feehul sat on the grass with his back leaning against Éiriú's body. He grew weary and struggled to keep his eyes open.
"Don't fall asleep, Feehul, or we could lose you too," said Seán. "Keep him awake there lads."

Jamie dismounted Banbha next to the fountain of youth. He walked slowly and quietly towards Caoilte all the while trying to see what he was doing. Caoilte was knelt down with the ore in his hand and lost to his thoughts. He stared into the pool of blue and wondered.
"What are *you doing?*" Jamie asked, approaching Caoilte from behind.
"I could ask you the same question," said Caoilte. He happily placed the ore into his inside pocket. "If you don't mind," he said, climbing onto his dragon's back.
"What have you just done?" Jamie asked.
"*I've slain* the goddess," he said, and flew away.
Banbha snatched Jamie from the ground, tossed him onto her back and sped through the air. She flew to Iolar on the mountain ledge.
"You see every creature that passes through this mountain," Banbha said.
"What is small enough to fit into a pocket, but heavy enough that it would not fall out in flight?"
"*Is this a riddle?*" Iolar asked, confused.
"*What could* Caoilte have pulled from the *fountain of youth?*" Banbha asked with greater urgency.
"What do you mean?"
"He said that he had *slain the goddess of Éire,*" Jamie said.
Jamie's words startled Iolar and she took flight.

Chapter 17

Son of Éire

Caoilte dismounted his dragon outside La Petite Maison Le Fèvre. He looked around but could not see his messenger. Then he heard the latch open on the cottage door and saw Rós. Caoilte nervously looked around him again and then looked up to the sky.

"Tá mé anseo," said Kubera, "I'm here." Kubera appeared on the rock outside the cottage.

"*I haven't much time.* Banbha's after me," Caoilte said, hurrying towards him.

He nervously looked across to Rós and then removed the ore from his pocket and handed it to Kubera.

"Are you sure about this?" Kubera asked, examining the piece of ore. Kubera looked over his shoulder to Rós and she nodded to indicate that it was in fact the ore that she had shaped from the stone that struck Elisa on the back of the head. Rós rolled her wheelchair closer.

"Make sure it gets to him," Kubera said.

Caoilte removed his breast plate and dropped it onto the ground next to him. He looked behind him and saw Banbha and Jamie approaching and removed the rest of his armour.

"Leave your helmet on," Kubera said.

"You *don't have to do this,*" Rós pleaded.

Caoilte looked at Rós and then quickly looked away. He placed his helmet back onto his head.

"Tell them that I loved them," Caoilte said.

"I will."

Caoilte then grabbed hold of his dragon's reins and mounted. The elf took one last look back at Rós.

"Slán," Caoilte said, and then flew from the hilltop to the meadow below.

"Slán leat," Rós whispered in a voice that mirrored her broken heart.

Kubera had disappeared from sight. There was nothing left for Rós to do than to retreat indoors. For Kubera, this moment meant that he must run as fast as his legs could carry him down the narrow path leading from La Petite Maison Le Fèvre. He saw Iolar gliding across the meadow and whistled, but she didn't hear him above the noise and chaos of the battle. Iolar flew low, scanning every inch of ground, but still could not find her messenger. Kubera whistled and then Iolar heard that floating whistle, looked behind her and swooped to snatch Kubera from the narrow path.

"Disappear," Iolar said, and Kubera vanished from sight.

"Will you be alright?" Kubera asked.

"I've dodged countless arrows and sling shots in my time," Iolar responded and sped through the meadow.

"There he is!" Jamie shouted, pointing to Caoilte in the distance. "Get him, Banbha!"

Jamie watched Caoilte's dragon land on the meadow as they chased after him.

"You have my dragons and you have my elves but your goddess lies almost dead," said Caoilte.

Iolar flew overhead and dropped Kubera without anyone other than Caoilte noticing the depression in the grass, and then she flew onwards in the direction of the woodland.

"It might be wise to remove the emerald from the sword," Caoilte said, smiling. "You *don't* want it to fall into the wrong hands."

Sinann was the elf of water and emotions flow like water through our hearts and our bodies. She took fright and then looked carefully at Caoilte and felt his emotions flow through her. Her heart filled with sorrow and confusion and fear. Sinann reached out and pulled the emerald from An Claíomh Solais. She stared at Caoilte with the concern of a mother for her child. Seán looked curiously in Sinann's direction and then in the direction of Caoilte. "After all, *it is* the sword of light – the sword that has never failed," Caoilte said with a wry smile and Seán dismissed his curiosity.

Sinann, however, did not dismiss her curiosity and was again confused. Caoilte seemed to her to be masking his true feelings with an alien smile. She searched for answers in her mind.

A distance away, Iolar pulled her wings tightly against her body as she pierced the veil and passed through. On the other side of that veil Fodarians were resting at campfires and eating and drinking their fill. Elfin children ran laughing between dragons and elves as they were being chased by the young fledgling dragons. The warriors removed their armoury and placed it on a large pile at the edge of the woodlands and happily returned to their families to celebrate their lives as free elves. The scene was in such a contrast to the battle on the other side of that veil and the fight the Kaphiens had to save their precious land.

Iolar searched the crowd until she found Ruan and Lir who at the time were distributing toys to the young elves and dragons. A young elf playfully hid from a baby dragon behind Ruan's leg when Iolar landed next to him.

"*What is it*, Iolar? I'm *very busy here*," Ruan said.

"I need to talk to you."

"You know I take my responsibilities *very seriously* and I have many more toys to distribute," Ruan said, almost toppled over by the dragon chasing after the little elf.

"It's Caoilte," said Iolar.

"*What about* my cousin?" Ruan asked, handing a rattle to the little dragon.

"I need to take you and Lir to him."

"I'm *not sure* that I want to see him. *That elf drives me mad!*"

"He's in trouble."

"What *kind* of trouble?"

Ruan looked at Iolar's face and that was enough for him to know that he must go.

"Grandmother Oak, I'm very sorry about this, but I…"

"*Go,*" Grandmother Oak whispered through the meadow grass.

Ruan dropped his sack and walked to Lir. He spoke to him quietly in the words that only brothers share. Lir then handed his sack to another elf and walked with his brother towards the veil.

"We don't have the time for that," said Iolar, snatching them from the ground.

She passed through the veil and onward through the gap between the hills and into the meadow. They saw Caoilte in the distance and watched something thrown into the air and struck by Setanta's hurl at the exact moment Caoilte removed his helmet. Caoilte dropped to the ground. Ruan and Lir were aghast.

Iolar flew faster than she ever had done before and dropped Ruan and Lir beside Caoilte. Ruan fell to his knees. He reached down to his cousin and lifted his head from the ground and cradled him against his chest. He cried out from the depth of his soul and no one was immune to that harrowing cry.

"*I didn't mean to,*" Setanta cried. "*I didn't mean to.*" Kubera appeared next to him. "I didn't mean to Kubera. He took his helmet off before I hit him. I…"

"Shush lad," said Seán.

The colour came back into Elisa's cheeks and she began to wake from her unconscious state. It was at that moment that Jamie stepped onto the meadow. He saw the scene in front of him and didn't know what to say.

"Caoilte!" Ruan cried. Caoilte touched Ruan's hand. "Caoilte! Caoilte, you'll be alright," Ruan said.

"Take me to the coast," he whispered. Ruan looked around.

"*Please* help him! He's my cousin," Ruan cried.

Dara gently placed his feet upon the meadow. He laid down and Banbha lifted Caoilte onto his back, and then Ruan and Lir climbed on board.

"Be gentle Dara. That's precious cargo," Ogma said.

Ogma and Méabh escorted Dara through the meadow and over the woodland to the coast. Caoilte held on though the life force was fast leaving him. He saw the treetops and the elves and the dragons' nests and drifted in his thoughts to the time of his youth. His eyes looked to the sun and his breathing grew heavier. Caoilte could smell the salt air and closed his eyes.

"*Don't leave us,*" Ruan called.

Caoilte opened his eyes. He heard the waves crashing against the coastline and saw the island. His head fell heavy in Ruan's arms. He was gone. Ruan's heart bled for his cousin and the tears rolled down his face. He could barely breathe he was so consumed by grief. Lir hugged Ruan and the three elves were inseparable at that moment.

"We'll bury him well," Ruan said to Lir. "No matter what anyone says. We'll bury him well. He was our cousin."

Lir nodded.

The dragons of the island watched the young Dara flanked on either side by his mother and father and grew concerned. Was this an omen of some kind, they thought. They waited to see what message these dragons carried, and it wasn't long before they caught a glimpse of the elves on Dara's back. They quickly made room for Dara and signalled to him to come to rest on the courtyard. Then the dragons took a step back and watched as Dara laid down. He stretched out his wings to allow Ruan and Lir to slide down either one if they so wished. Dara did his utmost not to make any sudden movement. He stilled his breath and waited.

"Good lad, Dara. I'm proud of you," Ogma whispered.

"Caoilte has passed away," Ogma said. "He is a Kaphien hero."

The dragons were shocked to hear the name of Caoilte. Was this not the elf that had left Kapheus for the east and not returned? They looked at each other.

"Caoilte is *our hero*," Ogma said, "join me in celebrating his life as we would if he were our very own kin."

The dragons lit the torches and surrounded Caoilte, Ruan and Lir in the light of those flames.

"We would like to give him a dragon's blessing," Ogma said.

Ruan and Lir held Caoilte tightly and slid down Dara's wing. They laid him at the centre of the courtyard; Dara stepped away. Ogma stood high and looked to the last few stars that remained visible as the day dawned. He called out to his ancestors to come and the dragon ancestors answered. They saw a shooting star across the horizon and then watched as Chiron flew to them and stood on the courtyard. The light from that streaming stardust opened a gateway and the dragon ancestors flew to the courtyard illuminated in a golden light. Dara looked but he was sure it couldn't be. He looked again. He saw a little dragon fly alongside the others with great determination.

"It's Fódla!" he exclaimed.

Ogma and Méabh looked around to see their dear Fódla come flying to them. He flew to Méabh and they embraced. Her heart was filled with immeasurable joy and unconquerable sorrow and so too were the hearts of Dara and Ogma.

"Boo, boo," Fódla said and Méabh laughed through her tears.

The ancestors laid down next to the three elves. Not for a moment was Ruan prepared to let his cousin go and he held him tightly in his arms. Ruan and Lir both watched as the dragon ancestors surrounded them in the courtyard and entered the dreamland. They watched as all the other dragons living on the island did the same.

"Boo, boo," Fódla called out to Ruan, and Ruan and Lir looked upwards to see the elfin ancestors walking towards them in a stream of golden light.

Caoilte's soul left his body. He stood up and hugged his ancestors who had left this world before him. He seemed so happy to see them all, and Ruan and Lir delighted in this.

"He'll be alright," Ruan said.

"Yeah," said Lir, "I don't think it's so bad on the other side."

Caoilte turned around and saw his cousins holding his fallen body. He nodded, smiled and then turned and walked into the crowd of ancestors and out of sight.

Caoilte's death did not only tear at Ruan and Lir's hearts but tore the heart and the soul of a young boy who had barely known this elf. The trauma Setanta experienced that morning in Kapheus was unspeakable. Setanta searched for solace in his mind but couldn't find it, nor could he find solace among the Kaphiens.

"*I didn't mean to,*" said Setanta, distraught.

"This was destiny, Setanta," Kubera said. "This was to happen today, and you merely played your part in the final scene of Caoilte's life," he said, walking to where Caoilte lay, "and by so doing, you saved Elisa."

Kubera reached down and picked up the ore that Rós moulded into the shape of the Spiral of Life.

"Ní thuigim," Setanta said.

"And you won't understand. How are you, a mere boy to understand something that is so profound that even me with all my years of studying the ancients texts and living my life by them fails to understand?"

"I didn't mean to," Setanta said, looking down at the point in the meadow where Caoilte fell. "*I didn't mean to,*" he said, completely distraught.

"Beidh sé ceart go leor, a mhac," a voice said.

Jamie looked around to see a slim, fair haired woman standing on the meadow dressed in the armoury of battle. With a bow hanging across her shoulder and a quill over her back.

"A Mham," Setanta said.

She opened her arms and embraced her son.

"It'll be alright," she said. "I'm *so* proud of you today. You're my brave boy."

Jamie saw Setanta hugging his mother and couldn't help but stare. Setanta was the same age as Jamie and he had forgotten that. He was sorry for making fun of him and disregarding his relationship with his mother. It was clear to Jamie now that Setanta's mother loved him so much and he loved her, and Jamie knew he was wrong to say those hurtful things. He watched Setanta's mother wipe the tears from his eyes and say something reassuring. He saw Kubera offering words of comfort too and he felt compelled to walk towards him.

"Setanta," Jamie called.

"Yeah."

"Setanta, I'm sorry. I didn't mean to hurt you in Rós' cottage. I'm sorry that I bullied you," Jamie said.

"You need to be nicer to Elisa," Setanta said, wiping his tears away. "She's *really good* to you."

Jamie nodded.

"You know Setanta, we wouldn't have been able to win this battle without you. You're the greatest warrior I've ever seen," said Jamie.

"It's not easy for me *either* Jamie. It's not easy being good at things. There's a lot of pressure on *me too* and now Caoilte is dead and *I killed him.*"

"I'm sorry."

"It's alright," Setanta said and he looked away.

It wasn't alright at all. Setanta knew that Jamie could go back to Éire and that no one there would know what he did in Kapheus but Setanta lived in Kapheus. He knew that everywhere he would go, people would remember him for killing Caoilte. He never thought that he would ever kill anyone. He was a killer. He knew the life he once had would be over now and that people would be more afraid of him than ever before. They were scared enough of him already, because he was a giant boy. Setanta was tortured inside.

"Setanta, when Fódla died I blamed myself for a long time. I was holding her at the time and she flew out of my hands... I didn't hold onto her tight enough," said Elisa.

"*Elisa,*" Setanta said, surprised to see her on her feet.

"I'm fine. I've just a bad headache... Setanta, I just want you to know that it's destiny. A second earlier or a second later and Fódla would still be alive," Elisa said.

"If only I had missed the shot Elisa, he'd still be alive,"

"Yeah, I know. I felt the same but he was destined for this," said Elisa.

"How do you know?"

"A second earlier or a second later... that's the only way I know."

"But Elisa, how could it be destiny when I killed him? *How Elisa?*"

"She doesn't know but I do," said Kubera. "Caoilte's life ended exactly as he wanted. His time was up. Maybe you and your mother will come with me to La Petite Maison Le Fèvre. I would like you to talk to Rós."

"Thank you for that invitation, Kubera. We would be happy to join you," Setanta's mother said.

"I need to go with my Mam, Elisa," said Setanta.

"Okay. I'll see you soon, I hope," said Elisa.

"See ya," said Jamie.

Setanta left for the cottage in the hills. It was then that Éiriú groaned while attempting to lift her weak body from the ground. Seán caught Geaspar in mid-air just in the nick of time.

"I have you little fella," Seán said, holding onto him.

"Maith thú, Elisa. You've done well," said Éiriú.

"Thank you."

"Banbha, did we succeed?" Éiriú asked.

"We did at a cost. Caoilte is dead," Banbha said.

Éiriú saw the wounded dragon lying on the meadow a short distance away.

"He's from Fodar," she said, "Feehul bring Geaspar with you."

Feehul left with Geaspar to heal the earth dragon. He tickled him a few times as they walked along the meadow and the little dragon squealed with delight. Suddenly a shadow crossed over them as the sun began to rise and they all looked up to see the phoenix in flight. She danced in the sky weaving, floating and gliding in the morning air.

"The battle is over," Éiriú said.

The phoenix came to rest next to Jamie and that beautiful bird of fire stared blankly at him.

"Squawk! Squawk!"

"What d'ya want?" Jamie asked.

"Squaaaawk!"

The phoenix looked at him again through her piercing blue eyes. She tilted her head to one side and Jamie copied her. Then she tilted her head to the other side and Jamie did the same.

"Elisa, do you know what she wants?" Jamie asked.

"Squaaaawk! Squaaaaaaaawk!"

"Argh! Do you have to be *so noisy!*" Jamie retorted, holding his hand to his right ear.

"Jamie, put our mother's heart back into your satchel. She wants it returned to its rightful place," said Éiriú.

"*Why didn't she just say that,*" Jamie quipped. "That noise pierces your eardrum," he complained.

"Squaaaawk!"

Jamie pulled the linen shirt from his satchel and wrapped it around the heart of Ernmas that lay on the ground next to Éiriú all the while being careful not to touch it. He then delicately placed it into his satchel and closed the buckles.

"Here, you can have it,", Jamie said, holding it out. "*Just don't* make that horrible noise."

The phoenix caught the strap in her beak and then pulled it over Jamie's head.

"I really wish I knew what you wanted. You *don't* make it easy," Jamie said, fixing the satchel over his shoulder.

"Keep it with you. There's probably something in it," said Seán. "If you don't mind, we'll be on our way," he said, and he and his fellow leprechauns left to gather their sacks.

"I'll rest here for a while," Éiriú whispered and closed her eyes.

Elisa looked at Éiriú sleeping. She seemed to understand her a little better now and not in the way Jamie did. She saw the mother of Kapheus in her. The elves looked up to her. She was their saviour, not Banbha, yet she was a raging and unpredictable dragon.

"Alright. I'll take Elisa and Jamie with me. We'll light bonfires to welcome Caoilte home," Banbha said. Éiriú nodded in her sleeping state.

"I'll stay here for a while," said Elisa. Banbha snatched Jamie and left before he could say a word.

Elisa watched the sleeping dragon and wondered who she was. She remembered her in the dreamland when Fódla died. She remembered her mother there too. Elisa watched her breathing. If this was her mother then why did she leave Kapheus for Éire and why was she a woman there and a dragon here? Was this true? Could she possibly be her mother?

"You're thinking too much," Éiriú said.

"Oh, sorry. I forgot you could hear my thoughts," Elisa said.

"Be the goddess you are and walk through the Kaphiens. My mother always did that. She believed that there is no leadership unless in service. She told me to always remember to be in service to the Kaphiens," Éiriú said and drifted into a deep sleep.

Elisa looked around. She saw the wounded Kaphiens tending to each other in the meadow. She looked to the hills and saw Setanta, his mother and Kubera walking towards La Petite Maison Le Fèvre. She saw Geaspar and Feehul and when she glanced at Feehul their eyes met. He knew what Elisa was feeling. He knew the responsibility of being the greatest medicine elf that ever lived, and he knew the responsibility Elisa carried in being the goddess of Éire. It was the journey all leaders walked alone, and he was not about to change that now. He didn't offer to walk through the meadow with her nor did he offer any words of wisdom to help her. For Elisa's wisdom needed to rise from deep within her soul as all the ancient texts had told.

Elisa smiled and walked on. She saw Mother Badger a short distance away and reached down to her.

"Are you alright?" she asked.

"Oh, it's merely a bruised ego," Mother Badger said.

"Have you broken your leg?" Elisa asked.

"I think so, dear."

"Let me show you how to mend a broken leg," Micah said to Elisa. Micah bent down and measured the perfect size for the splint.

"This is Grandmother Oak's splint," said Mother Badger. "I can feel her love. I know I'll heal well," she said and smiled.

"Elisa, if you like you can hold Mother Badger," Micah said, and Elisa held the badger tightly.

"I'll need to stretch it a little or it won't heal right," he said.

"Oh! The pain!" Mother Badger cried.

"Nearly there now. I only need to add the splint and… all done."

"Go raibh maith agat, Micah. Thank you."

"And thank you, my dear Elisa."

Scampering across the meadow to their mother's cry was the badger family. They lifted her up and together they carried her home to her sett.

"Here Elisa. You'll have enough in this," Micah said, handing her ointment, strips of bandage and a number of small twigs. "I want to check in on Rós. She was out of sorts this morning," he said, walking away. "Don't worry there are plenty here to help you."

Elisa walked to the injured elf close-by and offered her assistance. She rubbed ointment on his wound, and like the ointment in her mother's kitchen cupboard, it instantly healed the open gash on his leg.

"The arrow got me," the elf said. "Bhí an pian go h-uafásach."

"Buíochas le Dia go bhfuil tú ceart go leor anois. Tá alán daoine gortaithe," Elisa said.

"Yeah, a lot of people are hurt," a voice said from behind.

"Éataín!"

"Elisa, it's good to see you are not hurt."

"No, I was on Éiriú's back," said Elisa.

"She's not the worst dragon, I suppose," Éataín said. She looked at Elisa as if she wanted her to understand something about Éiriú, unfortunately Elisa didn't know what it was.

"This battle has awoken a lot of sleeping souls it seems," said Éataín and she looked to the boundary between the two worlds.

"Let's keep walking," Éataín said, walking towards the centre of the meadow.

There was a shimmer of light at the boundary and then Cathal stepped from Elisa's room and stood in Kapheus. He felt the meadow grass beneath his feet and the cool air against his skin. He watched the elves pass him by with their arms laden with armoury. He noticed other elves fill sacks and hand heavy loads to dragons who tossed them onto their backs. He saw the dragons fly away, and he rubbed his eyes. Cathal removed his hands from his face in hope that he would no longer see elves or dragons, but he did see them. For no known reason Seán felt a shiver down his spine. He looked towards the boundary and then nodded to Cathal and Cathal saluted him and then strangely wondered why. Seán didn't falter in his walk. As far as he was concerned, Cathal was a representation of Éire, and Éire was awakening.

Joachim took a very different view to Seán entering Kapheus and chased through the meadow with his pack following close behind. Cathal watched them gain momentum and began to panic. He looked behind him but all he could see was meadow. He looked all around him. It was a wide open plain. There was nowhere to run and nowhere to hide. Joachim and his pack bounded towards him and by now they were only a few feet away. Cathal fainted.

"Again!" Joachim complained. "You really shouldn't go on adventures that you *just can't handle.*"

The black wolf dragged Cathal's heavy body from the meadow and into Elisa's bedroom. He pulled him down the hallway to his own room and left him at the side of his bed.

"Maybe you'll sleep it off," he said. "If only Feehul had a potion to stem your curiosity."

Joachim walked down the hallway. He took one last look back at Cathal's bedroom and then stepped into Elisa's room and crossed the boundary into Kapheus to re-join his pack of wolves.

Joachim seemed to be in as much a hurry then as he had been before he entered Éire. He raced with his pack across the meadow and jumped over the Fodar dragon with the open wound on his chest. Feehul wondered what was so important as he watched each wolf jump over the dragon. He held Geaspar while he continued to heal that dragon for fear he would fall into the wound or succumb to a stray wolf paw.

"*What is* this place?" the dragon asked.

"It's Kapheus, the fantastical world of light. You're safe here now. You can live free," Feehul said. The dragon stood up and shook himself. "That direction," Feehul said, pointing to the coastline. "Your friends are all there." The dragon bowed to Geaspar and Feehul, turned and flew away.

"I think you've had enough at this stage," said Feehul, cradling Geaspar in his arms.

"A leanbh, mo chléibh, go n-éirí do chodladh leat (Child of my heart, sleep well),

Slán agus sonas a choíche 'do chomhair (May you always be safe and happy),

Tá mise le do thaobh ag guí ort na mbeannacht (I'm by your side praying for blessings on you),

Seoithín, mo leanbh… (Hushaby, my baby…)," Feehul sang softly.

Geaspar fought against the tiredness until he finally relented to Feehul's soothing strokes and gentle voice. The baby dragon fell into a deep sleep and Feehul carried him to Éiriú and placed him next to her.

"I'll get you iron for your blood. I won't be long," Feehul whispered and left them alone.

Éiriú opened her eyelids. The warm breath from her nostrils summoned Geaspar the extra few steps towards her until he curled his body against the curve of his mother's neck. Éiriú reached out and licked him clean. Her warm smooth strokes lulled Geaspar farther into the dreamland.

In the hills, Rós sat at her living room table holding a wooden clock in her hands when Micah walked through the door. Micah glanced over at his wife a number of times while taking off his coat and scarf and hanging them up on the coat rack next to the door. He couldn't help but feel sad for his wife, and to compound this, there was so much about Kapheus that he still didn't understand. He had no history in this place and couldn't completely know the depth of Rós' grief, but she was his wife and he loved her dearly, and for that reason alone, he grieved.

"The clock's stopped," Rós said.

She wondered how he died and where he died. Was it how Caoilte had planned to go? She rubbed her hand along the engraved wood that shone a light on Caoilte's life from an elfin child playing in the woods to a young elf leaving Kapheus for a new life in Fodar.

"He was alone," she said. Micah nodded. Rós looked up from the clock. "He didn't have a wife or children," Rose said. Micah shook his head. "He gave of his whole self to Kapheus and didn't draw anyone into his quest," she cried.

Rós' tears dropped on the clear glass of the clock-face. She saw her reflection and then wiped the tears away.

"Did he fall in the meadow as he wanted?" Rós asked.

"He did. They took him on that young dragon's back," said Micah.

Rós looked at him. She wanted to know everything.

"Dara?" she asked.

"Yeah, he and his parents brought him out to sea," Micah said.

"*What happened?*" she asked.

Micah sat down beside Rós and offered her his handkerchief.

"He was struck by the piece of ore you moulded into the Spiral of Life. He fell in the meadow… I saw Iolar fly to him with Ruan and Lir as he fell."

"*Were they* there? *Did they* get to say goodbye?"

Micah nodded. He remembered Ruan's cry and took a breath.

"I don't think I'll ever forget that cry," he said.

"*Ruan?*" she asked. Micah nodded.

"Was Elisa set free?"

"Yes, he saved her from the disease of the mind… He broke the hold the Dark One had on her."

"And Éiriú?"

"He told them how to save her without giving himself away."

Just then a knock came to their door. Micah stood up to open the door.

"*Rós.*"

"Yes, Setanta."

"Rós, I killed Caoilte," Setanta said and broke down in tears.
"Come sit with me. There are things you need to know," said Rós.

Down in the meadow, the Fodar elves approached the bonfires
with pieces of wood they had carried from the woodland. They
were welcomed by the Kaphiens who offered them a place to rest
and who sympathised with them for the loss of their leader.
Though they felt over-joyed to be set free from the shackles of the
Fodar regime, their hearts were filled with regret. Regret that they
had spoken ill of Caoilte, regret that they had thought that he was
sending their whole families to doom and regret that they did not
try to understand him.
"We *should have known,*" an elf said.
"If you had known then you would never had been set free. He
needed to keep you in the dark for as long as possible," said
Banbha. "Let's bury him well," Banbha said. "Set those bonfires
blazing. They should be here soon."

In La Petite Maison Le Fèvre, Rós placed the clock on her lap and
wheeled herself to the small mahogany table close to her work
station. She gently placed the broken clock onto the table.
"He died a hero," she said. "He's a son of Éire."
"What do you mean?" Setanta asked.
"Energy never dies it simply changes form", Kubera said. Setanta
didn't understand.
"Setanta, Elisa would have died with a disease of the mind," Rós
said, approaching him.
"How?"
"The energy that stone carried… it wouldn't have given up until
Elisa was dead. So, by Caoilte being struck by the ore contained in
that stone and dying, Elisa was set free," said Kubera.
"Is that how energy works?" Setanta asked.
"Yes, it is often as simple and as complex as that," Kubera said.
With all that Setanta had been told that morning he understood the
role he had played in Caoilte's destiny and his pain was softened a
little. There wasn't a Kaphien who did not feel sorry for Setanta.
After all, he was only a boy who had tried his very best to save

Kapheus. They all knew that this was a growing up moment for
Setanta and a moment that would define his life forever. It was up
to Setanta what he would make of his life from that point onwards.
He could succumb to feelings of guilt and shame and live a life of
self-destruction or he could do his best to accept life on life's terms
and continue to be the best person he could be. The silence was
deafening at that moment and Rós felt that she needed to say
something.

"Bury him well," Rós said. "*Make sure* to bury him well."

Rós approached the door of her home.

"You will need to welcome him home now. There's no point in
mulling things over any longer. It's best to move, best to keep
going," she said.

"What will I do with this piece of ore, Rós?" Kubera asked.

"Anything you like. It has lost all its power," said Rós.

Micah stood up and walked to the door to fetch his coat and scarf.

"Put on your coat, Rós. Wrap up well," Micah said.

Micah lifted the sled that lazily rested against the gable wall of their
cottage. He carried it to the door and sat it down. He looked down
to the valley and negotiated the path they'd take.

"We're going together," Micah said. "We built this life together.
We'll bury Caoilte well *together*. Are you right, Setanta? Let's go,"
Micah said.

"Umm… yeah… alright," Setanta said and helped Micah with the
sled.

On the island courtyard Ruan held tightly to the body of Caoilte.
He could not let him go.

"Boo, boo," said Fódla, and she nodded her head. "Boo, boo."

"It's time to go, Ruan," Méabh said. Ruan nodded.

One by one the elfin ancestors left the courtyard followed by the
dragon ancestors.

"Boo, boo," said Fódla, hugging Méabh one more time.

"Bye Fódla," said Dara with tear-filled eyes. Fódla then hugged
Dara.

"You be good now, Fódla," said Ogma, "I hope to see you when
the ancestors call me, but not before then."

Fódla nodded her head and then flew to catch up with the others.
"Will we ever see her again?" Dara asked.
"Yes. When it's our turn to meet the ancestors," Ogma replied.
"I'm sure I've a linen cloth in the woods. I'll have to find it… and
we'll need to ask Fachtna for a coffin… *only his best,*" said Ruan.
"Will I take you to the woods?" Dara asked.
"Ruan we have to go," said Lir. Ruan nodded.
"Yes. Take us back to the woods, Dara. It's customary to present
a fallen elf to Grandmother Oak," Ruan said, climbing to his feet.
Dara ran to the mountain edge, spread his wings and soon they
were flying across the sea to the woods of Kapheus. Dara came to
rest at the base of Grandmother Oak and presented Caoilte to her.
The spirit of the great oak tree stepped out from her bark. She
called to the elves to bring the linen and to Cillian to help Fachtna
with the coffin. There was a sacredness to everything that took
place in the woods that morning. Nobody entered, and nobody left
the wood until the body was ready. A wonderful feeling of peace
came over Ruan and Lir and although they struggled to do the basic
things or to even think clearly, they had their fellow elves by their
side to help them.
"Let us have some privacy now," Grandmother Oak said, "before
he leaves."
Ruan and Lir stood alone with their fallen cousin, Caoilte, listening
to Grandmother Oak. She told them of all Caoilte had sacrificed
for Kapheus and how his life had not been in vain. Grandmother
Oak told them of Caoilte's kindness and of how he created the elf
others perceived him to be with the ultimate aim to free his fellow
Kaphiens from persecution forever. She spoke for some time with
them, and when she had finished, Grandmother Oak gave Ruan
and Lir as much time as they needed to digest her words. When
the elfin brothers were ready, Grandmother Oak signalled to their
fellow elves to help carry Caoilte's coffin to the meadow.
"Fire brings everything into the light," Ruan said, "for good or ill.
Remember that, Lir," he said.
"I will," said Lir.
Ruan, Lir and the woodland elves lifted the coffin above their
shoulders and walked from the woodland.

"I'd say he hadn't it easy in Fodar," Ruan said.

"No," said Lir.

These few words were followed by a long silence until the elves tapped Ruan and Lir on the shoulder. The six pall bearers seamlessly stepped under the coffin and allowed Ruan and Lir and the four other pallbearers to take a break. As they walked alongside the coffin, Ruan thought of their mother and all the times Caoilte spent with them when they were little.

"Mam liked him," Ruan said, and Lir agreed.

"He wasn't a bad sort really," said Ruan, and again Lir agreed.

"Are you alright, Lir?"

"Not really."

"Neither am I."

At the veil of the Meadow of Discovery, the two brothers stepped under the coffin again and led Caoilte's body into the meadow.

"It mightn't be the best reception but just hold your head proud," Ruan said. "He was our cousin and we will bury him well no matter what they say."

"Alright, Ruan," said Lir.

Éiriú roared powerfully and stood high with outstretched wings on the other side of that veil to welcome Caoilte home. The Fodar elves and dragons lined the pass between the hills all the way to the meadow. The Kaphiens stood behind them and bowed as the coffin passed.

"Be proud," Ruan said to Lir with a crackle in his voice and tears in his eyes. "The goddesses of Éire are welcoming him. Caoilte is a son of Éire," he cried.

When they reached the wide meadow Banbha and Elisa stood waiting for them. Banbha stood tall and with outstretched wings she roared loudly.

"We can stop here for a second lads," said Ruan. "Banbha will lead us the rest of the way."

Banbha and Elisa walked ahead of the funeral procession and were soon joined by Éiriú.

"Are we too late?" Rós asked.

"No, the goddesses are only walking into the meadow now," said Micah. "We'll be in plenty of time."

The two parties met in the centre of the meadow where Banbha stopped to ask for the coffin to be laid where Caoilte had fallen.

"Thank you for coming, Rós," Ruan said.

"Go raibh maith agat," said Lir.

A short distance away, Jamie and Feehul stood, and as Jamie was about to step forward, Feehul pulled him back.

"Jamie, stay here," said Feehul. "Sometimes the greatest leader is the one who stands behind his dragons and allows their light to shine."

Jamie nodded. He watched Banbha and Elisa standing next to Éiriú and he understood that it was appropriate for him to let their light shine.

"All the dragons have fallen to the earth now," Lugh said. "A Kaphien hero…"

"What do you think they're talking about?" Jamie asked.

"A clock, I suspect," said Kubera, appearing next to them.

They continued to watch them talk next to the coffin and patiently waited for some movement to indicate that they could step forward to sympathise.

"Do you think Setanta will marry Elisa one day?" Jamie asked.

"I don't know," said Feehul. He laughed.

"Here they are now. They're ready," said Lugh.

They watched Rós and Micah step away from the coffin followed by Setanta and his mother. Then they saw Ruan clear his throat and with one reassuring look to his brother, he greeted the crowd.

"*Let's celebrate,*" Ruan said. "Let's give him a good send off!"

"We can step forward now to sympathise," said Feehul.

That day was filled with song and dance and story-telling of the life and times of Caoilte, the son of Éire. They ate and drank their fill and when the sun set and the stars filled the sky Éiriú called the three siblings, Feehul, Lugh and Sinann together. She silently walked with them to the pass between the hills and then stopped and looked back at the bonfires and celebrations. She scanned the hills and all about her for danger while the three elves stood waiting and wondering. They looked at each other and then looked back at Éiriú.

"I need you to hide the heart of Ernmas, the emerald of An Claíomh Solais and Geaspar's clock as far away from each other as possible."

"I…" said Feehul.

"I don't need to know where you've hidden the clock, Feehul. I just need to know that no one will find it and that he will die a natural death," Éiriú said. Feehul nodded. He stroked his hand along the surface of his leather satchel. Éiriú couldn't help but roll her eyes.

"Everything happened *so fast* and I just *didn't get the time* to think of a really good hiding place," Feehul said.

Sinann pulled the emerald from her pocket and held it in her hand, rubbing her thumb over and back along its surface. She thought hard about where she would hide it.

"*Don't* let your thoughts be known," Éiriú scolded.

Éiriú searched for Jamie amongst the Kaphiens and signalled to him to join them. Jamie nervously approached the white dragon.

"Jamie, you need to give Lugh my mother's heart," she instructed. Jamie pulled the red diamond from his satchel and handed it to Lugh.

"Jamie, could you get Elisa," she said. Éiriú watched as Jamie walked back through the crowd of mourners to find his sister.

"You'll have to leave tonight. The leprechauns may lose their compassion by morning and will likely follow you," Éiriú said. "Leave while everyone's distracted… and don't tell each other where you've hidden them," she said.

The three elfin siblings said nothing and left. They looked over their shoulders a couple of times and when they were a safe distance from Éiriú they spoke to each other.

"I hope this doesn't bring us bad luck," Sinann said.

There was silence for a short while as Sinann and Feehul waited for some words of wisdom from Lugh, who himself was sent to hide something precious by Grandmother Oak. Feehul looked a Lugh and then quickly looked away.

"I know what you're thinking. The last time I had to hide something it lead to years of torture and torment at the hands of the Dark One," said Lugh.

"Do you think we're doomed?" Feehul asked. "Has she cast a dark curse on us and on all those generations who come after us?"

"We can't let that happen. We'll have to come up with a plan," Sinann said.

"There can't be generations of secrets. I can't do that again. I can't… I've found someone who loves me, and I love her," Lugh said.

"Tara?" Feehul asked.

"Yes. Táim cinnte faoi."

"Well then, we'll have to think of a riddle or maybe we should go to Taragon and ask him if we could hide the riddle within the ancient texts," Sinann said.

In that moment, Kubera appeared next to them.

"Sinann hide yours in water. Lugh hide yours in the air element. Feehul…"

"I understand," said Feehul.

"I'll tell you now that Taragon will tell you no different," said Kubera. "Now, part company at the fountain of hope. There will be no curse if you use the elements as they were taught to you as children to hide these precious gifts."

"But what about a curse?" Lugh asked.

"There will be no curse, because you will hide them in the elements only to be found when they desire to be revealed… Now, part company at the fountain, like I said," Kubera insisted and then disappeared.

Éiriú waited for Elisa and Jamie to approach and wondered how she would tell them that Geaspar was their brother and that she was their mother. She watched the closeness of the siblings walking towards her. Despite all the conflict and all the struggle, they were still the best of friends. She wanted that for Geaspar too.

"It's too much to place on their shoulders. You'll tell them when they're better able to understand," said Banbha.

Éiriú nodded. Geaspar scurried along Éiriú's back and onto her head. She looked into this baby blue eyes, eyes that could barely recognised his own mother. She then passed Geaspar to Banbha.

"Take good care of him," she said and quietly left Kapheus.

Banbha watched her sister walk towards the woodland and then take flight.

"Hi Banbha," Jamie said. "Did you see *Éiriú?* She was looking for Elisa."

"She just left," said Banbha.

"Oh, I'll catch up with her," Jamie said.

"No need, Jamie. Leave her be... You don't have wings."

"But *she wanted* Elisa," Jamie said.

"She was looking for Fódla's satchel. Geaspar's getting tired," said Banbha.

"*Geaspar!*" Jamie called. The little dragon ran down along Banbha's neck and onto her shoulder and then took a leap of faith and flapped her tiny wings.

"He can *fly,*" Jamie exclaimed.

Geaspar flapped and flapped those wings with all his might but couldn't lift himself from his downward trajectory. Elisa quickly reached out her hands and caught Geaspar before he fell to the ground.

"You'll be really good at flying when you're older," Jamie said.

Jamie opened the satchel on Elisa's back and pulled out the teddy bear and Geaspar climbed onto it. Then Jamie carefully placed Geaspar inside and closed the fasteners. It was the togetherness of the three siblings at that moment that took Banbha by surprise and she marvelled at the comfort Jamie brought to his little brother, a little brother who was a dragon.

"What's wrong Banbha?" Elisa asked.

"Oh, nothing. Come on. I think you're all tired. Say goodbye to your friends before you go."

"Are *we not staying* until after the funeral tomorrow?" Elisa asked.

"No, you need to sleep in your own beds tonight. It gets quite cold at night in Kapheus."

Banbha walked with the three siblings through the crowd of dragons and elves and wondered if they would ever learn that she was their aunt. She wondered what it would have been like if she had left Kapheus to live in Éire. She thought about all her sister had gained and lost when she left her homeland.

"Your sacrifice was to stay. Her sacrifice was to leave. Neither of you are right and neither of you are wrong," Kubera said, appearing next to Banbha.

"Elisa, Jamie, you two go on and say goodbye to everyone. I'll want to talk to Kubera. I'll catch up with you shortly," Banbha said.

"See ya, Kubera," said Jamie.

"Slán," said Elisa, and the siblings ran off.

"Do you know everything?" Banbha asked.

"I know this thing but not everything," Kubera said.

"How will this all turn out?" Banbha asked.

"I don't think you need to worry about that too much, Banbha. You'll mind Geaspar for now and the children will return to their life in Éire with their mother and father."

"I wonder if there is something I could do to help Éiriú in some way."

"There's nothing you can do that you aren't already doing. She is her own worst enemy and the acts of the past two days won't change the conflict that resides within her. She'll have to deal with her rage and her woundedness before you can help her more than you already are".

Banbha sighed deeply and looked at the children saying goodbye to their Kaphien friends. She looked back again and Kubera was gone.

"Slán! Go dtí lá eile!" Rós said, waving goodbye to Elisa and Jamie.

"See you another time!" said Micah.

Elisa and Jamie stopped to speak to Ruan and Lir before they left, and when they did, Rós noticed something about Elisa. She thought it might have been that she stood a little straighter or maybe it was that she and her brother were united again, but she wasn't sure.

"Elisa has changed," Rós said, "I can't explain it. It's like she has a certain presence about her."

"Maybe she's raised her expectations," Micah said.

"Maybe."

They both watched Banbha call to the children and escort them home and soon they were out of sight.

"They're gone," Rós said, she then scanned the hills.

Rós had become more anxious with every hour that passed, and by now, she was unable to hide it. She searched the meadow and the hills again and looked as far as she could see to find her family, but there was no trace of the Tuatha Dé Danann.

"Have you seen the Tuatha Dé Danann?" Rós asked.

"*Your family?*... No," Micah responded and shook his head. "I haven't seen Dagda since we left the woodland that day in the snow."

"I really hope he's alright," said Rós.

"Well, he'll have *some explaining to do when he arrives back here.* There wasn't *even one member* of your *warrior family* here when we needed them in battle!" Micah argued.

Not too far from them, Dagda turned the key on the last lock and looked around.

"You're in Kapheus now," he said. "You're safe."

The gaunt looking figures of elves looked back at him, but they were too weak and too tired from a full day of walking through wasteland and tunnels to feel they were safe.

"We'll keep walking. We're nearly there," Dagda said.

The Tuatha Dé Danann lead the way along the outcrops on the boggy surface with hundreds of elves following in a line behind them. They were hardly recognisable as elves. Their emaciated bodies were clothed in mere rags and many were bent as they walked unable to stand up straight from the years of crawling in the small and often pitch-black tunnels of the silver and gold mines. Their eyes had grown dim from using only candle light to luminate their way when they chiselled. In all, they had suffered more than any elf should ever have to suffer and a life of freedom was deserved.

The dragons stirred in the meadow to the sound of the strangers approaching and they took flight over the hills.

"What's happening?" Ruan asked. He looked over at Rós. "Rós, *what's happening?*"

"Don't worry, Ruan. It's a good thing," Rós said.

One by one the dragons returned to the meadow with their cargo on their backs. They gently placed their feet upon the meadow and then lay down for the elves to climb down from their backs.

"Have you food and drink for these weary elves?" Dagda asked.

The Kaphiens stood up and rushed to help the elves down from the dragons. Their eyes were hollow, and they were the closest they had ever seen elves to death.

"*Where* have you come from?" Seán asked.

"The outskirts of Fodar," said Dagda. "We've been walking all night and all day," he said, "and now we need to eat and drink and give thanks to Caoilte."

"*Caoilte?*" Ruan asked.

"Yes, he saved their lives. They're now free elves."

The weak elves were helped the last few steps to the bonfires. Hot drinks and food were given to each and every one of them. Elves signalled to each other to pass blankets along to the emaciated strangers and they did their utmost to make them feel comfortable. An elfin child reached out to Rós for a piece of bread. She saw torn hands from the hard labour of the mines and his bleeding fingers. Rós handed him the bread and then asked Micah for ointment and rubbed it into the young elf's hands.

"Tomorrow, you'll all wash by the river and you'll all have new clothes to wear," Rós said.

"Aithnítear cara i gcruatan," Dagda said.

"*What was that?*" Micah asked.

"You know your friend in a time of need," Rós said. "A country without a language is a country without a soul. Maybe I'll teach you mine," she said.

"I'd like that … and sorry."

Dagda sat down next to Rós in a heap of exhaustion.

"It's good to see you sis," he said and smiled.

"Did the key open all the doors?" Rós asked.

"Every last one," he said. He looked at his sister and smiled even more broadly.

"You had the masterplan and we won the battle."

"At a cost," said Rós.

"Yeah, I know."

"We had Kubera too, and there's no doubt about it, that we would've been lost without him," said Rós.

"Where is he now?"

"The last time I saw him he was talking to Banbha. He's probably around here somewhere listening into a conversation," she said and smiled cheekily.

Dagda looked around but didn't see Elisa or Jamie. He stood up and looked even farther but still there was no sign.

"Here, Dagda," an elf said, handing him a bowl of soup and a piece of bread.

"Have you seen Elisa and Jamie?" Dagda asked.

"No. I haven't seen them since before the battle," the elf said and moved on.

Dagda approached another few elves and asked them the same question, but none knew of Elisa and Jamie's whereabouts.

"What's wrong?" Rós called out.

"I can't see Elisa and Jamie anywhere," Dagda said, distressed.

"They've gone home. Don't worry. They survived the battle. I saw Banbha walking them home a short while ago."

"Phew. I was a bit worried there," Dagda said and sat back down next to his sister. "They're probably drinking hot chocolate," he said and laughed. Dagda took a spoonful of soup from his bowl. "There's Kubera," he said. Dagda paused. "What did you ask him to do?"

"More than any gnome should ever be asked to do," Rós responded.

Dagda looked at Rós and then looked back in Kubera's direction.

"He must be feeling it," Dagda said, watching him leaving the gathering and walking home alone.

Kubera's head was dipped in deep thought as he left the gathering of Kaphiens for his home in Taragon's lair. He needed to be alone with his thoughts and needed space to feel. He disappeared from sight.

"Squawk! Squawk!" cried the phoenix, landing behind him. "Squawk!" she cried again.

Kubera sighed deeply and reappeared.

"I'm sorry I forgot to say goodbye," he said to the phoenix. "I wanted to be alone."

"Squawk!" called the phoenix and she bumped his back with her beak. "Squawk!"

"No, I didn't eat," he answered.

"Squawk! Squaaawk! Squawk," the phoenix called.

Kubera stopped and turned around and when he did the phoenix regurgitated her food and it landed on Kubera's boots.

"I've bread and cheese in my satchel," Kubera said. "If you really want to watch me eat then I suppose we should sit together."

They walked to the closest rock they could find and Kubera sat on it, and although the phoenix attempted to sit on the rock next to him, her rump was just too big and her plumage far too dense for the two of them to be able to share the same rock. The phoenix looked at the ground next to the rock and shuffled her rump a few times before she was completely comfortable.

"I could've eaten this at home, you know," Kubera said, offering the bird of fire some bread. She refused it and they both sat in silence for a while watching their fellow Kaphiens around the campfires.

"He sacrificed everything for Kapheus," Kubera said. "He even gave his life."

Silence fell between them again. Kubera ate a piece of his cheese although eating was the last thing he wanted to do.

"You've made your own sacrifices, Eve," Kubera said.

The phoenix looked blankly at him and it was as if a shiver had gone down her spine and she felt compelled to shake her feather body. The phoenix looked at the gathering and then in the direction of the boundary between the two worlds before turning her head to look up to the hills.

"An rud is annamh is iontach," Kubera said. He shook his head. "What's rare is beautiful and you may be the last of your kind."

The phoenix looked blankly at Kubera again. She tilted her head to one side and then the other.

"Squawk," she uttered in a low voice.

"What sacrifice will it be?" Kubera asked. "If you stay you could find a spot on those hills to nest and you could fly over the meadow and through the woods every day. But what if you are shot down for your treasured plumage or you are caught in a trap and spend the rest of your life in captivity? What life is that to constantly live in fear?"

"Squaaaaaaawk. Squaawk. Squaaawk," the phoenix cried, and silence fell upon them again. They observed the gathering and watched the fire flames.

"I know you've always loved him," said Kubera. "You could have married Cathal," he said, looking directly at her. The phoenix looked away and swished her long tail against Kubera's back.

"Where will you live?" Kubera asked. "Here or there... These sacrifices we make... *look at Caoilte* dead on the meadow, *Éiriú* without her newly born, and *now you* alone and without a place that you can truly call your home. *Will Éire ever awaken* from its slumber and *reclaim all of this as its own?*.. When will we be truly one?"

The phoenix stretched her wing around Kubera.

"Is it alright if I join you?" Cillian asked.

"Yes, please do," said Kubera.

"Go raibh maith agat," Cillian said and sat down.

"I went to Taragon's lair but you weren't there. He said that you hadn't been there all day," said Cillian.

"I was on my way when I met this phoenix," Kubera said, "I've your coin by the way," he said, pulling the silver coin from his pocket.

Cillian smiled and took the silver coin in his hand.

"This is the reason I went to Taragon's cave. I was told to meet you there when all was done," said Cillian.

"Who told you to meet me?"

"Do you not know the story of this coin?" Cillian asked, surprised. "I was sure you would've known."

Kubera looked at Cillian in a state of puzzlement and on seeing this Cillian felt that he should at least tell his side of the story.

"Well, the story is that Taragon gave that coin to my great grandfather or my great great grandfather, I'm not quite sure, and anyway, he told him to name his firstborn son Cillian and pass that coin to him. He was also told that this coin was to be passed down to every firstborn son in our family until there were no more," Cillian said.

He rolled the coin up and down between his fingers and pondered. It seemed to Kubera that Cillian had gone to some childhood place in his thoughts, and as such, he waited patiently.

"I'm the last of my family," Cillian said. "I haven't met anyone yet to continue my family line and there may be no more firstborn children to be called Cillian."

The phoenix became fascinated by the silver coin, and on seeing this, Cillian tightened his grip on it and closed his hand.

"That doesn't explain why you visited Taragon," Kubera said.

"When I was given this coin, I was told that when all was done to go to Kubera and that he will tell you everything," said Cillian, "so what are you supposed to tell me?"

"I don't know… This coin is a key…"

"A key?"

"Yes, it's a key to the heart of Ernmas," said Kubera.

"I don't know what you mean."

"This key opens the casket that houses the heart of Ernmas."

"But how did Jamie know that?"

"He didn't. I had the casket opened before Jamie found the heart. The heart of Ernmas' whereabouts is only known by the dragon ancestors."

"And you," said Cillian.

"Taragon knows the ways of the stars and the ancestors are found in the stars. The earth dragon was told in a dream to make the key you're holding, which he did."

"But it doesn't even *look like a key.*"

"That's probably so that no one would suspect a thing," said Kubera.

"I thought that after the fire it would be best that I make a camp in the woodland and stay there to watch for the signs," Cillian said.

"What signs?"

"Well, I was told that all these things would happen… and then when Mother Badger had that dream, well, I thought there has to be something in this."

Cillian searched Kubera and the phoenix's faces for answers.

"Prometheus was to come from the stars to bring fire to the earth. I saw it written in the ancient text. On this occasion, the unicorn foal brought fire in the form of the heart of Ernmas. The ancestors up there *in that starry sky,*" Kubera said, "allowed the fire element to come alive through the presence of the blood moon."

"*Poor Jamie* didn't know *what he was doing* in that case," said Cillian.

"Well, that's not entirely true. Jamie knew *exactly what he was doing*. He was greedy for wealth and power and when he saw the blood diamond, he believed it to be the answer to all his prayers. He just didn't know that it was Ernmas' heart."

"What now?" asked Cillian.

"You can do whatever you wish with that coin. It has served its purpose and its power no longer remains tied to the ancestral realm."

Cillian looked down at the large silver coin with the stag on one side and the harp on the other. He rolled it over and back between the fingers of his hand and then tossed it into the air and caught it as it landed.

"I think I'll keep it for old time's sake," Cillian said with a smile. He then stood up. "I'll leave you be."

Cillian walked towards the gathering of Kaphiens and it wasn't long before he sat with his friends at the campfire.

"Well, what's your decision, Eve?" Kubera asked. The phoenix looked blankly at him. "I'll leave you be. I want to go home," Kubera said. He walked a few steps and then disappeared.

The phoenix took flight and joined the others in the celebration of Caoilte's life. She floated above the gathering for a short while before coming to rest next to Rós.

"They've gone home," Rós said. "Banbha brought the children home if you're looking for them."

The phoenix shuffled her rump on the ground next to Rós until she found a comfortable seat. She then shook her feathered body.

"Here or there?" Rós asked.

"Squaawk! Squaawk!"

"I'm sorry. We don't need to think about Éire for one night, Eve. I'm really happy to be here with you."

Banbha reached her head through the drawing for one last look at Geaspar snuggling against Elisa.

"Only at night," Banbha said. "I'll take him early in the morning... sleep well," she whispered and withdrew her head from Elisa's room and returned to Kapheus.

Elisa had already fallen asleep and Banbha watched the two siblings for a little longer from Kapheus. Then she saw the handle turn on the bedroom door and immediately took flight. Footsteps crossed the bedroom floor to the little dragon on Elisa's bed. He gurgled when she approached. She lifted him into her arms and walked towards the door.

"Night Mam," said Elisa, still asleep.

Aideen looked back.

"Goodnight Elisa," she said and left the room, closing the door behind her.

Acknowledgement:

I wish to acknowledge the composer of Seoithín Seó, an old Irish lullaby. My research has lead me to understand that this lullaby was one of a number of oral songs collected by Amhlaoibh Ó Loingsigh (1872 – 1947) and entered into An tOireachtas, the Irish language cultural festival in 1902. Amhlaoibh Ó Loingsigh was from Baile Bhúirne in County Cork, Ireland. The name of the composer is unknown. Despite this, it is a testament to the beauty of its melody and the depth of its words that Seoithín Seó has stood the test of time and is now resting on the pages of this book.

I would also like to acknowledge the author of 'Is Mise an Ghaeilge'. It is a poem that tells the story of an Irish language that is almost lost and how it is so important for the people of Ireland to speak it. Despite my research, I have been unable to ascertain the name of the poet or the exact date it was written.